ADVANCE PRAISE FOR *THE RAGE ROOM*

Wow, what a ride! Lisa de Nikolits has written a pulse-pounding
thriller set in a troubled future that might just be ours. We see the
seeds of *The Rage Room* in our own digital landscape. Mind-bending
yet all too believable in the hands of a masterful storyteller.
—TERRY FALLIS, two-time winner of the Stephen Leacock Medal
for Humour

Leave it to the wild imagination of Lisa de Nikolits to bring us the
dystopian future of *The Rage Room*, an extraordinarily inventive
speculative fiction thriller with a decidedly feminist bent. Fast-paced,
funny, bold, and completely engrossing, *The Rage Room* is an allegory,
a cautionary tale, and a rollicking good read that will stay with you
long after the last page has been turned.
—AMY JONES, author of *We're All in This Together* and *Every Little
Piece of Me*

In her latest captivating book, de Nikolits proffers not only a roll-
ercoaster of entertainment, but also, sharp political commentary in
complicated times. *The Rage Room* is an intricately woven dystopian
world, rich in strong female characters who easily whisk readers
to a world of futuristic follies. Move over George Orwell—Lisa de
Nikolits shows us how the future can be scary, exciting, and above
all, female.
—KELLY S. THOMPSON, National Bestseller author of *Girls Need
Not Apply: Field Notes from the Forces*

In turns unsettling and very funny, Lisa de Nikolits's *The Rage Room* is a science fiction satire of toxic masculinity, narrated by your guide, Sharps, the neurotic, rage-filled Jason Bateman of the future. There are lines and descriptions that will stop you dead in your tracks and make you take notes.
—EVAN MUNDAY, *The Dead Kid Detective Agency* series

Dark, fun, weird, imaginative, *The Rage Room* is a dystopic ride perfect for the anxieties and conditions of the present day. The paranoia of Sharps Barkley seeps into you, propelling this thriller that will keep you guessing to the very end.
—DAVID ALBERTYN, author of *Undercard*

If dystopian speculative fiction is your thing, with the enticement of time travel, you won't go wrong with *The Rage Room*. The world Lisa de Nikolits has built is utterly fascinating, and quite horrific, yet believable. I sympathized with the main character, even though he is flawed, but that makes the story even more interesting. What a ride! The plot ratchets up like a train speeding down the tracks out of control. Gripping tension, and at the same time, highly complex, with multiple time travel redos and memories overlapping. I found that fascinating.
—MELODIE CAMPBELL, award-winning author of *The Goddaughter* Series

We've all wanted to go back to the past to fix the future—but Sharps Barkley has messed things up so much in his own high-tech future world that he has to do it. Lisa de Nikolits takes us—and him—on a wild, high-octane ride into other times and places so bizarre, blighted, funny and wise that they just might seem chillingly familiar. She turns time travel on its proverbial ear and you won't want to get out of the passenger seat until the last page.
—CATHERINE DUNPHY, author of *Morgentaler, A Difficult Hero*

With *The Rage Room*, Lisa de Nikolits takes a deep dive into dystopia. Prepare to be alternately chilled and thrilled as the hapless hero journeys backwards and forwards in time in his increasingly desperate attempts to right his terrible wrongs, and to find some sense in his rapidly disintegrating world.
—LORNA POPLAK, author of *Drop Dead: A Horrible History of Hanging in Canada*

Why would one go back in time? To make things right, of course. But every time Sharps visits his past, things change in ways he can't control, and he keeps changing from a worrier to a warrior. I loved all the witty characters, and original, daring twists in this genuine reality fiction beyond the imagination!
—SUZANA TRATNIK, author of *Games with Greta*.

The Rage Room is an extraordinary, astounding, and remarkable read. A to-and-fro tale, shrouded in mystery ... with ploys to destroy ... tracing trauma ... harbouring disharmony, mistrust, and betrayal, shattering at times.... Both terrifying and tender, nurturing and hostile by turn ... power pummeling ... altered realities and passages of change ... of transition.
—SHIRLEY MCDANIEL, artist

THE RAGE ROOM

We gratefully acknowledge the support of the Canada Council for the Arts and the Ontario Arts Council for our publishing program. We also acknowledge the financial support of the Government of Canada.

The Rage Room is a work of fiction. All the characters and situations portrayed in this book are fictitious and any resemblance to persons living or dead is purely coincidental.

Cover design: Lisa de Nikolits
Artwork by Saul Granda, Getty, RAGE font by iStock

Library and Archives Canada Cataloguing in Publication

Title: The rage room : a novel / Lisa de Nikolits.
Names: De Nikolits, Lisa, author.
Series: Inanna poetry & fiction series.
Description: Series statement: Inanna poetry & fiction series
Identifiers: Canadiana (print) 20200331205 | Canadiana (ebook) 20200331213 | ISBN 9781771337779 (softcover) | ISBN 9781771337786 (epub) | ISBN 9781771337793 (Kindle) | ISBN 9781771337809 (pdf)
Classification: LCC PS8607.E63 R34 2020 | DDC C813/.6—dc23

Printed and bound in Canada

Inanna Publications and Education Inc.
210 Founders College, York University
4700 Keele Street, Toronto, Ontario, Canada M3J 1P3
Telephone: (416) 736-5356 Fax: (416) 736-5765
Email: inanna.publications@inanna.ca   Website: www.inanna.ca

THE RAGE ROOM

A NOVEL

LISA DE NIKOLITS

inanna poetry & fiction series

INANNA PUBLICATIONS AND EDUCATION INC.
TORONTO, CANADA

ALSO BY LISA DE NIKOLITS

The Occult Persuasion and the
  Anarchist's Solution
Rotten Peaches
No Fury Like That
The Nearly Girl
Between The Cracks She Fell
The Witchdoctor's Bones
A Glittering Chaos
West of Wawa
The Hungry Mirror

To Bradford Dunlop and Colin Frings.
And to the world we really need to save.

REAL TIME

I COULDN'T LIVE LIKE THAT. And I couldn't let my children live like that either. There was only one solution. I had to go back and kill them. I had never been so certain of anything in my life.

I held my wrist out. The gates opened and through I went.

But when I opened my eyes, I wasn't in my house. I was in the rage room. I smelled plastic, oil, and diesel. I held a hammer and I was poised, mid-swing.

This was all wrong. I was supposed to be back in my house, back in the clean world where I'd be in control. What was going on?

And then it all came back to me.

BOOK I

TO THE MELTDOWN

1. THE RAGE ROOM

I DIDN'T KNOW WHAT YEAR IT WAS. We weren't allowed to know and, really, I couldn't have cared less. I was in my safe place, the rage room, focused on doing what I did best: breaking things.

Thwack. I brought the baseball bat down on what was left of a kid's wagon. The room was full of wagons, broken toys, junk furniture, and discarded office equipment—garbage, all of it.

The robo-voice made its usual announcement as I entered the room: *Screen-based materials are forbidden in the rage room. Glass cannot be utilized or destroyed in the rage room. We always consider your safety first! Because we care about you! All in accordance with Docket102.V, Health and Safety Code 0009: By Order of the Sacred Board, Gloria in Excelsis Deo.*

Yeah, man, I knew all the rules. And here's what I thought of them.

I attacked the wagon again, and the cheerful pink plastic replied with a slight *ughh* as if asking me if that was the best I could do, but it didn't give. I came down harder and scored a crack that mocked my feeble efforts. Story of my life.

My soundtrack was maxed. "O Fortuna" from *Carmina Burana* on repeat, volume pumped. Sometimes it's "War," by The Cult or "You Lied" by Tool or, incongruously, Vivaldi's *Four Seasons* with a disco twist and added bass for power. Rage Against the Machine is a good one too. *Thud, thud,*

thud, yeah. I chose my soundtrack, and I liked vintage—none of that auto-robo music for me.

Thinking about music choices made me think about my life choices or the lack thereof, and my wife's beauty badge, previously known as her profile pic, flashed unbidden across my crystal path. Celeste. She looked angelic, like vintage Farrah Fawcett in the days of *Charlie's Angels,* only a hundred pounds heavier, with two chipmunk teeth perching on the lower lip of her overbite. Celeste had ordered those teeth, paid premium to get her primaries longer than anyone else's. She thought it made her sexy.

I raised the bat higher and split the wretched wagon in two. *Sweetie, honey, baby, sugar. Thwack.* Was it possible for the woman to utter anything without coating it with saccharine, glucose and fructose, and then deep-frying it like an Oreo at a fun fair? Celeste had fried my brain all right. So why did I marry her? *Thwack.* Because she offered me everything I wanted, the sum of which boiled down to one thing: I wanted to be normal. I wanted to be The King of Normal. And, for her part, Celeste's marrying me was the act of a desperate addict trying to set her life straight, topped up with a deep-seated desire to please her father, Daddy.

I thrashed at an impervious lime-green keyboard, finally picking it up and slamming it against a workbench. I grunted as if I was up against the heavyweight champion of the world, and my thin white protective plastic suit tore like old wallpaper. But it was not all my fault; the suit was torn when I got into it. That's the government for you. Step into this used piece of shit—so what if it's slick with the sweat of some other angry dude who came before you? The rules say you have to wear it: *Docket809.V, Health and Safety Code 0009.12: By Order of the Sacred Board, Gloria in Excelsis Deo.* The rules should say you each get a fresh new suit, but that would cost too much money.

We looked like giant Easter bunnies, hopping insanely behind one-way mirrors, covered from head to toe in white disposable Tyvek coverall suits with elastic wrists, booties, and hoodie. All we needed were big floppy ears and little bobbing white pompom tails. Hop, hop, hop in a plastic room and break plastic shit to make yourself feel better for a tiny piece of your stupid, meaningless life.

I was a clean freak, and I liked my life to be scrubbed and tidy—it was an anomaly for me to find my safe place in a rage room—but I was also an anger addict, giving in to chaos at the drop of a hammer. And the hammer dropped a lot in my life, which I had come to accept. But what I couldn't accept was that the white suits disgusted me. They were damp when you pulled them on, and it was like trying to wriggle into someone else's just-discarded swimsuit. I also hated the smeared and greasy goggles with scratches as though some kid used them for skateboarding, which is still a thing.

I'd offered more than once to buy my own suit but it's against regulations.

It was also against the rules to self-harm in a rage room but more than one person has tried to commit suicide. I imagined them rushing in, falling to their knees, and hacking their veins open, wanting to die in a thick red sea of gushing blood while their fave hate song drums out the dying pulse of their lives. Trust me, I'd thought about trying too. It would have been a fitting place for me to meet my end, but the person behind the window watched just enough to not let that happen.

Sometimes I yelled profanities at the blacked-out glass window but I'm sure whoever's watching is so used to witnessing the pointless destruction that they don't even bother to look or listen most of the time.

I smashed on, chasing release and finding none. Then the music stopped—just like that—and a cop-car siren sounded. *Whoop, whoop, whoop!* Red lights flashed across the room. Green lights signalled go, red for when your time was up.

I was out of time, but release was denied. *Shit.* I pulled my face gear off, hearing only my frustrated breath. My face was dented from the goggles, and I ran my fingers along the ridges and bumps.

A guy opened the door and dragged in a trash can. He ignored me, and I just stood there. I wasn't ready to leave, but my time was up. The siren sounded again, *whoop, whoop, whoop,* and still, I stood there, goggles in hand, looking at the useless crap I had broken.

Another guy came, a big fella. "Buddy," he barked, "you know the rules. You gotta go. Come on now."

I turned to him, and I couldn't help myself—tears spilled down my face and I heard myself sobbing. He said, "Oh crapola, we got ourselves a wet one," and he left. The guy behind me carried on cleaning. I had nowhere to go so I just stood there, crying.

The big guy came back and handed me a roll of paper towel. I pulled off three sheets, blew my nose, and handed the roll back to him. "A bunch of us are going for a drink," he said. "You wanna come? You need a drink. Come on."

I thought about Celeste, waiting at home and about my baby boy, Baxter. I thought about how carpet needed vacuuming because the robovacs never got into the corners and how Bax wasn't eating properly and how Celeste wouldn't listen to me when I panicked about his nutrients. I needed my boy to eat properly, and no one cared but me.

"But honey," Celeste smiled, "we've got science, you know that. Science takes care of us. Minnie's got everything under control. It's not like the old days. We don't have to worry anymore."

She was right. It wasn't like back in the early twenty-first century when the news was filled with illness, devastation, human loss, and natural disaster. It was, however, thanks to the pervasive fears of that time, fears of illness, aging, and dying, that politicians had secretly funnelled billions from the taxpayers' pockets into the science labs, and the results, once uncovered, were astounding. The powers-that-be knew they were killing the world by denying the existence of global warming, and they'd collectively and secretly developed labs to create food and fuel, motivated not by altruism, but by the fact that none of them wanted to starve or die in a flood or drought or fire or get taken out by the newest raging disease, caused by alpacas or bearded dragons or, in the most deadly of cases, the family cat. Scientists had developed surgeries and scientific solutions for any manner of ailment or disease and Minnie, the Supreme World Leader, and her Sacred Board of Directors, shared this wealth of knowledge with the world.

So Celeste was right. Bax would be fine.

I was exhausted. All I wanted to do was lie down on the floor and carry on crying. Yes, the carpet at home needed cleaning and yes, I was worried about Bax not getting enough protein but, weighing on me more heavily than anything, was the fact that my paternity leave was over.

I was due back at work the next day, the thought of which tore through my gut like a tumbling drum of sharp nails and broken glass, all sloshing around in an icy pit of poisoned, oily water.

So I mopped my face and figured it would be best to follow this guy to a bar and pull myself together before I went home. I couldn't let Celeste see me like this. She thought I was Mr. Strong and Steadfast, solid as a rock, and I couldn't let her know any different.

But I realized I needed help, so I flashed a comm to my best friend, Jazza.

Need to see ya, buddy. Follow my CP.

I wondered if Jazza would even respond, given that I'd sorely neglected him since I ran out of the building into the waiting arms of my pat leave.

My CP. My Crystal Path. By logging in, Jazza could access my bio-hard drive, the neural implant microchip embedded in my brain. We all had them. Every interaction from my, and everyone else's, Crystal Path moved across The Crystal Lattice, which was like a large invisible digital spider's web around the Earth, connecting all the satellites and all of us. Even the weather was satellite-controlled and every strand of the information was part of the Crystal Lattice.

Implants became the norm shortly after Minnie took power. Even Bax had an implant that recorded his birth. The minute babies shot out into the world, red-faced and wailing, they were zapped and assigned a number. No race, no gender, just a number. There'd be no patriarchy or discrimination of any kind on Minnie's watch. We never used the numbers; I figured they were simply part and parcel of Minnie's extensive spyware. Hardly a reassuring thought, but there was nothing we could do about it. A lot of parents went wild with implants, hooking their newborns up so they could be monitored in their cribs, at childcare, at preschool, and in the playgrounds. It was important to keep an eye on the nannies, don't you know, and make sure that the robo-carers and humans weren't subjecting their beloved offspring to any horrifying abuse or disturbing discipline. Expensive software developments also allowed parents to access the kiddies' bio-stats to make sure their heart rates, blood sugars, and serotonin levels where all where they should be.

Of course, when Minnie took the throne, metaphorically speaking since royalty had gone the way of the dodo, she assured us that implants were optional, apart from birth record chip, but after she assumed control of the internet, how else were we to communicate? She dominated the service providers and established regulations that didn't let anyone else provide access. The Crystal Path wasn't exactly pure; it had its own form of the Dark Web, just like the old days, and despite my body being riddled with every manner of software that I could get my hands on, I wasn't sure I wanted Bax to have access to any of it. And yet, the creation of those implants were the very thing that gave me, and thousands of others, jobs.

The Crystal Path was like a map of screens that could be viewed at any time, all jam-packed with data and information that we could switch on or off, supposedly curated by ourselves. We were told that we could be the editors of our own content. What a joke that was! We were pawns while big business moved the pieces of our lives around the playing field.

When I went on pat leave, I shut Jazza out of my CP. You could do that, control who had access to what. Previously, Jazza had permissions to my path that Celeste didn't even know existed. I just hoped Jazza would heed my cry for help. God knew the guy owed me nothing considering how I'd dumped him when Bax was born.

I nodded at the rage room attendant. "Yeah. I'll come for a drink." I ripped my suit off, a petty act of childish fury that felt so good at the time but felt shameful later. That was me to a T: equal parts fear, guilt, shame, and anger.

The guy didn't say anything as I followed him. He had a man bun. Talk about retro. Why was I even following a guy with hair like that? But I went out to the parking lot and got behind the wheel of my solar-powered station bubble, an Integratron company car, courtesy of Celeste's father. The inside was full of yielding soft curves and cushions that moulded to my body. The round rolling ball of the car's exterior looked just like glass, but it was plastic, shatterproof polymethyl methacrylate to be exact, with a sunshiny yellow interior. Our car interiors came in a variety of colours: sky blue, fire engine red, or bubblegum pink. Pink was the most popular. The cars were cheerful, happy creatures, with scads more room than one might think, and they rolled along like soap-bubble spheres. My CP connected me to the car's displays and controls, and I could choose whether to drive the car or not. I always drove. The cars were silent and soundproof, and it felt odd, rolling along a busy suburban street or highway, and seeing other bubbles filled with reclining people who looked like they were talking to themselves, leaning back in their colourful seats and controlling the cars with their thoughts. There were no steering wheels or dashboards, just the flashview that connected the driver to the car via their CPs.

I sniffed my pits. I was annoyed with myself for skipping the post-session cleansing shower booth; my clothes had a rank, sweaty plastic smell. I'd have to do a wash down with wipes so Bax wouldn't smell me like this. I couldn't let my little guy smell the fear on me. I had to get a grip on things.

2. IN THE DIVE BAR WITH JAZZA

I FOLLOWED MAN BUN TO A DIVE BAR. He'd introduced himself as Norman. My heart did an arrhythmia dance in my chest as I drove, and I called my vitals up on my flashview. Heart rate, blood pressure, all good. When I pulled up in the parking lot, I looked around. Where was Jazza? I'd thought I'd see him waiting for me. Jazza. He was my best friend. He interned with me during initiation, and we'd been together through thick and thin, all the highs and lows of our careers. I guess that when I left for pat leave, I'd misguidedly hoped it was a case of *so long and see you never* when it came to the corporate world because I shot out of Jazza's life like a bat out of hell. And now, here I was, needing him more than ever.

I followed Norman into the bar and studied the drinks menu that flashed like a ticker tape in a fast blur, but I was really thinking about how Jazza and I had met.

I graduated from the Global International University with a Ph.D., in Optimal Communications and Life Branding, a Master's in Flexibility Optics and Mass Persuasion, and a bunch of other related psych and media relations majors. What the hell did any of that even mean?

University graduates got to audition at the three top branding companies, and I'd rated pretty poorly on the first two outings. Then, on the third, we were given partners to speed up the process, and thank god for that.

I realized, the second he opened his mouth, that Jazza was

a genius. His brain was filled with ideas the likes of which I'd never even gotten close to, glimpses that I was only permitted to spot by using the drive-thru, the lane he opened to me and only me through his CP. Brought together by happenstance, we stuck to one another, bonded by our desperate need to survive. We got hired by Integratron, my last kick at the can but, admittedly, the biggest prize. Integratron was a giant corporation linked to other global giants, tied to mass manufacturers around the world. Our job was to come up with innovative products, launches, dances, and clothing, basically any and every manner of tiny, stupid, fascinating things that obsessed people and gave their dreary, hopeless lives meaning.

Jazza and I made a great team. While I'd never had much confidence in myself or my ideas, Jazza was a chronic Asperger's boy with shameful secrets that meant he could never leave me. But he didn't want to leave me because I was the cool guy in his eyes. More importantly, I was the sales guy. I was the guy who could sell sand in the desert, water to a drowning man, a pork chop to a vegetarian—*ha ha* you get it. When I was in pusher mode, I was unstoppable.

Norman shook me from the shadows of memory lane and asked me what I wanted to drink.

"Raspberry hops, protein infusion, no alcohol," I said and Norman groaned. I called up my flashview and messaged Jazza again:

Where r u?

Would he even reply? I could see he'd accepted and read my message, and I waited for the tiny speech bubble to appear to show me that he was typing a reply. There was nothing. *Shit.* But then, came the reply:

Close

I could breathe again.

"Hi, I'm Knox," Norman's friend introduced himself. He was an over-friendly, in-your-face type of guy, vintage hipster to the bone, skinny, with a beach-ball beer belly and toothpick legs in tight jeans.

For some reason, I wanted to punch the shit out of him. But hey, that was just me. The whole world annoyed the shit out of me to the point where my mother had banned me from even using the word "annoyed" or any variation thereof. That didn't stop me from breaking shit and thinking about how "annoying" pretty much all of my life was.

"Kiddie fruity smoothie for my buddy here," Knox called out to the bartender, interrupting my thoughts. I caught sight of my reflection in the mirror and felt marginally cheered.

Thank god I had this handy mask to hide behind. People saw a handsome, reassuring man, with a cleft in his chin and a strong jaw that belied the reality. I had a thick head of hair, model good looks, and deep dimples that made it seem like I was smiling even when I wasn't. A trustworthy face. The face of a strong man. What a joke! Inside I was like Jello, afraid all the time, afraid of everything, and yet, also so damn angry with it.

Celeste loved my dimples. And the cleft in my chin. "So manly," she crooned, stroking my face like I was one of her FluffSqueaks. Since when did dents on one's face make you manly? But I smiled back at her and said encouragingly reciprocal things because that's what love was all about, right?

Knox and Norman were talking about hockey. I perked up. Sports were bigger than ever. We loved watching the steroid gladiators getting out there and pushing their bodies to insane limits. They were everything we'd never be. I tried to join the conversation, but Knox was like a shadow boxer, dancing and hopping to keep me out.

I was saved by the arrival of Jazza. I knew he had arrived because the mood in the bar changed. A hush fell, and there was a sense of freak-show wonder in the air. Jazza was a man unto himself. A six-foot-seven giant with a craggy face of folds and ridges that only a mother could love. Except that Jazza's mother didn't love him—she had vanished to live among the Blowflies, leaving him to make his own way through the various levels of state-funded care.

The Blowflies were the less fortunate economic sector who had been shuttled into the highrise condos built in the boom of the early twenty-first century. The rental wars had reached the point where no one could afford to save up for a mortgage, kids never left home, and the condos stood largely empty, save for overseas investors. And when those investors left, driven out by economic and viral disasters, the governments figured why not shunt the lesser-fortunate into the vacant skyscrapers because, among other things, it would make them easier to manage. *Affordable housing solutions at last!* cried the politicians, and thus, the inner cities of BlowflyLand were globally born. That caste kept to themselves in their tall glass castles. Admittedly the world population had dropped like a stone, thanks to all the diseases that flared up and wiped out millions. Way back in 2020, the world population was nearly eight billion. Eight billion, with the number of daily births doubling the number of deaths. Too many people! After the dust settled and we'd returned to a sensible and manageable two billion, the question was asked whether the rabid diseases had been biological warfare let loose to rein things back under control, orchestrated by Minnie's predecessors, but nothing was ever proven.

If you asked me, the Blowflies had it good. Food trucks kept them stocked with solid if unexciting fare, they had Welfare Streaming Channels twenty-four-seven, drugs kept them blissful and tame, and they even had schools for their kids. They were guarded by Welfare Ambassadors, aka security guards, because it didn't make sense to put the Blowflies to work since robots did a much better job than they did. They'd been dubbed the Blowflies by some low-grade journalist, and the name stuck.

I only knew about Jazza's mother's defection to the Blowflies by careful sleuthing. He never talked about her, and I reached a dead end without learning too much at all. I wondered if Jazza had ever tried to find her. If he had, he kept it a secret. Genius Jazza was full of secrets. For one, he liked wearing women's underwear. Big sheer granny panties, 1950's style, sheer and gauzy, with ruffled chiffon edging. And he had bras to match. I'd seen his stash, along with peach-coloured feather boas, cashmere sweaters, and fluffy angora scarves with soft fringes.

I often saw the line of a bra strap under his shirt, and I once saw the top of his frilly panties riding above his jeans. I didn't say anything then because I didn't want him to know I knew, but seriously, I couldn't let him near my Bax—are you kidding me? And I knew it hurt his feelings, but the man was an aberration even if he was my best friend. Separate the issues—work was work. He was my friend, but my kid was untouchable. That was why I ditched him. That and the fact that I really had thought I was escaping the workplace forever and that I'd never have to go back to Integratron.

"Sharps?" Jazza showed up at my side, parting the sea of people at the bar. He sounded understandably confused at being summoned, and he also didn't exactly sound warm and friendly. I guess he thought I could have visited him during my year off. But it wasn't only about the feather boa and women's underwear thing—there were his animals, too.

Jazza was a fiend for illegal real live fur babies. Genetically modified squirrels, sheep-like woolly cats, multi-coloured guinea pigs, and even a weasel. His apartment was filled with creatures, all of them scampering around and shitting everywhere. The place was a germophobe's nightmare, a fecal shit-fest of gargantuan proportions, and Jazza himself was a walking cloud of bacteria and fungi. I literally used BleachBuddy on myself when I got home from his apartment after my first visit. After that, I insisted we hang out at my apartment and, once I got married, we hardly saw each other outside of work.

So yeah, I acknowledged that Jazza's feelings had been hurt

when I excluded him from my perfect family life, but what else could I have done?

And now, a year later, he looked much the same, but he wasn't exactly enthused to see me. I thought about opening with an apology for neglecting him, but the whole thing was a can of rotting worms better left untouched.

"Yeah man, thanks for coming!" I leapt off my bar stool and hugged him, startling him by my spontaneous affection. My head rested on his big barrel chest, and he patted my head awkwardly.

"So good to see you!" I grinned. Knox and Norman were chatting up the bartender, a blonde girl, oblivious to me.

"You want a drink?" I asked Jazza, and he shook his head. "I'll get some food," he said. "Starved. I'll get us a bunch of stuff. Go sit over there."

He pointed at a booth in the corner, and I obdiently did what he said. How was I going to explain my panicked flash comm? My out-of-character summoning?

A few moments later, he settled himself into the booth and leaned back, arms folded across his chest. "They'll bring food. So buddy, you worried about coming back tomorrow?"

"Yes!" I practically shouted at him, and he looked startled. *Thank you, Jazza, for giving me an out.* Because it was that but it wasn't, it was everything. I was drowning. My life was suffocating me, and it was all of that and more.

"Everything all look the same?" I asked and he nodded.

Integratron, our hallowed place of toil and grind was a sci-fi Legoland, a sprawling estate housing hundreds of primary-coloured, dome-shaped bungalows made of interlocking durable plastic shiny blocks. The domes, or Sheds, spiralled out from the base of a two-hundred-storey, four acre, pink-and-blue skyscraper, Sky The Tower. And it was all plastic, which was par for the course. We had polybutylene terephthalate for cars; polyethelene terephthalate for clothing; good old Teflon polytetrafluoroethylene for pots, pans, and cookware; soft

polyurethane for foams and sponges; strong-bodied polycar-
bonates for appliances while acrylonitrile styrene acrylate bricks
replaced cinder blocks. We even used polylactide for medical
implants. Fluffy, furry, velvety, or glasslike, there was a plastic
for everything. Jazza and I had, out of curiousity, done the intel.
Lower eschelons worked in the Sheds, while movers and
shakers took up space in Sky The Tower. The Tower was cy-
lindrical with an open centre at the core, allowing light to flow
into the offices, and each pair of worker bees had their own
cell in the hive. No more open plan, no more shared space. It
had been proven that people, like bears, needed private caves
in which to think, hibernate, and create.

The dome-shaped Sheds, the ornamental Art Deco entrance
façade to Sky The Tower, and the giant animal statues dotting
the fake green lawns were intended to infuse the workers with
a sense of childlike joy, but they failed miserably. The inmates
were fearful desk sloggers who did the minimum and escaped
like scurrying mice as soon as the schoolbell rang.

"There are more Sheds," Jazza said. "And there's a waterfall
and atrium in the main foyer. Lots of Monarch butterflies. I find
them creepy." The butterflies weren't real, of course. Neither
were any of the plants in the atrium.

"Ah," I said and we were at a loss for a moment, silent.

"I guess we'll have to come up with a new campaign," I
finally said. "Unless you came up with something amazing
while I was gone." But I knew he hadn't because our boss and
my father-in-law, Mr. Williamson, known to me as Daddy,
would have told me.

He shook his head. Jazza wasn't being exactly welcoming,
and I needed to bring him on side. And how better than with
a little self-flaggelation, the revisiting of Jazza's successes, and
a spotlight on my failures?

"Best I don't screw up again like I did with the MDoggHot-
Body campaign," I said mournfully and I saw Jazza's craggy
face soften.

He unfolded his arms and leaned forward. "You gotta stop beating yourself up about that, buddy. Old news." He waved his hands around just as the waitress arrived, and he nearly knocked the food off the tray. Enough food to feed the bar. And it nearly landed on the floor.

"Sheee-it!" Jazza dived and saved the tray, coming up grinning. "Sorry!"

The waitress tried to avert her gaze from Jazza's misshapen face and rushed off. I felt badly for the way Jazza was treated in public, but he didn't seem to register the waitress's disgust and attacked his food with glee. He'd suffered from acromegaly as a child—his welfare family had not taken care of him as they should have—and the lingering giantism was evident in his features.

"Seriously, buddy," he said, his mouth full of onion rings and cheeseburger, "MDoggHotBody was a mistake—so what?"

So *what?* I had failed us. I had failed me. I had failed Jazza. I had failed my unborn son and Mother and Daddy. I'd brought the subject up to give us a bond, but in truth, it was never far from my mind. "Easy for you to say, genius boy," I commented. "You scored 123BlikiWin, which was historical."

He had the grace to nod modestly. "Yeah, well, by the time we got to present our shit, my brain had been working on a bunch of ideas for a while."

"Man, were we ever hot shit, then!" I said. "Home run, first time out to bat. The Board loved it!"

"Yeah, well, you sold it. They wouldn't have listened to a word from me. I don't have the visual asthetics to be a front man. Whereas you, everybody loves you!" He chewed, staring off into space, and I knew we were both thinking back to our early days, fifteen years prior.

3. GLORY DAYS

A PAY-TO-PLAY LOTTERY. Our first project. Targetted Shoppers, or TCs, had to rack up WinCreds by joining a points program that would score them a golden ticket to try out for the next golden ticket. If they won the round, they were promoted to a higher grade. There was a thirteen-level maze of lottery wins and points acquisitions and TC's had to shop their way through all of them. Finally, with the odds at one in three million, they got to be one of a dozen contestants on 123BlikiWin, the hottest reality program out there. Jazza and I created it. Correction, Jazza did. He invented the whole thing, and it was gold.

"We were a great team. We *are* a great team," I insisted. "And even more genius was us sitting on it for years, milking it. Did you score more vintage games while I was gone?"

He shook his head. "Nah. Minnie's cracked down even harder."

Great. Going back to work wasn't only going to be super stressful, we didn't even have games to pass the time.

"Hey," I said, "maybe we can do a rerun of ClothesKissez-Thugs?"

ClothesKissezThugs was Jazza's follow-up idea to the Lottery 123BlikiWin. He said it was inspired by the religious baptismal trucks that rolled out after Minnie the Great's Supreme World Leader inauguration, but instead of mimicking her Come-to-Jesus Marathon, we marketed Come-to-Style. We paced our pitches, riding the 123BlikiWin as long as we could before offering up the couture trucks of ClothesKissezThugs.

I loved Jazza's way of thinking, and at first we had fun, hanging out at work, gaming and eating crap and feeling like we owned the world, but then Mother kicked me out. She said I had to get my own apartment with her life and that she was cutting the umbilical cord. I asked her what that meaningful thing was because perhaps I could do it with her, but she just looked cagey and said I wouldn't understand.

And I got tired of cleaning up Jazza's mess at work. It was like the guy couldn't be in a room for ten seconds without making it look like *Hoarders* met *The Trashman from Outer Space*. About two days into our partnership, he looked over at me.

"Clean the shit up," he said, "if you need to. But don't expect me to do any of it and don't expect me to change."

Relieved that he understood me, I bagged his crap, wiped his sticky fingerprints off the surfaces, and sanitized the world endlessly. Cleaning brought me peace. Jazza said I was OCD and that there was a pill for that, and I said who cared, I had BleachBuddy, I didn't need pills or his psychoanalysis, thank you very much.

But, after career success, what was next? I began to feel empty. Bored. Lonely. I hit the rage rooms even harder.

The rage rooms were Minnie's idea. Three years after her ascent, an outbreak of violence spread throughout the world. People smashed up cities, rampaging with baseball bats, hammers, and wrenches. Minnie had outlawed firearms so at least no one got shot, but the damage was nonetheless widespread and extensive. Rioters tore down parks and buildings, smashed cars, and looted malls. Minnie called in an alarmingly large secret AI army. She tear-gassed the unruly and got things back under control. Who knew she had an army? We fell in line pronto. We thought Minnie would be furious and punitive in the aftermath, but instead she was sorrowful.

"I get it," she said with that honeyed voice, direct to our flashviews via our CPs. "Life is tough. Even when it's good, it's tough. Everyone has anger issues. You just need a place to express your true emotions. I didn't realize, when I banned the internet, that it was a drug you were hooked on. It was a place you could vent your opinions and feel like you had been heard." She didn't say that we were all idiots, addicted to expressing infantile opinions, but it was clear enough from her tone.

"But," she said, and her voice turned stern, "you misused the tools. I mean, my goodness, exchanging pictures of your genitals and having sexual relations willy-nilly! Encrypting messages so child pornography could thrive? You lost your way. And, by God and through God, it is my Divine Destiny to help guide you back to the path of Light. God handpicked me for this job, me, with Mama by my side, and we will help you!

"I thusly decree that rage rooms shall be constructed, places where you can express your most basic hatred and fears. Because I realize now that much of life is fuelled by hatred, rage, and fear. That is simply the way man is. You are fundamentally flawed. But, flawed though you are, you were created in God's image, and it is my Divine Task to help you shed the wages of sin and find your way back to that image, back to the perfect human beings that you were before you ate the apple and were lured by the snake."

And, at Minnie's side, her mother, Mama, leaned in and whispered something into Minnie's ear. Minnie nodded.

"Before the Advent of Minnie, the world was depressed, obese, and morbid. You spent your lives staring at screens and arguing with strangers about your ignorant opinions or pretending to love each other with likes or sad faces. Emoticons! Banning emoticons was one of my greatest triumphs. Learn to talk to each other; don't gesticulate like uneducated children flashing reader cards with stupid faces."

A wild look had come into Minnie's eyes, and Mama laid a reassuring hand on her shoulder. Mama whispered something else, and Minnie nodded again.

"But all is not lost. Every step is a step forward. So we are going to give you fun! We are going to make you happy! I thought sunshine every day would make you happy, but no! I gave you solid Vitamin D, not a cloud in the sky! Then you complained. *Why are there no clouds,* you asked! You people are so hard to please! Why are you so hard to please? So I got you clouds."

She shut her eyes, and Mama patted her again. "Right. There shall be rage rooms where you can express your rage and frustration to your heart's content."

In addition to the rage rooms, Minnie poured money into streaming new shows. Robots invented new dances and we became preoccupied, adult and child alike, trying to learn new moves and share clips of ourselves thus engaged. Once again, we found ourselves staring at screens, our viewing monitored by Minnie the Belle.

Minnie also gave us comfort centres. I tried them out too, but I've got restless leg syndrome and can't lie still for any amount of time without feeling like I'm going to go nuts, the ants under my skin wanting to eat me alive.

"Nope, we ran ClothesKissezThugs dry." Jazza grinned, bringing me back into the moment. "Ha, but we did good with CrystalMeBooty. Think about the good times, buddy. That was you as much as me."

I laughed. Despite the circumstances, it was good to be talking to Jazza again, reliving our glory days.

The follow-up to ClothesKissezThugs was CrystalMeBooty. Towering crystal-sided transport trucks rolled out with strobe lights and disco mirror balls, and the music became urgent, angry, and hateful, which only increased its appeal. Not everyone could place a purchase; TCs had to earn points to be considered Big Spenders, accruing a certain level of debt before being given access to the arenas of superior consumerism. And oh, the shame if you weren't that level. For some reason, the Big Spender and CrystalMeBooty made even more money than 123BlikiWin. Pretty soon, the whole world was in hock, just to be on the so-called right playing field.

Meanwhile, my life became increasingly utterly meaningless. I don't know what I would have done if Celeste hadn't come along. She and Bax changed everything. I finally knew my purpose. Family. My family was the only thing that mattered, the only thing that gave any kind of meaning to this sham plastic world. All I wanted was to be a stand-up guy. I wanted my boy to be able to say, *That's my Dad!* with a mixture of choked-up pride and overwhelming love. I wanted Celeste to look over at me, *There's my man, he's the guy, don't you know?*

But the minute I had Bax, my worries increased a thousand-fold. How would I keep up in this fiercely competitive world? And, increasingly, I couldn't afford Celeste. Of course, Celeste was a great fan of CrystalMeBooty and Daddy's money was, as he himself often reminded me, limited when it came to keeping Celeste in the style to which the world had told her she needed to remain accustomed.

And what about when Bax grew up? How could I make sure he had what he needed, to be part of the respected world of The Haves? How could I make sure he didn't get into drugs? There were rumours of strange sex clubs popping up like fungi in a forest, which was a bit rich coming from me, given my predilictions, but I didn't want Bax to end up an anxiety-ridden, anger-driven worrier like I was.

4. THE TRUTH INSIDE

JAZZA SNAPPED HIS FINGERS IN FRONT OF MY FACE. "Earth to Sharps! What's going on inside your alleged brain? Still wallowing about MDoggHotBody?"

I shook my head. How could I tell him about the fear I felt for just about everything? How I couldn't sleep at night, and when I finally managed to doze, I was beset by terrifying dreams of being publically humiliated at work, arriving for a meeting unprepared and having to flub my way through. I dreamed that massive white fire trucks, steel ghosts the size of buildings, tried to mow me down while I rolled out from in between their wheels with my colleagues laughing at me, their mouths wide and fingers pointing.

How could I tell Jazza that even when I looked calm, icy sweat was pooling in my pits and snaking down my sides into the waistband of my trousers? That my unflinching, sincere gaze was a mask and all I wanted to do was fall to my knees and sob uncontrollably? I had no idea why I felt so terrified all the time, terrified of everything. I'd always been afraid but ever since I'd had Bax, the terror had become rampant. It was as if the world's dangers were magnified and all I saw were monsters and demons around every corner.

"You've got Daddy," Jazza said, mopping up mustard with onion rings. "You're safe as houses, and you know it. Teflon Boy, that's you." He pointed at me with a french fry, and I nodded.

"True. But there's Ava." I shuddered as I uttered her name.

Jazza laughed. "She's not so bad," he said, and I looked at him in horror.

"Not so bad? She's a scorpion! What happened?" I leaned forward. "Since when did Ava become 'not so bad?'" I air quoted him.

He shrugged, and I swore I saw him blush. "Jazza?" I pushed him harder.

"She writes poetry," he said, sheepishly.

"And? So what? I wrote poetry too before I realized it was a lost cause."

"You did? When?"

"Ancient history. So how come you know aboout this poetry? And what's it about?"

"It's experimental poetry, about men and what shits we are, basically. Her book's called *And She Shall Rule the Day,* and it's about what cretins men are, good for nothing except for being big hot swinging dicks when a woman feels like a booty call or having a baby the old-fashioned way."

"You read it?"

"She read it to me."

"And you understood her? I can never hear what she's saying. I swear it's a power thing, how softly she talks. Fucking whispers everything."

"I understand her just fine."

He was right, he did. Even in meetings, he'd scribble down what she said when he knew I had no idea what was going on.

"It's brutal but good. I hate to say it, but she nailed our Neanderthalism to a T. It's a clever title. *And She Shall Rule the Day,* but it also means *He Shall Rue the Day*! And, mark my words, we will, Sharps."

I stared at him. "Jazza, you're really scaring me. I thought you were in my camp. I thought we were both batting for the same team, team you and me."

He pushed his food away, his second burger half uneaten.

"Ava likes me," Jazza said. "Okay, well, maybe not me. She likes my dick, I'll tell you that much."

"What?" I was speechless. "You fucked Ava? When? How did your dick not turn green and fall off?"

"Actually, she's pretty hot in bed. And besides hookers, who'd have me, Sharps? It's not like you've even invited me to your home." Ah. He finally cut to the chase. "I'm just the brain you ride. I don't have anybody, Sharps. You ever think of that? All you think about is being Mr. Perfect, Mr. I-Have-Everything, perfect little baby boy, a perfect little wifey. What do you care?"

I wanted to tell him the truth. "But it's harder than you think," was all I could manage, and I looked away. When I looked back at him, I saw the scepticism on his face and I realized I'd have to be more forthcoming. I had to sell him on Team Jazza/Sharps, which annoyed me. If I wanted his support, I was going to have to work for it. I sighed inwardly and leaned forward, my sincerity mask in place.

"Jazza," I started, and he laughed.

"You're shitting me, Sharps. I can see it. You think I don't know you? You called me here because you somehow knew about me and Ava and you wanted to find out how it would affect you."

"I had no idea about you and Ava," I said, and Jazza could hear I was telling the truth. "I asked you to come here because Celeste..." But I couldn't carry on. I couldn't admit that things weren't great. And what if I told Jazza and he told Ava, who told Daddy?

"Celeste what? You see, Sharps, that's you, you never tell me anything." Jazza got up to leave but I grabbed his arm.

"Please, Jazza," I said, and my eyes filled with tears. Jazza immediately sank back down.

"I just..." And then I was crying. Crying in a bar. Jazza slid into the booth next to me and put his giant arm around my shoulder. "I try so hard," I sobbed, and it was such a relief to get it out. "I'm worry so much, Jazza. I'm sorry I don't invite you home. There are things I can't tell you, things I have to deal with."

I felt Jazza's big body melt against his side, and a surge of relief filled my chest. I couldn't afford to lose him. I wound down, blowing my nose loudly into the napkin that Jazza handed me. He patted me on the shoulder until I had cleaned up and then he went back and sat across from me.

"There are meds for that," he observed, and I shook my head. "No. I don't want to go there. I'm just stressed. About going back to work, yeah, and then hearing that you've been banging The Whispering Queen. Kind of took the wind out of my sails. You really did the nasty with her?"

He nodded. "Where did you guys hook up?" I couldn't imagine precise, starched, pleated, and ironed Ava in Jazza's apartment, but of course I was wrong.

"My place, and hers. She loved my fur babies! And her place is really cool. It's like an underground honeycomb cave. The walls are made of stone quartz, and they change colour. And it smells good. There's no décor, just a mattress and a big screen that covers one wall with mountains or waterfalls, whatever you feel like. I said it was very monastic, and she said she didn't think in such gender-restrictive terms, she just liked the simplicity and purity. She also loves old Kung Fu movies. Man, we had fun!"

I wanted to ask how Ava felt about his granny panties but didn't feel I could go there.

"How many times did you hook up?"

He looked away. "I dunno. Lost count."

So that's what Jazza had been doing while I was hanging out with Bax, changing diapers and studying my kid's fecal matter for irregularities. "Lost count? Were you ever going to tell me?"

He hunched his shoulders, and I told myself to back down. "Like you cared. Anyway, like I said, I'm just a dick to her.

Literally." He paused. "Sharps, I don't have any real data on this, but I think Ava was, or still is, a Blowfly!"

"What? No shit! That's impossible! They can't infiltrate the outer perimeters. What makes you say that?"

"Clues in her book."

I cued my CP for *And She Shall Rule the Day,* but there was nothing. "I can't access it," I said, and he shook his head.

"It's print. Hard copy. And you're probably spelling it literally. It's *S(h*)E shALL R.U.L.E the day**" He wrote it on a napkin for me, and I studied it.

"Pretentious and incomprehensible. Just like her. Never makes sense. But wait. What? Nothing is in print! You saw a copy? Do you have one?"

"Nope. She wouldn't give me one. I only got to look at it when when she went to the washroom. It was published by The Eden Collective on behalf of The World Wide Warriors."

"Who? Are they Blowflies? It doesn't make any sense."

I wondered if this had anything to do with Jazza's mother, but I had the good sense not to ask.

He shrugged again. "I don't know for sure, but there were clues in the poems. It's also about how colonialism and patriarchy are still fucking up the world despite a woman being in power. We need to recalibrate and revolution is the only way. Pretty intense. "

"Why didn't you screencapcha it while she was gone?"

He looked away.

"You did! You've got a copy!"

"Yeah. But I won't give it to you." He looked petulant and frightened. "And you can't make me, Sharps. This is mine."

I'd seen that expression before with Bax and his favourite toy. I knew better than to trigger a black hole tantrum. I held up my hands in surrender. "I will never mention it again." Maybe I could hack into Jazza's drive.

"And don't think you can hack me," he said, reading my face. "I've got firewalls that will burn you backwards in time."

"Firewalls!" I laughed. "Talk about nostalgia." A red exclamation mark popped up in the corner of my eye. Incoming flash comm from Celeste.

Where r u?

I swiped it away, leaving it marked unread. "I gotta go," I said to Jazza, but I made no move. "Listen, buddy, I know I've failed you as a BFF. But we're a team, right? I've got Daddy, you've got Ava, and we'll rule the world, right?"

I needed Jazza like never before. I had wanted to stay home with Bax and somehow have Daddy support us—that had been my ridiculous fantasy—but Daddy said I had to go back to work. He said that the Board said Jazza and I needed to come up with something shiny and new.

But what if Jazza and I couldn't come up with anything? Daddy had also said I had to be his eyes and ears at the company because he'd heard that Ava was gunning for the top position and he wanted to nail her. As if that was breaking news, and besides, I didn't care about any of that. I wanted Bax and me to be together forever, alone. Me and my boy. But Daddy told me I had to be there, on the ground, to tell him everything I heard, so I had no choice.

Jazza nodded when I said that about us being a team but his body language lacked conviction. Great. One more thing for me to have to worry about.

"Wait," he said as I got up, and I sat back down. "I think Ava's gunning for Minnie."

"What the fuck? Minnie? The God Appointed Supreme World Leader? That Minnie?"

"That Minnie."

This I had to hear.

5. AVA'S PLAN FOR WORLD DOMINATION

I FLASHED A COMM TO CELESTE.
    Sorry hun, still at team mtg with Jazza. Get an InstaNanny if u
    need help. Sorry babes.
    "Back up," I said. "Minnie? I'm going to get us another
round of drinks. "Attacking Minnie is like attacking God,
only harder."
    "I think Ava's going to start by trying to bring back nature."
    I burst out laughing. "How, exactly?" Talk about living in
lala land. Ava didn't have a hope in hell. Global warming had
killed nature, and there was no bringing it back. Minnie had
taken the food labs from the early twenty-first century a step
further, and declared farming dead. It was time for humans to
take control and stop being at the mercy of Mother Nature.
Farmlands were transformed into football field labs, and the
world was studded with giant condom-shaped pustules birthing
perfect shiny red tomatoes, fire-orange flawless carrots, and
every kind of fruit and vegetable imaginable, plus new combi-
nations offering optimal nutrition and edible perfection. Here,
have a bananacot, an ingenious blend of banana and apricot,
with added protein. The result: a chubby orange fist-shaped
fruit was one of the more popular inventions.
    Meat was harvested in bioreactor labs using cloned animals
that had long since ceased to exist. Minnie said we needed to
discard the idea of the animal being the producer of food, and
she worked with cellular scientists to make it happen. Meat

proved easier to produce than eggs, which we soon forgot about altogether. Milk was replaced with an allergy-free formula that promoted growth, increased brain mass, and aided the fatty neurons that fired our intelligence.

As if we needed all that added intelligence. We weren't exactly doing anything with it except sitting around streaming shows on our CPs or shopping. The civilized world saw their lands divided into two: shiny plastic cities on the one hand, and plastic bubble farms on the other. The farms were auto run by robots, with two human foremen per, just in case. In case of what? It was inconceivable that anything might go awry.

"We can't go back to real nature," I told Jazza. "That would mean hijacking the satellites. We killed nature. There's nothing left. We'd all starve to death."

"It would be a struggle, at first," Jazza admitted. "But Ava said she'd make sure there were food reserves until the earth got back on its feet."

"Imagine having real weather," I mused. "I wonder what would happen?"

It was something I had thought about before. Major cities had been declared snow-free zones because studies had proven that most people didn't like snow, and besides, sidewalk ice was a health and safety hazard. It was too dangerous for children to toboggan down hills or skate on outdoor ponds, a law I'd thought ridiculous until I had Bax and then I changed my mind. Avid skiers were initially enraged by the loss of snow, but they soon adapted to skiing on virtual slopes, agreeing it was way better than the real thing. A protest by the Yuletide Purists changed the laws enough to ensure that a light dusting of flakes arrived at Christmas time. Three inches of perfect powder was deemed just enough to be aesthetically pleasing.

And, for our further health, safety, and convenience, it only rained at night because people voted that the rain was "too wet."

"Crazy," I said. "Ava doesn't have a hope in hell of getting to

Minnie's satellites. Remember Minnie's armies after the riots?"

"Minnie's not infallible," Jazza said. "AI armies can be hacked and, anyway, remember the water catastrophe? Epic fail for Minnie."

I nodded, running my tongue over my teeth as if to reaffirm they were still there. Due to a miscalculation during the Sacred Board's first stab at creating ionized, enhanced, immune-building, disease-lessening water, we lost our teeth and ended up with implants, steel rods capped with white titanium. Orthodontic perfection, built to last for a thousand lifetimes. It was weird how we all had the same smile, except for people like Celeste who spent big bucks on a deluxe designer variation.

"I always found it weird that Minnie never lost her teeth," I said. "She stuck with her crazy junk-yard smile. I always wanted to ask, hey Minnie, how come your teeth didn't fall out and why don't you want these shiny new ones?"

"Ava said the same thing," Jazza said. "But she said she's known too many people who asked questions and disappeared."

"Which is why going up against Minnie makes no sense! Minnie controls the world!"

"She understands the pervasive power of consumer capitalism versus that of free-market capitalism," Jazza said. I raised an eyebrow and he turned the colour of a ripe bruise.

"Okay, so Ava said that, not me. But it makes perfect sense. The religion of the dollar."

"And yet, Minnie professes to be on a mission from God."

"Her God. If you ask me, it's not Minnie we need to get rid of, it's her mother."

I nodded. "Good old Mama."

All this talking had made me hungry, and I waved the waitress over. I sensed Jazza had a lot more up his sleeve, and I wasn't leaving until I had the full scoop.

"I'd kill Mama first," Jazza said, returning to the topic. "I frickin' hate that woman. Leader of the Righteous Reform, my ass. What kind of woman would invent the Sanctified Priesthood? Lose my balls just to get a job for life? No thank you! I'd start by strangling her with her sapphire and ruby rosary. You know how heavy that thing must be? Still, it was the Holy Water of God's Light trucks that gave me the idea for our campaign, so thanks, Mama, for that."

Men who wished to join the Sanctified Priesthood could do so with one small condition: they had to have gonadectomies, in other words, have their balls chopped off. No desire, ergo, no sin. And since unemployment was at an all-time high, record numbers of men signed up to join The Renewed Catechism of the Righteous, cutely called the NewCats. You got employment, a roof over your head, and benefits for life. The thought of being a NewCatCenobite made me shudder.

"Even the Pope called Mama the salt of the Earth, a miracle sent by Jesus Himself," I said. "But you have to look at the positives. No suicide bombers. No racism. No more nuclear programs. And Celeste's a NewCat. I love going to church."

"You just like to sing. There's karaoke for that, buddy."

"You know where her power comes from?" I asked. "Minnie's? From her voice. You know the way sound vibrations make patterns in sand and can even change the shape of plastic? She does that to our brains. She hypnotizes us. I mean, she's an ugly little shit!"

"Yeppers. But hey, I'm not exactly an oil painting."

I felt shamed. How could I comment on looks when I was born so blessed while Jazza had been birthed on the opposite side of the spectrum? I had reached a new level of low.

"Well," I said, my voice an apology, "I still don't get how Ava plans to infiltrate all of this. Minnie is not only the Supreme World Leader, she is the Honoured President and Commander-in-Chief of the Sacred Board of Global Nations. She controls everything."

"Power comes and power goes," Jazza said.

"Can I see the capchas of Ava's poems?"

"No."

"Aw, come on! I'm your pal!"

Jazza laughed. "When you want to be. Anyway, Ava trusts me. I won't betray that."

Three red dots flashed in the corner of my eye. A level-two urgent message. I waved it away. Celeste. She was getting annoyed with me for taking so long. I ignored her and turned back to Jazza. "You won't win," I repeated. "And if you don't know by now, you'll never find out what's Ava's up to. She sounds beyond your level of code.

Jazza looked annoyed. "No one is beyond my level of code," he said, and his craggy brow furrowed. "I just have to find a way in."

And I have to find a way to survive all of this. How? All I wanted to do was crawl under the table and sleep for the rest of my life.

Sweetie!

Celeste finally used the emergency data pin to get me in a way I couldn't ignore.

Come home! We've got great news! Come on, honey! Come home!

Great. I sighed. "I've got to get going. See you tomorrow, Jazza."

He stood up, dwarfing me, and I could see the outline of a lacy bra peeking out under the sleeve of his T-shirt. Peach. "Sharps," he said, "look. We've been together since the start. I know I didn't tell you about Ava, but I was going to, I swear. I mean, I had no idea she wanted to have sex with me. After the first time, I felt embarrassed, like I'd been so stupid and I thought you'd laugh at me if I told you. And you would have, but then she came back and it was so great. It *is* so great."

"Are you in love with her?" I asked, and his face went the colour of a spoiled strawberry. "You are? Oh, shit."

"I know it's pointless," he said and he hung his head. "Wouldn't you be in love with her?"

"Ava? Shit, no way! She's like a bubble scorpion." Bubble

scorpions were vicious furry bumblebees with balloon bubble limbs in a game Jazza and I played. "I can just see her big yellow stinger waiting to zap me. She hates me!"

"She isn't fond of the way Mr. Williamson supports you." Jazza was tactful.

"No, she hates *me*. And even if she didn't, I wouldn't fall in love with her. My dick would fall off like an icicle if it even tried to enter the arctic cave of her vagina. Oh my God, I can't believe I'm discussing Ava's vag with you! Ugh!"

Jazza had a dreamy look in his eye, and I snapped my fingers at him.

"Jazza! Just let me know if she's going to stab me in the back, okay? At least give me warning."

"Yeah," he said mournfully and looking like a basset hound. I wanted to slap him into sensibility.

"What's the matter?" I asked.

"She's too good for me. She's way out of my league. You're right, Sharps, she must have wanted something from me. And I just have this feeling … like I've just lost something I should have taken better care of." He rubbed his head. "My head hurts too. I wish I hadn't told you any of this."

"Yeah, well, I don't mean to cut you off but I've got to go. I've been summoned by Celeste. Great news awaits at home, apparently."

"I think I'll just sit here for a while," Jazza said, and I left him to it, messaging Celeste that I was on my way home and getting into my car. But then I just sat there. I just couldn't put the car into drive. Too many memories flooded my mind. I needed a moment to myself. I set the seat to recline and tried to figure out how my life had become such a mess.

6. FINDING MY GLITTER BALL AND CHAIN

I WAS FORTY-FOUR WHEN I MET CELESTE. Over the hill. It was hard to believe, but Jazza and I had been a team for fifteen years. I'd taken my time getting to university, having suffered long bouts of depression in my teenage years, episodes that saw me bedridden, only getting up to smash the living daylights out of whatever was at hand and then crawling back into bed.

Years of nurturing by Mother, along with therapy, pills, and even electric shock therapy finally whipped me into good enough shape to get me through school and into university. I was quite content to remain a professional student for the rest of my life, eking out grants for as long as I could, but the government cracked down and booted a bunch of us out.

It wasn't even fair, who got kicked out. It worked via a lottery system, and I later wondered if that was where Jazza got the idea for the 123BlikiWin, because he got kicked out too. He was a math and science guy. He had his Ph.D. by the time he was nineteen, which is when we met. I was twenty-nine.

I'd always harboured a secret fantasy. I wanted to be seated at the head of the dinner table, with my family quietly eating their food, my wife dressed like a twentieth-century fifties movie star. She'd be smiling at me, supportively and kindly, like she got how hard it all was, and she loved and admired me for my ability to navigate the daily grind of life. I think it came from me never having had that as a kid. All I had ever wanted was a normal, safe, suburban life—no shocks, just cruising along with everything nearly in order.

"Here's to you, mister," my wife would say, lifting her glass of soda water with a twist of lime. "Thank you for keeping us safe today in a world filled with peril. How was your day?"

And I got my wife and I got my kid, but I could never tell them how my day really was and the furthest thing I felt was safe.

There was so much I hadn't known about Celeste when I married her. I didn't know that she'd spend hundreds of dollars on trending toys, like those god-awful fake budgies. Thank god the IridescentFlyShiny craze ended, and there were no more birds. I didn't know that she was so messy. Or that she'd be a bad mother. And a drunk. She was a frequent flyer on the AllGoodGetWell rehab program that was five-star all the way. She'd never worked a day in her life, and she'd lied about that.

I met Celeste at a party at work. I hated parties, but I had to go. The irony was that Ava had told me to go, and she herself never showed up. Since she wasn't what you'd call a people person, it was probably for the best.

The venue was typical of the time: a ballroom of mirrors with pale blue satin painted panels and carved curlicued sconces. Chandeliers dripped crystal and chrome, and everybody stood around fake smiling and wondering when they could get drunk or leave. I fell into the latter category.

I was leaning against the wall talking to a woman who had her coat buttoned to the collar and her backpack neatly in place, straps neatly parallel. I guessed she wasn't planning on staying long either, but at least I tried to look like I was participating, beer in hand, casual smile, flashing my dimples and talking about a serial killer series on the HumerusNumerous channel that was all the rage. Jazza preferred the ParityParallelUniverse channel or EchoSerialFree, but they were too gory for me.

I was calculated; I watched trending series so I'd fit in and have something to talk about. That, plus sports, and I was okay. And, at that moment, talking to the woman who was clearly less socially at ease than I was, I felt as comfortable as a prime time talk show host. I wished Ava was there to see me. I hated her but I also felt a weird desire to please her and that made me hate her even more.

And it was then, at that very moment, just when I felt like I could fit in, that I saw Celeste. How could I miss her? She was a battleship of cleavage and glitter, and she flipped her blonde hair back and laughed, just like the fifties' pinup I'd always dreamed about. A Marilyn Monroe smile, big white teeth and high cheekbones, so shiny and wholesome. I found out later that her avatar name was ShinyFangGlitterBaby, which really should have told me all I needed to know.

"Mr. Williamson's baby girl," backpack woman said. I knew the ill-at-ease woman was in pixel development or something, a part-timer in the Sheds, and I could never remember her name. I had a real job in the Tower, reporting to Ava who reported to Mr. Williamson, but I never knew he had a daughter.

"Oh god, here she comes," backpack woman said, and she ducked around me and scuttled out the door. I looked around and saw the glitter battleship heading towards me. Me! Buoyed by confidence with my encounter with Shed woman, I straightened my shoulders and sucked in my gut, although I worked out a lot so really there was no worry there. But then the beauty queen, a bit past her prime if one was honest, sailed right by me, and I was left standing and grinning like an idiot, my hand held high, a fool for all the world to see.

And they did see. My mirrored reflection told me that everyone had seen but were mostly just happy it hadn't happened to them. There was the tiniest pause, like the screen froze, but then it went back to noise and chatter and fake tinkle this and fake tinkle that.

I'd had enough. I put my glass down and reached for my coat.

"Sharps!" It was Mr. Williamson. The very guy we were there for. "Have you met my daughter, Celeste?"

The glitter battleship was back, flipping her hair and smiling. I wondered if she was on Feel, the latest drug to keep you comfortably numb forever.

"Delighted," I said, and I held out my hand. Celeste took it absently, but then her eyes focused and she leaned in closer. " Great dimples," she said, and her gaze actually held mine for two long seconds.

"He's my boy!" Mr. Williamson bellowed. He'd been a big fan since I was an intern; he made scads of money off Jazza's and my work. "Been with us forever," he told his daughter. "Will be with us forever if I have any say in it."

"Great to hear that, sir!" I beamed back at him.

"Say," he whispered, "how's Ava these days?"

A *bitch as usual*, I wanted to reply but I held my tongue. "Fine," I said and forced a smile.

"Good man. Listen, look after Celeste here for me, will you? I've got to do the rounds, make a speech *blah blah*. Don't know why they even had this thing. Forty-five years is a drop in the ocean. I'm not going anywhere for the next forty-five, *har har!* But drinks are good for morale and they're tax-free, so there you go!"

He left me with Celeste, and there was an awkward silence. She played with her bracelets, and I wondered why she didn't leave and schmooze with the rest of the room. I was sure anybody there was more interesting than me.

"You look like Jason Bateman," she said. "He died, in what, 2025? I love his avatar! So gorgeous! He still models for Armani and Givenchy and Dior."

"Yeah, I've heard the comp before," I said, trying to think of something fascinating to say. I was losing her. Her averted gaze had a vacant, dead-eyed look, the kind I saw in Ava's eyes whenever I started speaking.

Why did I even care what the glitter battleship thought? I cared because I was lonely and tired of being alone. I'd tried to convince myself that I was used to it. Sure I was, I worked out while streaming or I planned strategies for work or I tried to get Mother to return my flash comms or I talked to Betsy, my FurryFurlong avatar hedgehog. Yeah, I'm not ashamed to admit that I'm a hedgehog man. Betsy's the cutest thing! Her little tummy! But even with all of that, along with my ever-present, increasing preoccupation that I would be fired from work and fulfil my inevitable destiny as a Blowfly, I was lonely. Deep pockets of loneliness cemented my neatly sandwiched packages of time. That was how I saw time, boxes in a day, with each box having its allotted content, and you either filled the content neatly or you failed. I graded every box as a success or a fail. Mother said I needed to loosen up. She said I was getting worse, but I told her that the very thought of loosening up increased my anxiety.

Mother also said that I was too extreme, either cleaning things to high gloss or destroying them and creating a terrible mess. She added that she was getting unspeakably weary of having the same conversations with me. She said we both knew I had obsessive compulsive disorder, regardless of whatever kinder psych label was being bandied about. She urged me to return to therapy, but I ignored her. I told her that I had the rage rooms, and she replied that smashing things wasn't the same as addressing them. I retorted that I simply needed to clean more, which was the tipping point. Her interest in me started to wane as surely as the tides on my virtual seaside vacays pulled back and slipped away.

And, in the very same way, I watched Celeste embark on the great sail of her departure. Just as she was about to turn away, her father reappeared. "Say," he said, sounding slightly out of breath, "you kids want tickets to the hockey game?"

We both sprang to attention, beaming. Hockey tickets were hen's teeth in a barnyard of ducks.

"Pick me up at six," Celeste said, flashing her address to my CP. "We'll go early. I love hockey so much!"

She was all smiles, ear to ear, and in that moment, I was my travel avatar self, SmashingSablink007 carving through a big wave, power surfing. So much for Ava! I was the man! I was the chosen one! I had a date with Mr. Williamson's daughter!

7. GETTING HITCHED

OUR HOCKEY DATE WAS A GIGANTIC SUCCESS. Celeste was an animal, pounding on the glass, drinking beer, swearing like a sailor. She was a powerhouse, and all I had to do was be there.

She annoyed the people around us, blocking their view and spilling drinks on them, but I made her feel loved no matter what. I had, miraculously, got one foot in the door. I had to make this work.

What exactly did I mean by "make it work?" Marry her? Yes. Exactly. She could make my fantasy come true. I wanted to prove to my loser father that I could be the man he'd never been, and I wanted to show Mother I was a winner. I could already see the family Christmas Flashcard, Celeste and the kids in white, a silver-and-blue crystal Christmas tree in the background, me in a pale blue suit, grinning. Happy Christmas from the Barkley Family! Plus, marrying Celeste would secure me a lifetime office in Sky The Tower, Jazza or no Jazza. I'd be promoted to the hundred and fiftieth floor at least, and I'd be okay with that, being a middle-man, interviewing the interns that I had once been. I could put my feet up on my white Lego desk, or no, maybe not actually put my feet up, because I'd leave scuff marks, but I'd metaphorically put my feet up and enjoy the view.

So when Celeste spilled half of her fifth beer on me, I just laughed. No worries! *Har har!* I laughed just like her father did, with my head thrown back. We were having so much fun! Weren't we having fun?

"Oh baby," she said later, in the bubble limo Daddy had sent for us, "you're the best! Sweetie, I'm so glad I met you. I wasn't even going to come to that awful drinks thing, but I'm so glad I did! Listen, you wanna go to church with us on Sunday?"

Church? Celeste was one of Mama and Minnie's NewCats? I thought they were passé. I must have looked startled because she grabbed my hand and held it tight. "Yeah sweetie, we go every week. Mummy, Daddy, and me. And then we have brunch after. You'll come, right? I've never asked anybody before! Well, actually, yeah, no, I did but that was years ago." A sad look crossed her face, and I brushed the hair out of her eyes. I hadn't realized she used that much hair spray. I wanted to wipe my fingers on the car seat, but I didn't want her to notice.

"Yeah, we're NewCats. Mama's still around, still fighting for Jesus, and we have to too! Jesus would never give up on us, right? Come on, sweetie, and then we have brunch after— Mimosas and hot chocolate and eggs benny!"

"I'm not super religious," I said, not wanting to admit the extent of my atheism but trying for some level of honesty.

"Sweetie, you don't have to be." She was earnest. "Just come. Okay? It's only an hour and then food to die for! And you'll meet Mummy!"

"What must I wear?"

She thought this was hilarious, but I was serious. What did one wear to church?

"Seriously, Cee, what must I wear? I worry about stuff like that."

"And that's what makes you the gentleman you are, baby! Okay, specifics: no running shoes, loafers are good; a linen shirt, two buttons open, not more; no jewellery, not that you wear any; a blazer is good, blue is always in style."

I sighed with relief. "Thank you. It's the little things that get to me," I said, and I pulled her closer. "Keep me up at night. I worry, you know. I try to do things right. I want to do things right but sometimes the details are so vague."

"I'll always be specific with you, honey-pie," she said, and she snuggled in. "Like right now, I want your tongue in my mouth, nice and deep."

I did what she said, and I must have been okay at it because she moaned and groaned and I swear she had an orgasm in the back of the limo just from me kissing her and rubbing my hand on her crotch. I was worried she'd want to come home with me, but she had the limo drop me off and she blew kisses as I watched her being driven away.

The next day, she flashed me to say that Mummy and Daddy were so excited I was coming to church! She added I that could wear a tie but Daddy never did. I spent all Friday watching my bitch boss Ava, grinning, and knowing I had the ace up my sleeve. I just had to play it right.

It turned out that I loved church. I'd only seen the buildings from the outside, white-washed Dutch-style barns with a small gable at each end and a high-pitched red corrugated roof with ornamental rooster weathervanes.

The NewCat flag was clearly still flying high, with the parking lot spreading for miles and the service well attended. The church interior was a shock. The place was a neon carnival with white pews and white leatherette cushions. The Stages of The Cross flanked the walls while Jesus hung from a giant white neon cross at the front. He was surrounded by fluttering cherubs and angels while blood flowed convincingly from his face and side in a fluid neon movement. Jesus was a good-looking surfer fellow, and I was momentarily taken aback by his likeness to the ever-popular Chris Hemsworth avatar. Big blond Thor was the new Jesus? No wonder attendance was so high. No wonder Celeste was such a fan. The seats were comfy too. Memory foam, I bet. Once you sat your ass down, it was hard to get up.

Celeste's mother was thrilled to see me, and she kept showering me with double-wide smiles. Mummy's teeth were replacements of course, but they seemed weirdly small, which was odd since dentures were measured with such precision. Mummy'd had the work: implants, botox, facelifts, and dyed hair, with extensions filling out her thinning thatch. Mummy was a Swarovski waterfall of diamonds, clad in Chanel and her Wolverine manicure looked deadly.

But what amazed me was how much I loved church. It was so organized and clean and white and shiny with not so much as a dustmote daring to float on a sunbeam. The Williamsons were right to be NewCats. I wished I had joined a church before. I'd tell Jazza, maybe get him to come, but I quickly stopped myself. No. No Jazza. Ever.

And the songs! Gone were the ancient dirge-like laments, replaced by happy ditties. We sang "She'll Be Coming 'Round the Mountain" and "If You're Happy And You Know It" and "Jesus Loves Me, This I Know." I joined in, cautiously at first but with increasing gusto. Daddy and Mummy and Celeste were amused by my enthusiasm, and I soon lost my self-consciousness.

"There's a side to you I never knew," Mr. Williamson commented as we were leaving and I blushed. Had I let myself lose control? I was about to apologize when Celeste grabbed my hand and shushed her father.

"We're looking for men to join our choir," the priest appeared at my side. "I couldn't help but hear your wonderful tenor.

I nodded, close to tears with joy. His kindness hit me hard, and I just nodded. To be wanted!

The priest said he'd flash me the details, and, as we walked to the limo, I thought that even if things ended with Celeste, that I'd be okay. At the very least, I'd got the church choir out of it. I wished I'd thought of it before.

We arrived at brunch and left the girls, as Mr. Williamson called them, to their first round of drinkies in the main lounge. We headed for the men's bar.

"Wanted to chat to you man to man," Daddy said, tapping the side of his nose like an old-fashioned British spy. "Celly is a bit fragile. Likes to tipple a wee bit, but it's because she struggles in life. Mummy found a place in life with her charities, but Celly has always been a bit lost. We wanted an ordinary life for her, as much as one can have one—you know, kiddies and family traditions. Celly is an only child and getting on in years, and we'd both like grandkiddies, me in particular. I love the little chaps. I don't know why I never thought of you and Celly before. There you were, right under my nose and I never saw it!"

He beamed at me, and I was starting to wilt under the hothouse stare of his pale general's eyes. I was backed up against the bar, and the edge cut into my spine. I worked to maintain my grin while I nodded.

"Marriage and kiddies would make Celly happy. How old are you, son?"

"Forty-four." I forced the answer through clenched teeth. My back couldn't take much more.

"Perfect. Celly's thirty-eight. And we can get you help if she can't conceive."

Conceive? We hadn't been on a second date! Regardless, everything I'd ever wanted was all coming my way, albeit it somewhat like a freight train.

"Don't shoot blanks do you, son?" Daddy lost his good cheer, and the edge of the bar bit deeper into my spine.

"No, sir. At least I don't think so."

"We'll have you tested," he said. "Celly's fertile. We've had to get her out of sticky situations more than once. Losers she met in rehab and brought home. Those places weren't cheap either! Not sure how they let people like that in; they were practically Blowfly level! It took a while, but we learned our lesson and sent her to a private clinic, women only. She still makes friends—that's just who she is—and she's getting better every day. Listen son, to segue, be careful of Ava. She's in line for my title when I move up the ladder, but I'm going to throw your hat in the ring instead of hers. You've been the dark horse all this time, and I sense a winner in you. Plus, I don't like Ava one bit."

By now, I was bent over backwards and my back was ready to snap in two. I was going down two vertebrae at least. I was beginning to have my doubts about the whole thing. Take on Ava? Not a chance in hell. I was struggling as it was. And Celeste sounded like harder work than I cared for. Rehab? Sticky situations? Daddy must have seen the fear in my eyes because he gripped my arm and yanked me close, patting me on the back so hard I nearly choked.

"Don't worry son," he said soothingly. "One thing at a time. We'll get your swimmers checked out and take it from there. No point in putting the cart before the horse. Let's go and join the girls for eggs benny! Finest in town!"

He was right. The eggs benny were delicious. Daddy talked constantly, and all I had to do was smile. And luckily for me, I didn't shoot blanks. Celeste and I got married in the virtual Bahamas as soon as we heard the good news, but we had yet to consummate our carnal selves. I kept Jazza right out of the picture, only telling him once the contract was lodged in court and assuring him it had all been spur of the moment.

I didn't tell Jazza that Mummy and Daddy and Celeste and I were collectively panic-stricken that the bubble of goodwill might burst at any moment so we moved as quickly as possible.

To my surprise, Jazza wasn't angry with me, nor did he feel betrayed. He laughed like it was the funniest thing. "Takes the pressure off us for a bit," he said, chortling. "Yeah, baby, life insurance. Great thinking, Sharps buddy! Just one thing. When you move up, you'd better take me or I'll you kill you, man! Did you move in with her or her, you? Does she know how obsessed you are with cleaning? Have you actually done the horizontal rhumba?"

He was full of questions, but I brushed them off. "That's

classified," I told him. "But Daddy's buying us a house."

"Daddy! You call Mr. Williamson The Great, the Fourth and the Righteous-Up-Your-Ass, Daddy!" That had Jazza laughing the rest of the day. I gave up.

What he also didn't know, and what I'd never tell him, was that the prospect of sex had freaked me out to the point where I'd been honest with CeeCee. There was no way I'd be able to get it up so I had to come clean.

8. THE HOLE IN THE WALL

"I'M NOT MUCH GOOD AT IT," I TOLD HER. "Not face to face. I have to tell you, Cee, so you know. I haven't had sex with a woman in years. I go to the Lucky Hole bar, and I stick my dick through a wall and the woman on the other side talks dirty to me and jerks me off."

Instead of laughing at me or being furious and wanting to smash up the room, or calling me a liar and having the marriage annulled, Celeste was fascinated. And, more importantly, she was kind. She said it didn't matter, we'd figure it out. She wanted me to take her to the Lucky Hole and show her.

"The concept's old," I explained before we went to the club. "It was popular in Japan in 1980. Oh gosh, I don't know about taking you here. You're so innocent—I don't want to orrupt you."

She gave a deep throaty laugh. "Sweetie, I'm not going to tell you all my dirty secrets—not that there are many, mind you, but still. But innocent, I am not. And up for adventure, I most certainly am. And besides, there needs to be a level of honesty between us, always."

She turned me towards her, her hands on my shoulders. "Sharps, honey, we have a chance here, I can feel it. We both need something, and it seems we can help each other out. Don't ask me how I know, but I feel like we'd be better together than apart. And so if you need me to have sex with you through a plank or whatever, then that's what we'll do."

I was moved by her honesty. I bent my head forward to touch hers. "I feel the same. Come on then, I'll show you."

The Lucky Hole wasn't a place for women, and I had to do some persuading with the madam. The madam insisted, in broken phrases—meanwhile I'd heard her speaking the King's English—that women weren't allowed. In the end, CeeCee charmed her and lined her pocket, and by the time we got to the hole in the wall, I wasn't sure I'd be able to get it up at all. But, as the lights dimmed and the woman's voice soothed me and the music drifted in, I relaxed and soon forgot about CeeCee and the pressures from Daddy and that bitch Ava, and I came and life was good.

"That was very arousing," CeeCee said when we left. "Very erotic. Now, sweetie, I'd like to show you my way of doing things, if you don't mind?"

It was the last thing I felt like, but what could I say? I was drained from our whirlwind romance and our speedy marriage, not to mention the whole experience of showing her the Lucky Hole. I wanted to go home and have a short nap followed by a session with my weights. CeeCee and I hadn't moved in together yet because Daddy was still trying to find us the right house, and I hoped he'd take his time. But I had to oblige, and I forced a smile.

"Love to," I said, and she smiled. She drove me to a deluxe apartment set seventy storeys high, all decked out in crystal, steel, and black leatherette. A corner apartment with a view of the lake on one side and downtown on the other. It was nighttime, and the city sparkled like a spread of semi-precious glittering gems. I thought about how crazy it was that this was the first time I'd even been to her place and yet there we were, married. Daddy certainly hadn't wasted any time. It wasn't like he'd really given me a choice, but more like it had been a quiet clause in my job description all along, should he so choose. And while I liked CeeCee, there was something terrifying, too, as if she could castrate me by just thinking about it, if she ever wanted to. I just had to manage the situation, and it'd all be good.

Celeste poured herself a large gin and tonic from a pink Perspex drinks trolley, and I thought about what her father had said, that she'd met men in rehab, that she liked a tipple, and that she'd had a hard time finding her way in life. She seemed to sense my thoughts, and she raised her glass with slight defiance, as if daring me to say something. I was quiet. She was right; we were better together than apart.

I took a lime and soda and watched her navigate an army of FluffSqueaks, faux-fur round little robots, cute as hell, much like the Tribbles from Star Trek only four times the size and ten times as aggressive. They weren't cheap, and Celeste had at least a dozen in pink, lime green, red, and orange. They rushed around, squeaking and burping, bumping into each other, rolling around and laughing, their shag-rug hair wild and their eyes glittering and whirring.

Celeste's place was a ShyRichRollo compendium of the latest trending items. The ShyRichRollos were spinning neon wheels in upmarket shopping centres, listing toys for the super wealthy. Celeste had all of them, including the latest, PrayingMantisLuckyCharms, tiny plastic orchid-coloured insects that fluttered and settled in white-and-pink clouds on the edge of the sofa. I didn't like them, fearing they'd stick in my mouth, nose, and hair. Maybe they sensed my discomfort, because they swarmed me while I tried to unobtrusively swat them away.

Celeste downed the gin and tonic like it was orangeade, refreshed her drink, and held out her hand. I took it and she led me to the bedroom with a large bed. As I entered the room, my balls retracted and fled. I was immediately soaked in panicked sweat.

I was in a bordello. Chandeliers, red velvet wallpaper, mirrors, gilt and tassels, drapes, pillows, cushions, and throws. The bed was a giant lipstick-kiss in the centre of the floor. I looked up.

Yep, there were mirrors on the ceiling. Mirrors on the walls. A large naked Rubenesque Celeste eyed me provocatively from one wall. Lifesize, old-fashioned oil paintings daubed with flashing neon light accents looked down on the scene. I was going to throw up. I pressed my hand to my mouth. I wasn't the right guy for the job. Mr. Williamson had erred. I would be fired. My life as a Blowfly was coming at me sooner than I had thought.

Oblivious to my panic, Celeste pointed a remote towards a shelf, and a retro disco diva howled at high volume about feeling love. I was frozen, wretched with embarrassment, sweat pouring down my body. Celeste laughed and came over to me. She undid my shirt and ran her fingers over my body. "So fit," she murmured. "So tight, so nice. Hmmm." She didn't comment on the wetness of my shirt, and she genuinely seemed to like what she was finding.

I wouldn't say I was aroused by what she was doing, but I somehow managed to relax. I closed my eyes, and she undid my trousers and led me to the bed.

"One second, honey, let me get my box of goodies." I leaned up on my elbows as she walked over to the closet.

"Tell me," she said, taking out a bunch of outfits on hangers, "which one would you like?" There was a fifities film noir number with sheer organza and fluffy feather boa edging, a cheerleader outfit, a nurse's outfit, a nun's habit, and a domi-natrix skimpy affair in black leather and studs.

I pointed to the filmy affair, and she dropped the others to the floor. I was instantly distracted by the mess. The garments would be getting creased. I ached to get up and hang them up neatly, but I didn't feel I could. Meanwhile, the stereo had switched to a remixed version of "Tainted Love" with extra bass, and lights swirled around the boudoir while I wondered how many other men had lain exactly where I was. But mainly I wanted to pick those clothes up off the floor.

Celeste swayed in time to the music, dreamy-eyed and in

her own world. I wasn't sure what I was supposed to do—just lie there and watch her? Was this supposed to be arousing? I was bored out of my mind. Her eyes snapped open, and I was worried she had read my mind. *Sharps, you fool, you've a good thing on the make, get with the program.* So I arranged my face into an interested expression, with a touch of concern, was everything okay?

"Going to freshen my drinkie," she said, her second glass already emptied, and I gave a sigh of relief. She wasn't kicking me out.

As soon as she left, I scooted off the bed and hung up the clothes. The relief was instantaneous, like scratching a terrible itch. I was back on the bed by the time she came back, and she didn't even notice that the clothes were no longer on the floor. With the mess tidied up, I was able to relax slightly.

Celeste took a gulp from her drink and wheeled a sparkling aqua trolley out of the adjoining washroom. The trolley was piled high with sex toys. I watched, amazed, as she, like a sales woman, led me through the uses and highlights of each item. She had it all: dildos, chains, riding crops, terrifying bondage gear, lotions, condoms, massage gels, and candles.

"Uh," I stammered, "I'm intimidated, Cee, I gotta say."

"Don't worry, sweetiepie," she said. "I'm pretty good at pleasing myself. I'd just love for you to watch. This big boy's my fav!" She purred as she pulled out an eight-inch monster dildo and climbed onto the bed. "But you know what I love more than anything?" Her eyes snapped wide open, horrible with focus and sobriety in spite of her drinks. "I just love oral! How do you feel about oral?"

Oh god. Not oral. Anything but oral. The cave of the Red Vagina. I turned pale. What could I say?

"Um, well." I searched for the right thing to say, the thing that would keep me safe and yet keep us together. "I guess I'm not very experienced," I finally stuttered, and her eyes lit up. She must have been worried I'd tell her I was repulsed by it. "And," I added hastily, "I'm entirely not sure it's my cup of tea." A cloud crossed her face, and she slumped down ever so slightly.

"Oh."

We lay in silence for a bit, and I realized I had to fix things. "But," I offered, "I could try, if you like."

She sat up, joyful and jubilant. "Oh, honey! Would you? Thank you!" She immediately lay back and spread her legs.

My heart pounded as I took up the position. I closed my eyes, took a deep breath, and moved in. I'd take my medicine and do what had to be done. Since she'd lubed herself up for her vibrating cock, she didn't taste so bad. In fact, her cotton candy cunt wasn't fishy at all. But still, I had no idea what to do. I imagined an ice cream cone in front of me, and I slowly worked my way from a full cone to scooping out the insides with my tongue. I must have done okay because she bucked like a bronco before I was even finished.

"My god. That was SPECTACULAR!"

I was bludgeoned with relief. I crawled over to lie next to her.

"And look at you, silly boy," she said, stroking my hair. "Didn't think he had it in him. Sweetie, you're the best I ever had!"

Thank god! I passed the exam! I lay back, wondering if there was a protocol about timing. How quickly could I leave? I craved the privacy of my lovely pristine apartment more than ever, itching for my BleachBuddy and furniture polish. I had to be alone. I sat up slowly, ready with my exit line, but she pulled me down and snuggled into me.

"You'll stay the night, baby? Please? I want to wake up and find you next to me. Say you will, my hunky big love."

I murmured something and lay back, defeated.

Next thing I knew, she was out cold, snoring slightly. I maintained the position. The spinning lights swirled, and we must have looped the playlist because the disco diva was back to wailing about feeling love. My arm went numb, but I was on

the fast track to success—take that Ava! I've won the big prize!
Sweetie, where r u?

Celeste flashed the red light at me again. Oh shit. I'd yet to
leave the parking lot. My trip down memory lane had clocked
more kilometres than I'd realized.

Coming, hun! Sorry, I got caught up, Jazza nabbed me in the
parking lot. He's got woman troubles, would u believe?

I hoped she wouldn't be too pissed off.

Who cares? Listen, there's a party here with big news, baby!
Haul that sweet ass of yours home pronto! Lila and Christine
r here and so r Mummy and Daddy! We've got champers! Get
a move on!

Oh shit. Just what I didn't need. The prospect of a back-to-
work party hosted by Daddy with Celeste's obnoxious friends
in tow for the free booze and canapés. I flashed the time. To
my surprise, it was only early evening. My day had been so
hellish I'd have sworn it was close to midnight.

Sorry, hun! Coming!

But I still couldn't move. I reclined the car seat as far as it
would go and closed my eyes. I just needed a tiny bit more
time to myself.

9. GETTING PREGNANT

CELESTE AND I WORKED HARD AT GETTING her pregnant as soon as possible. She stopped drinking. We made our own sex props—a Lucky Hole wall along with her trolley of goodies—and we kept an eye on her fertility schedule. We both wanted to do it the old-fashioned way. I sold my apartment and was happy to throw a down payment on Mother's kitchen table, where I'd taken many a scolding.

I ate ice cream cones out of Celeste's cunt until I thought I'd die. We worked out a system whereby she whisked the wall away just as I was about to come and she jumped on top of me, taking my sperm and lying on her back with her legs in the air.

It didn't even take us long. Daddy was so proud of me. Ha, you should have seen that bitch Ava's face when Daddy threw a party for me at work! It was worth eating all the ice cream cones in the world. This was before the MDoggHotBody campaign went pear-shaped. Then, I was king of the world!

Celeste, pregnant, was cantankerous. She grew huge, monstrous. And, inexplicably, her appetite for sex grew equally as large. She binge-watched porn in between phoning me with her latest ache or pain or to tell me what kind of ice cream to bring home for dessert. At least she wasn't drinking. I hated the porn. At first I tried to pretend it was interesting, but it revolted me—all that skin and hair and genitals and groaning.

I tried to convince her that porn wasn't good for the baby. She needed to mix it up, watch some nature or shit like that or the baby would be a crazed serial killer sex addict. She just laughed at me. She treated pregnancy like a terminal illness, calling in massage therapists, a hair stylist, and even a make-up artist for god's sake! She said she was too tired to even lift a finger, but she lifted more than one when it came to food. She heavy-lifted all day! And when Bax was yanked from out of her, she was perplexed and furious as to why the weight didn't just drop off. So Mummy and Daddy sent her to a spa for three months. Three months! She left me with a newborn and went off to find her former figure.

When Bax was born, I was terrified. Baxter Hunter Williamson the Fifth Barkley, a ridiculous name for a tiny baby The nurse tried to hand him to me, but I shrank back and shook my head. "No," I said, "I can't." What if I broke him? I couldn't hold him, worried that my fear and rage would overwhelm me and I'd snap the child in two, then four, then six, just to spare him the horror of this world.

Eventually Daddy made me tell him what was going on. I cried and told him that I was afraid I would hurt the baby, that he was too small. I couldn't tell him my real fear, that my hands would betray me and I'd kill him. But Daddy said he understood and maybe he actually did because he took Bax and held him, all swaddled and tiny, then told me to cup my arms under his arms, not to take the baby but just to hold Daddy holding Bax. And it worked. When Bax made it into my arms, my whole life changed. I straightened up and held my boy close, and I swear that surge of love and protection was like nothing I have ever felt before or since. I'd never let anything harm that precious boy. Nothing. Ever. And I didn't want anybody else to hold him. When we took Bax home, I pushed the nanny away and let her do the cursory cleaning. I was so afraid that Celeste would take Bax away from me when she came back from the spa, but I didn't have to worry because she wasn't interested in Bax at all, treating him at best like one of her FluffSqueaks.

Granted, Celeste looked all svelte and smooth. She had dropped the weight, but she'd gained an entourage. Night after night, day after day, we were lumbered with her new-found friends, Christine and Lila. Christine was Celeste's art therapist in the clinic, and Lila was a nutritionist although she looked anorexic to me. I remembered how Daddy had warned me about Celeste's penchant for bringing losers back from rehab, and I sighed. I found I could summon nothing but hatred for my wife.

You can't hate her. She's Bax's mother. She's your wife. She's part of the deal. Shit man, she IS the deal.

In the next breath: *I hate her and feel like my head's about to explode, she's so noisy and so messy. She's such a slob.*

Lila and Christine didn't help. I heard them talking about me on the connecting audio, and it didn't take long for me to realize that Celeste was drinking again. How could I go back to work if she was drinking again?

I wondered, while I was bathing Bax and listening to them, if the three of them were sexually involved. I tidied up the towels while Bax gurgled and splashed, and I thought about that message on Celeste's portable flash comm:

Can't wait to smell your sweetness and lick your skin!

Celeste loved lesbian porn. Then there was the way the three of them were always hugging and kissing and touching each other. I asked her about the message, but she got angry and demanded to know what I was doing looking at her comm. I told her it lit up in front of me; it wasn't like I was spying on her or anything.

What would I do if Celeste told me she was having an affair? Probably nothing. My chest closed in tighter, and my ears buzzed with a ringing sound.

I heard Lila. "Our credit cards are totally maxed out. What a blow, being let go from the spa."

She'd lost her job? Christine too? Why hadn't Celeste told me? I had forgotten about the lives of consumers, the ones spending all the money I urged them to. If you asked me, the Blowflies were lucky, what with all that welfare living.

I told myself I too had to stop buying things for Bax. My credit cards were also maxed out, and Daddy had no idea.

The buzzing in my ears became a high-pitched scream. I gathered up my solid, fragrant little boy.

"Bax my boy, what would I do without you? You get it, don't you? Mama thinks I coddle you too much, but you're my boy. I never thought I'd feel like this, never. This kind of love, it's nearly too much. I would do anything for you, my boy, anything."

Downstairs Christine was putting the food on the dining room table.

"Is Sharps being better around Bax?" I heard Christine ask.

Better? What the heck did she mean? I leaned in to listen.

"No, he's utterly neurotic. It's quite ridiculous. I've got no idea how he'll go back to work," Celeste said.

"It's so destructive for Bax," Christine protested, and her voice rose. "He can sense it you know. A dichotomy between parents about baby regimens are one of the biggest causes of dysfunctional adults in later years."

WTF?

"I know, sweetie," I heard Celeste sigh. "But what can I do? I've talked myself blue in the face. So now I just live with it."

Live with what? What was she talking about?

"It's not fair on Bax," Christine insisted. "You owe him more. I see the consequences of this with my clients daily."

The consequences of what?

I heard Celeste sigh again. "I've got no say in anything. Listen to this one: Bax isn't allowed to have a blanket at night, in case he strangles himself. There he is, poor little guy, stiff as a plank in two pairs of thick pajamas, hardly able to move."

"Why would he strangle himself?" Christine was outraged. "Has that ever happened? I've never heard of it."

"It's possible in tiny babies, but what are the odds? But Sharps loves his boy—you can't tell him anything. I didn't tell you, but a couple of weeks ago, he woke up and thought Bax had been stolen in the night. He was hysterical. I tell you, there's no reasoning with him."

How could she tell them about that? I was aghast and my armpits puddled with oily cold sweat. I pulled off my T-shirt and wiped my pits dry. *I can't believe she told them that! How could she? I'd had a nightmare.*

I picked up Bax and carried him into the bedroom to get a fresh T-shirt.

I thought about my alcoholic father, his rages, the constant threat of violence and the ever-present tension in the family. Big hard man. Big hard drunk with a fist like iron. "Be a man, boy," he'd yell at me for no reason, breaking the silence like shattering glass. Or, "Grow a pair, will ya?"

All I wanted was for Bax to know that he was completely loved. I wanted him to remember his childhood as perfect, with everything shiny and in its place and with me doing things with and for him. I never knew I was capable of feeling so much love for one person. What did she know, that bitch, Christine? I clenched my fists. My scalp was crawling, and I wanted to put my fist through the wall.

I picked up my son and took him into his bedroom, and we sat down on the floor to play with his toys. I'd had a special carpet installed, pale blue with no loose fibres to clog his little lungs. His wallpaper was serene, marshmallow clouds on blue skies, sunshine, happy faces of smiling sunflowers.

But I could still hear them downstairs.

Celeste continued to trash talk me. "Sharps is so totally paranoid that something will happen to his boy that he can't leave him alone. He made me get rid of my FluffSqueaks, every single one of them!"

I hadn't made her get rid of them. I had wanted to, yes, because I didn't want Bax inhaling their neon plastic fur, but they hadn't gone far. They were in the basement, rushing around and bumping into each other, squeaking like a nest of angry little birds and making it nearly impossible for me to do the laundry. I tried to kick the shit out of them, but the little bastards were too quick for me and they seemed to love what they thought was a game.

Lila changed the subject. "I read about a Blowfly family," she said, "trying to integrate into city life, but they got caught and sent to the farms."

Blowflies integrating? I sat up straighter, horrified. I hadn't seen anything on the news about it. I'd follow up later. The Blowflies weren't allowed to encroach on our sanctity. They were scum, filth.

"Come on Bax," I said, "it's bedtime, my boy. Time for you to go to sleep."

But Bax wouldn't go down. I carried him downstairs to make a bottle, and I looked over at the three women. They were sprawled on the sofa, caressing each other, massaging one another's backs, hands, legs.

I made Bax's bottle and said a loud goodnight to the writhing orgy of limbs. "Goodnight ladies, if I don't see you leave." Having reminded them whose house it was, I turned to go upstairs when I remembered something. "Wait, it's garbage day tomorrow. Celeste, hang onto Bax for me."

To my happiness, Bax protested at leaving my arms and Celeste distracted him with a singing toy. "Sweetie," she said to me, "it's only eight at night. You've got time."

"What time do the garbage collectors come?" Christine asked.

"Oh, about twelve hours from now," Celeste said, "but Sharps is obsessed with the garbage."

"Am not," I said, slipping on my shoes and a coat. "I just like to be organized, not like some people I know." I smiled, three quarters wattage.

"There's organized and there's obsessed," Celeste called out, but I ignored her.

I closed the front door and I heard her discussing my so-called garbage obsession, and my chest ballooned with rage. I stood in the snowy night, listening to my wife gossip about me. I kicked at the light atmospheric Yuletide fluff and wished I was in a rage room.

"The more stressed he is, the more he cleans and organizes," I heard Celeste say.

I told myself that I didn't care what they thought. It wasn't like any of them had lives I wanted. I went back in and I finally got Bax to sleep while Celeste saw Christine and Lila out. I gathered up Celeste's mug of orange juice and vodka and poured the remains down the sink. I straightened up the sofa cushions and picked up the toys on the floor.

Finally. Peace and quiet.

"We need to have a chat," Celeste said, and my heart dropped.

She was kicking me out. She'd had enough. I felt bad for the things I'd felt and said about her. I couldn't lose this. I crushed a tiny fluffy rabbit in my hands, twisting its neck tighter and tighter, filled with panic. I'd taken things for granted. I'd sat in judgement of her and forgotten who was in control, who held the power. It wasn't me; it was Celeste. And there I was, thinking my biggest problems were Ava and my neighbour Strawberry Merv whose Christmas lights outshone mine. Celeste and I called him Strawberry Merv because he had a large strawberry-shaped birthmark covering half of his face. His real name was Mervin Hobbs, and he was clearly the least of my problems. My world was about to implode, and I had to apologize and convince Celeste that I'd try harder. I opened my mouth to speak, but she interrupted me.

"We need to have another baby!" Celeste beamed at me. "Baxie needs a little brother or sister. But I'm not getting fat and gross again. This time we'll go for surrogacy. And Christine's more then willing to do it for us. Daddy will pay her."

"Another baby? Christine?" I blurted out, my body slick with sweat at my narrow escape. I was dizzy with relief but equally stunned by what she had just told me.

"If she can't, then Lila said she will. We might try with both of them. That's what we wanted, right? A nice big family? Mummy and Daddy will be so excited, you'll see!"

The noosehold around my neck loosened. I wasn't being fired by my wife. We were still a team. I put my head in my hands and began to cry.

"Oh, sweetie," Celeste said. "Come here. Come let mama make you feel better. It's all good, baby, it's all good."

Reprieve. But work was still looming, I only had two weeks left of my pat leave. And was I going to have to have sex with Lila or Christine? No, of course not, they'd just need my sperm. I had to stop over-complicating things so much, stop worrying and overthinking.

10. LOOPING DADDY IN

AND THAT NIGHT, THE SAME NIGHT I learned about Jazza and Ava, it seemed like Celeste's plans had been put into motion a lot faster than I had imagined.

"Sweetie! We really *are* going to have another baby!" Celeste ran out to the car and banged on the bubble door. "What do you mean?" I said as I got out of the car. There, in the doorway, stood Daddy and Mummy and Lila and Christine.

"Sweetie," Celeste sniffed, "why do you smell like wet plastic?"

Oh shit. I had forgotten about that. "Rage room," I said, and I sounded lame. "Then Jazza had a crisis and I met him without cleaning up."

"Oh." Her eyes glazed at the mention of Jazza. "Well, anyway. Daddy thinks this is a great idea, and what's more, he's going to pay for Lila to have induced ovulation and make it all happen asap! We need you to go upstairs and jack off a great big lovely load of your best sperm. We've got a sperm transporter here and everything!"

Lila? I thought it was Christine? A sperm transporter? I was hardly in the mood to get an erection, but Celeste read my mind. "Come on," she said, winking at me. "I'll help you."

She led me upstairs, past Mummy, Daddy, Lila, Christine, the nanny, and a man in white coveralls who I assumed was the sperm transporter. The man handed me a white egg-shaped container. No one looked the least embarrassed by what was

going on, except for me. In fact, there was a real party atmo-
sphere. I was surprised there weren't balloons and streamers.

Celeste closed the bedroom door, popped a HardOn, the
newest performance-enhancing pill, under my tongue, and
wheeled out my hole in the wall. Pills or no pills, I was drained
and not up to the task. "Sweetie, why don't you have a quick
shower?" Celeste sniffed and waved a hand in front of her
nose. "You do smell rather awful. Skipped the rinse down at
your special place?" She was right, I had.

There was a knock at the door. It was Mummy and Lila
and Christine. *What now?* "We want to sprinkle holy water,"
Mummy said, "and light sacred candles and incense. We want
the church's blessing for the conception of this dear child."

If they all noticed the strange wall in the middle of the room,
they didn't mention it.

"I'm going to shower," I said. "And actually, it would be
helpful if you were all gone when I come out. I know what
I've got to do."

I closed the washroom door and heard them leave. I had to
deliver. It was tough because I kept thinking about Ava and
Jazza. Mainly Ava. Overthrowing Minnie? That wouldn't be
the worst idea in the world, but it was imposssible! One had
to admire Ava's arrogance. No wonder I was afraid of her.
Because she wasn't afraid of anything. And here I was, working my ass off, well, wanking my dick off, to bring another
child into the world. But what kind of world? A part of me
was curious. I wanted to ask Ava what she was up to, but the
idea of talking to her was like inviting a spring trap to snap
down on my unenthused member. I looked down at my poor
fella puddled in my lap. I had to stop thinking about Ava. She
reminded me of Mother. *Oh shit.* That wasn't a good route
to go down either. Mother, another fervent believer that our
world was shot to hell. Another Minnie-hater. I sat down on
the toilet and studied the creamy cleavage of Miss NewCat
March on the wall calendar in front of me. Yep, it was pretty

ironic that the NewCats had a nudie calendar, but it was a time of great contradiction, to say the very least. And the models weren't exactly nude; they did have strategically draped scarves, diaphanous and sheer with light accentuating curves and dips.

Live Your Abundant Life Today! Miss December proclaimed and I held my dick and prayed to the blue god of chemical delights. I thought about the party downstairs with everyone eagerly waiting, and my poor fella drooped even further. Stop it, I told myself, stop thinking about Ava or Mother or anything. But still ... there was nothing. I gave a sob of desperation and hunted in the cabinet for a second HardOn.

Come on, Sharps. I closed my eyes. What could I do? Thankfully, the answer came to me. I grabbed a pair of nail scissors and started hacking the rolls of toilet paper in the basket. *Stab as much as you can, slash that paper to ribbons, now hack a bar of soap, be careful now, we don't want an injury, ah yes ... there we go ... that feels better, stab, stab, let it all out, pump your dick with right hand, stab a towel with your left, get it done, nearly there, grab the container, let it out.* Sheer fucking relief. I leaned against the wall and surveyed the mess. For once, I didn't even care. I had the jar of jism!

"Good man!" Daddy said when I got downstairs. The only trouble was, the second HardOn had kicked in and my penis was a north-facing torpedo in my pants. I accepted all congratulatory hugs with a maiden auntie hug, my pelvis arched backwards.

"Sharps," Daddy said, handing me a gin and tonic, "let's you and I have a wee *tête-á-tête* over in the corner there. We need to talk a bit of shop, what with you going back to work."

He led me to an alcove with a love seat and patted the spot beside him.

"Ava's gunning for me. Son, you and Jazza have to deliver pronto. But," he said, casting a glance at Celeste who was three sheets to the wind, "Celly will have to go back to the spa. I don't think Christine's a good influence. She will henceforth be blocked, all access denied. Which is why I chose Lila to be the carrier. She's in financial difficulty—her husband hasn't had a job in years—and she's struggling. She's much more malleable. We like malleable."

I was relieved to hear that Celeste was going back to the spa.

"Daddy," I said, "I have to tell you something. I met up with Jazza, and he's gotten involved with Ava."

Daddy burst out laughing. "Involved? As in sexually? Now there's a scarring image. King Kong and the hobbit girl."

"I know! But it's not just that. Ava's apparently going to overthrow the government! She's written a manifesto and everything!"

"Hmm. Well, she can certainly try, but she will fail. Listen, son. I have to tell you something in confidence. Strictly between you and me. Back in the day, when I was at university, I was part of a boys' club. Phi Beta Kappa des Garcons, very hush-hush of course. It was considered good sport to visit Blowfly ladies of the night at their apartments, to get the full Blowfly life experience. But there were times when things went awry. You know, how boys will be boys? And one night, there was a group of us and one girl."

Oh my god. I glanced around. If my mother could hear Daddy, she'd have a conniption. She'd waste no time in pointing out that one didn't refer to adult females as "girls" but rather, as women. But I nodded.

"So there we were," he continued, "and admittedly, consensual-inducing chemicals were in the mix to smooth the waters. But things went badly. When we left, the girl wasn't in great shape, but we knew she'd survive. She was a Blowfly; they had doctors. But it turned out there were photographs. Evidence of a few of us in a compromising position. We had no idea that the woman had a child until that child showed up at my door, ten years later. Ava. She must have been nine or so when the unfortunate event occurred. She not only turned up, but she was also armed with copies of the pictures and full of demands that she work at Integratron. What could we say? Most of the Board members were there that night, and so we agreed, fine, Ava the Blowfly could have a job but that was it. We made it clear that we were playing nice. After all, we could have her more than blocked; we could have her deleted."

Around us, the party was in full swing, and it felt surreal to be having this discussion with Daddy.

"She worked hard," Daddy admitted. "She wanted to go to university before joining us, and we got her in. She got a Ph.D. I remember her thesis well: *Exposing the Hidden Connections Between Third-Wave Feminism and the Writings of Ayn Rand.* I was a great fan of Ayn Rand. Now there's a woman who knew how to write a man! The scene where Roark gets it on with Dominique and leaves her bruised and covered in quarry dust—it never fails to turn me on!"

I must have blanched because Daddy put a reassuring hand on my shoulder. "We all have needs, son. Anyway, my point is this: she and I had Ayn Rand in common but it turned out Ava's thesis was, and I quote, 'a deft evisceration of Ayn Rand's misguided patriarchal pretence at affecting feminism.'" Daddy got lost in thought for a moment, and I leaned against the wall, cold sweat soaking into my waistband. The noise became a muffled roar, and my vision blurred. I put out a hand to steady myself.

I had to go upstairs and lie down, and I was just about to excuse myself when Daddy grabbed my shoulder. "Anyway, after she graduated, we gave her a spot in the Sheds and she shot up the charts. She made us a bunch of money by helping sway female consumers, tapping into their insecurities and fears of aging. At first I didn't trust her. A feminist sellout? But she seemed sincere. Of course we monitored her like crazy. Was she there to blow us up and get revenge for her mother? Or turn the women of the world against us? But a decade later, all she'd done was work, nose to the grindstone. She hadn't attempted to access any privileged-denied files or shown herself to be a troublemaker in any way. So we stopped watching her. Until this, now."

"What happened to her mother?" My voice shook, but Daddy didn't seem to notice.

"Ended up in a permanent vegetative state. We admitted culpability by making sure she had all the medical attention she needed. However, we didn't know that she had a child and that there was evidence of that night. Those facts slipped through the cracks."

"Who took the pics?"

Daddy shrugged. "Boyfriend, pimp, who knows? But anyway, son, I'm telling you this because I need you to know what happened and just how dangerous Ava is and what her armory is. Poor girl actually, that Ava. Couldn't hold a candle to her mother in the looks department. Stunner, she was. Redhead. Bazookers out to here. And to be honest, we'd been with her a few times, talk about wild in the sack! Gets me hot just thinking about it."

Daddy got an odd and faraway look in his eye while I tried to process what he'd just said. He was part of a boys' club that raped Blowfly women and he got "hot" thinking about it? I felt sick. And Ava, having to fight her way up in a place like Integratron? No wonder she was such a bitch. She had to be. But why did she even want to be part of it? It had to be revenge. She'd been biding her time. Or was she another Minnie, a woman who sold out other women to get the money and power she desired? And did she jump Jazza's giant bones to get intel? Or did she like him?

"I really tried with her," Daddy continued. "I offered her all the surgeries in the world, told her I could make her look just like her mother. I thought she'd jump at it, but she just looked at me like I'd lost my mind. Then, purely for selfish reasons, I told her I'd treat her to the app that would change her appearance to other people, but she turned that down, too! Why would she care? I mean, fine, she's happy with how she looks, but we're the ones who have to look at her!"

So there was an app! "I've heard rumours of those apps," I said carefully. "But I thought they were urban legends."

"Nope. But still, they cost a bundle. And not only did she turn me down, she blocked me!"

I was curious. "If you bought the app for her, how would she look to me?"

"However she wanted you to see her. The host controls the view. You're only allowed one appearance per; once you pick your model, you can't change it. The result is absolutely convincing, fits your raw clay like real skin. That's what the designers call an unenhanced human body, raw clay. Anyway, my boy, we're getting off topic."

Something occurred to me. Daddy had quite the thing for the late Prince Charles. I'd assumed he simply had an uncanny resemblance to the man who had never been king, but now that I'd been alerted to the veracity of the visual distortion app, I couldn't help but notice that Mummy looked very much like Camilla. Daddy even talked like Prince Charles, *I say, old man,* and *what, old chap?* Good old ruddy Prince Charles who, unbeknownst to them, made the entire Royal family drink the lethal Koolaid shortly after he learned that Prince Will and his Duchess Consort Kate were being fast-tracked to the throne in a desperate attempt to keep the monarchy a socially relevant, lucre-pumping cash cow. But the monarchy was failing anyway, despite all of Will and Kate's efforts to maniacally grin at every farmer, schoolteacher, flower-bearing child, and weary-looking nurse. With the Royal family out of the picture, it was easy for Minnie to colonize the former superpower that had colonized the world. Talk about ironic. It was no longer called England either. For some unknown reason, Minnie and Mama had renamed the towns, cities, and countries of the world after lesser-known saints. The island formerly known as the British Isles was now St. Malo. America was now St. Isidore, and Canada was St. Hubert.

"Death before dishonour," Daddy had said, reminiscing about Prince Charles with tears in his eyes. "Mercy killing. The Queen had broken protocol; she had transgressed the Royal chain of command."

I heard a crash from the far side of the room, and I looked up. Celeste, giggling, was peering lopsidedly at her plate in pieces on the floor. Yep, she wasn't even in the same province as the wagon she had so whole-heartedly fallen off of. And how much raw clay was left there? Not much, I assumed. What if my wife was actually an eighty-year old woman? But she had borne a child. Still, anything was possible in that regard. The room swam before my eyes and I leaned against the wall. It was all too much to take in.

"Listen, son." Daddy forced my attention back to him. "Your intel is top-notch. You need to monitor Jazza and Ava, full surveillance. And we need to get this baby to fruition and get Celly sober. It's hilarious that Ava thinks she's going to have a go at Minnie—*har har!* Minette's got armies up the yin yang. So it's quite ridiculous. Anyway, old chap, I'm so glad we had this chat. Keep it under your hat, and we will not speak of it at work. The walls have ears and never, ever, message me about it. Be careful what you say; all audio is bot-monitored for trigger terminology, sensitive keywords *blah blah*. If you need to see me, flash the word *Vanguard* to my path and I'll meet you in the men's room on Sky Level 172. You need a pass to get in, so knock twice—*tap tap,* that's it—and I'll let you in. Anyway, enough shop talk. You deserve another drink! Here's to a new baby and a bright future!"

11. ONE FOOT IN FRONT OF THE OTHER

THE FOLLOWING MORNING, I LAY IN BED, smothered by the weight of my life. Dragging myself out of bed was harder than dragging a horse's decapitated head across a row of parked cars, the nightmare from which I had awakened.

I arrived at work buzzing with fear and exhaustion. It took sheer force of will to enter the main doors. I went to Jazza's and my office, sat down, and stared at nothing. Jazza always got in later than me, no surprises there. I felt anxious and wired, and my eyes were gritty and clouded. I drummed my fingers on the desk and wondered when Jazza would show up. I was about to fold my head into my arms and take a nap on my desk when a message flashed across my visuals, *Vanguard! SOS! Vanguard!*

I sighed and pulled myself up. I took the elevator to the Level 172 washroom and tapped twice on the door.

"Son!" Daddy dragged me inside. "The Board insists you get a copy of the manifesto! In fact, they're quite annoyed with me for not having contacted them last night. They consider Ava to be a real threat."

"But Jazza's not in yet, sir," I replied, and Daddy grabbed me by the shoulder. "Then get him in asap, get the file, and return here pronto."

I nodded and scurried back down to my office. I messaged Jazza on the way.

Where r u? Urgent!

No response at all. I rushed into our office, adrenaline firing through my body. And there, on the floor, lying on his back, was Jazza, with one arm thrown across his face.

"Jazza! Why didn't you reply? Listen, buddy, you've got to give me that capcha of Ava's manifesto, now! Come on, buddy! Get up! Code Eleven, buddy, come on!"

Code Eleven was our way of saying the shit was hitting the fan big time. But Jazza didn't move. I sat down on his chest—a weird move—but I had to get the guy moving. He stared up at me, his face red and swollen.

"She dumped me," he said. "She wiped our shared comms. She flashed me a note saying:

"Hasta la vista, baby! So long, and thanks for all the data.

She's gone, Sharps! I loved her and she's gone!"

"Gone? From work? Gone where?"

He shrugged and motioned for me to get off him. "I don't know. But she's gone from me. Gone." He started sobbing.

"Thanks for all the data...." My mind was whirling. "I wonder what data she meant exactly?"

I sat down on the floor, wondering how I'd break the news to Daddy when the big man himself rushed into the room and knelt down next to Jazza.

"Tell me you've still got the manifesto?" He must have been listening in. I leaned back against my desk.

Jazza shook his head. "Gone."

"What can you remember?"

"She will rule the day. That's all. She never told me how she would do it. Hack into Minnie's mainframe, I guess. She never told me the details. I loved her!" He wailed, and Daddy slapped him across the face.

"This is so much bigger than you, boy!" He thought for a moment. "We'll download your backups and histories and see if anything comes up."

"A brain scour?" Jazza jumped to his feet. "No way! People die from scours!"

A brain scour? I'd never heard of them. I felt like the only idiot in the room.

"I won't do it!" Jazza shouted. "You'll have to kill me first!"

"Not a problem," Daddy replied coldly, and I watched in horror as three wrestlers in surgical scrubs stormed the room and subdued Jazza, throwing him to the ground and spiking him with a needle. They carried him off as if he weighed nothing. I was stunned.

"Stop staring, son," Daddy said irritably. "Wait, incoming intel." He cocked his head and listened for a moment. "Received. Will do. We have to go to a meeting. Come on."

"Me?" I squeaked.

"Grow a pair, son. This is war. Come on."

"Will Jazza be okay?" I rushed after Daddy, who was marching down the corridor.

"Of course. The boy's a moneymaker. He'll be fine. We'll keep the parts that matter. We need him back in working order."

I followed him to the penthouse boardroom with an expansive view of the city. An enormous mahogany boardroom table floated in the centre of the room like a black lake. And there, at the table, sat Ava.

She looked calm. Impassive. Ava was tiny but formidable. Black bangs cut across her large pale forehead and she had weirdly rounded limbs, like a doll cinched by elastic bands. She's a tiny balloon toy, I thought. A poodle without any bones or angles.

She stared at me, and I shrank from her gaze.

"Called to order!" an electronic voice boomed into the room and I jumped. Ava didn't twitch a muscle.

"Ava Jane Jaccari, you have been found guilty of compromising the integrity of a fellow employee of Integratron, and you shall therefore be demoted with a commensurate pay grade cut and loss of privileges for the period of one year. What have you to say in your defence?"

Ava shrugged. Daddy took a seat and motioned for me to

do the same. I was shaking, and rivers of oily sweat snaked down my rib cage. Why was I always so wet? I wondered if I could get the glands removed or something. And I must have put on weight during pat leave because my suit was tight and my shirt buttons strained. I yearned for my track pants and hoodie. I reached for my acupuncture wire twist and started to slip it over my wrist, but Daddy saw me and stopped me with a look.

"Ava Jane Jaccari, what do you have to say?"

"He was a good fuck," she said, and she folded her arms. "Probably more man than you ever were, you and the club of boys who raped my mother."

"You've used that card," the electronic voice said coldly, "well beyond the expiry date. Perhaps you seek expiration yourself, or deletion, or you'd like to work on a Farm? I know you know all about them. Hmmm?"

Ava went white, and her large eyes widened further. "No," she whispered. "I seek neither expiration nor deletion nor the farms."

"We want a copy of your manifesto."

"I destroyed it. You can look for it. Scour me if you like. You won't find a thing. Besides, you need me. And you know I deliver the highest dividends. The numbers speak for themselves. No one understands the female psyche like me."

It was true, and I found myself nodding. Wait, I was agreeing with Ava? I stopped myself, but not before Daddy turned around and glared at me.

"I realize I overstepped my boundaries," Ava sounded chastised. "Let me make amends. It was nothing more than primal lust. I let my female hormones get the better of me. I knew the rules and I broke them."

What? What was this? She-tiger turned tiger moth? Where was the real Ava? She had to be playing them.

"You think we're stupid, girl," the voice boomed. "We're not stupid. You and Jazza Frings will be assigned to work under the direction of Sharps Barkley, here present, and he in turn will report to Charles Phillip Arthur George Williamson the Fourth, here present. Your goal is to develop a new campaign that will deliver no less than thirty-three percent of the total global dividends of the corporation."

What did that mean? I was never good at math. But Ava clearly was.

"Impossible!" she said. "You want us to earn over ten billion dollars in the next nine months?"

"Or be deleted, trying. Message received?"

"Message received."

A strobe light flashed into my eyes, blinding me. I was trapped in a cave of darkness, and I slowly blinked my way back to the shadowy present.

They'd lowered the blinds and dimmed the lights to an eerie twilight. If these were their intimidation tactics, they were working.

"Any questions?" Daddy asked.

"Yes," Ava replied flatly. "When do we get Jazza back?" I noticed she was no long referring to him as the employee. "And you'd better not have damaged so much as one brain cell on him. If this cardboard cutout quarterback's all you're giving me, I can't deliver." I was mildly flattered that she'd likened me to a quarterback.

"We only need Frings for a day. Both of you take the rest of the day off and report for duty tomorrow."

I stood up. Even my jacket was soaked. I was hardly able to stand. "See yourselves out," Daddy said. "Sharps?" I turned to look at him. "Remember you've got a bunch of balls in the air on this one and there's only so much I can do."

I leaned on the table for a moment, aware that I was leaving a palm print on the spotless surface. I was trying to reply when a purple light hologrammed around Daddy's body. He turned a weird shade of green and deflated like a dehydrated prune into a haggard, ninety-year-old man with sunken, ravaged hawklike features and sparse teeth. Three seconds and he'd turned into a centenarian. The stress of the moment must have eroded the data, overwhelming the app that made him look like a younger man. I was looking at his raw clay instead of the image he projected to our visual cortices. But then he shimmered again, and the light turned pink, then yellow, and a sixty-year-old Prince Charles rippled back into place with big goatlike teeth and pale blue rheumy eyes.

I couldn't think straight. I nodded. "Yes, Daddy, I mean, Mr. Williamson, sir." I saw Ava's mouth twitch as if she was going to laugh at me, but she was silent. Had she seen his crazy metamorphosis? Most likely, but knowing Ava, she wasn't surprised.

She and I rode the elevator down together. I wanted to say something. That I was sorry about what had happened to her mother. I wanted to ask her if she had used Jazza or if she had felt any kind of fondness for him. I saw her differently now. I'd feared her, but she'd revealed her own passions and weakness, and we were in the same boat now.

"You and I are nothing alike," she said as she pressed the STOP button. I sank to the floor, trembling, the walls instantly closing in. I suffered from terrifying claustrophobia, and I knew Ava knew that. She knew everything about me.

"You're the angriest, saddest man I know, Sharps. I see you and your futile anger. I see how you clench your fists when you're talking to me. I see you doing everything you can to hold back from hitting me because you hate your life. Has it ever occurred to you that you could change things? No, of course not, because you're a company man, Sharps. You, in your too-tight shiny suit. I see you."

She sank down close to me. "Don't ever think you know anything about me, you weak little man. I see you, with your pretend gym-boy muscles. I know you're afraid of everything." Her breath was warm, like cinnamon toast. I covered my face with my hands and wheezed as she leaned in closer.

"By the way," she added, "I know your mother—she's an amazing woman."

What? Mother? When had they met?

"What did she say about me?" I managed, my head buried in my knees, my mouth filled with sandpaper, and my heart a panicked mouse on a hamster wheel. My brain was going to explode all over the mirrored elevator walls. "Ava, please let me out. I'm going to die here."

"You won't die! And you should ask her what she said," Ava laughed. "Great woman, your mother." She poked me with her finger, and I looked up at her. "I would have expected more from a son of hers."

"I'm pretty sure she did, too," I whispered and then I fainted. When I came too, I was lying alone outside the Level Two elevator. I got to my feet and leaned against the wall.

Then I left the building and went to find Mother.

12. MOTHER

I PULLED UP AT MOTHER'S HOUSE and took a deep breath. A certain kind of bravery was needed to see Mother.

Mother never liked Celeste. But then again, Mother had spent most of her life trying to convince me that it was okay I was gay. Only I wasn't gay. Or asexual or metrosexual. I had a sex drive all right, I just had a weird way of expressing it. Mother said I'd be so much happier if I just embraced my true self and let myself hang loose. Hang loose? When she said that, I put my fist through the wall, quickly followed by my first anger management session. I was fourteen—who wouldn't have lost their temper?

My father was a Real World Athlete, a RWA Gladiator. His body, unable to endure further punishment, forced him into early retirement and he reluctantly turned to coaching. Cage fighting and body-building were his specialities. I had no idea how my parents met or why they got married. They were close to forty when they had me, so I guess it wasn't so weird that I had my kids late too. Following his retirement from competitive sports, my father remained a health nut. He ran twelve kilometres a day, getting up at four a.m. on the dot and doing two hundred push-ups and two hundred chin-ups as a warmup. He was also a steady alcoholic, a fact which none of us was ever allowed to mention. When he was drunk, a solid funk of hatred rose off him like the early morning fog off a swamp. He had a sharp angular face—a tough guy best left alone.

One day, he went out and he never came back. Mother said she figured he went on a bender and decided to stay gone. She didn't care, and I certainly didn't miss him. I preferred it when it was just Mother and me. She was a neat freak too, and I loved that about her. So why did she hate me for being the way I was? You could lick her carpet and come up clean. As a kid, I used to do that, lick surfaces around the house, just to test. Mother said that wasn't normal, but then again there were kids out there literally eating dirt, so why take issue with me? She said I resented my father for leaving, and the therapists agreed. They said that was the root of all my problems, my issues of abandonment. But if you asked me, I had bigger issues with the fact that he was an asshole. And hey, the whole world was angry, it wasn't just me. Then Mother grew annoyed by my increasing fondness for BleachBuddy. She said I was over-the-top obsessive compulsive, and it annoyed her when I followed her around, spray bottle in hand.

So it wasn't exactly a gaggle of kittens at a picnic when Mother met Celeste. They both froze and became icily polite, like they'd collided in a grocery store and were forced into an awkward conversation while gathering scattered cans of creamed corn and mushroom soup. At first I thought it was funny because I'd never thought Mother loved me enough to fight for me, but then I realized it wasn't that. She just didn't like Celeste and the things that she stood for. And after we had Bax, things didn't improve. She didn't visit, nor were we allowed to visit her. Who doesn't want to see their own grandchild?

"I'm not babysitting," she said when I told her Celeste was pregnant. "I've done my time. I'm not saying I regret having you, but the results were ambivalent. I just want to do something meaningful with the rest of my life."

What was I? A science experiment? And an ambivalent result? What did that even mean? And why wasn't I meaningful? Why wasn't Bax meaningful?

"Why don't you love me?" I asked plaintively. We were

drinking coffee at the plastic white table, and the kitchen was not as clean as it was when I lived there. I wanted to dart up and grab a cloth, and Mother caught my eye. "No, Sharps," she said. "That's why you had to leave, remember? That, and breaking things. So sit still and grin and bear the filth."

She was being sarcastic. The kitchen was impeccable by most people's standards, but I spotted fingerprints on the stainless steel kettle, a dusting of crumbs under the toaster, and the drying rack needed a good bleach bath soak.

I studied my hands to distract myself, but I could also see that the floor under the fridge hadn't been vacuumed since I left. And I knew I didn't want to look inside. "I wish we saw each other more," I blurted out. "I miss you."

"Do you, Sharps? That surprises me. It's not like we ever really talked to each other. I cooked and you cleaned, and you stayed in your room or we watched some streamed program together."

"Yes, but now I'm married and I'm going to be a father!"

"And I'm happy for you. Look, this won't be easy for me to say or for you to hear, but I'm going to be honest. It's like you're not really ... well, doing anything with your life. I feel like I don't even know who you are. I've never really known. And that makes me sad. We never talk about things that matter. What can I tell you? I wish you all the best, I do, but I can't change the way things are."

"You wish me all the best," I echoed, pushing my coffee away from me. "Wow. That's brutal, Mother."

"That's not my intention," she said. "I just can't fix things for you anymore, Sharps."

"It's not my fault I'm the way I am," I exclaimed. "And I try. We're each other's only family. Through the good times and bad. I care about you!"

"Look, Sharps, I need some space away from you." Mother looked wrung out by the last admission. "I'm sorry, Sharps. It's not like you're stupid—you're not. In fact, your IQ is off the chart. And you're a fine-looking man, handsome. And now you've got yourself a family. I want you to leave the nest, fly and be happy. You don't need me to be happy."

"But I do!" I cried. "You're my mother!"

"You keep saying that like it's some kind of magic charm. It's not. I'm just an elderly woman, getting older by the day, wanting to find some real meaning in my life. I'm entitled to that. I looked after you all these years; I'm owed my time to think about what matters to me. My time of not being responsible for you."

Which is when I got up and left. Well, I meant to leave. Instead, I stood up and reached into the cupboard that housed her special occasion Queen Elizabeth china. I looked at her calmly while my body throbbed with red anger and my scalp prickled with static fire. Without stopping to think, I smashed every single piece. Teacups, saucers, plates, a coffee pot, side dishes, and even a gravy boat.

Mother didn't say a word. She sat and watched me. At one point she folded her arms and sighed. When I was done and there was nothing left to break, I left, vowing never to return. But here I was.

I walked up to the house. Was this a bad idea? Most likely. But it had to be done. I still had a key to the place but I rang the doorbell and waited. "Sharps!" Mother looked surprised to see me. "What are you doing here? In the middle of the day?"

"How do you know Ava Jane Jaccari?" I didn't mean to shout, and she flinched.

"In a mood, are you?" she said. "Fine, come in."

I marched into the living room and stopped dead.

"Plants!" I said. "What the fuck, Mother?"

"Language, Sharps," she said. "Are you going to report me? Turn your own mother in for an illegal hibiscus?"

But it wasn't just one plant. The room was full of them. It was a veritable jungle.

"Have you lost your mind?" I asked. Gardening was against

a whole slew of decrees by the Sacred Board. Astroturf ruled. Real grass was declared a noxious weed. Green belts had been cleared to make room for suburban mansions. Trees were replaced by tall slim plastic chimneys that inhaled carbon dioxide and exhaled oxygen. The blue-and-green candy cane trees were pretty, with stencilled leaves for artwork. Plant Guards patrolled, looking for rogue weeds and plants and eradicating them with poisons. Parks were filled with sculpted evergreen faux topiaries and lush, exotic flowers as large as dinner plates and as colourful as souvenirs from Mexico or Spain. Birds had long since died, falling from the sky, their tiny corpses quickly incinerated by Anti-Nature Guards. Bees and butterflies became extinct, and we didn't even notice until one day they were simply gone. The oceans and lakes were vast lukewarm baths, devoid of fish, coral, or seaweed. Mother Nature tried to fight back. Tendrils, roots, bushes, and branches fought their way into the drinking water and pushed through the plastic asphalt, but the guards were vigilant in their eradication duties.

But gardening? Mother had lost her mind.

She sighed.

"This is why you didn't want me to visit with Bax!" I said. "You're *gardening!* How long have you been doing this?"

"I started as soon as I could dissuade you from visiting," Mother said and she sat down in between two potted ferns.

"Where did you even get them?"

"Oh, for heaven's sake, Sharps! I may be getting on in years but I know how to find my way around the world! Has it never occurred to you that this plantless world is an aberration? Don't you ever miss nature? You grew up in it—real grass, real trees, flowers."

"I can honestly say I never missed it. Oh shit, Mother."

I sat down and looked at her.

"And as for Ava Jane Jaccari, she and I met at a writing workshop."

That Mother was a writer further stumped me, and she saw

that. "I'm going to make some tea while you process all of this for a bit."

I sat and tried to make sense of what she'd said. And what was I going to do about the plants? Minnie had decreed that plants were evil, that they were trying to take over the world, destroy mankind, and take back the earth. Minnie said plants possessed an innate DNA that made them want to survive in a way that put our species at risk. The Anti-Nature Guards would incinerate Mother's entire house with her in it if they found out.

"I'm moving them out of here soon," Mother said, returning with a tray. "Do stop worrying. You won't have to do anything. Put this out of your head."

It was hard to do, but I had more important matters to worry about than illegal foliage. I studied a small rose bush and sniffed it. It was pleasant. And when I touched the flower, it felt different from the fake replicas; it was soft and silky, and it smelled amazing. I stroked it and then jerked back. What was I doing?

When I looked up, Mother was holding out a small book and I took it from her.

"*Single Girls Go Mad Sooner.* You wrote this?" It was a slim volume with Ruben's Hero and Leander descending into their watery depths on the cover.

"I did." She laughed. "It's pretty bad. I wrote it while I was at university. It's a bit of a rant, but it proved quite popular."

"Why do single girls go mad sooner? Doesn't that imply that all women go mad?"

"They do when they are forced to follow the mandates and dictates of mankind. You see that, Sharps? 'Man'dates. 'Dick'tates. 'Man'kind. Do you see the subliminal patriarchal influences we are all subjected to from the very time of our birth? Young women, particularly in my day, were encouraged to get married and have children. It was our primary purpose, our ultimate destiny. Anything else was considered meaningless.

But the quest to communicate with men, to find a partner, to have a meaningful relationship took its toll. Single girls had to go on countless dates and endure more of those awful encounters, to the point where they thought they were insane. In fact, they were simply trying to connect with a species ill-equipped to reciprocate in either thought or emotion. Finally, exhausted, the girl either capitulated with the most suitable partner she could find, or she became weary and gave in to whoever was nearest. In so doing, she finally became a woman in the eyes of the patriarchal world. But look what she gave up. She agreed to a lifelong sentence of being misunderstood and subjugated."

"I see." I didn't, but I wasn't sure what else to say. I bent over slightly in my chair as if my dick needed protecting and Mother laughed. "See how instinctively you react? Must protect the precious family jewels above all."

"But," she said and she was serious, "I loved you. Above all else, I wanted to be a good mother but I failed. I must have failed you since you are so unhappy. I take responsibility for being a bad mother. But I tried. I really did. And yet still, I failed."

"I'm not unhappy," I objected miserably, uncomfortable with the way the entire conversation was going. "And you were a good mother. But right now, what's more important to me is Ava. She wants to bring down Minnie and destroy this world."

"Don't we all?"

I must have looked horrified because she laughed. "Oh, Sharps, look at you. You see. That's what I mean. You don't think. You just accept. You accept your job and the world as it is; you accept the drones that control the satellites that control the weather, and you accept the rampant materialism and self-obsession and vacuity and vanity and greed. And not only do you accept it, you propagate it! You package, market, and sell it! You see what I mean about not thinking?"

"But there's nothing we can do about it! I'd do something if I could! You think I don't worry about Bax's future? And whatever other kids we have? Of course I worry!"

"Not enough to do anything. Only enough to try to keep up. How do you know about Ava's manifesto?"

"Jazza fell in love with her. They had an affair."

"And she told him about it? She must have fallen for him, poor girl. And he told you about it. Hmmm. And of course she found out that he had."

I told her everything. She leaned back and folded her arms. "I'm surprised at Ava," she said. "Trusting a man. After what your father-in-law did to her mother."

"You knew about that?"

"Ava told me. I think she sees me as a surrogate mother and I'm very fond of her. She's going to do great things with her life, you'll see."

"Yeah, like increase the amount of women who buy useless shit for their useless lives," I said, and Mother shook her head.

"Give her time, Sharps. Rome wasn't rebuilt in a day."

"How come you discourage me from writing when you write?" I asked her, and she looked surprised.

"I didn't," she said. "What made you think that? Your father said that."

"I was ten when he disappeared! Or left or whatever you'd have me think. I don't think I'd remember what he said."

"Oh, you remembered. A bunch of your therapists all commented about how scarred you were from your relationship with him. I'm sorry about that."

I shrugged. I didn't want Mother feeling sorry for me about anything. "Why did you marry him?" I asked. "An unlikely combination, really."

"He was so handsome! Like a movie star: lantern jaw, big muscled man! I saw him coming out of a swimming pool, the sparkles catching on him like he was ablaze. And he walked straight up to me! I was a looker in those days, Sharps, with legs longer than the month of May. I got caught up in the romance of it all. I never thought about what *They Lived Happily Ever After* even meant. I thought it was a given. But you know how well that worked out. I fell in love. It happens, Sharps. And one day, it will happen to you too."

"I'm already a very happily married man, Mother," I said wearily. "So, back to you and Ava. A writing group. How long have you known her?"

"About ten years."

"You met her the same time you kicked me out?"

"Around then, but that had nothing to do with Ava. Well, it did in that I wanted to reconnect with who I was, Sharps, and yes, that was part of what my writing group advocated."

"They told you to kick me out?"

"It wasn't them; it was me. I realized it wasn't healthy for me to have you live with me any more. You were a grown man. Listen, Sharps, this is tedious, to be honest. Okay, so I know Ava and now you've met my plants. You know my worst secrets. Anything else?"

"Do you have a copy of Ava's manifesto?"

She laughed. "No, and you can tell Mr. Williamson that from me, if that's why you came." She stood up. "While it's been a nice visit, you need to leave now. And if you so much as touch one of my flowers, I'll face-plant you on the carpet."

I followed her to the front door. I stood on the step and faced her. I wanted to say something that would change our relationships for the better, forever, but I couldn't think of anything. She patted me gently on the shoulder and closed the door.

13. SUCKING IT UP

THE DAYS THAT FOLLOWED WERE AWKWARD, to say the least. Jazza returned from his brain scour. He was mean and bitter but more brilliant than ever.

They moved the three of us into a boardroom and closed the door. Daddy had one parting shot before he left. "God helps those who help themselves," he said. "But if you ask me, may God help you." He gave me a meaningful glance and left. I had the most to lose, and everyone in the room knew it.

The Board had given us every manner of research and design equipment imaginable. We were in a giant lab. Display panels flashed statistics, ratios, trends, and images. Consumer holograms filled the room, walking among us, pointing, laughing, and buying. These were our Targeted Consumers, our TCs. But what were we going to sell them?

Another floor-to-ceiling wall screened reruns of our previous campaigns, flashing in all their brilliance. Of course, there too, with it's own special display, was MDoggHotBody with a massive rubberstamp FAIL at the centre, in a disaster font. As if I needed reminding.

And there we were, the three of us, silent. I wanted to run, but I had nowhere to go.

Ava got up and placed three silver pyramid paperweights on our desks. "Scrambles the audio," she barked at me. "They'll hear a script that will keep them happy, a bot-collected dialogue from other meetings. We can say whatever we want." I wasn't sure why she was even speaking to me.

Jazza flipped a switch, and floor-to-ceiling blinds shut down the room. My throat closed with panic, but he waved at me. "Door's open, run away any time you like."

Then he swung around to Ava and glowered. The gloves had come off. "You bitch," he said to Ava. "You hacked into my personal optics. I was *scoured* because of you."

"You told him my secrets," she fired back. "I told you not to trust him. I told you not to tell anybody."

"But you hacked into me first! I trusted you!"

They came out from behind their desks and faced each other, Ava seemingly the same height as him, such was her voltage.

Meanwhile Jazza looked shaky, Frankenstein's monster hoping someone would throw him a bone.

But Ava wasn't in the mood to play nice. "Yeah? Well, I hacked into you hoping you'd prove me wrong. But you proved me right. You told him everything. All he had to say was, 'Jazza, I'm so stressed,' like a big cry baby, and you leapt into his lap like the good little puppy dog you are. You're just like every other dickhead on the planet. A total waste of space."

Ava clenched her fists at her side, and they started shouting. I realized she must have hacked into Jazza's audio the night he and I met in the bar and she was none too happy about him spilling the beans. I tried to tune them out. I held my hands over my ears, feeling as childish as Bax. How had it come to this?

"It fucking hurt to be scoured," I heard Jazza shout. "And it was all because of you! I don't feel like me anymore! I feel…" He stumbled and fell silent.

"You deserve the pain," Ava snarled at him, baring her teeth like a tiny Rottweiler.

It occurred to me that the thing they wanted the most was to rip each other's clothes off and have crazy sex on the floor. I felt uncomfortable even being in the room, and I decided to try to diffuse the situation.

"Tell us, how do you feel, Jazza?" I asked soothingly, into

the silence that had fallen. I kept my voice low, using the same strategy that many a therapist had tried on me. "It must have been very harrowing for you."

"Oh, shut the fuck up," Jazza said. He threw a Fluffsqueak at me, and I caught it neatly with one hand.

"Hey," I said, "You wanna play Slam the Squeak?" I held the blameless Fluffsqueak high. We used to make basketball nets and throw activated squeaks into them, finding their simulated pain squeals hilarious.

"No. I fucking do not want to play Slam. I do not want to fucking do anything with you fucking ever again."

Okey dokey.

"Well, we can't have our asses fired," Ava pointed out, and she sat down behind her desk. "We've only got nine months. We'd better get a move on."

"I know what we've got to do," Jazza muttered. Ava replied but it was drowned by Celeste's voice in my head.

Sweetie! It's time for u to take me to the spa! I hope u didn't forget?

Shit. How had she bipassed my audioblock? Had she heard everything Daddy had said? It was best not to think about it.

"It's Celeste," I said to Jazza, and then replied to her.

No, hon, I didn't forget. I'll be right there.

And u have to take Lila to the clinic. Flashing u the address.

Yep, I knew that too. I'm on my way.

I swiped her incoming data out of my peripheral vision, wishing I could swipe my life away.

"I gotta go," I said, and Ava snorted.

"Just like you," she said. Jazza nodded without looking at me.

"Meanwhile we'll stay here and do all the real work," he said.

I'd had enough. "You know what, Jazza?" I yelled. "Man the fuck up. You fucked up, or you fucked down or sideways. Your PrivaKarmaSutra's none of my business...."

"Kama, not karma," Ava corrected me, and I glared at her.

"Whatever. I've got no idea what positions you guys got into, but you both fucked up, not me." I looked at Ava. "Neither of you guys like me, and you sure as shit don't respect me. But let's not forget one thing. I'm in charge, so we will all play nice. As much as you two are the brains, trust me, I've got a role to play and you know that I deliver what I need to, when I need to. So let's behave with some cordiality, how's that? We all on board?"

They nodded, and peace flooded my system like the sweet scent of BleachBuddy. Jazza would figure out how to make money. Ava would figure out how to get it to armies of eager women. And I'd ride that wave while taking care of my boy and keeping my wife in rehab for as long as I could. I felt a lot more cheerful than I had in a long time.

I tried to dial up Mother to tell her that despite her beliefs to the contrary, I really was very happy with my life. She didn't take the call, and all I got was a widely grinning hologram that was so unlike Mother. The hologram informed me that Mother was out of town and not to leave a message. *Out of town? For real?* I bet it had to do with her gardening. She was putting herself in danger, and while she'd clearly washed her hands of me, I still loved her.

And now she had disappeared. Great. I added that to my list of things to follow up on.

I settled into my lava-lamp seat inside my bubble car and got ready to face Celeste. She, in preparation for her journey, would be soaked in a hundred-proof spiced rum. I'd drop her off and have Bax all to myself. Things were going to be just fine.

I got Celeste settled into her spa, delivered Lila to the clinic, and then played with Bax to my heart's content.

I returned to the office the following day with trepidation. To my surprise, peace prevailed and what's more, they even had a plan.

"Here's how it's going to work," Ava told me. "The PeachDi-amondDelux Program. You won't understand it, so don't even try. Just sign where Jazza tells you to. I'll work my magic, and we'll all get out of this hell, you to your new baby—and yes, we all know all about that—me back to my nice big private office, and Jazza will do whatever it is he wants to do with the rest of his life. Got it?"

Taken aback, I nodded.

"We're going to flash ads everywhere, Sharps, on every wall and building. We're assuming control of personal Crystal Path viewing. All viewed content will henceforth be sponsored. Through the viewer's eye, the world's going to look like a kaleidescope of logos tossed its cookies in Real Life Las Vegas, but it'll work and we'll generate the revenue we've been tasked with."

It sounded unthinkably ugly. "You're turning the world into a virtual catalogue? That kind of hard sell is illegal! Advertising has to be hidden, experience-driven! That's how 123BlikiWin, ClothesKissezThugs, and CrystalMeBooty worked! We never advertised directly! It was all about being a player in the game! Direct merch sales are banned!"

"There are ways around things," Ava said. "A way into allowing direct advertising onto personal devices. Your Mr. Williamson is one of the masterminds behind it. I never knew he had that kind of legal savvy. I have to admit I'm even mildly impressed. He spotted a loophole and dove right through it, opening up a whole new world. Maybe he knew it was there all along and was saving it for an ICE situation, which, admittedly, this is."

"ICE?"

"In Case of Emergency. But really, it's IA. Intrusive Awareness, Sharps. Get it tattooed on the inside of your eyeballs. Although actually, you won't have to because you'll be seeing whatever we want you to see. We can't market it like that, obviously. The trick is direct selling but not direct selling. Got it? You'll still have to disguise the hard sell as entertainment, but that's your sticky jam. You'll have all kinds of brainiac ideas, won't you, Sharps? I've got a stack of reading matter for you on the legalities of it, which you'll need to distill and turn into cheery

PR for advertisers. Going through the data will make you want to kill yourself if you don't fall into a coma first. I bet that's why they passed the law because no one actually read the full legislation to the very end."

She leaned forward, her sharp little foxy face intense, her big black eyes cold and dead. I shrugged, wishing I could grab her by the hair, yank her head back, and tell her to never talk to me that way again. "I'll do my best, Ava. I always do."

Her eyes narrowed into slits. "That's so you, Sharps. Your best had better be shit hot and shiny as diamonds. Your last big hit—or shall I say, miss—was the MDoggHotBody, which cost us a bundle. I know I wasn't supposed to mention the elephant in the room, but screw that, the cards are on the table here."

"Fine," I shouted. "I screwed up. I get it! I'm sorry." I sank into my chair and stared at my wall of shame. FAIL. Was it really necessary for her to flog me like this?

I looked at my initial pitch. *When You're Hot, You're Hot!* And *Oh, Mama, You Are One Hot Diggety Dog!* I'd thought the idea was genius. I figured women hated seeing themselves naked under the unforgiving stare of florescent lights while avatar shopping was such fun. Here was the hook: you looked like a million dollars in the virtual store, and when the suit was delivered, it fit like a glove. In your mind's eye, you were that supermodel strutting the cat walk or lying on beach sands inside football-sized beach malls, complete with waves, surfer boys, coconut oil, and palm trees. The trouble was, when the suits arrived and no one looked fabulous but remained their lumpy dumpy selves, women were enraged. We had the highest returns in the history of Integratron.

Jazza shared the loss and shouldered the blame, although he'd told me in no uncertain terms that the idea was a loser before it left the gate. He said that he knew he looked like a half-baked hairy dough ball that had rolled out from under the fridge and that even if he got to look like Mr. Gorgeous online, when it came to reality, one had to face the facts. He told me I was a pretty boy who'd never heard the fat lady sing. I brushed his objections aside, and, fortunately for me, the losses coincided with my marrying Celeste. Daddy told me not to worry, that no one's record was spotless. He'd promised me he'd make it go away, a promise clearly unfulfilled.

"I learned a lot from that one." I stared Ava down. "Research dropped the ball. Which is why they ended up in the Sheds processing data for the rest of their lives. They should have caught the flaws. I'm not going to let that happen again."

"You're right, you won't. And how you even got the word 'dog' into the campaign is beyond me, but let's not even go there. Is that what women are to you, Sharps? Dogs to come when you call them and play fetch, roll over, and have their tummies rubbed?"

I shrugged.

"This time," Ava said, and her tone made my balls retract up my spine, "you'll just do what we tell you to."

I looked at Jazza, but he was staring at a screen. I pressed my fingers to my temples. I was caught in the undertow of something I couldn't control and could barely understand. Maybe, just maybe, if I could just keep my head above water, I'd come out of this okay. But it seemed like a long shot.

14. A TERRIBLE LOW

CELESTE GOT SOBER. LILA MOVED IN with us so I could keep an eye on her pregnancy. Without Christine egging her on, she wasn't too awful to be around. Soon my little angel, Sophie, was born. Lila pocketed her cash and quietly vanished, and our little family of four was complete. Daddy couldn't have been more proud of me. The PeachDiamondDelux Program seemed to be going according to plan, and the Board even gave us another few years grace. They realized that the deadline they had given us was unrealistic, but to our credit, we nearly hit the target.

Mother reappeared from wherever it was that she had gone. She surprised me by coming to see Sophie, but there was a distance between us and I had no idea why she'd made the effort. Was she watching me, waiting to catch the pieces when I finally fell apart? I, in turn, visited her a few times, and her home was spotless, with no signs of gardening or mention of her writing. When I asked about Ava, she changed the subject.

Jazza and Ava channelled their passion into a mutual working fury that saw them in the office twenty-four seven. To my discomfort, not that they cared, they practically sat on top of one another while they worked, whispering in a huddle. I was spared from seeing it too often as I was on the road a lot. I'd always believed that selling needed to be done face-to-face. Holograms didn't cut it. Virtual me just didn't have the fire power of real me, and I felt euphoric after a great sales pitch.

Good days on the road even made Celeste bearable when I got home, and she, in turn, clearly enjoyed the sight of me in my charcoal pinstriped, double-breasted Yves McGaultier power suit, making a killing. Her sex drive had fallen off, much to my relief, and we seemed almost like a normal family. All my dreams had come true. Nanny Flo was a gem, and I trusted her with the kids in a way I'd never thought possible.

The years went by, and I began to relax, increasingly confident that things would work out in the long run. Of course, that's when it all fell apart.

It began with Celeste's gentle yet insistent increase in vodka consumption. Then Daddy told me that some of his investments hadn't worked out and I had to take care of his share of Celeste's expenses. Right, like that was even possible. I poured every cent I earned into my family, blowing up one credit card after another. At four, Bax was a quiet, distant little boy while Sophie stole my heart. Sophie was so happy. I had no idea what fuelled her easy-going grin, but right from the start, Sophie was a shining, delightful angel. At least Nanny Flo stayed loyal, and we had a round of babysitters helping out, neighbourhood kids from what I could gather.

But sales slowed down. I had fewer pitches, and interest in our program waned. Jazza and Ava continued to pour good work after bad, but the results for the PeachDiamondDelux Program fell off. The kiss of death came when a hacker figured out a way to block the broadcasts. I had to spend more time at the office, and the tension of being around Jazza and Ava sucked me dry. I knew they were contravening the Geneva convention as mandated by the Board and were humping each other like rabbits every moment they could. Although it was more like a squirrel humping a grizzly. I walked in on them one time—sweet Jesus, it scarred me for life, the sight of tiny Ava attached to big old Jazza, her legs wrapped around his waist, both of them howling away. I'll tell you this for nothing, orgasms when not artistically directed are not attractive.

Even then, I find the whole thing embarrassing. I backed out and flashed Jazza.

Next time, lock the door, buddy, for Pete's sake.

I wished I could play hooky, showing up only to sign whatever documentation Jazza told me to, but Daddy said I was office bound to keep an eye on things.

Only Bax and Sophie brought me any joy, but I was so worn out by the end of the day that I couldn't even bring myself to give them the love and attention they deserved. Besides, they had all those kids looking after them, as well as Nanny Flo. It wasn't like they were neglected.

Tired as I was, I still cleaned. Polishing and spraying soothed me. I often found myself—clean wipes in one hand, Bleach-Buddy in the other—staring into space, forgetting what it was I wanted to clean. I punctuated my life with visits to the rage room, but even within the plastic walls of my haven, I was often too tired to do anything except lie on the floor, baseball bat in hand, listening to the soundtrack of my life and wondering how I was going to drag myself home. And slowly but surely, I started to sink even further.

I started sleeping more, having naps as soon as I got home. I just couldn't seem to rally. Celeste told me I should play with Baxie, that he missed his dada, but I was too tired. I was happy to kiss a fragrant little Sophie and ruffle Bax's hair, but I was smothered by a thick dark cloud. I wanted to float down to the bottom of a pond and close my eyes. Even the upcoming prospect of the annual Christmas lights war with Strawberry Merv failed to excite me. I slept like the dead, plagued by nightmares of a relentless Ava gnawing at me with her sharp teeth and Jazza, hating me because it was my fault he'd lost her even though she couldn't stop herself from banging him.

Daddy stopped by the office for a board meeting now and then. I tried to tell him I was struggling, but he just looked off into the distance as if he was seeing a future that had nothing to do with him. He was getting on in years, and I got the impression that the Board had found ways to sideline him after he'd failed to react with immediate action and appropriate force after learning of Ava's manifesto.

He responded by packing up Mummy and running off to Real Life Florida. I'd have thought they'd want to stick around for their grandkids, particularly after all the expense and work it took us to get them, but they lost interest after Sophie was born. They'd taken up real life golfing and were addicts. Daddy didn't even seem to care about Celeste any more.

One night, struck by inertia, I was late getting home. Nanny Flo was nowhere to be seen. Celeste was passed out cold on the sofa, with Bax playing quietly in the corner. Toys were everywhere, and the smell of burnt toast filled the air.

Sophie was in her playpen, wailing, covered in snot and I reached in and picked her up. Her diaper was full and dripping.

"Oh no, you're all wet. How did you get so wet, baby girl? Where's Nana Flo?"

I changed her and soothed her and made her and Bax supper, and then I cleaned up and put them both to bed.

Celeste slept through it all. I flashed a bunch of messages to Nanny Flo, with no reply.

I finally shook Celeste awake, and she sat up, drool covering one side of her face. Deep sleep creases lined her cheeks, and her one eye was droopy and weird.

"Where's Flo?" I shook her and she was like a rag doll. "Cee, are you high? What's going on?"

She noticed that it was dark, and she stood up and pulled down her blouse which was twisted around her belly. A fleshy doughnut circled her like a water tire. She must be eating as well as drinking.

"Honestly Cee, what's going on? Where's Flo?"

"I think she left."

"Left? What do you mean, left?"

"Gone. Home. To wherever she's from. I've got no idea. An emergency. Or something. I couldn't cope. I had one drink, then another. I know I had too much, Sharps. You don't have to look at me that way. It's very tough, being a stay-at-home mother—you've got no idea. You've got your career and your sense of purpose, and it's so easy for you."

Easy for me? A sense of purpose? I wanted to hit her. "What I've got is a drunk for a wife who does nothing but spend, spend, spend. And you just expect me to pay. I'm not your father! I've never had that kind of money, Cee, you know that. My career? I'm struggling to keep my job. I have ALWAYS STRUGGLED!"

"And you know I had EXPECTATIONS!" she shouted at me. "You were supposed to have my back, Sharps. You knew the deliverables. Daddy TOLD YOU!"

That was when I slapped her. "Fuck you, Celeste, fuck you."

She held her hand to her face, but that wasn't the worst of it. The worst was the little face watching me through the bannister.

I sank down to the floor. I wanted to die.

"Good job, Sharps," Celeste said. "Well done, big guy. Nice."

I buried my face in my hands, and I heard her go up the stairs. I heard her pick up Baxter and murmur things to him that she should never have needed to say.

I lay on the carpet, surrounded by mess and filth and chaos.

And then a message flashed across my visuals, overriding accept or decline.

WTF? Hundreds of K missing. UR dead. TMR. 9am.

Ava. I sat up.

What r u talking about?

TMR. YOU SHIT. U are SO burned.

WTF do u mean?

Right. Play dumb. U thought we wouldn't find it?

Find what?

TMR.

And that was that.

I sat there, staring into space when a second comm shot across my visual space. It was Jazza.

Sorry buddy. My bad.

Jazza? WTF? What happened? Ava flashed me a comm. What's going on?

Jazza? Jazza?

Nothing. Radio silence.

I threw up. I threw up on our cream carpet, the one I'd kept so pristine all these years.

The next morning, Celeste, clearly hungover, was downstairs making breakfast. The mess made me cringe, but I went up to her.

"Cee…" I was lost for words. "I'm so sorry. That will never happen again."

"I know, sweetie. It's okay. Listen, you're under a lot of stress, I know that. And I know I haven't been supportive or even aware in the way I should have been."

She'd covered the bruise with concealer, but I could still see it.

Bax eyed me cautiously from the table.

"Baxie, give Dada a big kiss," Celeste said, but Bax just looked me and then at his piece of toast.

"Daddy lost his temper last night," I said to my child, and I got down on my knees next to his chair. "And he is very, very sorry. Isn't that right, Mommy?"

"Quite right," Celeste said cheerfully. "Life is hard for adults too, Baxie, you'll see. Daddy's said he's sorry and he is. When people are sorry, we forgive them and we say it's okay."

But Baxter stared at his toast, and I wanted to throw up the bile in my belly.

"He'll be fine, sweetie," Celeste said. "Kids are resilient. Don't worry about it. You go and do your day."

I stood up. I wanted to touch my son, but I knew it would only make things worse so I reached for my man bag instead.

"Good luck, sweetie," Celeste said. "Flash me later. Listen, Sharps, we'll be okay. You know that, right? We'll fix this. The kiddies and I will finish decorating. Don't you just love our tree, sweetie? We'll do the rest of the room to match.

It's Christmas Eve. Our special night. When you come home, everything will be perfect.

"Okay." I pecked her on the cheek, filled with gratitude for her kindness, and then I rushed headlong into the day I dreaded.

I sat in traffic and tried to tell myself that it wouldn't be so bad. I waited for the car in front of me to move, and I felt numb and terrified at the same time. It took a while for me to hear the angry horns behind me, and I swiped the car into drive.

And I was right. When I got to work, it wasn't as bad as I thought it would be. It was a thousand times worse.

15. THIEVERY

"I'VE GOT ALL THE PROOF I NEED." Ava was smug. "I haven't told anyone yet in case you've miraculously got an explanation, but you don't, do you?"

We were in the Aurora boardroom and I wondered where Jazza was. I'd sent him dozens of texts.

> Where r u? What do u mean? Help me out buddy, what's going on? Come on Jazza, talk to me. Fuck u Jazza, wtf?

I looked at Ava. I didn't have a clue what she was talking about.

It was nine thirty. I was late for the meeting. I walked into the Aurora boardroom and sat down gingerly across from Ava, who had spreadsheets displayed on the crystal screens. She led me through half an hour of torture, flicking through spreadsheets and documents. I had no idea what I was looking at. "You see the discrepancies?" she kept asking. "Which, when added up over three years, equal millions of dollars. And you signed off on them. You got lucky banging Celeste and popping out a couple of kids, but your goose is so cooked, it's not even funny. What do you have to say?"

I had no idea what to say. "Does Daddy, I mean Mr. Williamson, does he know?"

She smirked. "Daddy does not know. I've called a meeting of the Board for later this afternoon. All shall be revealed there. And you'll be at my side, telling everyone what you did with the money and explaining yourself. What do you know,

Sharps? I'm psychic! I see an arrest in your near future. You may not even make it home for dinner. Christmas for you, Sharps, might be cancelled this year!"

I looked at her and opened my mouth to speak, to tell her that I had no idea what she was talking about. Just as I did, the fire alarm went off. At first I thought it was the cops coming to arrest me, and my heart nearly burst, but it was the fire alarm. *Whoop, whoop, whoop!* Thank god. All two hundred floors had to evacuate. The building was so safe that fires and fire drills hardly ever happened, and I thanked all of my lucky stars. The thought occurred to me that Jazza had started a fire to save my ass, but either way I didn't care. I grabbed my man bag and started to shove my portable comm into it, but Ava waved at me to stay where I was. "It's just a drill," she said. "Sit. Ignore it. I'm not leaving until you admit what you did." *Whoop, whoop, whoop!*

I looked around in desperation. Why weren't we leaving? But the boardroom across from us was fully populated with earnest Integratroniers who carried on working, and I had no choice but to force my gaze back to Ava and the wall-sized screen.

Whoop, whoop, whoop! The siren was insistent. "Explain yourself!" Ava yelled over the noise, and I forced myself to stare at her screen. I hated spreadsheets. What was I even looking at? Rows of shit that made no sense. The screen swam in front of my eyes. Where was Jazza, for fuck's sake? The siren was honking like a goose trapped under the wheel of a bus, and I wanted to scream. *Whoop, whoop, whoop!* Ava was talking, but I couldn't hear anything she was saying anymore. *Blah blah*, those red lips moved, and she pointed at her screen. *Whoop, whoop, whoop!* I nodded but the noise was a suffocating blanket. No, worse, I was drowning, I was under an overturned boat, bobbing in black water with a fog-horn blasting in my ears. *Whoop, whoop, whoop!* I wanted to stick my fingers in my ears, but of course I couldn't.

"Make a note of this one," Ava said. "The primary account. You'll have to…" *Whoop, whoop, whoop!* And then the words were drowned out, and all I heard was "Where's the money, Sharps? Did you spend it on your cupcake wife and heirs to the throne?"

I watched the boardroom empty behind us. *Whoop, whoop, whoop!* The emergency response guy opened the door and waved us out, shouting. And still, Ava shook her head.

"We must finish this," she yelled. "I want to KNOW!" *Whoop, whoop, whoop! Whoop, whoop, whoop!* She forced me to sit there, with the howling smashing at me like a baseball bat. I was trapped. I closed my eyes.

There goes my life. I should have tried to get another job but there wasn't anything out there, and then Celeste and Daddy had come along and I had thought I was safe.

Whoop, whoop, whoop! I kept my fists clenched tightly by my sides. I dug my nails into my cuticles as if the pain would distract me, and it did for a while, but Ava still wouldn't shut up. The fire alarm was still honking *whoop, whoop, whoop!* and she kept on talking. I was trapped in that boardroom with Betty Boop and her dead black eyes, going on and on, and her mouth was moving but I couldn't hear what she was saying. *Whoop, whoop, whoop!*

Eventually, the EmrGuard kicked us out of the boardroom, refusing to take no for an answer. "Leave," he yelled. "Out, now!" I wanted to run out of the building and never come back. What was I going to do? I was soaking wet, rivers of cold sweat ran from under my armpits, down my rib cage and pooled in the waistband of my trousers. My heart, a flattened balloon, chose that moment to inflate in my chest like the inner tube of a bicycle tire full of toxic air. I had to get out of the building, run away from Ava, find Jazza, and figure this thing out.

A red light flashed in my peripheral vision. Jazza. Thank god. But there was no good news.

By the time u read this, I will be dead by my own hand. Sorry Sharps. I couldn't face it. I let you down. I let me down. Call the SSOs. I don't want to rot here or have my furballs eat my face. Sorry buddy. Best Wishes.

Best Wishes?

Whoop, whoop, whoop! I read the flash comm again, shaking while Ava herded me towards the stairwell. She pushed her way in front of me, carrying her laptop-sized portable comm and her purse, tottering on high heels.

I paused at the top of Stairwell 9, shoving my arms into my twisted jacket while Ava trotted ahead. *Whoop, whoop, whoop!* My thoughts were spinning. What the fuck had Jazza done? Ava and I were alone in the stairwell, the rest of the building had emptied, and there was no one else inside.

Ava was half a flight down when I saw my opportunity. It wasn't so much a conscious thought as a fully fleshed-out realization. *Lose your footing. Crash into her. Solve this problem. Get rid of her.* I'd risk my neck by crashing into her, but it would be worth it. I had nothing left to lose. And if she didn't die in the fall, I could tackle her and strangle her and hope that no one noticed. "I fell, in the rush," I could say. "It was an accident." And no one would know any different.

I rushed down towards her. She had her back to me. I figured that if I got her at the turn, at the very top of the stairs, she'd tumble the full length and achieve maximum damage. The stairwell in Sky The Tower was like any other, steep and narrow, with a railing on one side.

I had once heard it said that pushing a person down the stairs was as easy as opening a door, and it was. I hardly had to do anything, and there she was, tumbling down, down, down. The bicycle tire in my chest flew away as if it never existed. I grabbed the railing while I watched, and I couldn't help but smile.

Bounce, bounce, bounce, there she was, nearly at the foot of the Stairwell 6. But a terrible thing happened. The door to

Stairwell 6 opened and a woman stepped out into Ava's path. Ava careened into her, like a luge sled going off track, and they both tumbled down the stairs, like spinning laundry, coming to an abrupt stop at the bottom of Stairwell 5.

I froze. I waited for them to move, but they didn't.

And all this time, the siren was still wailing, but I was so overcome with horror that the sound was muffled, an underwater moan from far away. I sank to my haunches and watched and waited. The fire alarm pounded along with the message my heart was banging out, *what did you do, what did you do?*

Adwar. What was she doing in Sky The Tower? She was a low-level accountant from the Sheds who had no place in our hallowed grounds. I only knew who she was because she'd won the annual Christmas Shed Bonus Lottery and her face was plastered across our CPs, highlighting what good Christian folk we all were, helping the disenfranchised. We were told that she'd emigrated from Saint Genesius, formerly known as Ethiopia, to earn money and help her family and that she sent money home every month. Her name in English was Sophie, just like my little girl. I'd killed a good woman who'd never harmed anyone in her life. And Ava was dead. I stood there in the stairwell and realized that I had to do something. I had to take control.

I fumbled around in Ava's jacket and found her portable comm. Jazza had told me her password. *AvaQueen007!* I deleted the texts she'd sent me as well as my replies to her. I grabbed her large portable comm and rushed down to Stairwell 4, hiding the comm deep in the clean wipes trashcan in the washroom. I took a moment to calculate. Fire drills usually took about an hour. Ava had kept me hostage for about fifteen minutes. If the fire drill had started at nine forty, I had twenty minutes.

I ran back up to Stairwell 5 and called #Emr, a shortcut for emergency calls. "We left the building in a rush," I'd say.

"Ava was running down the stairs in those killer heels and she tripped. And Adwar came out at that very moment. It was terrible."

And no one would know about my role in the money scheme. Shit, I hadn't known—it was all on Jazza. He'd admitted as much to me. I deleted my texts to him. There was a way out for me! I had Jazza's admission of guilt, and Ava was dead. Relief filled my chest. I could do this!

What is your emergency?

Accident in the stairwell, two women unconscious, one fell down the stairs into the other.

Help is on the way.

I needed to weep. I needed to look like I cared, but I wasn't an emotional guy at the best of times. I tried to force a few tears, but I stopped. No, it was better to play this the silent way, jaw clenched, stoic, shocked.

And that's what I did.

Ava and Adwar were carted away. Ava was still alive but barely. Adwar had broken her fall. Adwar's neck was broken, and her head hung sideways away from her body. I wanted to throw up.

"Go home," Mr. Williamson's boss said to me. It was the first time I'd met him. He was a tiny wizened gnome of a man with a dome of dandelion hair. He introduced himself as Nix and nothing more. "Take the afternoon. What a thing." It was lunchtime by the time the scene had been cleaned up and the rest of the building let back in. "Come in tomorrow and we'll talk. Get you in touch with EmoHealth and have them set you up with a compassion counsellor. I know Ava wasn't easy to get along with but regardless, it's a shock to us all." He didn't seem upset by what had happened and even seemed tacitly approving, although perhaps I was projecting.

But it wasn't that easy to get away. The Safety Services Officers, the SSOs, wanted more than I was willing to give. Minnie had thought that Safety Services Officers sounded more positive than homicide detectives, but milder moniker or not, these two Pinkertons were intense. They wanted a detailed statement. I refused to give them more than the Coles notes version, seemingly incoherent with shock.

"We'll come back tomorrow." They finally agreed when Nix insisted. "Ten a.m. See you then."

I nodded and grabbed my coat. I took the elevator to the fourth floor, retrieved Ava's computer, and made a run for it.

A red light flashed, an incoming comm. *What now?* It was Celeste. The BlossomVents in the house had died. She and the kids couldn't breathe. What, like five minutes of real air was killing them? Celeste had a lavender and rose blend gently pumped into the high-oxygen regulated air flow, which she sometimes switched to lilacs or lilies. She said she didn't know who to call, so I had to come home and fix the air. And Baxie had tripped over Sophie's toys and chipped a tooth against his lip, gashing it open, and there was blood everywhere. She was hysterical and could hardly talk. That she'd prioritized flower-scented air over Bax's tooth made me want to throttle her.

"Well, so far my day's been pretty rough too," I said distantly. She didn't listen to me, so I yelled, "Celeste! I've got my own shit to deal with. Ava fell down the stairs and nearly died. She took another woman with her. Jazza didn't show up for work and I'm in deep shit. I've got to go and find Jazza. I need you to step up. We both know you can do it."

This was not greeted favourably. More hysterical sobbing ensued. I would have called Mummy and Daddy, but they were in Real Life Florida, most likely teeing up on a gentle hilly mound surrounded by flawless greens.

So I had to do the hardest thing ever. I had to ask Mother for help. "Cee, I'll call Mother."

Silence. The sobbing stopped. "Must you? Why can't you come home?" she wailed.

"Because," I hissed, "as I explained, I have multiple quadruple emergency situations of my own. I'll get ahold of Mother and call you back."

I took a deep breath and flashed a comm. Mother picked up on the third alert. "What do you need, Sharps?"

"I'm in a crisis, Mother. I need you to go and take care of Celeste. Long story, I can't get into it. Please, just help me. There's no nanny. Celeste will most likely be drunk by the time you get there. Bax chipped a tooth, the BlossomVents are dead, and god knows what else is going on."

There was silence. "Mother," I said. "Please. It's life and death, and I do mean that. I'm not being dramatic. Help me out and I'll buy you a NeptuneSupremeBodyFountain. I know you've always wanted one instead of the chipped old bathtub."

"Okay," she said, quick as that. "Deal."

I swiped the comm closed.

Thank you, Mother, thanks very much. What did I ever do to you? All I ever wanted was to be loved.

A wave of self pity washed over me, and tears filled my eyes. Finally, emotion.

"It's not fair," I said out loud, and a passerby looked at me oddly. "I just want things to be easier. I just want Mother to love me."

I flashed Celeste.

Mother's on her way. I'll be home as soon as I can.

16. WHAT JAZZA DID

I MADE MY WAY TO JAZZA'S APARTMENT. I hadn't been back since that visit when I found his underwear and his zoo of hairy creatures, and I shuddered to imagine the state it was in now. Jazza had given me a key for safekeeping in case he lost his or locked himself out, which he did at least a few times a year.

I glanced around the lobby and pressed the elevator to the seventh floor. The corridor was empty. It wasn't even three in the afternoon and the day had already been an unspeakable nightmare. I had no idea what level of horror to expect inside Jazza's apartment.

I put my key in the lock. Part of me wanted to run, not see whatever was inside. I could delete Jazza's text, pretend I never saw it, and go home once I had let Mother sort things out. I could go and sit in a deluxe coffee shop and get myself a macchiato with extra cream—no, maybe not since I hated cream—but I could get something, a treat of some kind and wait this out. I thought about running away, but I had no money. The credit cards were maxed. I stood pondering my options and decided I had no choice. I had to see what Jazza had done. Curiosity more than compassion forced the key into the lock, and I opened the door.

"Jazza?" I called out. There was an ancient wailing howling sound and I froze, sure my heart would explode from terror. Was that Jazza? "Jazza?" I whispered. "Jazza?" The ungodly howl sounded again, and I was about to run when I realized I was being an idiot. It was just one of the hairy creatures, and it sidled around the door and rubbed against my leg. I realized it was a cat.

Sadie. Sexy Sadie, Jazza had told me about Sadie and her ear-splitting yowls, and now I had met the beast in person.

I went inside the apartment and closed the door behind me. Sadie kept rubbing against my legs, and then she gave another gut-wrenching scream.

The place was a HazMat zone of shit, kitty litter, kibble, and piss. The acrid stench was so powerful that my eyes watered and I clamped my hand over my nose. It was worse than I ever could have imagined. Containers covered every available surface, balancing on the arms of the sofas and chairs. The garbage was piled high, stacks of Jenga towers. How the animals didn't knock the shit down, I had no idea.

Squirrels darted across the sofa, and there were several cats and—was that a weasel? Yes, it was a weasel. And a big mama raccoon with a bunch of babies peering out from under the coffee table with their Lone Ranger faces. Dear god. I stared, speechless, at a cage full of guinea pigs and hedgehogs, but where was Jazza?

The full-length curtains billowed, and I dug my hands into my winter coat and shivered. Why was I so cold? Because the door to the small balcony was wide open and Jazza's ratty brown drapes were gusting back and forth.

I couldn't face the balcony yet. I went to Jazza's bedroom in the hopes he had passed out on the bed. *Oh shit.* Instead of a coverlet, a moving colony of rabbits twitched and fidgeted. I closed the door as quickly as I could and I pulled my sweater up to my nose and breathed through it. The faint scent of dryer sheets and fabric softener helped settle me. I plunged into his washroom next. Hedgehogs lay asleep in a towel inside the basin, and a chipmunk peered up at me from the bathtub, rummaging through a bag of sour cream and onion chips with tiny paws.

I backed out to the galley kitchen to gather my thoughts. What to do? I mindlessly opened the fridge. A single beer sat at eye level, all by its lonesome. Propped in front of it, was a letter with my name on it. *Hi Sharps! Read me!*

I reached in and grabbed the letter. The rest of the fridge was crowded with black lettuce, fuzzy grey carrots, rancid mustard jars, calcified butter, and mouldy condiments. There was only that one cleared shelf, with a beer and a letter.

I opened the letter. It was neatly typed and printed, but OMG, *Comic Sans*? I'd had figured Jazza for Palatino at least or perhaps Bebas. We had endless discussions about typography—it was another weird obsession of ours—including exactly what kinds of plastic built our world. But since when did he have a printer? And Comic Sans? Really? More proof that he'd lost his mind.

Sharps. How did I know you'd poke in the fridge? Same way I know everything else about you, buddy. I use that word loosely. I was YOUR friend, but what was I to you? Nothing but a sicko, a slave. You think I didn't know what you thought? I knew. And I know you thought I was so desperate I'd take any level of friendship, and I did and I hated myself for it. And by now you're wondering when I'm going to get to the point.

He was right, I was.

Even now, it's all about you, you, you. I stole the money. Why? Because Ava asked me to. The day we were put in the same office and you left to taxi Celeste around, Ava told me her plan. She sent me encrypted messages, in case you're wondering how Daddy and the Big Boys didn't find out.

It worked to her advantage, them putting us together like that. She had us in the palm of her hand. Well, me anyway. She got a lot more out of it than if she'd just carried on dating me and again, I use the word loosely. Her plan, all along, was to fund a female army who will reclaim the world. I know the army's real because my mother was a she-soldier.

Even though my mother abandoned me, she kept in touch until she was killed guinea-pigging an alternative energy-creation technology. It's got something to do with the rage rooms that you love so much, but I don't know exactly what. Ava wouldn't tell me. I wanted to help Ava because she knew about my mother, but I did it more because I loved Ava and I thought that if I did what she wanted, she'd love me again.

Because I believed that she did love me once, but you ruined it, and despite everything I did for her, she never loved me again. She said mankind is fundamentally flawed. Not womankind, mankind. She said I'd broken her trust, and she was right, I had. And for what? For you. You, who only ever used me.

She set things up so you and Daddy would take the fall while she collected every dime. You'll never trace it to her because she flowed it into a bank account in your name and then into an untraceable trust in Saint Drausnius.

But here's the stinger. Guess who hacked the PeachDiamond-Delux Program? Ava! It was the ace up her sleeve the whole time, but she waited until she stashed all the dough she wanted. I had no idea it was her, and she couldn't wait to tell me. She was so proud of herself. She was proud of how she'd ruined me, never mind you and Williamson, The Not So Great.

But you know what? I also did what I did because you were so smug and stupid and selfish. You could have made me Bax's godfather or invited me to your home but you never did. You never asked about me. It was always only about you.

So now. Go to the balcony. I'm waiting for you. But before you go, know this—your perfect life is over. Celeste is evil.

Best Fucking Wishes Forever Amen, Jazza

I pocketed the letter. I eyed the beer. Oh shit, why the fuck not? I was parched. I cracked it and downed it in one long swallow. *Thanks Jazza, good brew.* I wiped my mouth and turned towards the balcony. My flash comm buzzed, and I jumped six feet high. It was Mother.

> All under control. Lavender air is restored. Celeste took a pill and is asleep. Kids are watching cartoons. When will you be home?
> Soon.
> When is soon? I've got a meeting tonight. HAVE to leave at midnight. Be here or be square.

Be here or be square? Was I the only one losing it or was the rest of the world along for the ride?

I took a deep breath and peered around the balcony door. There, true to his word, was Jazza. Hidden from the neighbour's view, the bastard had gone classic Kurt Cobain style. A needle in his arm and a bullet to his brain. His head and face were all but pulverized. I rushed to the balcony railing and spewed the beer, retching until it hurt. Since when did Jazza do drugs? And a gun? I guess he wanted to make sure he died. He was unrecognizable, except for that huge body and lacy underwear.

I leaned on the railing, trying to figure out what to do. Sexy Sadie rubbed against my leg, and I patted her absentmindedly.

I thought about Ava. She was still alive, which was bad. She'd no doubt recover, and I'd be charged with double manslaughter. Plus Adwar was dead. Plus the evidence showed that I had stolen hundreds of thousands of dollars of company money from the PeachDiamondDelux Program, and who'd believe me when I claimed that Jazza had given the money to Ava? Plus Celeste was well and truly off the wagon and Mummy and Daddy were safely in Real Life Florida and I'd bet my bottom dollar, not that I had one left, that Daddy would be protected by his boys. Plus Nanny Flo was gone. And here I was, standing over Jazza's cold body. I should have called the SSOs as soon as he messaged me, instead of acting like the selfish, sociopathic, psychopathic moron that I was. Oh, and I'd forgotten the big fat cherry on the sundae of my rotten life: I'd struck my wife in front of my son. Then there were the maxed-out credit cards although, given the rest of my life, who cared? I'd been counting on a big bonus when the program reached fruition, but instead I was facing bankruptcy.

I went back into the apartment and looked at the horror of Jazza's life. But was mine really any different? It was true that my surfaces were BleachBuddied and sanitized whereas his were shit-smeared and foul, but we were both losers. We'd had a lucky run, but our time was up. There was no rescue in sight. I'd have no choice but to turn myself in and face the music. But then something caught my eye. The spare bullets on the coffee table.

I knew what I had to do. I grabbed the gun from the balcony floor. I was hardly a gun afficionado, but I recognized a silencer. Jazza had planned this carefully. I tried not to look at him but couldn't help myself. The blood and bone made me want to throw up again. I had imagined blood would be brighter and thicker, like spilled ketchup, but it was dark and watery, which somehow made Jazza seem sad and vulnerable. His body was twisted to one side, and his Dalmatian-spotted towelling gown opened to reveal a sexy satin peach cami with feather edging and spaghetti straps cutting into his flesh.

"Jazza," I said softly. "What a couple of losers, you and me. This wasn't your fault. None of it was. I'm sorry I was rude about you. I never said it, but you were right, I thought it. I thought I was better than you. I should have been a better friend."

I went back inside to look for the printer, but there were too many animals and I had to get out of there as soon as I could. I found a pad of paper instead and wrote a note of my own.

Then I pocketed the gun and scratched Sadie's head and she purred. "See you never, you hairless Sphynx cat freak," I said, and I slipped out, locking the door and praying that no one would see me on the way down.

I studied my reflection in the scabby elevator mirror. Who was that wretched soul? A man in a bind left with few choices.

I had to go home, but I wanted to wait until Mother was

gone. I was counting on her to leave before midnight to go to her meeting. I flashed her to say that if I missed her, I'd be there minutes after she left. I just couldn't face seeing her, and I think she understood because she flashed me back an okay—short, sweet, and to the point.

I had a few hours to kill so I headed for a rage room, not my usual one but a sanctuary none the less. Oddly enough, I didn't smash anything. I just lay on the floor and let the time pass.

I knew Mother would have restored perfection. The kids would be bathed and fed and asleep, with every toy tidied away and every surface polished and shining. The Christmas tree lights would be twinkling and the carpet would be spotless, with track lines where the vacuum had cleared a path. There was so much beauty in the symmetry of vacuum patterns. There might even be carols playing, although no, Mother didn't like noise. The anticipation of that beautiful quiet, the heavenly serenity of the cushions arranged just so, and the untrampled virgin carpet pile made my heart swell.

I carried that image with me as I drove home and when I arrived, it was just as I had imagined. I checked on my family, and then I carried my sleeping boy downstairs to sit with me in the quiet of midnight.

Everything was in place, gleaming in the soft lights of the Christmas tree.

I looked around. If things could be like this all the time, life wouldn't be so bad. Why couldn't it be like this all the time? Because real life didn't work that way. I'd tried and I'd failed. But I knew a way to capture this perfect moment forever. Celeste need never know the truth. And Daddy would never know because I'd pointed the finger at Jazza. Overwhelmed with guilt at his thievery and by how he'd betrayed such a good and loyal friend, Jazza had committed the most unspeakable of crimes. And if Ava lived, I'd find a way to visit her in the hospital and finish the job, tie up the loose ends.

While I, devastated by the loss of my family, did the only thing I could: I ran from the horror of it all. Ran away. Who wouldn't? Who would stay in that situation? No one.

In the stillness of my perfect house, I felt as if I'd been waiting for this moment my entire life. I even felt a kind of joy, an exultation. Everything was going to be fine. Things were going to be neat and perfect forever.

I lay Bax on the sofa and went upstairs. Celeste was snoring heavily, lying on her back. How she disgusted me. No more ice cream cones, ever. I leaned over her and caught a wave of her alcoholic stench. I took careful aim at the middle of her forehead and shot her neatly.

Then I went to Sophie's room. She sensed me and opened her eyes, mewling softly. I stroked her head.

"I love you," I said, "but this is for the best. Say nighty-night to Daddy now."

I covered her little face with a sunflower cushion and aimed the gun. Once it was over, I arranged the coverlette perfectly and folded her little hands on her chest.

I went back down to the living room and before I could stop to reconsider, I held the gun to my precious boy's head and I did what I had to do.

"Daddy loves you more than anything in the whole world," I whispered, tucking his favouite bunny into his armpit and pulling his special blankie over his head.

And I finally felt peace.

17. LEAVING DODGE

QUIET FILLED THE HOUSE. The vulture in my chest released its talons and flew away, and I could breathe. I went upstairs and packed as much as I could. I took anything of value, which turned out to be less than I'd thought although Celeste's jewellery filled a small tote bag and would see me fed for while. I shoved energy bars, bottled water, and NutriSmoothies into a bag and quickly loaded the car, hoping that nosy bastard, Strawberry Merv, hadn't seen me.

It felt surreal, leaving the home of my dreams and knowing I'd never be able to return, but it also felt resolved. Sophie and Bax were sleeping peacefully, the house was shiny and clean, and the thought of never having to see Celeste again made me grin from ear to ear.

I figured it was a good idea to ditch the car. There were no individually registered licence plates; cars were issued serial numbers by Mobile Production in the same way as toasters or microwaves, and fobs were issued for each vehicle. Because all personal data was loaded onto the dashboards via the CPs, theft was practically non-existent and registering ownership with The Vehicular Bureau was a protocol ignored by most. I just needed a fob and, with it, a new ride.

I parked outside a dive bar to stake out the perfect victim. Two hours later, a bunch of giddy middle-aged women pulled up in three different vehicles. They parked alongside one another and began to shout about all the fun they were going to have. I followed them inside, and it didn't take long for them to get more than a little tipsy and tottle off to the washroom together and one woman left her purse on the table. I immediately swiped it and left the bar.

Mission successful. I transferred my bags and logged onto the woman's car as an anonymous guest, thanking my lucky stars that her security was so lax. I'd scored well—the bubble was a deluxe model. I trashed everything I could on the dashboard hard drive apart from the driveable essentials, and I blocked the woman's home control and tracking app.

Next up, I needed to change my appearance. I picked up a pair of lightly tinted sunglasses, a baseball cap, and supplies from an all-night convenience store, then I stopped to shave my head in a cheap by-the-hour motel. Next on the list was cashing in on Celeste's jewellery, so I ventured to the outskirts of Blowflyland where pawnbrokers worked all hours and asked no questions. Who knew I was so resourceful? Take note, Mother, I had everything under control.

And thus began my life as a fugitive, living in my stolen car and thinking I'd let the dust settle before I took a stab at what came next.

It took a long time for the SSOs to piece the whole thing together. At first their pieces were like the mismatched leftovers of a SparkleExchange puzzle: some seemed to fit, others didn't at all. I followed their progress on my CP avidly as though I was watching a series on Jazza's favourite serial killer channel, EchoSerialFree. Crime had been another of Jazza's and my fascinations, and we had the complete range of Safety Services apps as well as a bunch of dark channel streams.

Jazza and his apartment caused more furor than the murder of my family. That such a den of filth and illegality could exist within such an innocuous building had the whole city in an uproar. An extermination task force was set up to find Jazza's furbaby dealer, and Anti-Nature Guards were given carte blanche to enter anyone's home at any time to check for illegal cargo. Jazza's animals were ruthlessly deleted. That wasn't on me. Jazza had killed himself and left them to the mercy of the world. Then there was my dead family and me, gone. And of course, Adwar and Ava and the money. So much disaster, a clusterfuck the authorities had to untangle and solve.

Then Ava died, thank god. And, thanks to Jazza's revised suicide note explaining how I had been set up from one end to the other, the SSOs did a forensic investigation of the accounts and they saw that the funds had been transferred into Jazza's bank account before making their way into an account under my name, which Jazza had set up and operated. Although Ava, had she lived, would no doubt still have insisted I'd known about it and was complicit, I could counter that authorizing money transfers was an act of trust and stupidity, not thievery. After all, I didn't end up with any of the money, did I?

But the money was the least of my worries. The SSOs didn't buy into Jazza killing my family. They said the timeline didn't fit, that Jazza had died hours before Celeste and the kids. My fingerprints were all over Jazza's place, but in my defence, we were work colleagues and friends, so of course I'd visited him. And while the SSOs claimed I took Jazza's gun and killed my family, there wasn't a single shred of evidence to prove it. Daddy told the SSOs that it made sense to him that I had fled the scene. I was obviously traumatized by everything I'd been through. Daddy said I didn't have the gumption to kill a fly.

They found my car, but no one remembered seeing me at the bar and there was no trace of me after I stole the woman's station bubble.

But the SSOs insisted I had killed my family, and they said they'd prove it.

And I had no idea what on earth to do next.

BOOK II

CHASING THE PAST
TO CATCH THE PRESENT

18. ON THE RUN

SHANE'S THE NAME I'M GOING BY NOW. I learned via EchoSerialFree that you need to keep your name as close to your own as possible, so when people start saying "Hey Sh...," and you turn to answer, it makes sense. So, Shane Bailey's the new and shiny me. No more Sharps Barkley.

I keep my head shaved too. It's tougher than you'd think to successfully shave the back of your skull. I rubbed my head without thinking, and Knox winked at me.

Yep, it didn't take long for life on the run to find me back in the bar near the rage room, the same one Norman had taken me to all those years back. I had thought my life was such a mess then, but I'd had no idea. A lifetime had passed. So much had gone so horribly wrong.

"Shaving your head's new to you, right?" Knox said, and my face went white with panic. How did he know? I stammered something, and he laughed.

"Super pale, man," he said. "And you missed a spot." He pointed to the back of his head, above his ear, and I reached up. He was right.

Knox gestured for me to grab a bar stool and I hauled myself up. A widescreen blasted *The 24/7 News Shack*, an ambulance chasing streaming channel that pub crawlers loved. They were addicted to its neverending loop of trending deals and city crime updates. *Oh shit.* There was me, weeks later, still a featured headline, with a picture of my smiling former pretty boy self. I rubbed my head. Wished I'd worn a baseball cap. But what with the glasses, the shaved head, and the beard, I looked so different. It was okay. No one would recognize me. *Oh god.* There were pictures of my family. Little Bax looking pensive, Sophie smiling sweetly, and a glam shot of Celeste at her retouched, high-cheekboned best. I flinched and turned away, watching Knox chat up the bartender, Shasta. He nodded eagerly and scooted over to me. He couldn't sit still; the guy was a bouncing stringbean of static-carpet energy.

"She'll see me later," he said. "I feel like a kid about to pop my cherry! Look at her, man, wow! I tell you, I love this girl!"

I watched Shasta mixing drinks and smiling at the world. Something about her seemed familiar.

All of a sudden, I was exhausted. I didn't want to be there with Knox and the wall-sized screen and the crowd of drinkers who had boring, happy, normal lives. I wanted to be in my car where I could sleep and escape. I'd no idea life could be this relentlessly demanding.

"Gotta go," I said, jumping off the stool. Knox lost his smile.

"Ah, stay a while, buddy." He looked at the clock on the widescreen. "It's hours before she gets off. Stay and talk a while."

All he wanted was a patsy to talk at. I shook my head.

"See you tomorrow? I'll be here later tomorrow night. And if not here, then the pub up the street. Come find me."

I agreed, with no intention of ever seeing the guy again.

I drove to an underpass, parked, and then climbed into my sleeping bag. As scheduled, the late-night rain began to fall and at first, the sound was comforting on the roof of my bubble, but then it made me think of Baxter and how he was so afraid of the rain. *Make it stop, Daddy, make it stop,* he cried, burrowing into me like a soft furry animal, smelling of baby powder and his own pureness. I hugged him and told him he was safe. Daddy would keep him safe from everyone, from everything. Then Daddy turned out to be the worst monster of all.

19. ALONE

I WOKE IN MY CAR, GAGGING LIKE A CAT trying to hawk up a furball. I couldn't breathe; the back of my throat was superglued tight. I reached for a drink of water next to my bed, and instead I flung my hand hard against the window. I scrambled around for my bottle of water and chugged it down. I had been dreaming of Celeste and her kiss-shaped big bed and her trolley of toys, and how in that moment I'd felt such triumph over Ava. I'd felt like my whole life lay before me, a race to be won, with cheering crowds and cameras to catch my slo-mo joy as I crossed the finish line to claim my happy-ever-after.

The rain had stopped. I kicked off my sleeping bag and ran my fingers over my prickly scalp. I missed my hair. I missed so many things.

I buried my head in my arms and I cried. I finally cried for everything I'd done. I cried for the loss of Baxter and my dear beloved sweet Sophie. My chubby, smiling girl, always so happy, with a big smile on her face for Dada. And my boy, Bax, a worrier just like me. Born to worry and to fear everything. I cried for the man I'd hoped to be. I was nothing but a homeless loser, covered in dirt and crying for all the mistakes I'd made. I was worth less than a Blowfly. I had been right. I knew I would end up in the dirt, and now I had.

And then I knew where I could go. I could go home, to Mother's. She'd let me in. She'd help me. She had to.

20. VISITING MOTHER

I ARRIVED AT MOTHER'S HOUSE, but I couldn't face her. I parked a few blocks from the house and scooched down in the seat with the baseball cap pulled low on my head. I felt sick to my stomach. I couldn't remember the last time I ate. I'd considered going to a drive-thru and grabbing something from DinnaBoi or a VendaRipple dispenser, but the thought of food made me feel even worse.

I girded my loins and sat up in my seat. I was about to open the door and go and see good old Mother when I spotted the car. Actually, I wouldn't have spotted it, but Mother came out of the house and went over to a black sedan that just screamed SSO. She was carrying a tray of coffees! WTF? I slid right back down again. *Oh shit.* Of course the SSO would be at Mother's place. And of course Mother wouldn't be in my camp. And how could I blame her, this time? I didn't blame her. But where else was I supposed to go?

I froze. I had driven up so casually, not a care in the world. Now how was I supposed to get out of this mess?

I slid back up the seat with enough of the windshield in view that I could see Mother still talking to the officers. Of course they'd suspect I'd come back for a visit, stupid me, and there they were, waiting. Why didn't they look around and see me? *Oh shit.* That's all I could think. *Oh shit.*

I shut my eyes, distracting myself with one of my favourite memories of Bax and Sophie playing in a little splash pool in the back garden. I must have dozed off or even passed out for a moment from hunger and exhaustion, because when I woke, it was dark and the sedan was gone. I was lucky they hadn't seen me. My childhood home was in darkness except for the porch light. I checked the time on my CP. Past midnight. What to do? If Mother was carrying trays of coffee to the enemy, the chances of her having my back were slim. But I had to have a respite from my car and my life. I just needed a couple of hours to get cleaned up and catch my breath. Mother would be asleep. She took sleeping meds and was out cold from midnight to three a.m. I had just over two hours grace.

I got out of the car as quietly as I could and walked quickly down a side lane. I climbed over the neighbour's fence and cut across our backyard. I held my breath as I searched for the key. Mother had three hiding spots. She thought I only knew the one, but I knew them all, just like I knew that she went outside every night when she thought I was asleep to drink a small sherry and smoke a cigarette. I always knew Mother's secrets.

I got it on the third try. I slipped inside the kitchen and took my shoes off. I needed to get down to the breaker box. I went down to the basement, feeling my way slowly, knowing which stairs creaked. I made it around the corner and fumbled along the wall. *Oh shit*. Knocked over a can. Mother must have moved things around. I just hoped the flashlight was in its usual place.

I grabbed it, and just as I did, light flooded the room. *Oh shit*. I was standing there, a sitting duck, the flashlight in my hand and the world lit up like Strawberry Merv's Christmas display. I lunged for the fuse box and flipped the switches. Darkness fell so fast that even I lost my focus. Just as quickly, I flicked the flashlight on. I had to find Mother. What if she had flashed an #Emr?

I rushed up the basement stairs and there, at the top, staring at me and looking more like Norman Bates than any kind of mummy, was Mother in a pink towelling bathrobe, a godzilla masquerading as a fluffy toy. Her arms were folded and she was staring at me, and when I shone the light at her, her eyes were sad and confused.

"Oh, Sharps," she said. "I knew you'd come back." Her expression overwhelmed me. "I knew it. Oh, what did you do? How could you?"

I launched myself up the stairs towards her, a wild beast. I barrelled into her and pinned her down. She was smaller than I'd thought.

"Did you flash emerg?" I demanded, but she didn't reply. She just lay there, staring at me with such sadness and disgust that I couldn't bear it, so I hit her on the head with the flashlight and knocked her out cold. It's not like I had any choice. I couldn't stand being looked at like that. I got up and dug in the miscellaneous drawer and pulled out the scissors and twine.

"Thank you, Mother," I said, "for always being so meticulously tidy. I can always rely on you." I tied her up and stuffed a kitchen towel in her mouth, tying it tight with the twine.

"Let's see if you've changed your password, Mother," I said, logging into her path. "*TidyMa000*. Really Mother, *tut tut*. Still, lucky for me."

No flash comms had been made, no alarms sounded. I had no idea when the officers would come back, perhaps it had been a shift change and there was already a new crew stationed outside. I had to be careful.

A part of me just wanted to go my room, pull the covers up over my head, and go to sleep. I could do that. I could give up, give in. Get one good night's sleep and give myself up. But then I'd have to face the music, and it was a pretty terrifying tune. No. I had to carry on. I'd come this far. I had to kick things into action.

I made sure Mother was well and truly tied up, and then I showered, scrubbing and cleaning like there was no tomorrow. I shaved my head, leaving no rough patches. I looked thinner, but a few weeks of hardly eating would do that.

What was I going to do with Mother? The question roiled around in my brain, and I stared at my reflection. I went to my bedroom, pulled out some clothes, and sat on my bed for a moment. I knew the room inside out even in the dark. It was all blue: light blue comforter, dark blue walls, and navy carpet with a pale blue throw rug. Just like Bax's room. Hockey posters once lined the walls, but I'd ripped them down in a fit about something, I couldn't even remember what. I had a lamp once, but I broke that too. The only things I hadn't destroyed were my books: *The Great Gatsby, Catcher in the Rye, Catch-22,* and my Graham Greene collection.

I slipped into jeans and a hoodie. A pair of red-and-black running shoes. Clothes from before I was a married man and a dad. Why hadn't Mother given my things away and packed up my room? I knew why. Because I'd screw up and need to come back. She knew it all along. I was so confident that I'd show her and show the world, and I guess I had shown them all right, oh man, I'd shown them all.

What choice did I have? Mother had seen me. She knew I'd shaved my head, and she'd tell the world. I went downstairs to address the situation. After all, I really had no choice, but I could make it as painless as possible. It was the look of pity in her eyes that drove me to it. I had no idea I could feel this ashamed, and I had to make it go away.

21. MOTHER IS DEAD

IWAS ALL OVER *THE NEWS SHACK*. A repeat flash comm. MOTHER, KILLED BY THE "PERFECT" SON. Under the words: a picture of me and Mother on a sunny day, both of us looking cheery. I had no recollection of when the pic had been taken. When had we ever been that happy?

I wondered about that comma. MOTHER KILLED BY "PERFECT" SON VERSUS MOTHER, KILLED BY "PERFECT" SON. It fried my brain trying to figure out the difference.

After I left Mother's place, I drove to the rage room. I had to let it out, smash things. Norman booked me for a double session and I went wild in there, leaving nothing but smithereens of plastic dust. Norman didn't comment. He just played my soundtracks and let me have at it.

Finally, spent, I looked down at the floor. Unbelievable. There was one bright red spot. I examined myself, nope, I was intact. Great, just great, someone else had bled all over the floor. Disgusting. Bleeding was against the rules. Blood carried disease. How had it snuck through the disinfecting process?

I leaned down to examine the offensive splat. It was fresh blood, bright and sparkly. What the heck? Alien blood? I nudged the droplet and it moved. It was a sequin, not round as I had thought, but hexagonal with a pin-prick hole in the centre. A sequin. Someone was bleeding red sequins. This made me think of Sophie and my heart slammed shut, squeezing the air out of my lungs.

Sophie, my angel. She would have bled red sequins, not like Celeste who would have spilled thick red motor oil. I couldn't bear to think about Bax, and I was overwhelmed by pain and remorse. All I could see were their baby faces shining with love for me. Their pure innocence. How I missed those chubby little hands, those feet; their fat little tummies and the way they smelled. Skin so soft and those tiny bones, so achingly fragile. Tiny, perfect little humans. I had been right to fear myself when Bax was born. I'd known then about my potential for terrible destruction. But how could I have gone through with it? And now, how could I live with it? I missed them so much my very cells felt lanced with burning pain. I was an inescapable poison to myself. How could I go on?

So when I pulled off my goggles and stripped off the suit, and Norman asked me if I wanted a drink, I said sure, why not?

So there we were again, me, Norman, Knox, and the bartender, Shasta. It was mid-afternoon and we were all getting wasted.

"Man, you know you look like shit," Knox said cheerfully.

I shrugged. "Can't sleep. My brain's shot. The other day I couldn't even remember where I parked my car."

Knox nodded sagely. "There's a memory app for that," he said eagerly. Knox was a know-it-all who always had a better story, and I wasn't in the mood to hear it. I finished my beer and ordered a scotch. I needed to drown my sorrows. Wasn't that what tough guys did? Didn't they drown their sorrows by throwing back hard liquor and wincing at the taste?

The News Shack was still running me. The headline had changed to MOTHER KILLER ON THE LOOSE. A mother who killed? These guys needed a grammar app. There was a recent pic of Mother looking like a vintage grandma hippie. And good old Celeste with an avalanche of creamy breasts, a milky crevasse into which I could bury my head, softness fragrant with vanilla and coconut and a hint of bitter orange. I'd grown to like Celeste's expansive breasts. We'd had a few good years, her and me, after Sophie was born, and Celeste stayed sober, and the PeachDiamondDelux Program was flying high. And look, there were my kids. My blameless little kids.

I ran to the washroom and puked up my scotch and beer.

"Yeah, man." Knox had followed me. "That son of a bitch screwed up big time. And now he killed his mother. Wrote a message on her back. *Sorry, Mother. I guess I wasn't the perfect son. Sorry I disappointed you. Guess what? You disappointed me too.* What a sicko. Neat handwriting. They've been showing it nonstop. How they haven't caught him, I've got no idea. Pretty boy like that. Probably in St. Isidore now or St. Malos. They're welcome to him. So hey, Shane, there's a guy I know who can help you with the memory thing."

I got up from kneeling over the putrid toilet bowl and washed my face. How could Knox not recognize me? And yet, I could hardly recognize myself. I walked back to the bar with Knox following me.

"Norman was telling me," Knox rambled on, "about this guy who's like this cyborg—biohackers they call themselves. They go way beyond Minnie's shit. This is all black market stuff. Tell him, Norm, tell him!"

Norman shrugged. "Yeah, I heard of a few things." But he didn't elaborate.

"There's other things people do." Shasta joined the conversation, and Knox looked all perky. He shuffled closer to her, grinning. "Porn contact lenses where people get together and they put contact lenses in, and it changes what they see, collectively. Like you're on a beach and everyone around you is screwing like rabbits, and the lighting is out of this world and you feel like you're really there. But those were contact lenses, not chip implants." She shuddered. "Porn sucks large. I had a really sick experience with one woman. It was so fucking twisted, I can't even talk about it." She looked haunted.

"I'm sorry." Knox pulled her in for a hug and she let him, staying close, and Knox looked like he'd been visited by the rapture.

"The biohackers want to become more machine than human," Norman said. Shasta pulled away from Knox to listen. "They want robot limbs and to be able to overcome biological limitations. It started out with people just wanting toys, like the guy who had a magnet implanted in his hand just for the thrill of it—a cheap thrill if you ask me—or the guy who implanted glowing lights in his forehead. That was kind of stupid, but the merging of man and machine makes sense in a way. It would make us stronger, fitter, faster."

"None of that shit appeals to me," Knox said, first sensible thing I'd heard the guy say. "Now time travel, yeah, baby, that'd be cool. I'd go back in time, win the Universal Bingo Draw, and take Shasta here to buy the best ShyRichRollyPolly shit she wants, and smoke the best weed in the world!"

Shasta grinned. "Yeah, baby," she said. "But if you had that much money, I'd do coke twenty-four-seven, not pot."

"Too much coke will fry your brain," Knox argued. "I love it too, but it's a slippery slope. Miss MaryJane's medicinal, keeps you level and happy. Let me doctor you, baby, I'll keep you high in all the right ways."

"I don't think you can go back in time to win money in the future," Norman said, sounding reflective. "You can take a future action back into the past, but you can only go back into the past and change the future."

"You're wrong." Knox was certain. "Winning ticket numbers don't change. It would work, for sure. There was that guy in 2003 who said he came from 2256. Andrew Carlssin. He made it big on the stock exchange, and he did it by time travel. Turned eight hundred dollars into three hundred and fifty million!"

Norman laughed. "Don't tell me, vintage YouTube. *Ha ha!* The crap you can find on there! I saw that one too."

"He was arrested by the FBI," Knox argued. "But then he disappeared. I'm telling you, he made money by time travel."

"He was a gambler on the stock exchange, and he was

killed by the mob he ripped off. No mystery there." Norman corrected him.

"I'd go back in time and get revenge for what happened to me," Shasta said, and we turned to her and I inwardly sighed. She was, no doubt, back to her bad porn memory, but I wasn't interested. I had real things to deal with. I'd go back and fix them, and Mother was only one of them. I'd definitely undo what I did to Celeste and the kids, and since Mother came after that, it would naturally follow that she'd live, too.

And then it hit me like a tidal wave. They were never coming back. I'd lost them forever. I'd killed them. I got dumped so hard that my lungs filled up and I couldn't breathe, and when I surfaced, it was like a heavyweight champion of the world had come back from the dead, walked into the bar, and punched me in the gut. That's how hard it hit me, the knowledge that I would do anything, absolutely anything, to be able to undo what I had done.

The only thing I wanted in the entire universe was my old life back. I wanted to turn into my driveway and see the lights on at home, the Christmas lights twinkling, and even if Strawberry Merv, the asshole neighbour, had won the War of the Lights that year, I wouldn't care. In fact, I'd give anything to have my ass handed to me by Strawberry Merv.

I'd go over, a bottle of tequila in hand, because I just knew Strawberry Merv was a tequila kind of guy, and I'd confide in him and tell him how I'd maxed out my credit cards on Christmas lights and gifts I couldn't afford. I'd spill my guts about how worried I was that I wasn't going to make it through the next year. I'd tell him how work was going to hell in a handbasket with sales sliding daily. I wouldn't tell him that Celeste was a full-fledged drunk, only close to sober on Sundays for an hour when we took the family to Church.

I'd tell Strawberry Merv congrats on a great year of lights and hey, that maybe the next year, I'd come close. We'd get a bit drunk on the tequila, and then I'd stumble back to my house, my belly filled with the warmth and camaraderie of men sharing men's problems.

And I'd look at the warm glow coming from the living room window, and know that Bax and Sophie were playing with their toys while Celeste warbled on about the Baby Jesus or streamed channels of Christmas carols, three sheets to the wind. Yes, I would do anything to get back that moment, to be able to open the door and hear the carols playing, see the Nativity scene near the fireplace, and the tree in all its magnificent glory.

Because that was the moment of sheer and utter perfection, and for that moment, warmed by tequila and good conversation and how proud I'd be to have eaten humble pie so graciously with Strawberry Merv, my life would be everything I wanted, flaws and all.

"I'd like to have an app that goes forward and back," I heard Knox say. He turned to Shasta. "I'd spend my whole time fast forwarding and rewinding, only to be with you."

I heard her giggle, and I felt myself wrenched back into the present, the harsh and lonely present where I had nothing but bludgeoning memories that I couldn't escape.

I ordered another round.

22. FINDING THE PAST, PRESENT, FUTURE

"HEY FELLA, YOU PASSED OUT," I heard a voice say. I tried to sit up. "Buddy, your friend here passed out."

I opened my eyes to see Knox standing over me. I was on the washroom floor of another bar, one with an animal name—what was it? It seemed crucial that I remember. Right, The Barking Frog. We were in The Barking Frog. We left The Bar None and came here. I turned my head to the side and threw up, and Knox and the guy jumped out of the way.

"You don't look good, fella," the guy said and I struggled to sit up.

"Sorry," I said weakly to Knox, and he helped me to my feet.

"We'll get you a coffee," Knox said. "Come on, Shane. It'll be okay."

He led me back to the bar, and I sat down. Man Bun was there. What was his name again? Norman. Right, Norman. Had he been there all along? How had we got here? I tried to focus, and Shasta put a coffee in front of me. Did she work here too? Nothing made any sense. I sipped the coffee, and my vision started to clear slightly. I held my hands out in front of me. I was trembling like an old guy, and it was unnerving to see.

"So listen," Norman said. "You guys. This is going to fry your brains, but I do know a guy who sells time travel."

That got my attention. I focused and swung around to him. "For real? What do you mean?" Why was he telling me now?

He'd seemed so circumspect. What if it was true? What if I could go back?

Shasta and Knox leaned forward too.

Norman looked around. "He says he can. He could be lying."

"Tell me what you know," I said. I grabbed his shoulder and shook him.

"Easy, Shane," Knox said. "Maybe we should go for a smoke before we get into this."

"No," I said through gritted teeth. "You don't understand. I need to know now."

"He lives about two hours from here," Norman said. "St. Adrian's. There are some underground tunnels there, and once a year they have a secret biohacker convention."

"A secret and yet you know?" Shasta was skeptical. "And here you are, telling us."

"Shane needs to know," Norman said. "I haven't told anyone else."

"How super-intuitive of you." Shasta was sarcastic.

"Will you let the guy talk?" I was getting desperate.

Norman shrugged. "Not much more to tell you. But we could go there if you like."

I jumped up. "When?"

"Now, if you like."

I was surprised. "What about work?"

"It's Friday night! We've got the whole weekend!"

I had completely lost track of time.

"I want to come too," Shasta said, and Knox stood up, grinning.

"Me too," he said. "Road trip."

I was wary. "Why do you all want to come? Norman, how many devices or whatever does this guy have to sell?"

"No idea. I don't even know how it works."

"And you're sure this guy's even still around?"

"Yeah, man. I just flashed him to check." Norman pointed at his portable comm. "He said he'll be there."

"How much?" I asked, and Norman raised an eyebrow.

"Twenty thou cash. You good for that?"

I was. The jewellery I'd grabbed before leaving had gotten me plenty of cash. I nodded, and Knox looked delighted.

"Next round's on you, buddy," he said and waved the bartender over. Shasta grinned. "I'll have a Manhattan!" she yelled.

"I thought we were going now?" Norman asked.

"We are going now," I said, no argument allowed.

"Aren't you being like just a bit too trusting?" Shasta asked me. "I mean, time travel, for real?

"I've got nothing left to lose," I said. "Let's make like Donald and duck." It was a stupid line and one I'd wanted to use all my life. I grinned. I felt happier. Still hungover, still drunk, but happier.

"Hey," I said. "I'm over the limit. The car will prohibit me from driving. Oh shit. Norman, you're sober as a church mouse—you drive."

Knox threw back the rest of his drink and Shasta grabbed her purse.

We piled into my station bubble that was a bit rank from me having slept in it for weeks. No one commented on the smell or the mess of fast food containers, although Knox dug out a plastic bag from somewhere and started cleaning up the debris around his and Shasta's feet. Knox was in seventh heaven. A road trip with Shasta would give him all the time in the world to convince her that he was the man of her dreams. Only Shasta grabbed my pillow from the back, leaned against a window, and fell fast asleep. I saw the look on Knox's face—he was sunk in disappointment—and he suddenly looked far older than he did when he was his fired-up animated self.

Norman settled his bulk into the driver seat and turned on the car. The nightly rain was falling, and the sound of the windscreen wipers was reassuring as they slapped back and forth.

The highway to St. Adrian's was lined with long-haul trucker trains, wall-to-wall, flying by and spraying roosters in the red brake lights. The oncoming lanes were steady with big loads pushing through the night.

I was trying to figure out what to do when I time travelled. Which would be the best point of entry where I could make it right? I needed to pinpoint the spot when it started to go so wrong. Meanwhile my brain kept worrying that the whole thing was a hoax and that there was no time machine. It will be fine, I told myself. Why would Norman lie?

"Can we you tell him we're on our way?" I whispered to Norman, not wanting to wake Shasta or Knox, who had also fallen asleep.

"Sure," Norman said, and he activated a speech comm, murmuring too low for me to understand what he was saying, even although he was sitting right next to me.

"It's on," he said.

"And he's definitely got the gadget or whatever?"

"He's got it. Goddamn this road is boring."

We didn't speak again until we stopped for snacks and a pee break and I took the wheel.

"Turn right here," Norman told me an hour later, just outside of St. Adrian's. I figured he was getting directions via his CP. The sun was rising. There was a peachy glow to the world, and the sky was baby-blue and cloudless. Distracted for a moment by the beauty and knowing how fake it was, I wondered what the real world would be like, without all of Minnie's weather control.

We turned down a side road, and the bubble bumped along the rutted lane. Shasta and Knox woke up. "I need to shake the snake again," Knox said, and Shasta laughed.

"Me too."

"You gotta a snake?" Knox joked. "I never noticed. C'mon, Norman, three minutes to let us let a load off."

I pulled over with an exaggerated sigh, and they got out. I thought of pulling off and leaving Knox and Shasta as their dilly dallying was bugging the shit out of me.

"Shane," Norman said, "you gotta ease up, man. Jaxen's there. It's all good. Lighten up buddy. This is going to take a while. We can't just ram in there, throw the money down, and start using the gadget. We also need to eat. You need to chill. They'll want to talk to you, bond a bit. You get it?"

I gave a loud groan, and Norman dug into his pocket. "Shane. Sharps." I looked at him with horror.

"Sharps?" I squeaked.

He shrugged. "Yeah, I know who you are. I'm the rage room guy, remember? I know you. I know everything. You need to take one of these."

I eyed the pill he was holding out with suspicion. "I need to have my faculties about me," I said.

"And you will. This will level you out. Heightened powers of concentration along with nerves of steel and the calm of a sleeping baby. Trust me, Sharps. You're outta control. You need this, man."

"Where are those guys?" I replied and leaned out the window. "WTF! They're having sex! Wasting time! Hey, you guys, WTF!"

Norman pulled me back into the car and grabbed me by the throat. I thought he was going to strangle me, and my eyes bulged in fear, but he stuck his thumb in my mouth with one hand while he shoved the pill down with the other.

I choked and swallowed. "Fuck's sake! Are you for real? Did you just feed me a pill like I was a puppy? Goddammit Norman, you don't have the right to do that!" I tried to retch, but nothing happened.

"For your own good," Norman said calmly, and he was right because almost instantaneously I felt a strangely removed sense of calm, along with an equally strong sense of power. I was the man. I had this. I was the king of the world. Norman watched me and laughed.

What's the hurry, man?" Knox showed up at my window. "Just trying to start Shasta's day off with a bang. Shaz, we'll pick that up later." She grinned at him, and I didn't get it. One minute she was hot for him, the next she was ice cold. She was a lot younger than he was, as far as I could tell, and he was a drifter, a drinker, and a pothead. But then again, Shasta seemed pretty aimless too, happy to float around whichever way the wind blew. I couldn't care less; I wasn't even sure why I'd let them come.

"Make a left here," Norman said, and I slowed. "Where?" I couldn't see a road.

"There's a trail. We'll get a little way in and have to walk from there."

I pushed the car through as far as I could. "This is it, Norman. I won't be able to get us out if we go much further." We were in a real life forest. I was astounded. I thought they'd all been destroyed.

I pulled the car to a stop and went around to the trunk to get my backpack. It occurred to me that I was in the middle of nowhere with three people I didn't know from Bob your uncle, about to pull out my life's savings, or Celeste's nest egg from the sold jewellery. I was all alone, so they could jump me, take the car, and kill me, or leave me to die in the woods.

I looked around, fully expecting to see them surrounding me with truculent war expressions, but Knox was chasing Shasta around a log and she was laughing like it was the funniest thing, and Norman was watching them with an indulgent grin.

No one was even looking my way, and I felt slightly hurt and unloved. "Got it," I shouted to the trio and locked the car.

"Follow me," Norman called out and we fell in line.

An hour later, we were still picking our way through the forest, tripping over tree roots and twigs. "Crappy real nature," Knox complained. "No wonder they got rid of all this shit. How did they miss this place? Whole place makes me itchy as shit." He kept slapping at his head; the mosquitoes were biting, as were the black flies.

"I thought the whole world was nature-free?" I asked Norman.

"Nope. Couple of hours out of the city in any direction and

there's all this. People just never bother to explore. They believe the lies they are fed."

"You could have mentioned there was a nature hike involved," Knox complained.

"I'm so thirsty," Shasta added.

"How much longer?" I was ungracious, and my power chill pill had definitely worn off.

Norman didn't reply. He just kept pressing on.

A shot rang through the bush, and Shasta grabbed Knox and pulled him to the ground, her eyes wide and terrified.

Norman laughed. "Keep your panties on. They're just having some fun. It's important you get a sense of these guys. They're generally not open to strangers coming in. I vouched for you. I've been with them forever, and my sister runs the place. She's been a biohacker since she was seven, trying to make her body like Wonder Woman. Drove my parents nuts. She wants to be a cyborg made of metal. She even had a leg removed so she could have a metal one. Nuts, right? Her goal is to replace her entire body, as much as she can, with steel and metal. She gets off on it. But she's clever too, studied bio-medical engineering, but she said they were too slow for her. So she started this convention. Jaxen, the guy with the time travel gadget, he made the most advances."

"Did he invent the machine?" Shasta asked, still firmly ensconced on Knox's lap. He looked like he'd died and gone to heaven.

"Nope. He was at university with my sister, and they discovered it. The military had tested it and decided it was too dangerous to use, so they destroyed the whole operation. At least they thought they'd destroyed it, but Jaxen and Janaelle, that's my sister, found a laptop with the software and core data. They stole it and disappeared. They've been living out here ever since, and it's been tough. Life didn't turn out like my sister thought it would, all shiny and electronic and amazing. She hates the way the world is run, all of us with the Crystal Paths in our heads and satellite dishes controlling the weather."

"I would have thought she'd love that," Shasta commented. "Have the whole world be electronic."

"She did too. But she says they've leached the life out of the planet. Instead of humans becoming faster, stronger, more clever and doing amazing things, the world got lazy and sick and lay around finding ways to shop while eating junk. She was depressed for a long time. I was worried she would kill herself."

"Heavy shit, man," Knox commented. I noticed he hadn't moved a muscle. He was obviously thinking the longer he stayed exactly as he was, the longer Shasta would remain in his lap. His legs had to be killing him, and maybe Shasta realized that because she climbed off him. Although he looked sad, he also looked relieved, and he thrust his legs out in front of him and rubbed them.

"Yeah, heavy shit. But my sister's got a plan."

"Do you know what it is?" Shasta asked.

"I do. But I won't say. It's a biggie. You'll see one day."

"Why me?" I asked. "Why are you letting me into this club? Is it so easy to time travel that you hand it out like candy?"

Norman doubled over laughing. "Uh, no, buddy, it's not easy at all. Not many people can do it. You might not be able to do it either. They'll need to check you out, run tests, and see if you're a viable candidate."

I lunged for him and tackled him to the ground. "You never said that! I wouldn't be here if you'd said that. You said I could do it!"

I raised my fist to punch him, but Knox pulled me away. For a stringbean, Knox could handle himself. I glared at Norman, my chest heaving.

"Because I knew you wouldn't come if I only said it was possible. And I never met a guy who needs it more than you do, Shane," Norman said, and I noticed he didn't use my real name in front of the others. "And Janaelle agreed when I pitched you."

"Why didn't she and Jaxen use the time travel to fix the world?" Shasta asked. "They could have done anything they wanted."

"Time travel, as our friend here will see, and as the military saw, isn't the magic pill everybody thinks it is. Time travel is a moody bitch, full of paradoxes and quantum conflicts. We're nearly there. Remember, this is a privileged world—you guys are lucky you're being allowed in."

Norman got up off the ground, and we followed him. I had no idea what to expect, and even Knox and Shasta had fallen silent. We marched along behind Norman, with Knox still swatting his head. My brain was spinning with what Norman had told us.

23. GOING UNDERGROUND

"WE'RE HERE," NORMAN FINALLY SAID, and we slumped down on the ground in relief.

"My feet are killing me," Shasta said, and she pulled off her shoes. Her feet were a mashed-up pulp of blood and ooze.

"Why didn't you say?" Knox looked ready to cry. "I would have carried you. Norman, this is ridiculous."

But Norman wasn't listening. He was inserting a huge old-fashioned key into a massive oak tree, and we watched, open-mouthed, as he swung the tree half open, revealing a small elevator.

"Can we all fit?" Knox asked. "I get claustrophobia. Can I go down first or after you guys? We can't fit."

This was a first, something Knox and I had in common. I hated the thought too.

"We all have to go together," Norman said, and Shasta looked doubtful. She peered into the carved-out tree. "It's not real," she said, stroking the tree.

"Of course it's not real," Norman said. "Listen, we can't leave the door open much longer—a security breach will sound. Get in or don't."

I leapt in and Shasta followed. Knox took a deep breath and jumped in, holding onto Shasta and burying his face in her neck. Norman was last, and we made for a tight squeeze as he pulled the door closed and pushed a button. The elevator was lit with soft blue light, and cool air rushed down, as did a familiar chemical fragrance. I sniffed the air in appreciation, focusing on the fact that we were moving. As long as we were moving, we were okay; I could do this.

"Permethrin," Norman said. "Bug spray. It was a regular feature on airlines back in the last century. It was approved by the World Health Organization, but people objected and they eventually stopped using it. But Janaelle likes us to be cootie-free, although, as you will see, the process has only just begun."

"How much longer?" Knox asked. He was beginning to hyperventilate. Shasta pulled him close and whispered to him, but his body language stayed taut and he was shaking. He was sweating like a pig, and despite the bug spray, his stench filled the small space. Four bodies in need of a shower and a few bars of lye soap.

The door opened, and we spilled out like wound-up sardines sprung from a can. We sprawled on the floor, gasping for breath. I sat up first, rubbing my eyes, and the others followed suit.

We were greeted by a robot who regarded us impassively. "Follow me," it barked electronically, and we got to our feet. Shasta grabbed Knox's hand and hung on tight. The robot looked like a titanium Terry's Chocolate Orange, its petals neatly folded inwards with triangular panels forming a base. It looked like a moving flower or a petalled sea crab with two bright blue stalk-eyes sticking off his ball head, eyes that seemed strangely expressive. I swear the thing even blinked.

"It's a Roundabout, modelled on a MorphHex, first made by Kare Halvorsen," Norman said. "Cute though, isn't it?"

Shasta nodded, her eyes wide. "You're crushing my hand," Knox said, and she loosened her grip but pressed closer to him.

"I didn't imagine it would be this futuristic," she whispered. "Or this underground. Are you okay?"

Knox nodded, although he didn't look convinced. "Trying not to think about it," he said.

The Roundabout led us into a room, and without warning, a door slammed shut, locking us in. Knox slammed his hand against the door and quickly discovered it was steel. I could see Knox was about to lose it; he was nanoseconds away from screaming and pounding the door when giant sunflower-shaped shower heads dropped from the ceiling and the room filled with steam and hot spray.

"Cleansing cycle initiated!" the Roundabout announced, volume high. "Remove outer garments now! Remove outer garments now!"

"Take your clothes off," Norman yelled. "And close your eyes. This won't hurt! Stand still!"

"I'm not getting undressed," Shasta shouted, and she screamed as the Roundabout raised itself up to six feet tall on spindly legs, extended spider arms, and ripped her clothes off. Its eyes didn't look that friendly anymore.

I kept wiping my eyes and trying to sneak glances at what was happening. We were covered with pale green shaving cream that smelled like cedar and pine with a touch of Old Spice, still a bestselling male fragrance. I figured out why the scent was familiar—it was like the after-rinse detergent at the rage rooms. Where were we? I was sure that was no coincidence. Was this a government-sponsored initiative? But Norman had said these were biohackers, geeks.

"Rub your bodies," the Roundabout announced, disturbing my thoughts. "Rub your bodies." We did as it said, motivated I guess, by fear that if we didn't, it would.

"Cleaning cycle complete, rinse cycle initiated. Rub bodies to remove excess residue from cleansing cycle." Caught under the steaming waterfall force of the rinse cycle, I welcomed the opportunity to rinse every pore.

The water stopped abruptly, and panels extended from the wall offering stacks of thick white towels, neatly-folded track pants, a hoodie, a T-shirt, white slippers, and an additional small metal tray with toiletries.

Shasta pulled on the clothes while she was still wet.

"Where did our old clothes go?" Knox asked. "I was kinda fond of those jeans, man. It's really hard to get good jeans these days. And that hoodie, I got it on the set of an ad with a Justin Bieber cover version, and the guy even signed it. It's worn off, but still. And my shoes man, NikesNewCentury. I can't afford to replace them. And this shit," he tugged at his white garb, "makes me look like a mental patient."

"You'll get them back," Norman said. "Shasta, you'll get replicas. You guys need to relax. This is a safe place. Janaelle's just got a thing for cleanliness."

"Where did the water go?" I asked, and Norman pointed to the edges of the room. "Drains. So cool, right? Shall we move on?"

The door had opened without us noticing, and the Roundabout, reduced to its former ball size, rolled along like a ball-bearing.

We passed an enormous warehouse lab with floor-to-ceiling windows and technicians in white suits studying computers. I stopped and stared. "Norman," I said evenly, clenching my fists at my side and barely stopping myself from pounding the shit out of him, "you've got some explaining to do."

I was looking at a massive ball suspended in the centre of the room. The ball was at least the size of four station bubble cars, and it rotated slowly. The surface was a matrix of edge-to-edge angled screens, like a dragonfly's eyes. The whole thing looked like a peeled pomegranate, enough to make a trypophobe run screaming, but that wasn't why I was glaring at Norman. It was the content on the screens. Each screen showed a rage room, with a man or woman, hitting or screaming or smashing things. Hundreds of rage rooms.

I stared at Norman, and he studied his fingernails and gnawed at the edge of this thumb. "That's The Eye. Janaelle will explain everything," he said, walking away. I had no choice but to follow him.

We heard a strange noise, a gurgling sound, and we all looked around, including Norman. "My stomach," Knox apologized. "I'm hungry."

"We're here," Norman said.

The Roundabout stopped at a glass door and extended a bony steel finger. The door opened.

"You said you were hungry?" Norman asked Knox, and he gestured to a long mahogany dining room table with full crystal place settings, complete with place cards and starched napkins shaped like swans.

"Janaelle loves swans," Norman said. He found his name card and sat down. "Let's eat."

"You've forgotten something, little brother," a voice rang out into the room, a deep, husky, lounge-room voice. "Naughty boy. What did you forget?"

"To say grace," Norman looked shamefaced. He held out his hands. "Come on, hold hands, and don't argue."

We all grabbed each other's hands.

"Dear Humankind, we have thus far failed you. We have failed you with our greed, our selfish preoccupations, our lust, and our laziness. There is only one Creator and Her Name is Truth, and we shall set Her free. Namaste."

"Namaste," we muttered, not wanting to look at each other.

I unfolded my napkin. "Is there a menu?" I asked, half-joking, and Norman shook his head. "Grilled cheese and tomato soup," he said. "Take it or leave it."

"I'll take it," Knox said, and he looked around expectantly. "More robots coming?"

But instead, a tiny woman walked in, wearing a long skirt and wheeling a food trolley.

"No," she said, and her voice was the deep chocolatey lounge-room tone we'd heard over the loud speakers, at odds with her tiny, birdlike body.

I peered around to look at her steel leg, but her skirt covered everything. She caught my stare, and I blushed. She was around thirty, and her hair was thick and black, almost blue, lustrous, falling to her waist. She looked familiar to me, and I stared at her. I knew I had met her before. But where?

"So, Shane," she said, cutting to the chase. I shook myself back into the moment, thinking I'd figure it out later. I knew her. I just had to figure out where we'd met. "Norm here says you need to travel through time. What makes you so special?"

"You tell me," I fired back. "I saw you guys, with the rage room footage. I'm not here by coincidence. You guys picked me. Not the other way around. What's the deal?"

She passed around plates of sandwiches, and Knox and the others fell on them. I tried to hold back, like a man of principle, but my hunger got the better of me and I grabbed my sandwich. Janaelle ladled out bowls of soup and took her place at the head of the table.

"You're right," she said, not eating but watching us. "Norman said you're the guy. And the lab technicians agree. They say if anyone can go back and change the past and therefore the future, that you're the guy to do it. I've got my doubts, but I guess we'll see."

"Do you guys own the rage rooms?" I asked, and she shook her head.

"No. But we hacked into them to study the world. We're trying to find a reason to have faith in mankind. You've got to have faith in something. Don't you agree, Shane?"

I stared at her, cheese stuck to my chin. I wiped it off. "I don't know. I'd like to think so, but I don't know. You've seen the evidence of my life. I can't tell a lie."

"Lying is pointless, you're right. You did respond well when Norman told you there was a chance you could save your family. You insisted on taking immediate action. That was a good sign, although I can't say I'm completely sold on you."

I jumped up and threw my bowl of soup against the wall. The bowl didn't smash, but the red soup ran down the pristine wall like blood and dripped to the floor.

"When in doubt, smash something," Janaelle observed. "Not exactly an award-winning move. And that was just a small test. You fail so easily, Shane. You don't seem to be a man of strong mettle to me. A man who comes looking to time travel should be of strong mettle. You realize this, don't you? You're a weak man, a man looking for the easy way out, the simplest solution. Time travel isn't that. If we do bring you in, you'll need to get your emotions under control. And you'll need to learn some science. Can you do that?"

I was trying to think of a convincing way to tell her that I could when Knox interrupted me.

"What about us?" he asked. "I'm just here because of Shasta. I don't like being underground."

"Is it worrying you now?" Janaelle asked, and Knox closed his eyes.

"No," he said, surprised, "it isn't."

"We gave you a bit of help," Janaelle said smugly. "We patched you up. When you were in the shower, the Roundabout pinned you with a tranquilizing microfiber patch to help lessen your claustrophobia. It immediately entered your blood stream. Pretty good, huh?"

Shasta jumped up, angrier than I had thought possible. "Bitch! You drugged me? I want outta here. Fuck you, bitch. Let me go, now!"

"You can check out any time you like," Janaelle sang, "and you can always leave. Bye bye, birdies. Your clothes have been restored, and Norman will escort you off the premises."

"Shut the fuck up and let me out," Shasta yelled. "Now!"

"No, don't go!" I shouted. "They could kidnap me or hold me hostage or kill me."

Janaelle nearly fell off her chair laughing. "Yeah, right. Listen, we were going to let your friends go anyway. They're not part of this. And Shasta, honey, all we did was patch you and your boyfriend with a forget-this-ever-happened drug so you won't remember a thing. Nada. I hope you had a good dinner. Good soup, huh? Old family recipe, although I add sherry. It's the sherry that makes it so delicious."

"Knox!" I shouted, and he wouldn't look at me. "You can't leave me!"

"Sorry, buddy," he said. "Gotta go. Good luck. Come on, Shaz."

They left without a backward glance, and I was left alone with Janaelle.

24. DESCENT INTO HELL

JANAELLE WAS BEAUTIFUL IN A FELINE kind of way, and her incisor teeth were capped with silver. She was wearing steel-rimmed glasses, and I wondered what technology they housed. She was probably reading my mind right at that very moment, scanning my brain and somehow implanting controlling micro-fibers. Maybe the soup had been bolstered with micro-fibres, extra roughage. *Hey look, you can lose your mind, but don't worry, you'll have a great bowel moment, ain't life grand?*

"I'm going to give you what you want," Janaelle said. "I don't have the faith in you that Norman has, but then again, he knows you much better than I do. To my mind, the data's ambivalent about you, but if Norman says you're it, then you're it."

"I'm what?" I barked at her because Mother had used that exact word too about me. Ambivalent.

"Never mind. Because you either are or you aren't ready. But what you have had is a long day, and you need to rest. We're going to give you a crash course in relativity, both special and general, quantum mechanics, and wormholes."

"Isn't there an app for that?" I wasn't joking. "Why can't you just download the info on my CP?"

"Unfortunately, we cannot. While we can manufacture apps for all kinds of things, you'll need to do some old-fashioned homework. Norman told you that we're pioneers of biohacking? I'm sure Norman told you about my steel leg?"

"He did."

"I now have two. Much better. Have you ever looked at feet? Disgusting things. Toes. My god. The worst. And knees? The god who invented knees—what was It thinking? I'm far happier without my knees and my feet. I'm much speedier too."

Next thing I knew she was standing right by my side. "You travel at the speed of light?" I joked, but my heart was hammering. How had she done that?

"Joke all you like, Sharps, if it eases your discomfort."

"But seriously, with those long skirts too, how did you do that?"

She grinned a vampire smile, and there was something attractive about her in a gothic, terrifying sort of way.

"Do you have faith, Sharps?" she asked. "Stupid question. You can't or you wouldn't have done what you did. The world's going to change; that's all I'm going to say. Try to remember that at some core level, although you will only remember some parts of this and not others."

"Patchy microfibres?" I joked.

"No. Human interpretation and subjective memory of any given event. That's primarily what we study with the rage room profiles. Every human being has a number of experiences in any given day, but how they interpret them, internalize them, react to them, and remember them is entirely unique, unpredictable, and unmappable. You'd think we'd be able to map memory and plot predictable behaviours, and sure, serial killers killed animals when they were kids, but which memory will stick in your brain as being a good one versus which one would annoy the heck out of the guy next to you, we cannot say. Science is exact, but humans are the exact opposite."

"I try to remember the good stuff, but there wasn't much," I said, feeling sorry for myself. "My father was a drunk and he left. I was a loner at school with no special talents and no interests in life. Nothing. My mother never liked me."

"It's true that you missed out when the happiness gene was

being handed out. And I know you tried. And Norman knows it too. You just wanted to be a normal guy, a perfectly normal but perfectly perfect guy, and that, Sharps, is where you went wrong. Unrealistic expectations. Although I do salute your affection for cleaning products. I also thought Celeste lacked attention when it came to personal hygiene."

"You knew Celeste?"

"I've said too much. I'll take you to your room, and we'll reconvene tomorrow. I would say don't worry it will be fine, but that's a lie and you know it. But it will be an adventure, and you might come out of it a better man."

She walked me down a hallway and opened a door to a bedroom. The bed was large and soft and I wanted nothing more than to face-plant and fall into the nothingness of sleep.

"Faith," Janaelle said to me as she left, "may seem at odds with my chosen career in science and the clinical surroundings in which I live, but I abide by, and respect, the fundamental principles of human morality, not to mention a sense of order within the world that was created by a being more extraordinary than we can ever imagine. But that's just me. Sleep well, Sharps. More tomorrow."

She left, and I kicked off my slippers and face-planted as planned. It felt exquisite for a moment, but the bed bottomed out and I fell from a great height into the maw of someone else's horrific nightmare.

A man came towards me, and I immediately recognized him. It was the Hockney man, the one from the print I loved so much, *I Saw in Louisiana a Live-Oak Growing*.

The print hung on our bedroom wall, much to Celeste's dismay. I was no art aficionado, but I came across the print when I was just a teenager and it was one of the few things I'd never destroyed. Besides, Celeste kept her horrible Rubenesque neon atrocity on full display. I told her it was unseemly for Bax to see his mother's lady parts splayed out like that, her enormous nipples glaring like two full moons, but she just laughed. "Good for the boy to know where he came from," she said, and I shuddered.

What did I love about the Hockney man? His starkness, his aloneness, the decapitatedness of the scene. The topsy-turvy of reality, the vitriol being spewed from his thick, white, closed lips. The tiny half-buried head that screamed for help, the muted colour palette of putty and green, and the broken earth, speaking of the fissures of life.

As a child, I'd loved books and art. It was a guilty pleasure in a world where such things were treated with derision and scorn. Crtainly my father thought I was an idiot for my fondness of such "irrelevancies." I couldn't stand contemporary music, and I treasured the few print books I had collected. Books in the twenty-second century were no more than audio feeds read by robots with dead voices. The print industry had long since died, and art galleries had closed. There was no new fine art and no one to love the old art. But I kept my precious print, and I told Celeste that it had to come with me. It was odd that I stood firm about so random a thing, but it wasn't random to me. The picture gave me voice. I knew the Walt Whitman poem from which Hockney had titled his art. When I was a boy, I wrote poetry. When my father found my poems, he laughed at me and ripped them up, and I heard him telling Mother that her foolish son fancied himself Shakespeare. After that, I hid my efforts from the world, although I got Jazza to get me black market downloads of all the Penguin classics. To his credit, he never laughed at my love of literature. I'd meant to mention that to Mother when she'd told me of her writing aspirations. Why hadn't she defended me against my father? I should have asked her.

And now the Hockney man stood in front of me, spoiling for a fight. "We've met before," he said, and his tongue was like raw flesh.

The blood drained from my face, and my breath was short and sharp and loud. I hated that, disgusting mouth breathers.

"How do you know?" I asked, and my voice was a whisper. Before he could answer, all I could think was that I was dying and the Hockney man agreed. He smiled as I felt myself fade.

I rose above myself and watched my sad and crumpled body lying in a puddle of flesh, clothed in ridiculous white sweat pants and a matching hoodie, innocuous garments I'd so naïvely assumed would see me through another day.

The Hockney man tied a piece of rubber tubing tightly around my upper arm and told me to make a fist as he picked a syringe up from a small silver tray.

"I thought there weren't going to be any drugs?" I asked, and my voice was filled with suspicion.

"Helps the machines read the data," he said as he inserted the needle, and I watched the fluid flow into my body. He put a HealPatch on the tiny dot that the needle had left. "You're set up. Have a good night. Don't let the bedbugs bite."

I lay on the queen-size bed with nothing for company but my cries of self-loathing and fear. A war raged on in my head, and I was about to sit up and rip off the cords and pads and leave. I was going to scream that I couldn't take it anymore when the lights went out and I was smothered in darkness, just like that. The machines stopped humming, the air vent stopped blowing, and a syrupy silence hung in the darkness. I waited for the emergency generator to kick in, but it didn't.

"Hello?" I called out loudly. "Somebody?"

I wished I had taken note of the Hockney man's name, but I hadn't figured I might want to see him again.

Hello! Hello! I shouted repeatedly. I put my full weight behind it, and boy, it felt good to yell like that. I screamed as loudly as I could and kept it up, *Hello, hello, hello!*

But no one answered and no one came and there was no reprieve, no light.

I pulled the monitor off my finger and tore the wires and pads from my head, shoulders, back, and legs.

I patted my way over to the chair as a blind man would,

touching things gingerly and feeling for shapes. I opened the door and walked down the hallway, turning into an empty reception area lit by a grey computer screen, a backlit fog trapped in a box, glowing with an unearthly amount of light. And when a telephone rang, I screamed like a girl. I looked down and saw a vintage aqua phone with a large circular dial. Shamed by my weakness, I shivered back into myself and picked up the phone, certain, or rather hoping, that the person on the other end of the line would clear up what was going on and put the situation straight. *Congratulations! You've won a free night at the Sky The Tower! All you have to do is phone 1 888 Integratron and give us the promotional code* BINGO *and you'll receive your free night!*

I stared at the receiver, incredulous, and then a strange thing happened, as if the night hadn't been weird enough already.

My teeth—my perfect, white, titanium-based teeth—crumbled into sea-shell shards inside my mouth. I spat bloody mouthfuls of broken shell enamel into my hand.

I ran my tongue along my molars, and my tissue-fragile teeth broke even further. I spat out more bloody crumbs. I stared at the sharp ruined mess in my hands with disbelief and watched as the shards fluttered upwards. Moths. *Ah, no way!* My mouth had been filled with moths.

The moths rose from my hand, leaving a stain of dried blood on my palms. The rose petal moths flew like wedding confetti, then died in a single breath, falling softly to the floor and dissolving into the cheap harsh grey weave of the carpet. I collapsed to my knees and examined the carpet in the thin milky light of the monitor.

I ran my shredded tongue around my mouth. I was left with one incisor and that was all. My tongue was a torn ribbon and my chin was sticky, covered with layers of dried and fresh blood.

I lowered my forehead to the carpet. I, like my teeth, was broken. I had no idea what was going on, but I had no reserves to deal with any of it.

Just when I thought it couldn't get any more bizarre, The Beach Boys cheerfully lit up the airwaves, yodelling about a surfing safari.

I shot up on my knees like a rabid squirrel and clapped my bloody palms to my ears. It wasn't even a good funk remix for god's sake. "Make it stop," I shouted. "Stop it. What is going on? Why is this happening?"

Wham! decided to take over, howling about waking up before you go and go and hanging yoyos. Why couldn't I wake up or escape this nightmare? Were there clues in the songs?

I stood up, jello-legs. The door. Why hadn't I rushed for the door? What was I thinking? I had to escape. I had to leave. Once I reached the sidewalk, maybe the nightmare would end and my life would be restored to me.

I rushed around the curved reception desk and grabbed the door handle.

PUSH.

I pushed with my body, ready to exit, but I only succeeded in slamming full-tilt into the glass and crushing myself against the steel door handle.

Winded, I fought to catch my breath. I tried to see through the glass, but there was only my reflection, my blood-covered chin and my staring eyes.

I was a madman.

"Venus" by Shocking Blue pulsed into my eardrums. *Oh god.* I loved that song once.

I opened my mouth as wide as I could, and spikes of shark sharpness stared back at me from a black oval. My ribbon-shredded eel tongue was covered with lumps of black blood. I clamped my mouth shut. I forced my eyes to lessen their crazy-man glare, and I backed away from the glass doors just as Madonna started wailing, wanting me to get into the groove and prove my love to her.

The phone rang over the sound of the music, and I rushed around the desk and snatched it up. Even that automated cheery voice would help right now, but there was nothing except for a slight hissing sound. And then a voice said, "He's coming," a voice that made my sphincter contract right up into my spine. A thin line of cold sweat ran down my spine, and the line went dead.

"Who's coming?" I shouted into the dead phone and I shook the receiver like a rag doll.

A strange whooshing sound brushed by my ear, and I looked up, clutching the dead phone to my chest like Bax cradling his favourite bunny when the night got too dark. I looked across the room. A painting swung wildly from side to side, swinging with such force that I couldn't see the picture. It was no surprise when the hook came loose and the painting fell to the floor.

The rectangle shape-shifted and folded into sharp angles, and an origami figure came to life—look, a bird, a plane—oh holy shit, it was the Hockney man. He was back. He'd never left.

The phone rang. I was already holding it. How could it ring? It was Celeste.

"Sugarpops babykins, how are you?" She sounded calm, and I was frightened. There were hidden depths to her voice I had never heard before.

"I'm fine," I said, but my voice shook.

"YOU ARE SUCH A LIAR!" she shouted down the line, and I wrenched the phone away from my ear.

"Stop lying! Just stop it!"

I sank down into the receptionist's chair.

"Fine," I said. "I was going to lose my job. They were going to fire me for being a thief. And now I've lost my teeth and I've lost my mind and I think I'm dead. Are you happy now?"

"Well, honey, it's a start," she said.

I started to cry. "It's so dark," I said. "And I don't know where everybody is. My tongue's ripped to shreds by my teeth. I don't even know how I'm still talking. Stupid music keeps playing through the loud speaker, and it's so dark and I'm all alone."

"Yeah, that's kind of how I felt, being married to you, honey. Admit it, you're sorry you married me, sweetie, aren't you? Go on, say it."

"No, no," I lie. "I love you."

"YOU ARE SUCH A LIAR!"

I couldn't help but notice that the glimmer of warmth in her voice the first time she'd uttered that phrase was gone. She was stating a fact without any compassion.

"Tell me the truth," she said. "I want the truth."

"No," I said, and I was crying. "All I want is to be home with you and the children." And it really was the truth, and maybe she heard that because she didn't call me a liar.

"It's too late," she finally said, and she sounded as if she was musing. "You killed us, remember, honey?"

"It's not too late," I said with as much fervent desperation as I could muster. "I'm coming to find you. I'll come back in time and find you, Cee. But why did you stay with me when you seem to hate me so much?"

"There was a tiny moment when I thought I loved you and I hoped that could return. When we met, I thought you were so sophisticated and witty and funny and handsome and debonair. And you were the future father of my children. You made Mummy and Daddy so very happy, and you set me free of their eternal scorn. But you deserve everything that's happening to you now. You treated me like an idiot for years. You think I didn't notice? Oh, I noticed. Everybody noticed."

"I…" I tried to say something but nothing came out.

"Yeah, big man, so good with words, cutting little nasty words, words like broken teeth. Yeah, baby, feels nice when you can't say anything, doesn't it?"

"I'm sorry," I said.

"For what?"

"Everything," I replied, and she snorted.

"So what happens now?" I asked. I noticed smoke swirling around my ankles and covering my slippered feet.

"You're going to let me die in here for being honest?" I asked, standing up. "That's not very nice or fair."

"Oh, honey, do you think you've been nice or fair?"

"You could have left," I pointed out, and it was clearly the wrong thing to say because the smoke rose to my knees, as thick as mud. I tried to pull my legs up, but I couldn't move; the suction was like quicksand.

"What can I do?" I tried to sound calm, but I heard the panic in my voice. "What can I do to make things right?"

"I don't think there is anything," she said.

"There must be," I told her, desperately grasping. "We can be a family again. A proper family. Please, Celeste, give me one more chance. Please, I'm begging you."

The smoke curled around my waist, a python fist squeezing the air out of me. My heart tightened as life left my body. I was slapped onto the surface of my beloved painting with a strange wet suctioning sound, but just before movement became impossible, I glimpsed a reflection of my face.

I had become the Hockney man.

25. TIME TRAVEL ON THE BRAIN

"WE THOUGHT WE'D LOST YOU," Janaelle said as I tried to push my way to the surface, clawing through grey muck as I went. "Your body struggled to acclimatize to the insertion of the device. You may have felt a period of temporal displacement and altered consciousness as well as a sense of disturbed time."

"You could say that," I replied caustically, the experience still running loops on my frontal lobe. "It wasn't fun."

"No pain, no gain," Janaelle said cheerfully. "But we nailed it."

"Nailed would be accurate. I've got a headache the size of Jupiter. Any chance of an Advil?"

Janaelle shook her head. "We need to monitor you sober. Anyway, it's time you met Jaxen."

I gaped as a poster boy for *Call of Duty* marched in wearing full military gear, his rolled-up shirt sleeves boasting impressive biceps. He was a pumped-up muscle boy with a square jawline and a cleft in his chin. He had a handsome, manly nose and high, flat cheekbones. He strode up with such force that I thought he was going to go right through the bed and halve me, but he ground to a sharp halt an inch away from the bed frame.

"Jaxen Killingsworth," he barked, offering me his hand. I took it cautiously, expecting a crushing show of machismo, but his hand was warm and reassuring.

"I hear there were some issues getting the device fitted. We lost a man once. Good for you for sticking it out."

I wanted to point out that I'd had little choice.

"Why don't we let him rest for a while?" Janaelle suggested. "Then we'll feed him, explain time theory, and send him on his way."

"I don't want to rest," I said. "You guys ... I mean I lie down to sleep and you drug me and do who knows what? I don't trust you. I had the worst nightmares."

"You want to time travel," Janaelle reminded me. "Besides, now that we've invested in you, we're not going to damage our product, are we? You need to trust us."

"I'm getting up." I sat upright, a mild movement that nearly killed me. "Or maybe not." I sank down. "Shit, this hurts."

Jaxen waved his arm at a window that I hadn't noticed, and blackout curtains fell silently into place. "Janaelle's right. You need quiet and darkness."

I closed my eyes. Every inch of my body stung with pain. I felt something soft and heavy cover my body, and my muscles immediately relaxed.

"A weighted blanket," Jaxen said. "Re-engineered Deep Touch Pressure Stimulation technology. Filled with non-toxic glass beads." His voice was soothing, and he patted my shoulder, which made me feel even better. I wondered about him and Janaelle. The minute he walked in, I'd had visions of them engaging in rough Marine-style sex—*wham, bam, thank you, ma'am*—but now I could see him being all gentle and considerate, bringing her to multiple orgasms by murmuring scientific facts and laying his hands upon her. I was still imagining them together when I drifted off.

I woke two days later. I knew it was two days because they told me.

"We monitored your brain," Janaelle said. "We needed to let you wind down. There was a lot going on in there. The inside of your skull looked like a snow globe on acid and speed. Poor guy. We did a detox recalibration, as much as we could anyway."

"You people!" I sat up. "I told you I didn't trust you! Detox calibration! Stay the fuck out of my head."

"No longer a possibility," Jaxen said, handing me a plate with peanut butter and jam toast. I particularly welcomed the hot coffee, and I wolfed it all down.

"We need to ascertain the exact moment of your return," he said.

Oh shit. I hadn't given that any further thought, not that they'd given me the opportunity to. "I'll think about it," I said. "What happens once I decide?"

"We log in the date and time. Look at your left wrist."

I did, but I couldn't see anything different. Oh wait, there was a short, thin grain of rice under my skin. I wanted to touch it, but I stopped myself in case I unleashed something else I wasn't equipped to handle.

"That's your magic button," Jaxen said. "You simply hold your wrist out to the pass point at St. Drogo's subway station, and *voilà*, the doors to the past will open. All you need to know is that every moment of time is mapped out and exists in the past. You just have to know where to look for it, which we do. In the same way that energy can never be destroyed, time can never be deleted. It all comes down to code. Life is code."

I had no idea what he was talking about. I had finished my second cup of coffee. My body felt punished and bruised, and I had a menacing headache. I tried to concentrate. "What do you mean, every moment of time is mapped out and exists? Exists where?"

"Sting Ray Bob will tell you the ins and outs." A tall man slipped into the room, his white coat neatly buttoned and a row of red and blue ballpoint pens in his top pocket. I screamed and scrambled back on the bed, knocking the tray to the floor. It was the Hockney man. I pushed as far away from him as I could, jumping off the bed and cowering in the corner.

"I'm Sting Ray Bob," the man said, and he smiled, if one could call it that.

"It's entirely normal for you to have an adverse reaction to Sting Ray," Jaxen hauled me to my feet. "He's digging around in your neurons, and you had an awareness for sure. Let's go to Janaelle's office; it's more peaceful there."

I followed them, keeping a wary distance from the Hockney man. I rubbed my tongue along my teeth, checking they were still intact, no bloody shards. I wanted to ask Jaxen what Sting Ray Bob had to do with the Hockney man, but we had reached Janaelle's office, a glass cube in the middle of the forest with a sparkling waterfall to the east and a sunset to the west. I stared, mouth open. Moss-covered rocks and brightly-coloured birds made the place idyllic. I went up the glass, wishing I could lie in the cool shade of a magnolia tree in full bloom.

"Yeah, Janaelle likes pretty," Jaxen climbed into a swinging basket chair and crossed his legs like a zen guru. "She's sentimental that way."

"I thought we killed the birds? Along with the weather, natural farming, and mountain streams. This is gorgeous. It can't be real?"

"It's not real, not yet," Janaelle admitted from behind her rose quartz desk. "Our goal is to revive the world you see out there, but it's slow going and given the data we've gathered from the rage rooms, we're not optimistic. The world's getting dumber and dumber and angrier and angrier, but we won't give up. And you're part of that future. If we can change the trajectory of your past actions, there's hope."

"It has to work!" I immediately insisted. "If my family lives, things will be better and other things will change too."

"That's the theory," Jaxen said. "Sting Ray Beebop, I can see you're just bustin' a gut to start this guy's tuition. Time-travel for Dummies 101—let the lesson commence!"

Sting Ray Bob was silent for a moment. "Go to St. Drogo's, stick your wrist out, and jump."

"That's it? I thought I was getting a lesson in science?"

"Frankly, I don't believe it will be helpful for you to know any more than you need to." Sting Ray Bob looked defiantly at Janaelle and Jaxen, ready to challenge their objections. He was a beanpole of a man, exactly like the Hockney man, only Sting Ray Bob had a mullet hairdo and was a walking tattoo covered in chemical formulas and mathematical equations.

Jaxen gave Janaelle a glance. "He's probably right," he said, and she nodded. "But he does need to know more than that. Come on, Bobbo, give him the nuts and bolts."

Sting Ray Bob sighed. "You've got five visits, and the duration of each visit is a week. Time will appear to stop on this side so that when you return, the same people will be in the subway station and it will be the exact moment you left. A word of warning: travel takes a physical toll. You have to rest for at least two weeks in between jumps. Every time you jump, you eat away at your body. One guy literally fell apart; his fat and flesh dropped off him like pulled pork."

I shuddered. "And do I have to leave from the exact same location in the past?"

"No. You will be brought back from wherever you are. Now, if the device fails…"

"It could fail?" I interrupted him and shot up in my chair, my heart hammering in my chest.

"The likelihood is low. If it happens, you must stay calm. Look at your wrist."

I did as he said.

"That's the activation device. You'll need to aim that in the direction of gate activation software. See it as your boarding pass. If it fails to work, you'll have to dig it out of your wrist with a scalpel and reset it. Get it out and wash it in saline solution or water. Then look for a tiny raised area on the surface. That's the software reset button. Press it hard with your nail and count to ten, then release. Then stick it back in and pinch the flesh to hold it in place until you're back and we can effect repairs. Digging it out will hurt like hell, but worse than the pain is the discomfort of being stuck in the vortex of displaced time. It could feel like you're trapped in the spinning ball of death—you know the one—the rainbow-coloured wheel that used to go around and around on old-fashioned computers when they were trying to load data? Some nostalgia software programs like to mess with people by using them as a joke. *Ha ha.*"

I nodded, shrinking back in my chair. I knew the spinning ball. What I hadn't known was that time travel would necessitate this level of bravery, and I was beginning to have my doubts that I was the right man for the job.

Sting Ray Bob continued. "Yeah, well, it could be like that. Trying to get stories from people about what it was actually like in displaced time is tough because memories fade fast, like bad dreams. I've heard it's very grey, like being in a fog, and you feel stuck, like you can't make anything happen. Just remember, don't panic. Know that we'll be working on it from this side."

"What was the longest they were stuck?"

"Two days. One woman came back dehydrated and hallucinating wildly. She lost her sense of gravity. We put her in a decompression chamber for a couple of weeks and she's fine now, although she never regained her balance. But from a data-gathering point of view, her experience was invaluable. The facts we mined were incredible, and all of them will be used to help you."

"How many people have time travelled?" I asked and Sting Ray looked at Jaxen.

"Over three dozen," Jaxen replied. He sounded like he was lying, but I couldn't exactly call him out on it. "Any other questions?"

"Jazza's mother. He said she died in a rage room accident. Are you guys going to pretend you don't know about that?"

"All we know is that she was a pioneer in the industry," Jaxen replied and folded his arms. Subject closed.

"And what about Ava and her manifesto? You guys are

involved with her, right? And Mother? How does it all fit in?"

"Ah, buddy." Jaxen looked firm. "That's all on a need-to-know basis, and at this particular moment, you do not need to know. Above your paygrade, so to speak. Sorry, buddy. The day will come, believe me, and you will be fully looped in, but today is not that day. Any other questions pertaining to the actual jump?"

I thought hard. "So if I go back and I do not kill my family, then I will arrive safely in my future in which my family will be alive and Jazza will be alive and so will Ava and Adwar?"

"That is correct. Other things may be different. Jazza may have made other choices subsequent to the date on which you killed your children—who knows? And Ava too. And even Celeste. You cannot change other people's actions, only an action of your own. So things will be different, but your children will be alive."

"I get it. At least I think I get it. I've pinpointed when I want to go back. Let's get this show on the road. I'm getting tired of talking. Let's do it."

"Not so fast, buddy boy. You still need to rest. We plan to hook you up with electrolytes and flood your system with goodies from the lab. Get rid of that headache and make you feel strong." Jaxen was firm.

"You're going to drug me again?"

"You don't exactly have a choice but to trust us, isn't that so? What are you going to do, run?"

Bastard. I stood up, resigned to my fate.

"But on the plus side," he said cheerfully, "we've got a bunch of classic time travel movies for you to watch while you heal. *Memento, Back to the Future, The Butterfly Effect, Sputnik's Children.* My advice would be for you to sit back and enjoy yourself while you can."

I half expected him to say, *Interview terminated.*

I had no choice but to do exactly what he said, and I let Sting Ray Bob lead me away.

26. THE FIRST JUMP

IT WAS TIME TO DO THE FIRST JUMP. I was terrified, but I had to do it. It was all mapped out. I was going to go back to that fateful day when I returned to work and let Jazza and Ava take control of the PeachDiamondDelux Program. I wouldn't sign off on anything. And I would have to find out how to make Nanny Flo stay. I'd also ferret out whatever Celeste was hiding. I hadn't forgotten Jazza's comment. And I wouldn't kill Mother. Or Adwar. I'd probably still kill Ava. Nope, only joking. No killing. I'd have the whole situation under control, and I'd have my kids and my life back. Maybe it wouldn't be perfect, but that was just fine too.

Jaxen dropped me off at St. Drogo's. "We'll be waiting for you when you come back," he said. "But in case there's a delay, hang onto this." He handed me my fob and a token for a Parkette, two streets north of here. I was confused. "Your car's got money and supplies, just in case. We'll be here, but if for any reason we're not, go to your car and we'll hook up there."

I nodded and shoved the fob in my pocket. He waved and drove off, and I was left alone. I'd been hoping he would come in with me and help see me off, but he left me. It reminded me of my first day of school when Mother marched me up to the main gates, pointed vaguely towards the gothic arched entrance, and left.

Really, Mother? Couldn't you have stayed to see me safely

inside? The sheer terror of walking up those stairs all by myself and feeling so lost and out of place flooded my mind now, and I was that kid again.

St. Drogo's was filled with early morning commuters, their GrumpyCatAvatar expressions firmly in place. I flashed back to being one of them. Did I really want to go back and have to be part of the grind? I thought about what Knox had said, about winning the lottery. Was there a way I could do that? Only if I could find the winning ticket number. Hmmm. I suddenly wanted more time to think about this, but then I remembered something. I had five jumps! I didn't have to solve world peace or my finances in this jump; all I had to do was go back and fix those pesky murders.

And then when I was back in real time, I'd note the winning lottery ticket number, jump back, buy it, wait a week, jump into real time, and collect my winnings! Great! But that would have to wait. This jump was to clean up my mess. Hey wait, was that Shasta? I twisted around, but in their hurry to get in and out of the station the wave of annoyed commuters shoved me in between two fare collection booths. I yanked up my sleeve and bared my wrist. *Okay, here goes nothing.*

The gates sprang open. I hesitated, and then I leapt through, fully expecting nothing to happen, nothing at all. I thought I'd land on the other side and have to pick a lane of those swift-moving bodies, go east or westbound, and that I'd better make it fast or the commuters behind me would mow me down.

But I landed in my house, exactly like Sting Ray Bob had said I would. Time travel me looked down at my sleeping son. I walked past our bedroom, where Celeste was fast asleep, snoring. It was weird, doing my day on rewind, and I shook my head like a dog after a swim. I forced myself to carry on and not get distracted by how surreal it all felt. I went downstairs to say goodbye to Nanny Flo. And, once back at work, I tried to nail down Ava and Jazza in the shared office they'd set up for us. Daddy had just left, issuing his parting shot. "God helps those who help themselves," he said. "But if you ask me, you need God's help most of all." He gave me a meaningful glance and left. He was right. I had the most to lose, and everyone in the room knew it. Jazza had just returned from his brain scour and he was seething. Ava was Mount Helena ready to blow. She put the silver pyramid paper weights on the desks to scramble the Board's audio, and she and Jazza faced each other, ready to attack.

"Guys, wait," I said urgently. "Listen! We have to take control of this because if we don't, we'll all end up dead. You have to listen to me!"

They both ignored me and started screaming. I opened my mouth to mediate, but Celeste flashed me and I had to leave. *Oh shit*. I'd miscalculated and wasted a bunch of days. I should only have come in after I'd deposited Celeste and Lila in their respective clinics. Now there was nothing to do but wait it out until I got to the moment when Ava brought up the program.

The days passed with nail-biting slowness, and I finally got to the point where I could address things and make a pivotal change.

Ava was in full spiel. "We're going to flash ads everywhere, Sharps, on every wall and building. We're taking over personal Crystal Path viewing. Henceforth, all content will be sponsored. Through the viewer's eye, the world's going to look like a kaleidescope of logos tossed its cookies in Real Life Las Vegas, but it'll work and we'll generate the revenue we've been tasked with."

I stuck to my script. "You're turning the world into a virtual catalogue? That kind of hard sell is illegal! Advertising has to be hidden, experience-driven! That's how123BlikiWin, ClothesKissezThugs, and CrystalMeBooty worked. We never advertised directly. It was all about being in the game. Direct merch sales are banned."

"There are ways around things," Ava said, as expected. "A way into allowing direct advertising onto personal devices. Your Mr. Williamson is one of the masterminds behind it. I never knew he had that kind of legal savvy. I have to admit I'm even mildly impressed. He spotted a loophole and dove right through it, opening up a whole new world. Maybe he knew it was there all along and was saving it for an ICE situation, which this admittedly is."

I saw my opportunity to rewrite the narrative and I jumped up. "Ava! Listen to me. We can't do this. If we do, we'll all die. Well, I won't die, but I'll kill you."

She burst out laughing. "Yeah? In your dreams." Even Jazza laughed at me.

"Seriously guys, it's true," I insisted. "Ava, you want Jazza to steal money for your army so you can change the world. You want to pin it on me. And believe me, the consequences are disastrous. You guys can't do this. And you're in love, even if you won't admit it to yourselves."

"Now you've really lost your mind," Ava spat out, although Jazza perked up when I mentioned mutual love. Ava slammed her hand on the desk, and I jumped.

"Listen to me, Sharps, you insignificant little shit, sit the fuck down. Never, ever mention words like 'army' in here, even with our decrypting devices. If you do, we'll all end up on the Farms, never mind the Sheds. Do you hear me? The fucking farms! Forced labour, drugged."

She looked over at Jazza. "I did believe we had something," she said softly, and Jazza melted. That was when I knew she was playing him.

"Don't believe her!" I yelled. "She just wants you on board with her and not me! She'll say anything to make you do what she wants! But you'll end up dead!"

Ava walked up to Jazza and put her hand on his shoulder. "You know me better than that. Yes, I was angry, but I understand. Sharps is an idiot, but he is right. We're in love."

"Don't believe her! She's lying! She's playing you!"

"But you said it first!" Jazza was torn. His massive blood-hound face swung from me to Ava and back. "I'm not listening to either of you right now. I'm going to work on the plan. And Sharps, Ava's right, shut the fuck up or we'll end up on the Farm."

He sat down, and I could see his expression was lighter. He believed her. He'd do anything she wanted. If anything, I'd made things worse. He was more sucked into her honeytrap than ever.

I looked down at my wrist. I could see the tiny node of the implant and the faint scar from where it was placed. I was trying to change my life. I was trying to change my future, all our futures. Why wasn't this going more easily?

"Okay," I immediately replied. "You guys are right. Sorry. I panicked, okay?" I held my hands up in agreement. "My bad. Give me my homework. But," I added firmly, "I'm not signing off on any shit I don't understand."

They both cracked up laughing. "Sharps," Ava said kindly, "when the fuck have you ever understood anything? You'll sign where we tell you to."

To my credit, I tried to really figure out what the PeachDiamondDelux Program was about. Something to do with hacking into the users of our other programs and creating bots to send them individualized shopping plans with bonus incentives. The bots would access the users' bank accounts to see where they shopped the most. I wondered what the Union of Ethics and Trustworthy Communications, the UETC, would have to say about that. But Ava had mentioned that Daddy was the one behind the loophole, so the whole thing must be legal or it wouldn't be happening.

Yeah, I knew that was me being naïve and stupid. So that's how Jazza ripped off so much money. He not only stole from the company, he stole from the users too. Wrong on so many levels.

I grabbed a portable comm and went to a shared space filled with VendaRipple dispensers and cheerful jellybean-coloured plastic sofas. I sat down on a teal sofa in the corner and tried to figure out what to do.

This program, and Jazza and Ava, were the dominos that made the whole house of cards of my life come crashing down. So far I had proven two things: I couldn't stop Jazza and I couldn't stop the program. So, what could I do? The only thing I could do was let it move forward, and then, on the day in question, not kill Ava, not kill Adwar, and, when Jazza left his suicide note, let it fall on him. I'd have to wait to go back to the future and come back on the day of the killings and pin the whole thing on Jazza, and obviously, I wouldn't kill anyone.

Yeah, I'd still take the fall for signing off on the money, but at least I'd have my family. I wouldn't have a job, but I'd win the lottery later, wouldn't I? I had to let things roll as they were. I'd thought I could cut Jazza off at the pass, but I couldn't.

What if I resigned now? But I wouldn't find another job. There were no other jobs. Shed jobs were minimum wage and I couldn't afford that.

"Making lists?" A voice spoke behind my ear. Startled, I inadvertently let out a little scream.

It was Daddy. I leapt up, clutching the comm to my chest. "Daddy! I mean Mr. Williamson! So good to see you, sir! Listen, sorry to trouble you, but do you have a moment?"

"Not really, son. I'm off to a meeting of the Sky Trust. Can't keep them waiting. Saw you sitting here, and I just wanted to say hello and see how things were going."

"Not well, sir," I blurted out. "I need to be reassigned, sir. Ava's gunning for us both, sir, and we can't win. Trust me, we'll end up losing everything. Jazza can't be part of the project, because he'll do anything Ava wants. I'm worried that, because I don't understand the specifics and they want me to sign off on it, I'll be the fall guy and so will you. You've got no idea how much Ava hates you."

Daddy looked at me. "Calm down, son. Walk me to the elevator."

I followed him, and he pushed the button. "Sharps, my boy, you need to calm down. Jazza and Ava have looped me in. The PeachDiamondDelux Program is sound. All you need to do is sign where they tell you to, do you see? You're our front man, which is how I keep a roof over your and Celeste's head. I'm very fond you, my boy, you know that, but you're not the sharpest tool in the shed, *har har!* I've wanted to use that joke for a while, but I never wanted to hurt your feelings, but there it is. You're a good husband to my Celly, and Bax is a gem. And we've got a new kiddie set up to bake. But son, where do you think you're going to get another job like this? Or a woman like Celly? She's high maintenance. Which means you need to step up even more. She's costing me a bundle and Mummy's set her sights on a condo in Real Life Florida, so I've got my own problems. You need this job, and it's a good one. You need to keep Celly on the straight and narrow. That's your job, my boy."

"But Ava and the kiddies and Jazza end up dead!"

Daddy looked at me as if I'd lost my mind. "Sharps, coming back to work has clearly involved some trauma for you. Listen, son, no one's going to die. I've seen the program. It's all sound. Run with it! Run hard!"

Oh shit.

I cast around for something else to say, but the elevator arrived and Daddy held the door open. "Son," he said, resting a big hand heavily on my shoulder, "you've been given a goose that lays the golden egg. Just let it do its job and you do yours. Simple. We'll not have any more of this hysteria, roger that?"

"Roger that," I echoed as the door closed, my enthusiasm pale and wintry. So much for my big bold idea of trying to save my world.

I went to the men's room, shut myself in a cubicle, and put my head in my hands.

There had to be another way. But what? I couldn't exactly kill Ava or Jazza now. Besides, I wasn't a homicidal maniac. I had to figure out a peaceful solution. But what? I was trapped. Fine. I'd let the rest of the week run its course, then I'd come back and let Jazza take the fall.

I was a little annoyed that Daddy saw me so clearly. I'd thought I had him fooled. I'd hoped he thought I was more impressive than that, but clearly not. The only fool in all of this was me. But I'd still do what I could to find out about Celeste's secrets and Nanny Flo's family.

I went back to my desk, but I couldn't concentrate on the remaining thousand documents outlining the program. I was supposed to read all of it? I groaned out loud. It wasn't even three in the afternoon, and I was bored out of my mind.

I messaged Nanny Flo for the seventh time.

Bax okay?

All good, Mr Sharps!

I drummed my fingers on the desk. Across from me, Ava and Jazza were working closely. She was practically sitting in his lap. It made me want to throw up. She was playing him more than ever, and I only had myself to blame. Why hadn't I figured things out better? I could have gotten him onside. Because I had no proof of anything, that's why. I didn't have a leg to stand on.

I got up. I needed to vent. So to the rage room I went.

27. TRYING TO MAKE ALTERNATIVE PLANS

I HEADED FOR THE NEAREST RAGE ROOM to thrash the shit out of crap. And yet my mood didn't improve.

I peeled off the suit and stood under the cleanup rinse wishing I never had to leave. I still felt grimy after the shower and I rubbed myself down with some of the HandiWipes they provided. There was a small cut on my hand, proving that the government-issue gloves were useless. I squeezed the tiny cut, maximizing the flow of blood. I was happy I was bleeding. Look, I bled too. I was human.

"Here," the rage room guy handed me a MediWipe. "You shouldn't have cut yourself. I'll make sure the ProtectGear doesn't fail again. We keep our patrons safe. That's our promise to you, to provide a safe haven for your anger."

WTF? I didn't hear a word he'd said. It was Norman.

"What do you know about time travel?" I blurted out, jumping into his face, and he laughed.

"Nothing, man. *Dr. Who*, shit like that. It's not real, but it sure is interesting. Who knows in the future though? Anything can happen. Here's a HealPatch."

I took it and peeled off the covering. When I looked up, Norman was gone and another guy was standing there. "Gonna give you a refund today," he said. "There should be no injuries. Our bad."

"Can I get a job here?" I asked. "I'd love to work here."

"We have a BotList I can flash you," he said. "But I'm telling you now, we're pretty full up. Union job, good pay, benefits, and six weeks furlough a year, and as much access to comfort centres as we like."

It all sounded appealing apart from the comfort centres. CCs were spa-type setups catering to every un-hostile emotion. If you needed to be pampered, massaged, manicured, pedicured, acupunctured, or hugged, you just checked in at a comfort centre. I went once at Mother's insistence, but it felt claustro-phobic and intrusive. I never returned. The comfort centres also offered small narrow booths where you could chat to an "unseen friend," kind of like a confessional in that you never actually got to see the person behind the small, purple, velvet curtain. Your unseen friend murmured comforting affirmations that you were loved, that you were important and respected, and that you were worthy of that respect. I had no time for all that empowering, feel-good bullshit.

But people loved the centres, and there were often long lineups to climb into the white chaise lounge that reminded me uncomfortably of dentist chairs. It was all designed to encourage honest dialogue, although really it was just people venting the same old shit. The purple curtain never opened. The chair hugged your body, the lights dimmed for your twenty minutes, tiny stars glowed on the walls and ceiling, and you voiced your greatest fears and your worst sins. No matter what you said, the voice was kind, but you had to display voice moderation control, and physical displays of anger were not permitted under any circumstances. I had proven this to be true.

I'd screamed obscenities and pounded on the glass. My actions were immediately curtailed. The lights flashed on highbeam, and the voice, no longer friendly at all, told me to check in at a rage room because my aggression had no place in this oasis. I'd also proven that the only thing behind the velvet curtains was a funhouse mirror that made your face look weird.

It was weird how much everybody loved the CCs, as they

were called, because, while we had recourse to help lines on our portable comms and you could flash chat with a virtual EmoHealthExec any time you wanted, it was the personal touch that people craved, having a real person listen to you. Only I was pretty certain that the only thing listening to you was an EmoBot.

If you liked, on your way out, you could get a real life hug from an EmoHealthExec. Each CC had a serene suburban living room filled with plush sofas and soft cushions, and you could take your pick from a group of professional huggers. There were limits to how long you could hold the hug, and any off-colour behaviour such as buttock fondling, breasts feels, or an inappropriate pelvic distance saw you banned for life. Hugging was one of the highest-paid careers. Between the rage rooms and the CCs, Minnie had created vast employment opportunities.

"I'm not a fan of the CCs," I told the rage room guy. "Hugging is out of the question, but man, I'd love to work here! Hook me up with the BotList, and I'll apply. I'll do anything to change my life. I'm sick of the shit I deal with."

"Yeah, I know what you mean. But I gotta be honest, you need a referral or relative on the voting board. My father-in-law got me in here. It's the only way, these days. I mean, you can submit your experiential profile—they legally have to let you—but pretty much none of the applications make it past the RoboFilters without a verfiying in-house signature. You tell me one business that doesn't work that way. Unless you've been there since when you interned, you don't get in."

I nodded. "I interned at Integratron after I graduated from the Global International University. I've got a Ph.D. in Optimal Communications and Life Branding, a master's in Flexibility Optics and Mass Persuasion, and a bunch of related psych and social media majors. I'm educated up the yin yang, but I'm looking for something new." I'd always been aware of the ironies. Me, a psych major? What a joke.

"Take some free advice from me. Ride the horse you've been given until he drops dead. If he keeps going, you keep going too." Great. I was talking to a philosopher. Plus, he wasn't telling me what I wanted to hear.

"Thanks, man," I said and wandered out to my car. I wanted to go home, but I wasn't ready. I still had too many pent-up feelings. So I made my next mistake, which was to go and visit Mother.

I parked outside the house. Was this a bad idea? I thought about how I killed her in the future and wrote on her body with a thick, black, felt-tipped pen. What was it that I had written? I didn't have any idea, no memory whatsoever. An apology?

I got out of the car and locked it. I walked up the long path and rang the doorbell.

"Hello," Mother said when she answered, and she sounded neither pleased nor displeased to see me.

"Can I come in?"

She opened the door, and I went inside.

"My room's the same?" I asked even although I knew the answer, and she nodded.

"Why? You don't want to see me and yet you kept my room?" I wanted her to tell me it was because she knew I'd screw up. I was hoping we could talk about it. Maybe she'd be able to help me be different and do different things. But she changed the subject instead. "Is Celeste still drinking?"

Ouch. "She's in rehab. We've all got our own issues, Mother. At least she's trying, and a new baby will help."

"Oh sure it will," Mother said and I wanted to hit her.

"What's wrong with you, Mother? Should we stop pro-creating? What's your great and marvellous plan for our future? I know you've got one. You and Ava and the army!" I was shouting, but Mother remained calm. She didn't ask me where I'd got my information, and I couldn't remember if we'd had the conversation before. I felt confused and sick, and I couldn't remember anything. "Just tell me!" I yelled.

"I've got a right to know. No one tells me anything! I'm not stupid!"

"All right then. We let it run out. The world, us, and the mess we've made. In the meantime, we'll do the best we can, whatever that means, but we need to admit that as a species, humanity has failed. Life is a rage room, Sharps, you know that better than anyone. That's all it is. Angry people flailing about, hitting things and destroying rubbish from the past. Your children will grow up useless and depressed unless things change. We need to run dry and start again. No apps, no robots. Let the weather be the weather; let it fail us, reward us, and be real again. Let real crops grow again and make clothes from fibres found in nature. Ban plastic wherever possible. Have a real world again, instead of this fake, sterile tedium where everybody lives in a virtual reality that isn't real at all." She came to an abrupt stop.

"You're right, Mother," I said, and I sank down into a chair and folded my arms. "I hate my job, and it's going to end badly. My life is going to end badly, and I want to try to change things. Things will end badly for you and for my family. Isn't there anything we can do, you and me, to change the course of my life?"

"You may think you want to change things, Sharps," she said, "but in the end, you won't do a damned thing. And nothing I can say will change that, which is why I can't get too involved with Bax and your future child. The lives that you and Celeste live are polar opposites to my moral principles. Poor little Bax is doomed, and it's too horrible to watch. So much of the world is angry, but we, my group, we're not. We understand the way things are, and we accept. We accept and we don't partake or participate. And one day, we will unplug it all and reboot the system."

She sounded like she was repeating something a fanatic had written. No wonder she and Ava got on so well; they were both on the same crazy page.

"So, you don't care about dying?"

"Well, of course I don't want to die, Sharps. None of us do. But that's not the point. It's the awful pointlessness of living that I'm trying to deal with."

It occurred to me that Mother was seriously psychologically damaged and needed help. But for the level she was at, I knew what kind of help she'd get: pills, pills, and more pills until she couldn't take a shit by herself. No, if you were that messed up, it was better to keep it on the down low because once you were in the system for failing even a low-level EmoPsych, it was over for you. They kept you pumped full of meds, ramming them down your throat in increasing doses to keep you "safe," which meant controllable.

I'd passed all my EmoPsychs, which only proved that I knew how to play the game.

"But Mother," I burst out, "you do want things. You say you don't, but you do. Why on earth would you agree to a NeptuneSupremeBodyFountain if you didn't want things?"

She looked at me as if I had lost my mind and, in a way, she was right. I had spoken from the future. *Oops.* But Mother looked delighted. "Now that you mention it, it that would be lovely. There's nothing like the healing power of water. Feel free to gift me with that for Christmas, Sharps. Good thinking!"

"I don't have the money," I said morosely. "I don't know why I said that. I don't even know why I came to see you, but I'm glad I did. You cleared up a lot of things for me, Mother."

"Good. Because I have to go," she said. "Do you need to break anything before you leave?"

"No, Mother, I don't. But thank you."

I walked down the path and got back into my car. Nothing was going my way. I was trying everything I could to try to steer things onto a better course, but there wasn't any give. Once inside the soundproof little bubble, I screamed and pounded the dashboard with my fists.

28. TRYING, AND FAILING, TO CHANGE THINGS

I DROVE HOME, EXHAUSTED. I wondered if I'd remember my conversation with Mother when I got back to my real present. And my efforts with Jazza—would I remember them too?

When I got home, not even my boy's joy at seeing me could lift my spirits. I played with him and bathed and fed him, but I was sunk in gloom. Mother was right. What kind of world did we live in? I tried for the most part not to see what was going on out there, but it was all so messed up. We'd let ourselves get dumbed down, and the world was full of people walking around as if protected by giant water wings. Why did we need to be constantly shielded? Because we couldn't be trusted? I'd never thought about it before. I had simply accepted things.

Mother was right about the loss of meaning. Celeste steadfastly maintained that Christmas was all about Jesus, but it was more like the old cult movie, *Brazil,* a 1985 classic I'd watched with Jazza when we decided to vape some weed and get high and act stupid. Neither of us had particularly enjoyed the experience, but the movie was good. I'd loved the "Consumers for Christ" Christmas parade that parodied consumerism as wolves in sheep's clothing. And that was *then!* Consumerism was still our god. All we did was shop, eat, and sleep—the new Holy Trinity.

And the best Bax could hope for a was a job like mine, where he'd shuffle through his day until he could go home to eat,

drink, and shop, and pretend to be someone else by donning
his avatar self. No wonder we were so angry. One way or another, Bax's life would amount to no more than a placeholder
for meaningless productivity while he channelled the hours of
his day. We had failed to create a better world. I crushed my
knuckles against my temples and groaned.

"You all right, Mr. Barkley?" It was Nanny Flo. I seized the
moment.

"Yes, I'm fine. Just a tough day at work. Listen Flo, how
are *you*?" My fervent question startled her, and she looked
around, uneasily.

"I am fine," she said, and she looked ready to run.

"Where is your family? Is everybody here in St. Polycarp's?"

"No, Mr. Barkley, they are in St. Barbara's. I send them
money."

"Your husband and your kids? How many kids?"

"I have five children. And my sister has four. We have no
husbands; they left."

"So you're supporting ten people?"

"More than that. My parents and my grandparents are still
alive too." She laughed. "We have a very big family."

I tried to remember how much we paid her, but Celeste was
in charge of that. I'd have to speak to her about it. Did we
pay Nanny Flo enough?

"You know you can come to me if there's ever anything you
need," I insisted, and she looked confused.

"I mean if you're ever in trouble, don't leave us. Please never
leave us, Flo." She looked more startled than alarmed, and I
let her go before I made things worse.

I decided to chat to Celeste via the portable comm. Maybe
she'd make me feel better. I dialled her up, and she answered.
She had a green face mask on and seemed in a good mood.
"Sharps, sweetie, are you okay? You look a bit weirded out?"

"The world's a mess," I sank into the sofa and switched the
view from my portable comm to my CP. "We won't be able to

protect Bax. And I don't want to protect him. I want him to be a real human, a standup guy who can fend for himself. But then what? What kind of life will he have? Relationships? Will he have kids of his own? Will he have any kind of religious faith? What will keep him going?"

I came to a stop, and Celeste laughed. "Oh, honey. What's the point of thinking about any of that? Was work today that terrible?"

The awful trajectory of my doomed life flashed before my eyes, and I choked back a sob. "It was bad. And it's going to get worse. Nobody wants to hear anything I've got to say. I'm a pawn, CeeCee. Nothing but a pawn. A stooge, a joke, a bit player in a stage show where everybody else knows what they're doing and I don't have a clue."

"Oh, sweetie, you have had a bad day. Do you want to take me upstairs and get some of the old Lucky Hole? Although wait, I'd need to really be there for that. But I can walk you through it, help you find release?"

"No. I don't want that. It's the last thing I want. I want to try to figure things out, make things different, and create a different outcome than the one I know lies ahead. CeeCee, do you have any secrets from me? Please tell me. Tell me everything. I won't be shocked. I won't. I'll always love you."

Would I? Did I even love her now? We were more like tacit partners hiding behind a façade when really we were robots just like the rest of the world, keeping time to the marching band of trending politics and social dictates we were powerless to change.

"I love you, too, HoneyBear. I do. Listen, you're worrying me. Why don't you take a pill? Just one, for tonight. You're so on edge. I heard that things went well with Lila, and I'm doing well. Things are moving along, sweetie—they are! Do you want a pill?"

"I do NOT want a pill!" I jumped up and heard Bax start to cry upstairs. "Oh shit. I'll go and get him. But Celeste, do you have any secrets from me?" I shouted, and she flinched, clutching her hand to her chest and looking at me, wide-eyed from the comm. "No, sweetie, I don't. Listen, get Nanny Flo to get Bax. You're too wound up. You need to go to your special place or something. Go and calm down, okay? Go and work out maybe. I don't know, but do something."

She was right. I had to get out of the house. My body hadn't seemed to suffer any ill effects from my having come back. If anything, I felt an agitated restlessness.

We logged off. I grabbed my keys and got into my car and drove to a place where I could see St. Polycarp's skyline.

I sat in my car. Skyscraper city lay before me, sparkling and shiny, futuristic and impersonal. It could be any country in the world. And another stack of cubic zirconia, home to millions of little rats and hamsters, each living a pointless life, obediently running on the wheel in front of them and falling into the sawdust that lined their cages. I could even imagine the smell of sawdust, the sweet fragrance of the freshly sawn wood shavings.

I leaned back and closed my eyes. I had been right to kill my family. There was no point to their awful ungodly lives. Little rats and hamsters. I'd let the week run out. I'd do my time and go back to my future.

Shit. My future where I had killed Mother and was on the run. Right, that wasn't so great either. Maybe I had been right to spare my family this awful existence, but I still needed to figure out a plan for myself. A plan in which they were spared this terrible meaninglessness but one in which I escaped the eye of the police. And I knew from Celeste's response to me that she was lying. She had secrets, and there was something rotten to her core. And Nanny Flo would leave, so the kids had no hope. I wished we hadn't brought Sophie into the world—it was selfish and wrong.

Was that what I was supposed to do this time around? Was the answer for me to go back to a pre-Celeste time? I couldn't do that. My time with my kids was the only thing that had given my life any meaning.

And I didn't want to cancel Sophie. I loved my time with her. She was my sweet little angel. She enjoyed all the things a baby should. I ended things before her life became polluted and I got to appreciate her pure joy, her sweet, unsullied essence.

I wondered if I should kill myself, on the other side. But I felt strangely empowered by what I'd done, and I wanted to live, perhaps for the first time ever. I had gotten off the hamster wheel! I was living a different life, the life of a killer on the loose, yes, but there was a vitality to the whole thing and I wasn't ready to die yet.

I went home and ran a bubble bath, filling the room with scented candles, my unmanly guilty pleasure. I added lavender epsom salts to ease my aching muscles, and I lay in the flickering darkness with a lime and soda at the ready.

I studied my toes at the end of the bath, and finally, soaked out and worn out, I put on my striped pajamas and went to bed.

Tomorrow was another day. I'd face the future when I had to and not a moment sooner. I still had a few days left. I'd come up with a plan. I had to. That's what I told myself anyway, and I even felt a glimmer of hope and happiness and a ridiculus feeling of invincibility. I'd come up with something. Why not? Good things could happen to me, right? I was the master of my own destiny.

Very funny. I thought about the whole thing six ways to Sunday. I didn't stop thinking about it, but I couldn't come up with anything. I faced the facts: I was loser. And life was what it was. I'd already tried to change my luck by marrying Celeste and having kids. I'd had my shot at my perfect life, and it hadn't worked out. The play had been called. Life would go on its way, inexorably dragging me along like a cat caught in the rain. No one had any faith in me, so how could I have faith in myself?

I went through the motions in the remaining time. I called Celeste back and reassured her that I wasn't losing my mind. I was just another loser; none of this was her fault. I was so considerate and loving that she asked me if I was having an affair. At work, Jazza asked me if I'd developed a terminal disease because I'd gone so quiet.

I felt strangely rooted in time, as if the future wouldn't come, that terrible future. You know when you know something's going to end badly but you're not in that situation yet and so you begin to believe that things will be fine? You settle in and you settle down. The thought of going back felt unreal. Maybe I'd dreamt up the whole thing about me killing my family. It didn't feel like me because I couldn't imagine having that kind of energy. But perhaps my coming back was a miracle, a gift from Celeste's Jesus. Beautiful, blond, toned, and buffed neon Jesus had cleared my tab, restored my family, and sent me back so that they could live their lives. And I'd take that. Maybe He'd done it for them, not me. Maybe all I had to do was nothing, which was something I was pretty damn good at.

29. BACK TO THE FUTURE PRESENT I AM THROWN

S O IT WAS WITH SOME SURPRISE that I did go back to the future. Or the present. I'd hoped that it was Jesus's miracle that I was delivered to my past, and I thought that it would stick, and that I wouldn't have to go back or forward or anywhere.

I wasn't even thinking about my life when I jumped. I was just sitting at my desk when next thing I knew I was back in St. Drogo's being mowed down by early morning workers who growled and hissed at me for standing in their way.

I was dizzy, flooded with confusion and nausea. I managed to reach a wall and leaned against it. Sting Ray Bob had told me how awful I'd feel coming back, but I'd thought he was exaggerating. I'd never suffered from hangovers and I'd been certain it would be the same with time travel, but not so. I sank to my haunches and retched, which cleared a path around me pronto.

I heard a familiar voice, but I couldn't look up. I slid onto my side. I heard someone groaning in pain and a distant part of me registered that the noise was coming from me, but I couldn't move. Drool snaked down my face, disguisting and sticky. I bit my hand to try to quell the nausea. I couldn't bear it. Could one die from nausea? But it wasn't nausea, it was time travel.

"We've got this," the voice said, and I felt myself being lifted up onto a stretcher. I was still in the fetal position, moaning, my eyes squeezed tight.

The man spoke again, but I couldn't make out what he said. I was lifted aloft and bumped along, every movement agonizing.

Doors slammed, and then Jaxen spoke. "It's okay, Sharps, you'll be okay. We're here for you."

Then darkness hugged me like a weighted blanket, and I floated away.

I woke in a hotel room with Jaxen, Janaelle, and Sting Ray Bob. The blinds were drawn and the three of them were talking in hushed tones.

From what I could see, the place looked swanky, cream and grey with touches of silver and coal. An IV needle bit into my elbow, tightly taped and pinching my skin. The room was cold as a butcher's locker, and I shivered and jerked. Was I having a fit? My legs spasmed uncontrollably, and my teeth were chattering like half a dozen jackhammers firing on all cylinders. I groaned, and the three turned towards me as if they were surprised I was still alive.

Sting Ray Bob rushed over, yanked the IV out, and handed the end to Jaxen who pumped it with a syringe. The shaking stopped almost instantly. Warmth flooded my body. I was parched, but the memory of the nausea was so strong I was reluctant to even swallow my saliva. Jaxen put a straw in my mouth and urged me to drink, but I twisted my face away.

"It's okay," he said. He put his hand on my shoulder, and then I knew it would be okay. Jaxen was there. I could trust him.

I took a small sip, and I swallowed just fine. There was no nausea, and I nearly cried with relief.

"Sorry it was so bad," Sting Ray Bob said. "The data on your tolerance levels didn't suggest this level of hyperemesis gravidarum. We've run more tests, and it won't happen next time."

I sat up slowly. "You're right, it won't. Because I'm not going back. There's no point. I tried. I went back and I tried. The only data, as you would put it, is that I'm an official loser. And the world's a terrible place. It's better for my kids that they don't live."

"You don't get to make that choice for them!" Janaelle shouted at me, and I was startled. She leaned in so close I could smell the sweetness of her chewing gum. That or she used the world's most citrusy mouthwash.

"You don't get to choose that for them!" she shouted again. "And the world will get better. It will! It always does. You think these are the worst of times? Everybody thinks that, no matter when they are born. You thinking it doesn't make you special. And you do have the potential to change. We all do. That's the whole point of this experiment, you idiot, to prove that we can change the future by going back and fixing our mistakes. We've been looking for a successful candidate for years and Norman said it was you and I believed him!"

I couldn't believe it, but the gothic little bitch was crying. I looked at Jaxen, and he shrugged. "Norman was wrong," I said shortly. "Believe me, I've thought about it from every angle. Sorry, I let you down, but it's what I do. I thought I could do it. But just like everything else in my life, I failed."

"Why don't you talk us through it?" Jaxen handed a box of tissue to Janaelle and then sat on the edge of my bed, rubbing my shoulder.

His warmth and tender kindness shot through me like an AK47 pumping into my chest at close range. Tears filled my eyes and spilled down my cheeks. Before I knew it, I was howling and snot was flowing down my face like a waterfall.

"I'm so sorry!" I cried, and Jaxen pulled me in for a hug. I grabbed him and sobbed my heart out. "I tried so hard. I really did. Nobody could have tried harder. I knew my limitations and I thought *fake it till you make it,* but I didn't make it and it broke me. It's my fault. I know that. And," I pulled away from Jaxen and turned to Janaelle, "and you're right—it isn't up to me to choose, but I can't change things."

"We know you did your best, buddy." Jaxen handed me the box of tissues, and it took a fistful to mop things up. "We watched the live feed. You did try."

"You watched me?" Just when I thought no further humiliation was possible, I sank to a new low.

"Of course we did. We thought you knew that. You gave up any right to privacy when you let us staple you with implants," Sting Ray Bob pointed out, and I shrank back.

"What else did you 'staple' into me?"

"Nothing," Jaxen said. He glared at Sting Ray Bob, who shrugged.

"For starters, the nausea won't happen again," Janaelle said. "So forget about that. And we'll help you by brainstorming some actionable alternatives for when you go back. We've got time. You need to stay in bed for two weeks to heal."

"Two weeks!" I was horrified. "I can't stay in bed for two weeks! And anyway, I told you, I've thought about it from every single angle."

"Not with us on board you haven't." She was confident, and I closed my eyes. I was trapped.

"Can we at least get me some food for starters?" I said rudely as I lay down and pulled the blankets over me.

"Of course, buddy," Jaxen grinned. "Your wish is our command. Meanwhile, we'll log in algorithms and get started on a plan for success strategies. You aren't alone. Go team!"

That didn't make me feel better. I was sick of the whole thing. I'd made a mistake messing with time travel, and now these guys had me wired up like a turkey and I was beholden to them, a prisoner of their experiment.

Sting Ray Bob flashed me a comm:

QuikDine menus.

I flipped through the options. "Fettuccine Alfredo with garlic bread. Extra cheese. Extra butter. Three times root beer, tall bottles. Vanilla ice cream with hot chocolate sauce. The last meal of a dying man."

"Fats and carbs are good choices," Jaxen said. "But you aren't dying, buddy." He turned to Janaelle. "Maybe we should give him a comedown dose of valium?"

"No! Mood enhancers will render the results of the experiment null and void. He'll be fine, but Sting Ray Bob, I'm thinking you should give him a shot of sodium thiopental. We need him emotionally unpolluted to gather information."

"That's truth serum! I'm not stupid!" I shouted at her, and she put her hands on her hips—her rather broad hips, I noticed, for such a tiny woman. Mmm, nice boobs and shapely arms. I wondered what her legs were like under those long skirts, and then I remembered they were steel from the hips down. One leg or two? I couldn't recall but regardless, the thought was arousing. I got a huge stiffie and I shifted, hoping that no one would notice, but Jaxen did and he grinned. "From what I've heard, a very worthwhile experience," he said quietly, and I hoped Janaelle hadn't heard him.

"Come on, Sharps," Janaelle said, taking the syringe from Sting Ray Bob. "Let's get to the bottom of why you think you are so unlikeable and such a loser. It all goes back to perceptions of the self, and I'm guessing you had issues with your father."

"Jaxen's got a Ph.D. in psychiatry," she added, settling into an armchair in the corner of the room with a large portable comm in her lap. "While you guys go hunting around Sharps's damaged childhood, I'll run algorithms of potential action scenarios that we'll marry to your findings. You make him want to return, and I'll give him a map of what to do when he gets there."

"You can't make me go back!" I shouted, and I turned over and refused to look at them. I heard them whispering, but I couldn't make out what they said. The food arrived, and I decided to eat first and fight later. I was so ravenous I hoovered off the entire order in fifteen minutes.

"What do you want to know?" I asked Jaxen, finishing off one of my root beers. "Let's just do this. I know you won't leave me in peace until you get what you want."

He dove right in. "What's your first memory?"

"I don't know. Learning to skate I guess. I wanted to learn

to skate, but my father didn't know how. So he asked the neighbour to teach me, down at the arena."

"How old were you?"

"Um, three or five I think. I don't know. But I remember the skates. I loved them, and I loved being on the ice. My father came to watch me. He was drunk and he shouted at me, 'Look at you, jello legs, you call that skating? Look at your friends, they're much better than you but wait you don't have any friends!'"

"Why would he be so cruel? And what did the neighbour say?"

"He told me to ignore my dad, but it was hard. Admit it, Wally, you're not cut out for athletics."

"Wally? Who's Wally?"

"Wally was me. It's what my father called me. I haven't thought about it for years. He hated the name Mother had chosen for me. He said it sounded like I was a tool in the shed and not the sharpest one either. You can imagine the jokes. And even Mr. Williamson mocked me about it. It is a stupid name. Maybe Mother deserved what I did to her just for giving me such a ridiculous name."

"To get back on track, if you'll pardon the pun, you stopped skating?"

"My father took me home after my tenth lesson or so. He stood me in front of a full-length mirror, and he said, 'Be honest now, does that look like a sporting kind of guy? You're too emotionally weak, son, useless. I've seen you, with your head buried in a book. You're a dreamer. Thank Christ the legislation will come soon, axing books, music, and faggot theatre. We need to attend to the serious things in life. We need hard workers. Work is the engine around which life is built. We'll help you find your place, Sharps, although god knows it won't be easy.'"

"Sounds like a gem, your father," Jaxen said sympathetically, and I nodded. "There was no talking to him. And when I annoyed him, which was often, he'd make me stand in front of the mirror and say, 'You see that guy? Is there anything likeable about that guy? You're right, there isn't but we're going to change that, aren't we, Sharps? We're going to bring that guy into line.'"

"And how did he do that?"

"He got hold of psych evaluation tests from somewhere, personality tests. He said that the tests would identify traits of weakness and that he could train them out of me. Math and logic questions, drawings, measurements in spontaneity, risk aversion, and peer acquiescence. You want to know the results? He concluded I was a daydreamer with my head in the clouds. He said I had no talent for anything useful in this world. I showed an aptitude for the written word, which wasn't even on his totem pole of worthy achievements."

"Then what?"

"Mirror exercises. What do I see? A loser. An unlovable loser. My father's theory was that it would snap me out of my funk and get me behaving like other boys. He said he never wanted a boy, but I was like half a girl which was even worse."

"How weren't you behaving like the other boys?" Jaxen asked, and I shrugged.

"I don't know exactly. Father disappeared when I was ten. He went to work and never came home. Mother filled out a missing person's report, but nothing came of it. He didn't withdraw any money before he left, nor did he use his bank accounts afterwards. There were no sightings of him, and he took no belongings. His employers didn't understand it either. Mother was happy. She said he was a sex maniac and she was tired of him constantly screwing her literally and emotionally. She said men should just stick it in a hole in the wall for all the emotion and respect they show for the act. Oh my god. The Lucky Hole! How disgusting! Argh!"

I heaved, and out came the fettuccine Alfredo, the bread, and the root beer. Sting Ray Bob grabbed a trash can and shoved it under my face.

"The Lucky Hole," I explained, once I was composed and had rinsed out my mouth, "is the only way I could have sex. Oh my god, Mother was even worse to me than my father. She ruined my sex life!" I shouted.

Jaxen looked thoughtful. "You suffered a lot of damage, and your anger runs deep. So when things became chaotic and uncertain, your go-to solution to control the situation was to clean. In the most extreme way, your brain saw killing your family as tidying up."

"I was protecting them," I shouted.

"I believe you honestly thought you were. How do you feel now having told us all this?"

I rubbed my face. "Humiliated. Embarrassed. Disgusted. My father was right. I saw the truth on the other side when I went back. I'm nothing. Nobody. Worthless. I couldn't change a thing. Maybe I should go back and kill myself, only I bet I wouldn't have the guts. If I go back, can you kill me in that time zone? Can you reach through and kill me? That way my family will live. You're right, Janaelle. They don't deserve to die. And so what if everyone knows I failed? I wanted to control the narrative, but I just proved myself to be more of a freak than ever."

"You need to stop thinking now." Janaelle came over. "Sting Ray Bob, why don't you and Jaxen go to the lab and start correlating alternative action plans for when Sharps does go back"

"I'm not going back," I objected weakly, but they weren't listening. Jaxen and Sting Ray Bob gathered equipment, and Sting Ray Bob took the IV out of my arm. "Between you and me," he whispered, "your parents were a real piece of work. You deserved so much better."

His words helped clear some of the shame away, but my self-loathing was a suffocating strait jacket and I wished I could bang my head against a wall until I bled, just to create an opening for the blackness inside me to escape. Because I couldn't get away from it.

I got out of bed and walked over to the window, opening the blinds and looking down at St. Polycarp. "The world is so rotten," I said to Janaelle. "There's nothing left to live for."

"There is this," she said, and I turned to face her. She had unbuttoned the bodice of her long gown, and she stood before me, shapely and perfect, her steel legs like an artist's sculptures. She looked at me, waiting.

I laughed, but she didn't flinch. "You think you can help me have sex, no Lucky Hole style? And even if you do, once, then what?"

"I told you, stop thinking." She moved in close, and I smelled that sweetness again. And her lips looked so soft and her breath was so sweet and pure that I leaned in and my cock was hard but I didn't even care—all I wanted to do was kiss her. I wanted to ask her if she had sex with all her experiments and didn't Jaxen care? Weren't they a couple? But she kissed me so hard and so deep that I forgot the questions I had in my mind. It turned out that the missionary position had quite a lot going for it. I loved how she wrapped those beautiful steel legs around me, so cool and smooth.

We lay on the floor afterwards and Janaelle stroked my head. "I can't fix those years of self-hatred," she said. "Your mother felt like that about herself and so did your father. And they would have had their reasons too—everybody does. But sometimes, stripping it naked and looking it in the eye is the first step towards taming the beast. You reacted to how they made you feel, according to their feelings, based on their perceived reality of life. If you'd had a brother or a sister, their interpretation of your parents could be the complete opposite to yours and that's not your fault."

"Please can I not think about any of this for a moment? I actually feel marginally happy, and I'd like to enjoy it. I'd love to sleep now, really sleep, and not think about anything except how good I feel."

"Of course," she said. She sat up and I grabbed her arm.

"Janaelle..." I wanted to ask her if this was pity sex to get me back on track, but I couldn't find the words. She stroked my cheek. "I do like you," she said. "I did, from the start. And I don't mean when Norman told us about you. I noticed you on The Eye and I felt drawn to you. I felt a kinship. I don't know. So no, this wasn't me trying to fix the situation to make you go along with our plan. Which is your plan too, even if you don't feel that right way now."

"But will we...?" Ever see each other again, or see each other at all? I wanted to ask. She leaned and kissed me and my cock sprang to action and before I could think any further about any of it, we were at it again. Her skin was so soft and smooth and she smelled like lilacs and peaches and I lost myself inside her.

Once we were done, she said, "I guess that answers your question?" She laughed and got up. "I'm going to shower. I'm glad you didn't find my legs off-putting."

"Everything about you is stunning and exquisite," I said, and I meant it. I heard her turn on the shower, and my happiness left me like a sheet yanked from my body. What was going to happen next?

Because I had just added a whole new dimension of things I would lose. And never recover from.

30. HEAD OFFICE CHIMES IN

"THE COMPUTER CANNOT COMPUTE," Jaxen announced when he and Sting Ray Bob arrived back at the hotel room.

"What do you mean?" Janaelle asked, and a frown cut a vertical crevice down the centre of her forehead.

"Sharps's journey back changed things. But we don't know what changed. There's no way to track the variables. We can change Sharps's arrival time, but we can't help him plan anything."

"Great." Janaelle sank down into a chair. "So there's nothing we can do."

"Head Office has a suggestion."

Head Office? This was the first I'd heard of Head Office.

"OctoOne said we need to change his timeline."

"OctoOne? Will someone please tell me what's going on?"

"Need to know, and you do not need to know, Sharps. But we've been advised that if you go back on the day you killed your family, you can perhaps change things by not going into work. That way you'll avoid pushing Ava down the stairs and that will save her and Adwar. You must go to Jazza's place instead. And," Janaelle looked off into the distance and fell silent for a moment. I reached over and prodded her. "And what?"

"And you have to save Jazza. Jazza is not allowed to die. Ava and Jazza both have to live."

"Why?"

"They just do."

I was getting annoyed by this game of cat and mouse, and Janaelle saw it. "Listen Sharps. You need to save your kids. You know you do. You hate the world as it is, but you love your kids and if you do this, things *are* going to change. You may not believe this, but you were a great dad."

"I was?" Tears filled my eyes and spilled down my cheeks. "Really? You're just saying that."

"Nope. You were gentle and loving and kind and caring. You loved them more than life itself, and now you have to save them. Save them so they can be a part of the new world."

I saw my babies' faces. Bax's narrow, earnest little face, his fine features, and Sophie's wide brown eyes, her little button nose. "Sure," I said. "But..."

"But what?"

I looked at Janaelle. "I won't have you." I said bluntly, not caring that Sting Ray Bob and Jaxen were there. "I want you."

"Not part of the plan," Janaelle said. The sliding doors of her face closed, and she stood up. "You need to save your kids, Sharps. This is bigger than you and me. You can't be selfish. Who knows, maybe there's a way that we'll connect. I guess we'll see."

"You can't mean that!" I jumped up and grabbed her, and she didn't flinch. She looked right at me, and I knew she could see the desperate panic in my eyes. "I just found you," I said. "You're the one for me. You and me. You know it, too."

"Sting Ray Bob, please sit Sharps down, hook him up, and adjust the time." Her voice lacked any emotion. "I'm leaving now. Sharps, I'm not sorry we took a bend in the road. I'm not. And in case you think I don't care, you're wrong. I care. But like I said, this is bigger than you and me."

She left, and I turned to Jaxen. "Help me," I said, and he shook his head.

"No can do, buddy, sorry about that."

I was about to turn to Sting Ray Bob to beg for his help, but I felt a sharp prick in my neck and I crumpled into Jaxen's arms.

"Gotta feel a bit sorry for this guy," I heard Jaxen say, and then I saw the Hockney man coming for me. I screamed and ran down a long tunnel of white light, but he was gaining on me—man, that sucker could run. "No pain, no gain!" he yelled as he jumped me and tackled me from behind. "You're going to save the world! We're topping up your immune system; you might feel a small level of discomfort."

I wanted to tell him that I didn't care about saving the world. All I wanted was to taste Janaelle's sweetness and kiss her so deeply that I lost my mind. An agonizing pain seared my body, and I heard a high-pitched howling—me, as the flesh was ripped from my bones. *A small level of discomfort?* What an ass that guy was.

When I woke, the room was dark. I was afraid to move. What new horrors awaited? Nausea or pain? A broken heart. I sat up slowly. I felt good. Rejuvenated. Strong and powerful. I took a deep breath. No nausea. I stood up, walked over to the window, and pulled the blinds apart. It was night, and the city sparkled below me. I was reminded of the first night I went to Celeste's apartment. How naïve I had been. How cocksure and full of myself. Fake it till you make it. I'd thought I had a game plan when really I'd had a shotgun in my mouth the whole time.

I turned to the mirror and inspected my body. Ship shape. I actually looked great, more defined than my toughest gym periods. I ran my hands down my legs, up my back, around my ribcage. All good.

There was a note on the dressing table.

You're set to go back to the day of. There won't be any nausea on re-entry. You're booked into this hotel for the next week. In case you've lost track, you've been back for seven days. You healed more quickly than we anticipated, so you don't need us anymore, but you STILL NEED TO REST. We loaded your CashExchange. Stay out of trouble.

That was it. Nothing from Janaelle. I looked over at the pile of clothes on the chair. Jeans, running shoes, a hoodie, and T-shirt. I pulled them on. I had to get out of the room. They were nuts if they thought I was going to stay in that prison all alone. I stuffed the money and the fob into my pocket.

I hailed a Taxiio on the street and gave the driver the address. The Bar None, Norman and Knox's stomping grounds.

On the way over, I thought about Janaelle. What choice did she have? I understood that she couldn't be with a man who had killed his children. But I was trying to fix things, undo what I had done. I was angry with her. She had all kinds of technology at her disposal, surely she could think of a way for us to be together? She wasn't trying hard enough. Why had she started what she couldn't finish? I had no answers to all the questions whirling around my brain.

31. THE DREAM TEAM REUNITED

THE BAR NONE WAS PACKED, bodies pushing against each other in waves, heat rising despite the air conditioner. I saw Shasta behind the bar and Knox talking to her, grinning.

"Hey guys," I said. I thought I saw a wary look come into Knox's eyes, but I didn't care. "How's it going?"

"Shane!" Shasta looked delighted to see me, and I realized that was why Knox looked equally as miserable at my arrival. He didn't want to have to compete for her attention. "Where've you been?" she asked. "I get off in a couple of hours. You guys want to do something?"

Knox looked annoyed, like I was raining on his parade. "Sure," I said, more to annoy him than anything. "I'll have a beer, Shaz, lager on tap, whatever."

She poured me a drink, and I motioned to her to pour one for Knox, too. He took it grudgingly. "So what have you guys been up to since the forest?" I asked, and they both looked blank.

"St. Adrian's! We went to St. Adrian's together."

Shasta nodded and looked away while Knox looked very confused. "Not us, buddy. You are beyond confused." He laughed. "Man, you were a mess the last time we saw you, on the floor."

"I'm fine. Better. You don't remember anything? We were there together, remember? The long walk with Norman, the shower, the robot in the underground lab, the grilled cheese and tomato soup, Janaelle?"

They both shook their heads. Right. They had been erased. I sighed.

"When last did you see me?" I asked, and they both looked confused.

"At The Barking Frog, buddy," Knox said. "You fell over. You look way better, by the way. You actually look kind of healthy. What've you been up to?"

"Not much. Just hanging out around the St. Drogo's, *ha ha,* living the high life, long story."

"What's at St. Drogo's apart from Blowflies?" Shasta leaned towards me.

"Nothing, forget it. Knox, you been working?"

Knox shook his head. "It's like so dead out there right now. I'm super strapped for cash. Which reminds me…" He shook his head like he was trying to get water out of his ears. "You've got cash, right buddy?"

"Not a whole lot," I lied. "But enough to get us another round."

"And enough to buy us some weed?" A gleam came into Knox's eye. "I've been starved! Hey, how about we go and score us some of the good stuff and then come back here and get Shaz?"

"I can do that," I replied. Heck, it wasn't my money. What did I care? I had nothing better to do with my time. My heart was in shreds. I hated getting stoned, but if it would help me forget Janaelle for a moment, I was game. I wanted to get wasted beyond all recognition.

"And some coke," Shasta said eagerly. "Just a bit. Come on, Shane!"

She smiled brightly, and I nodded. "Okay."

"We'll see you back here," Knox said to Shasta. He downed the last of his beer and jumped off the bar stool.

I followed him out onto the street, and he got us a Taxiio. "Corner of Duchess and Queen," he told the driver. "Step on the gas!"

"That's Blowfly land," I objected, and Knox waved a hand in dismissal. "We'll be fine."

We got out and walked up an alleyway, and Knox headed towards a man in a red cocktail dress who was standing in the shadows of a streetlight.

I'd never been so deep in a Blowfly zone before. I scanned the area, convinced we'd be mugged at any moment, but there was no one out. It was eerily quiet. The fake trees and the park benches were covered with graffiti, but otherwise, it looked like the rest of the world. I wasn't sure what I had been expecting.

I handed Knox a couple of hundred bucks, and he and the man had a quiet exchange. We turned to leave, but as I turned towards the street we had come from, Knox grabbed my arm. "Let's go through the park that way," he said. "Shortcut. And we can get a head start."

He sat down on a bench and fished a straw out of his pocket. "Straw bag," he laughed. "Trouble with doing it this way is you can do too much. *Whazza!* I'd better leave some for Shaz or she'll kill me." He snorted and threw his head back and howled at the night sky. I wondered what I was doing with him. Such a dick. I'd made a mistake coming to see him and Shasta. I had counted them as friends, but they were just random party people, strangers. I got up to leave, and next thing, Knox was in front of me, in my face, breathing hard. "Where are your car keys?" he asked. His breath was sour, old bourbon, weed, unbrushed teeth.

"What?"

"Your car. You've got money in it. I can't remember how I know, but I know. And I know something else, too: you're that guy who killed his family. There's a reward out for you. But I won't turn you in if you give me the money in your car. Fair's fair. I could have turned you in at the bar and got the reward but I didn't. To be honest, I didn't think I'd ever see you again, and then when you showed up tonight, I had to think fast. I guess I should have asked you where your car was and have us go right there." He looked around and seemed to be thinking about the mistakes he had made. I immediately tried to make a run for it, but he grabbed my hoodie and yanked me back. "You've got some nerve, walking around when you did what you did. I won't turn you in. I just want your casheroo."

WTF? I tried to play it cool. "Knox, buddy, you're losing it. I've got no idea what you're talking about. Let's go and find Shasta and have some fun. I just want to have some fun. There's no money in my car and I didn't kill anyone. You're stoned and messed up."

"I need the money!" he yelled, and then he grabbed me and punched me in the gut. He was pretty feeble, and I came back at him with a violence that surprised us both.

"Don't touch me!" I yelled. "Who do you think you are? Loser! You're such a fucking loser!" I pounded him, pushing him to the ground and grabbing him around the neck. He thrashed around. I should have stopped myself there, but I couldn't. I'd lost Janaelle, I had nothing left in this world worth living for, and now this guy wanted to pull this kind of shit? I squeezed harder and harder and I yelled and spat in his face and suddenly I was still shaking him but he was limp and heavy. *Shit.* I'd killed him. I hadn't realized I was that strong or that it was that easy to kill a man with my bare hands.

I jumped to my feet. The dealer had seen me with him. So had Shasta and the Taxiio driver. The entire world had seen me with Knox. I was up to my eyeballs in boiling water. *Shit, shit, shit.*

There was only one thing to do.

I had to jump immediately. I had to go back and fix this thing. I turned and ran towards St. Drogo's.

32. THE SECOND JUMP

I KNEW I WAS JUMPING TOO EARLY, but I had no choice. I landed in my kitchen, wearing my suit, my hair slicked back, ready to face my shitty day. Right. I'd hit Celeste the previous night and she was making breakfast, her face covered in makeup. The kitchen was a mess and I was in no position to say anything. I had a meeting later with Ava, and Jazza would text to say he was sorry, and I'd take it from there.

"I'm so sorry about last night," I apologized to my wife and my son. "Bax, what Daddy did was very wrong. And he's very sorry. Please, my boy, forgive me."

Bax gave me a nod of sorts and darted a look at Celeste. I was surprised by his allegiance. I thought he was my guy. Didn't he see what a loser Celeste was? I hated myself for pitting myself against my wife for my four-year-old's attention, but he'd turned on me for one mistake.

"It's okay, sweetie," Celeste told me. "He'll be fine. Go and do your day. We'll make things lovely for when you get home." I hoped she'd clean up the mess properly and I wanted to comment, but I bit my tongue. Knowing her, she'd get the OpalineCleanShines in, even though she knew I thought those robots did a shitty job.

I sat in traffic on the way to work and thought about my life.

The girl of my dreams had sent me back to save my kids, thereby making it likely I'd never see her again. How could my life as Sharps Barkley, husband and father, ever intersect with hers, Janaelle, leader of the underground resistance, residing in St. Adrian's?

Regardless, I had to fix things. I'd inadvertently turned into a killing machine, and I had to find the command undo key and sort my shit out. How had it even happened? Was I born a killer or had life pushed me too far? Could I blame genetics? Was this my father's fault? Perhaps I could change things. Janaelle thought I could, so I would certainly try.

Head Office had instructed me to go to Jazza's place, but I had a better plan in mind. I wouldn't kill anyone myself, but that didn't mean someone wouldn't die.

I met with Ava. I pretended to study her wall screens and spreadsheets while I waited for the fire alarm to go off. I sat through her yelling at me over the alarm while the building emptied. I waited patiently, wanting to hit her stupid vapid face, and I followed her to get our coats. Then I ran down the stairs with her and out into the crowd that had gathered outside in the park, waiting to be let back in.

I watched as Adwar emerged from the building. All the while Ava shouted at me and everyone saw it, and I took it, a slight smile on my face.

"What the hell's wrong with you?" Ava yelled. "Do you think you'll have Mr. Williamson's protection? He's on his way out!" She raised her voice even louder, and heads were turning towards us. I waited for my portable comm to buzz, and when it did, I grabbed it.

> By the time u read this, I'll be dead by my own hand. Sorry, Sharps. I couldn't face it. I let u down. I let me down. Please get the SSOs. I don't want to rot here or have my furballs eat my face. Sorry, buddy. Best Wishes.

I called #Emr. Ava was still shouting at me but even she heard the words "EMR, what is your emergency?" and the colour drained from her face. Maybe she thought I was calling them about her harassing me.

"I think my friend might have hurt himself," I said, trying to infuse my tone with fear and panic. "I got a flash. He's at 767 Marquis Way, Kingston and Johns. Apartment 302. Please send someone. It might be nothing, but I'm worried for his safety."

I ended the call. "I've got to go," I said to Ava and she nodded, for once at a loss for words.

"Where's Jazza?" I heard her shout over my shoulder, but I ignored her.

I had realized something. I didn't owe Jazza anything. He had set me up. I needed him to die so he'd leave the suicide note. It was the only way to clear my name. OctoOne, whoever the hell that was, wanted him alive, but I needed him dead.

I'd collect the suicide note with the police as my witnesses and my name would be cleared. That Ava! She'd be eating humble pie very soon, having to admit I was innocent and the guy she worked so closely with had stolen all the money. She'd be implicated, not me! She'd be banished to the Farms. And I'd track Janaelle down. I had figured out how to find Janaelle while Ava was shouting at me. I would find her through Norman, the rage room guy. I'd find him at my usual spot; he had been there the last time, and he'd lead me to her. I had it all figured out. And, with my name clear, I'd leave Celeste, prove she was an unfit mother and a drunk, and Janaelle and I would live with my kids and raise them with good values. Who knows, maybe even Mother would be a part of that. I'd like that. I'd prove myself to be a good boy, a good man. A good son, a good father. Janaelle had said I was a good father, and she had no reason to lie.

The SSOs were at Jazza's place when I arrived. Two officers took me aside, and I tried to stop myself from being too cheerful and chatty. The one guy was bald as an egg; the other was the exact opposite with an extravagant mullet.

"Mr. Barkley?" I nodded.

"We've got some bad news. We found a suicide note, and we've got some bad news."

I forced a solemn sad expression on my face. "Is he gone?" I asked, a tremor in my voice. The officers exchanged a glance.

"What's going on?" Things suddenly didn't seem that simple. Why weren't they telling me about Jazza? "What happened?" *Oh god.* Jazza pinned the thievery on me. I was going down after all. There was no salvation. I grabbed the officer by the arm. "Tell me what's going on."

"There's no easy way to do this," Mr. Mullet said, and I wanted to hit him. "Do you have any close family we can call?"

"My wife, Celeste." I pulled out my portable comm and rang Celeste, but it went to voice-mail. I went to leave a message, but the officer took my comm and hung up.

"What the hell?" I was incensed. "Give me that." But then it occurred to me that something was very wrong. Why hadn't Celeste called me about the furnace and Baxter's tooth? I stared at the detective.

"He killed your family, Mr. Barkley."

"What? Who did?"

"Jazza Frings. We found his note when we got here and we called it in, but unfortunately we were too late."

"I don't understand a thing you're saying. What note?"

The SSOs exchanged another glance, and I grabbed one by the shoulder and spun him around. "Stop messing with me! What happened?"

"Here's the note." The detective held out a Police Services CrystalFlashDrive, and I took it from him and read the note.

Sharps. I thought about it very carefully. I thought maybe they deserved to live their lives because it wasn't their fault. But I just got so sick and tired of hearing about you and your perfect life. You deserve to lose everything.

I'll bullet point it for you since you've got the attention span of a gnat.

• It was your idea to steal the money. I went along with you because I was desperate to be your friend. You knew

I'd take any level of friendship you offered and I did. I hated myself for it.

• It's in a bank account in your name. The statements are all on your kitchen table at home.

What the hell was he talking about?

He gave the money to Ava and her army. I didn't want to read any more, but I had to.

• You could have made me Bax's godfather, but you didn't. Or Sophie. You never invited me to their christenings or birthdays. You were ashamed of me. I was good to score games and shit for you, but you never took me home. I was your slum buddy. Remember what you said to me? Jazza, my boy, you know you need me! You wouldn't have a job without me. You said that the day they promoted you. But Ava knew I was the brains. She knew and Mr. Williamson knew and you knew too, and I was never given any credit.

• Have you ever had your brain scoured? No, you have not. You have no idea what it does to a person. It changed me, Sharps, and you never even noticed or cared because all you wanted was the money.

• There are things about Celeste you don't know. You know how she loves money, but you don't know what else she loves.

• Ava will flay you and hang you out to dry.

Best Wishes, Jazza Frings

33. DOING HELL IN PRESENT TIME

I WAS STUNNED. I COULDN'T SPEAK. I turned to Mr. Mullet, waiting for him to tell me the entire situation was as crazy and stupid as his hair. What the fuck had gone wrong? And that's when I realized the truth. I changed Jazza's trajectory with the first jump. I'd done this to myself. That was why OctoOne had instructed me to go straight to Jazza's apartment. And I'd thought I'd known better.

I stared at the note. "I didn't steal any money," I whispered. "I didn't know about the money. He did it. He's setting me up. It wasn't meant to be this way."

The SSO officer cleared his throat. "We'll be looking into that," he said gently. "But your family is dead, Mr. Barkley. Your mother is waiting for you at the station. You don't want to go home. They're taking your family to the morgue. Your mother will take care of you. Jazza also killed a woman by the name of Florence Garcia, do you know her?"

"She's our nanny. Oh god. Not her too." But then his words registered, and I shivered like a dog in a hailstorm. "No! Not Mother! I can't see Mother! What about Mr. Williamson and Mummy? His wife, I mean."

"They've been contacted."

I leaned against the roof of the cop car. It was snowing prettily, although I wasn't in the mood to admire how atmospheric it all was. Big white flakes settled on me, and I welcomed the cold, turning my face up to the sky. My mouth opened in a silent scream, and I pounded the car with the palm of my hand, slapping it again and again, not feeling the stinging burn. And then a thought occurred to me.

This was only jump number two. My goose wasn't cooked! I still had a few aces up my sleeve. I just had to let time play out.

I would see Janaelle again! I deserved real love, with Janaelle. And on the third jump, I'd come back and save my babies and Janaelle and I would end up together. This was all temporary. I was still in the game.

"What happens now?" I turned to Mr. Mullet, who was standing next to me. I was exhausted. Regardless of what had happened, I wanted to go home, chew a couple of Celeste's sleeping pills, and escape. I wanted to be alone. They'd taken my family away. I'd pretend they were all out shopping, per-fectly fine, and coming home soon.

I groaned, and the officer laid a sympathetic hand on my shoulder. "I know, it's devastating. We're very sorry for your loss."

"Losses, plural," I wanted to tell him. *Oh shit.* I had no way of calculating how the future present and the consequential past would be affected. What would I find on the third jump?

But first, I needed to play out the current time until the clock ran dry.

I descended into hell. They made me stay with Mother, who seemed baffled as to how to deal with me. The police made me see a doctor, and thankfully, he numbed me. Pills for the day and pills for the night. Integratron, while sorry for my personal loss, were investigating the theft. And none of it pointed to Jazza. I had signed off on every single thing. Mr. Williamson and his wife, Mummy and Daddy to me no longer, refused to speak to me. Mrs. Williamson was sedated up to her eyeballs while Daddy, they said, had lost the will to live. From the moment he heard the news, he stared into space, unmoving. He had, however, said one thing: "I should never have trusted that boy with my princess. He was worse than a Blowfly."

"I'll take you to your room," Mother had said, when the SSOs delivered me into her care. She gave me tea and toast and watched me take my meds. "I knew you'd be back one day, Sharps. Because you're a weak man. I tried so hard to make a feminist of you. Make you into a man. But you were so flawed, just like your father. He came back too, you know."

"Wha...?" My tongue felt thick in my mouth, fuzzy and fur-coated. My eyes were closing and it was hard to stay awake.

She nodded. "I never told you. He left us. He ran away but he came back and said he was sorry. Sorry! As if that made everything all right. He just as well could have said, 'Oh, right, I backed over you with a truck and broke every bone in your body but I'm sorry!' Apologies are for losers."

"When?" I tried to keep the conversation on track.

"Six months after he left. He had committed a fatal error by leaving. There was no way to make it right. What kind of man does that? Just leaves?"

"Wha... happen...?" Wow, these meds were strong. I hoped I'd remember this conversation in the morning.

Mother shrugged. "It was easy actually. He vanished without a trace and then he reappeared without a trace and then he vanished equally easily again. It was the only thing he ever did that I appreciated, being so traceless. I exterminated him, and no one knew any better. You were at camp. Remember camp?"

I remembered all right. I hated it. Real life camp. The pits. Covered in black fly bites, I pierced my thumb with a fish hook and needed stitches, and let's not forget the poison ivy. I was sent home early by the camp nurse.

"I didn't like it."

"Of course you didn't. But fortuitously, your father turned up while you were away. Talk about good timing!" She sighed. "I guess I'll have to organize the funerals. The Williamsons are a mess. They aren't even coming back from Real Life Florida for the burials. I'll take care of it, like I take care of everything.

We'll figure out what to do with your house. I gather you'll be facing prison time for the money."

I nodded my head. "Be sent to a Farm, I guess."

I knew Integratron would back both Daddy and Ava. It was all on me. Jazza was irrelevant to Integratron, and Ava had stood up for him, saying Jazza hadn't known a thing, that he had snapped after being scoured. For someone who hated him, Ava was spectacularly gutted by Jazza's suicide. EmoHealthExecs at Integratron had sent her to a Grief Counselling Spa, and I had no way to contact her, not that I'd have had anything to say to her.

And now, here was Mother, telling me she killed my father. I'd been doomed from the start. I cradled my heavy head in my arms. Janaelle would know what to do. I had to get back to her.

"I'm not sorry I killed you, Mother," I said, and she looked confused.

"You didn't, I'm here," she said gently.

"You'll see." I pushed myself to stand. "You'll see. I'm going to lie down. You'll see, Mother."

"Oh, Sharps," she said, sadly, her face old and tired. "Do you know that we picked you out? You were handpicked. Well, I picked you. I admit you weren't your father's first choice."

I turned and looked at her. "What?"

"Never mind. Go and lie down and try to sleep."

I went to my room, leaning against the wall the whole way. I had to remember this. But how? I had to write it down.

I scrabbled around in my room for a pen and piece of paper. I couldn't find anything to write on, but there was a pencil in the back of a drawer. I pulled my bed away from the wall and wrote a note where Mother wouldn't see it.

MOTHER IS NOT MY MOTHER!

FATHER NEVER WANTED ME! FIND OUT MORE!

Then I lay down and waited for time to pass.

34. THINGS GET JUMBLED

"WELL, THAT WAS FUCKED UP," I said to the gang when I got back, or forward, or whatever. They'd been right—the jump was fine. There was no nausea, but Sting Ray Bob found internal bleeding when he scanned my brain and Jaxen was pissed off with me. "Why did you jump so soon?" He snapped at me.

"You know why. Because I killed Knox. And I know, I shouldn't have gone to see him, but I was lonely." I looked at Janaelle pointedly. "You guys left me alone. But what the hell, Jazza killed my family. I had no idea. Did you know?"

"Of course we didn't," Janaelle sounded short. "We would have told you. We're on your side, but who knows what side you're on, Sharps. You keep screwing up. You were supposed to go to Jazza's place first. Why didn't you?"

"I'm sorry. I had no idea what would happen if I didn't go and see him. I thought I had a great plan figured out. I tried really hard. And I found a vital clue to my past." Darn it. What was it? "Hang on," I said, screwing up my face. "It has to do with Mother." I closed my eyes, but it was a blank. "Oh shit. It was important. I know it was. Didn't you guys record me when I was over there?"

"No. The capacitor failed because we weren't ready. You weren't supposed to jump when you did, remember?"

Jaxen stood up and walked around. I could see he wasn't about to forgive me any time soon. I was back in the hotel room and eating enough food for half a dozen people. "Look," I said, my mouth full, "there has to be a way around this. I've got three jumps left, right?"

"Maybe." Sting Ray Bob was still flipping through X-rays. "This time you're under house arrest until we get you healed. The way you're going, you'll last one more, tops. And given your failure rate, you're going to need more than one."

"Ease up on him," Janaelle said, and I looked at her gratefully. "Time travel is a bitch," she said. "We all know that." She chewed her lip and stared out the window.

"Do the cops know I killed Knox?"

"They do. Your mug shot is flashing on every optic nerve in the city on the hour. We'll have to disguise you the next time you go to St. Drogo's. What matters is that the device is still working. The diagnostics on that are sound, but your body is failing, Sharps. You lost ten pounds in your last jump."

"If all else fails, you can use time travel as the new weight loss schtick," I joked, but no one else thought it was funny. Losers.

And then it happened.

The lights went out. Not just in our room. The entire world rippled into darkness as if a dropcloth had fallen from the sky.

"What's going on?" Janaelle sounded annoyed. I couldn't see her until Jaxen turned on a flashlight, and it was great to see their faces. We moved into a comfort scrum, hearts pounding. At least mine was anyway.

"No news flashes," Jaxen said, tapping his temples, trying to jolt his optics into action. "Blackout." He shone the flashlight on Janaelle's face. "Do you think they went ahead without telling us?"

"I don't know. Looks like it. The fuckers!"

"What and who are you talking about?"

"The World Wide Warriors. It's an underground international group we subscribe to. The Eden Collective is St. Polycarp's chapter. There was a plan to shut down the satellites and restore the Earth to its natural rhythms and let it detox. Goodbye

Crystal Path; goodbye controlled weather patterns. No more fake digital life."

Panic pierced my heart like a sword. "But," I stammered, "what about my kids?" And where had I heard of the Eden Collective before? From Mother! Mother was involved in this. And Ava! This was all Ava's fault. The Eden Collective had published her book. She wasn't at any spa for grief—she was rebooting the world, using funds I had supposedly given her! "It's all Ava!" I yelled. "She's doing this! And Mother too! We have to send me back. I have to get Bax and Sophie to safety."

Sting Ray Bob cut me off. "Oh, so now you care about your kids," he said sarcastically.

"Of course I care! I thought I had three more tries! None of us knew that Jazza would kill them! And if you had known, you should have told me. Yeah, maybe I did want to come back to see Janaelle, but I didn't think it would mean leaving my kids forever! You know that's true! Oh, man!" I went to the window and stared down at the blackness. hit my head against the glass until Jaxen came and got me.

"Dude," he said, "we've got generators. We're ready. We still need you to follow through. And maybe this will instill a greater sense of urgency in you. You've been cavalier and all over the map. And," he cast a glance at Janaelle, "our leader dropping her panties didn't exactly keep you focused. Sorry," he said to Janaelle, "but it's the truth, and you know it."

Janaelle didn't rush in to tell him it was worth it. In fact, she kept distressingly silent.

"I don't regret that," I said.

Sting Ray Bob laughed. "Course you don't, buddy."

"Guys!" Janaelle reined us in. "We'll have to head back to St. Adrian's. It will be good for Sharps anyway. He can get some rest."

"But we'll have to bring him back again," Sting Ray Bob said. "He's programmed to jump at St. Drogo's. I can fix a lot of things, but not that." He sounded like a whiny little kid. I wanted to laugh at him, but it wasn't funny.

"We'll bring him back," Jaxen said.

As he spoke, the lights came on. "We're going back to St. Adrian's." Janaelle was firm. "We've got time. Sharps needs to rest and think. Sharps, we can try a form of hypnotherapy to try to reach what it was about your mother."

"Sure, as long as it's not the Hockney man digging around with a scalpel and chasing me." I was about to elaborate about what that meant, but it was too much effort.

"And there's another thing," I said while they were gathering up their equipment. "Jazza said there was something about Celeste I didn't know. He said it both times like it was really important."

"There's no way for us to know if you don't," Jaxen said, and I felt stupid, a kid who had asked the wrong question.

We drove back to St. Adrian's, and the world looked weird. The Disney chemiluminescence of our world had been snuffed out. The other-worldly glow that had characterized our life was no more. Generators were starting to kick in, but the world had lost its shiny all-powerful neon radiance. Cars moved slowly, and the city was like a scared beast, crouching in the shadows.

I hoped we wouldn't have to walk for two hours through the forest to get to the tree elevator, but I needn't have worried. We entered via a bridge under a railway, moving into shadow as an electronic gate slid open and closed silently behind us.

The others were silent as we unpacked the car, and the mood was grim. I was relieved when Norman came running out to the car and threw his arms around Janaelle. "I heard there were no casualties, but I was scared shitless," he said. "It wasn't supposed to do it now, was it?"

Janaelle shook her head. "And no one's said anything. Radio silence, although the communicators are wired for sound and good to go. None of us knows anything except that the

Vatican has been hacked to hell and gone."

"They should have told us." Norman was angry. "We voted on it. But some people always think they know best. We're not ready, none of us."

Janaelle shrugged. "We'd never be ready. Maybe it's better they went ahead." We heard the sound of thunder and looked at each other in alarm. Rain in the middle of the morning? It was unscheduled, unheard of. And thunder had long since been programmed out because it disturbed dogs and children and some old folks.

"Viewing tower," Janaelle shouted over the noise, and I followed the others at a run to the far end of the building. We crammed into a tight elevator. I, by all rights, should have been told to stay behind, but I wanted to know what was happening. It took forever for the elevator to get to the top, and I thought Knox would have imploded, if he'd been with us.

We were on the top of a tall smokestack, thankfully under cover, and we were squeezed closely together. By happenstance, I was next to Janaelle. I loved the feel of her body against mine. But what I didn't love was the landscape that lay before me. Day had turned to night. Lightning shot out from the black sky, and the rain was a torrent, a waterfall, relentlessly pummelling the earth. As we watched, rivers formed and swept through the forest, flattening the earth it left in its wake. Black clouds slammed across the sky, speeded up and wild, flashing their anger at having been held in check for so long.

"When will it stop?" I asked, and Norman shook his head.

"We have no idea. This is Real Life nature. We've got no control. And no way of tracking the data. Meteorology died when the satellite dishes were given control of the weather system."

"But surely you and the Warriors were ready for this?"

"We didn't think it would be as immediate," Jaxen admitted, "or this intense. The most widely held view was that the weather was in a holding pattern and would carry on doing what it had been guided it to do, but clearly we were very wrong."

I was about to ask about the Eden Collective and if she knew if Mother and Ava were in charge—and if Ava was actually OctoOne, which I was beginning to suspect, but she turned and left. "I'm going to try to contact Head Office again," she shouted, and I ran after her, leaving the others on the platform.

We got into the elevator and then Janaelle surprised me. She stepped up close, fast and smooth, and she kissed me. I grabbed her around the waist and pulled her as tight as I could. We kissed the whole way down, and what had seemed like a long trip up lost no time in getting to the ground.

35. PUT IT IN WRITING

"AH, SHARPS," SHE SAID WHEN WE GOT OUT and the elevator doors closed behind us, "bad timing. You and me. I don't know why, but I do like you. More than like you. Maybe it's chemistry. Maybe it's just your body and my body and no more than that. I've tried so hard to be more than a body, to conquer it, and not be a slave to its needs. But it hungers, aches, and tires. I hate it for that frailty. And now it seems it wants you."

"No," I said and hugged her close. She'd blown so hot and then so cold. I wasn't going to let go of her this time. "We have a thing. We have a connection, a mental and emotional connection, a spiritual one—yes, spiritual. The essence of me connects with the essence of you, and even though there will be fundamental differences in the way we see the world and how we react to it, we're connected."

We were still standing outside the elevator, and she buried her head in my neck. "Maybe," she murmured. "But really, this is very bad timing."

The elevator pinged, and Jaxen and Norman came out.

"Lovebirds," Jaxen said, and he sounded amused. "Get a room, why don't you? Seriously, we've got time. The rain will fall and we will gather data. Norman and I will be the responsible ones keeping an eye on things. You two go and get the carnal longing out of your system."

"Yeah, the sexual tension is killing us," Norman agreed.

Janaelle grinned and grabbed my hand. "See you tomorrow," she said, and we hurried down the hall. She pulled me onto her bed, and for a fleeting moment I was convinced my dick would fail me, that the Lucky Hole dysfunction would raise its flaccid head, but it didn't. We had encore after encore, and I was in heaven.

"We have to figure out how to meet up after I save my kids," I said as the clock struck midnight.

"We will," she said, and stroked my hair. "And we won't leave it up to the computers. We'll do it. Humans have always been superior to computers; we just got star-struck by our own creations. We'll take back control."

"I've got an idea," I said. "I'll run away with the kids. It's the only way. On that day, I'll tell Celeste I was sorry for hitting her. I'll arrange for her to have a spa day at the LetItAllGo spa where they serve non-stop cocktails, and she'll go for sure. I'll take the kids, and we'll go somewhere—St. Theo's where they've got that great kiddies' carnival. I'll get them out of the house and keep them safe through the day. Then I'll go home with them and life will go on and we'll have changed the storyline. But how will you find me? You have to find me, Janaelle."

I lay back and thought about it.

"I know what to do. It's like that old movie, *Memento*. We each write something on the other that only we'll know is real and true. We won't wash it off. Then when we meet again, we'll have proof of us. I have to believe in destiny and that we'll be together."

"But what if you don't know what the message means or where it came from?"

"But I've remembered you every time I've been back to the past," I insisted.

Janaelle was silent. She got up and got dressed. "Let's go downtown. I know a friend who runs a twenty-four-seven tattoo parlour. I think this might work."

"A real tattoo? I hope it won't hurt too much," I said, and Janaelle laughed. "You're such a baby. What's more important is what we're going to write. It needs to be something I'll immediately understand and respond to."

We were silent on the drive in, both of us trying to think of the perfect message, me also thinking about the pain that lay ahead. I wasn't a big fan of needles. In fact I felt dizzy at the thought, but I didn't want to tell Janaelle that. In the end we decided to get Janaelle's name stencilled on the inside of my right wrist, like a rubber stamp, with *Time Warrior* below it. The only problem was that the woman got as far as the J and I fainted. "Sorry," I gasped when I came around.

Janaelle was laughing. "I don't know if you can handle the rest. Let's just leave it at the J."

"No!" I was determined. "I won't look. Carry on." I clenched my jaw so hard it hurt and turned my head away. The pain went on forever and tears seeped out of my eyes.

And finally, it was over. I was red-eyed and puffy-faced, and Janaelle couldn't stop laughing. By the time we got back to the lodge, I was annoyed with her. "Enough," I said, looking up where the deluge continued unabated. "Mummy Earth is pretty angry with us," Janaelle said. "And so she should be. Hey Sharps," she said. "Look." She pulled up her long sleeve and showed me a bandaged wrist. "I got one too, with your name. I thought if we had matching tats, we'd stand more of a chance."

"Gosh. And there was me, fainting and crying while you never made a sound."

"Which is why I love you," she said, and the bottom dropped out from my world. I was hanging, weightless in space, waiting for her to take it back or say she didn't mean it, but she didn't, so I got weepy and told her I loved her too. And she laughed and I got annoyed again and it seemed so ridiculous and perfect that we both laughed, hysterical maybe, high from the sheer delight and craziness of it all.

"The honeymooners have returned from their secret agent business," Jaxen said when we got to the lab. "Got it out of your system, I hope. Time to get down to business. Head Office says they have no idea what's going on. It's all utterly out of control."

"If you find who did this, can you restore world order?" I asked.

"Maybe. But we'd rather not. It wasn't meant to happen like this, but now that it's here, it needs to play itself out. The world needs to run its course, and if it means spitting us out, then so be it." I looked at him. I had heard that before, but where? I sat down.

Oh shit. "My brain feels confused," I said, and it was true. "Things are getting mixed up. Like I know I've heard what you just said, from someone else, about the world running its course but I can't remember where. I can't think straight. I feel really weird." I couldn't breathe, and everything sounded weird, as if I were underwater, sitting at the bottom of a swimming pool. I was drowning, but I couldn't find the words to express my panic.

Janaelle looked at me in alarm. She faded from my vision, and I crumpled in a heap on the floor. I heard shouting and Jaxen talking, and then the Hockney man was in my face, pulling off my T-shirt, applying paddles to my chest. *Thud, thud.* The voltage shot through me, and I was pulled along the violet current of light, *thud, thud,* and then, nothing.

Then, ice-white light in my eyeballs, burning, and I flinched to the side.

"He's back," I heard Sting Ray Bob say, and I wanted to move but I couldn't. "Severe cranial hemorrhaging. Must have been all that sex. He blew a fuse."

"Not funny," Janaelle said, and her voice sounded shaky. "Sharps, are you awake?"

"I'm good," I said. I wanted to touch her, but I was trussed up, wired from head to toe and strapped down like some kind of mental patient. I started to panic, struggling against the straps, and Sting Ray Bob rushed to release me.

"We had to tie you down. You were having seizures," Jaxen said, and he handed me a glass of water with a straw. The cool liquid hit my palate with a thrill.

"How long was I out?"

"Four days. Sting Ray Bob put you in a coma to help you rest."

"And for once I didn't dream of you," I told him. "There was nothing. Just me on the floor and then me now. Do you think that's what death is like? Just nothing? Is that what I did to my kids? Extinguished them like two little candle flames that I had the power to blow out? What's happening in the world? Can I go back now?"

"Easy fella," Jaxen said. "You're not going anywhere for ten days. No negotiations. I'll tie you down if I have to. And no rambunctious sex. Janaelle has to go to St. Drausnius anyway. Bed rest for you, buddy."

"St. Drausnius? Is that safe?"

"Safe as anywhere." Janaelle shrugged. "A meeting of the Houses has been called, and the country formerly known as Switzerland is still, after all these years, a port in a political storm."

"The Houses?"

"The Sacred Board has been dismantled. I have to go."

I was filled with panic. "No, you can't," I said, reaching for her and pulling on my IV. "You have to stay here. Do you know what's going on yet and who's in control?"

"Not yet," Jaxen admitted.

"Where's Minnie?"

"Not a peep from her or Mama. They were last spotted six hours before the lights went out. Everyone's wondering if she had something to do with this and if we'll be hearing from her. But we do know that Head Office seized all her data and it's in safe hands."

"You can't leave," I implored Janaelle. "You have no idea what or who you're dealing with."

But Janaelle was implacable. "Wheels up this afternoon. I'll be fine. I know how to take care of myself. Don't you worry about me."

But I did worry. Meanwhile, I'd be stuck in the room for ten days. I was still exhausted and battling to keep my thoughts in order. I'd managed to make sense to the others, at least I hoped I had, but my voice sounded muffled to myself, as if it were bouncing around a long tunnel and strange things were happening to my vision. Shards of light flashed and danced, blue streaks with glints of yellow and gold. It was unnerving to say the least. I didn't want to let on how bad I felt, but the others knew.

"You're pretty broken," Sting Ray Bob said bluntly. "There's bleeding in your cortex, and I hate to be the bearer of bad news but we found growths on your brain."

"Growths?" I sounded like an idiotic parrot. "What growths? Malignant?"

"They appear to be benign. But your right carotid artery is wrapped around them, which makes it impossible for us to remove them. They won't kill you, but they may be exerting pressure that will affect your thinking. We're going to try to reduce them via laser surgery, but your brain, the host, is suffering from the parasitic relationship. What is interesting is that your anger levels are down. Which indicates to us that rage is a physical phenomenon and we can actually lessen anger levels via physiology."

"Fascinating." I was sarcastic. "Glad I could be of help. Isn't lessening anger via surgery called a lobotomy? Let's try to avoid that if we can. What's the plan? I admit, I don't feel great."

"We sedate you again. We pump you full of healing steroids and antibiotics."

"We haven't had antibiotics in years!" I said. "And I don't know that I trust you messing with the arteries in my brain."

Sting Ray Bob grinned. "I don't know that you've got much choice," he replied. "I'll increase the sedatives to lessen the Hockney man effects. I looked up that painting after you mentioned it. I can't say I'm flattered, but I guess there's a likeness there somewhere. There's something weird about your brain that keeps a part of you conscious, where other people would be out cold. I've never encountered it before."

"Will you be back when I wake up?" I asked Janaelle.

She shook her head and kissed me lightly. "I've got no idea how long my trip will take. But I'll try my best."

She and Jaxen turned to leave. "What about hypnotizing me," I called out weakly. "To see what it was that I found out about Mother? She said something else, something important, but I can't remember."

"You're too fragile," Sting Ray Bob said, loading up a massive syringe that made me shiver. "We might be able to do it, but I doubt it. Maybe it will come to you while you're out. We'll be scanning your brain constantly, and although we can't isolate and nail down exact thoughts, we track visuals and record the visuals as you dream."

I flushed bright red and looked at Janaelle. "Have you watched them?"

She came back to the bed and took my hand. "You have no secrets from me."

I was annoyed and embarrassed. "So you guys know exactly what goes on inside my brain, and I know jack shit about any of you?"

"Face it, Sharps," Jaxen snapped me back to reality, "we're on a more elevated bandwidth than you. We weren't supposed to get emotionally engaged, but one of us did." He looked pointedly at Janaelle.

"And you yourself told me you were more engaged with Subject Forty-nine than you should have been," she shot back at him.

Subject Forty-nine? There were forty-eight before me? "What happened to the other forty-eight?" I asked in a small voice but no one replied.

"The most important thing you can do is heal." Sting Ray Bob shot the vial into the tube in my arm. "Let it go, Sharps, all of it. I'll fix you."

His voice faded in tandem with the image of him and I slipped away. And, while I didn't fade away entirely, it felt quite pleasant, like I was bobbing on a soft warm sea under the stars, with moonlight above, and Janaelle by my side. And there was my boy, Bax, and he was smiling at me like he did before I hit Celeste, like I was the best thing in the whole world. And Sophie was gurgling, my sweet girl, the sweetest girl in the world, with her fat little wrists and a smile from ear to ear, her big brown eyes soft and trusting. I was happy to stay there in that world forever, but Sting Ray Bob yanked me out of those warm waters and declared me fit for duty. It was time for Jump Number Three.

Janaelle was nowhere to be seen, and neither was Jaxen. I got the feeling Sting Ray Bob didn't like me too much, which was confirmed by his parting words as he dropped me off.

"Go to Jazza's apartment," he said, shortly. "Do not pass Go. Do not collect two hundred stupid and novel ideas of your own. Stick to the plan. Over and out. Got it?"

I nodded and got out of the car. There was no wave from him as he did a U-turn and took off. I watched his car vanish into the distance. I was alone again. I had to nail it this time. And I swear, I was going to stick to the plan, but I hadn't counted on a passenger riding shotgun with me. No one had figured that might happen, least of all the omnipotent OctoPuss or whatever the fuck her name was.

36. JUMP THREE SHASTA RIDES SHOTGUN

STINGRAY BOB HAD DROPPED ME at St. Polycarp's city limits. He hauled a bicycle down from the rack. "You'll have to ride from here," he said. "The roads are covered with debris. The cleaning robots, parking guard robots, auto-police, traffic monitors, they fell right over when the power died. Their circuitry went down, and they're cluttering up the roads. No robots to clean up the robots! Oh the cruel irony. Anyways, this is as far as I can take you. Here's a lock for the bike. From what I heard, people will do anything to steal a bike, so if it's gone when you come back, so be it. It's only been ten days since the Evolution, but the world has fallen apart. There's no martial law, not yet, but the governments are threatening. Which is hilarious. How do they figure they're going to whip a bunch of out-of-shape, unmotivated kids into being soldiers? Those MinetteGens haven't even learned how to blow their own noses." He got back into the car. "And remember, Sharps, you've only got twenty-four hours this time, make it snappy." And with that, he drove off.

I zipped up my slicker and walked the bike for a while, trying to get my bearings and thinking about what he had said. Martial law. Wasn't Minnie rumoured to have had armies? But where was she? I'd bet my bottom dollar countries like Real Life China and Real Life Russia were armed to the gills too.

The lake roiled and heaved to my right, a wash of oil and dark anger, with mile-high surf waves crashing onto the shore.

A summer gazebo pulsated with bodies, and the echoing ugly screams and shouts sounded like a riot. I stopped to watch a stick-brandishing mob of people chase another gang across the park and my gut tightened. I tried to pick up the pace.

The roads were packed with dead robots just like Sting Ray Bob had said. There were hundreds of them. Yellow, green, red, and blue. All twisted and wrecked, like old coat hangers, eyeballs hanging askew from bird's nest wiring.

I threaded through abandoned bubble cars, their doors open, seats deflated like leftover bridesmaid party balloons. Cyclists and harried humans scurried by with shopping carts and strollers filled with canned goods, bottled water, diapers, and toilet paper. The Crystal Path had died, all news and marketing implants were silent. The world that Integratron had ruled no longer existed. So long 123BlikiWin, ClothesKissezThugs, and CrystalMeBooty. No more FluffSqueaks or PrayingMantisLuckyCharms, but, thank god, at least no one would ever talk about MDoggHotBody again.

I wondered if my car was still in the Parkette. I had forgotten to ask Sting Ray Bob. Not that I needed it now, but the money might come in handy down the line, as well as a place to sleep. I had no idea what my future held. But, looking around me, I figured the Parkette was a thing of the past. Best not to even consider it as an option.

Coal skies clashed overhead, thick and threatening, with the temperature continuing to rise. It had hit forty-four degrees days ago, and garbage flowed around the robots and abandoned cars, carrying the foul, sour stench of sewage. Drains were backed up, and rivers of refuse and offal flowed down the streets. Bloated raccoons and squirrels, dead birds and cats, bundles of hair and bone and bloody flesh floated by, and I wished I had a bandana to wrap around my face. I had no idea there were that many illegal animals still in the city. I, like all other humans, thought they'd all been eliminated. Well, they were certainly dead now.

Walking was too slow, and I got on the bike, wobbling like a small child. I couldn't remember the last time I had even been near a bike. I had forbidden Celeste from getting a tiny plastic bike for Bax in case he hurt himself. Now I saw how stupidly obsessive and weird I had been with my boy. I vowed to be different when I got him back. I'd have to be, judging by the condition of this world. It didn't look like anti-bacterial wipes were high on the list of must-haves. I wondered what Celeste would make of this new dystopia. She'd probably try to head to Real Life Florida to join Mummy and Daddy, although from what I'd heard, St. Isidore was in worse shape than us in St. Hubert. In my opinion, the Eden Collective, the World Wide Warriors, Head Office, and the rest of whoever had started a war had left us to pick up the shrapnel and die trying to survive.

I wobbled along, pedalling unsteadily through the people and the garbage. Rain poured down my face, stinging my eyes and making it hard to see. I pulled my hoodie up, and it was immediately water-logged, but at least it helped funnel the rain away from my face.

It took hours to reach St. Drogo's. When I finally got there, I was beyond exhausted. I slid down onto the muddy front garden of the church next to the subway station and threw the bike down next to me. The world had lost its mind. It was still raining, a solid curtain of gauze. People were zombies covered in mud, indistinguishable from one another. Most were angry, shouting. A few were bemused and didn't seem to know what to do with themselves. I wasn't alone on the muddy ground, and I kept a wary eye on my neighbours, hugging my backpack close to my chest while I regrouped. I'd munched on a few energy bars on the way and chugged bottled water that Sting Ray Bob had given me. He'd also given me chewable energy pills, a mix of ginseng and caffeine and acetaminophen, and I'd shamelessly fuelled my tired body as it fought the elements and navigated the chaos on the roads.

I tore the wrapper off my last energy bar, ignoring the starving, pleading eyes of the man staring at me, but I gave him half a bottle of water as I left.

I locked the bike up against the fence, gave it a pat, and forced my way through the milling bodies into the station. What a revolting mess. I leaned against the wall for a moment and closed my eyes. The station was a nightmare of homeless people seeking refuge from the weather. The trains had stopped running, but Sting Ray Bob said that the time-travel technology would still work and that I couldn't go any other way. But how was I going to get down the stairs? Bodies were jam-packed, six to eight on a stair, huddled over one another. The escalator was the same, stacked wall-to-wall with stinking bodies, crying babies, and vacant-eyed old people.

I stopped pushing for a moment and took a breath, which I immediately regretted, wishing I could spit out the stench of the foul thick hot air. I told myself that one good thing about the sudden onset of premature dystopia was that I didn't have to worry about being nailed for killing Knox. A drug murder, in light of the entire world falling apart, no longer mattered.

I took a deep breath and tried to make my way down again, but I was blocked. People hissed and scratched at me, and one woman even drew blood. Could she give me tetanus? Nope, that was rusty metal. But one could get infected from humans if they bit you. Note to self: do not get bitten.

I was forced to leave the station on the east side, and I struggled to the smaller gate on the west, the one under the bridge. I pushed through another solid wall of bodies, wishing I had a taser to jolt and shock them out of the way. I remembered Sting Ray Bob warning me about keeping my body hydrated to ward off the dreaded nausea, and I reached into my bag for my last bottle of electrolyte water and drank it to the last drop. I had nothing else left. No food, no water, no pills. I had to make this happen. It was now or never.

Filled with renewed determination, desperation, and panic,

I became rough and feral. As I approached the rear entrance and faced a new mountain of starved, wet, angry humans, I realized I had to be cruel and wily, so I went low.

I crouched and pushed through them, forcing my way between their legs and barrelling forward with my head down, mowing them down like bowling pins. They fell, growling and cursing. I met the gaze of more than one filthy small child, standing stoically, eye-level to my bent-over form. I tried to apologize by way of a glance, but my look was met with hatred and I tried to forget what I had seen.

It took hours to reach the electronic gates. My tongue was dry as sandpaper, stuck to the roof of my mouth, and my eyes were stinging. A rancid fog rose off the prone bodies that had sought shelter into the subway; there were dozens lying on the tracks. A train was stuck halfway in the station. It too was filled with people, and there were more clambering and jostling on the roof.

A mere ten days had passed, and it had already come to this. I couldn't tell which people were dead and which were alive. Tiny mice scurried across the bodies and either people had gotten used to them or they were dead.

I closed in on the electronic gates and reached my arm forward. Dear god, I couldn't wait to get out of this world and back into the past. I didn't care what anyone said. This world was so much worse than anything we'd previously encountered. But perhaps the Warriors wouldn't see it that way. Perhaps they still believed that this would help the planet detoxify, regenerate, and heal. Maybe they were right in the long run, but for now, it was a terrible place to be.

I stretched my arm towards the gate. Only my wrist had to be within range, not my whole body. And as I leaned forward, I saw a girl reach up and throw her arms around me. It was Shasta, and her timing was such that when I landed back in my living room, she was right there with me.

37. SHASTA'S FIRST LANDING; SHARPS'S THIRD

EARTH TO SHARPS. I WAS FACE DOWN on the carpet. Rough carpet. Sandpaper fibres scratched my face. Drooling. I was drooling. My vision was blurry and my head felt hungover. My head was thick, dense, heavy. I sat up. What happened? My head was killing me. *Oh shit.* I was in my living room and there was Shasta. Right, she had jumped with me. Stupid girl. We shot through the gates the minute they opened, before I could shake her off. We just made it. The glass doors snapped tight, lobster jaws clenching tight, slamming shut.

I motioned to Shasta, who looked stunned, wide-eyed. "Get under the sofa," I hissed at her, and she did, rolling quickly and flattening herself among the dust bunnies that shamed me. I thought I had vacuumed there only days earlier.

And then I heard Celeste's voice. "Sharps, sweetie, honey, what are you doing on the floor?"

"I fainted," I lied, and I pushed myself into a sitting position.

"Oh, sweetie, you are so stressed out. Please, honeybun, don't worry so much. Daddy's got your back. I've got your back. Listen, I was going to take the kiddies to Silly Bunnies for pancakes and milkshakes. I know you think it's junk food, but they need a treat, right? Especially our boy after what happened last night."

"What happened last night?" I croaked. I tried to remember, but I couldn't. I looked at her, dazed.

"Sharps," she whispered, "you hit me. You struck me across

the face and Bax saw it. You don't remember."

"Oh, Cee." I tried to stand, but I couldn't. "I must have blacked out. To be honest, I can't remember anything, not even what day it is. What day is it? I hit you? Why did I hit you? I would never hit you."

"Well, you did, honey." And there was ice and finality in her tone now. "And our boy saw it. Which is why I wanted to get him a treat."

"But wait, um, I was thinking..." I wanted to say that I needed her to leave and the kids to stay so I could take them away from her and Jazza, but I knew that nothing I said would make any sense whatsoever. Besides, I was supposed to go to Jazza's. But now Shasta had thrown a great old giant monkey wrench into the works.

"What time will you be back?" I asked instead.

"Mid-morning, I guess. We'll go to Kiddie Mart too and buy some toys. I sent Flo home. Listen sweetie, like I said, I know you're under a lot of stress." She smirked. "I saw the texts from Ava. She sounds really mad."

"You read the messages on my comm?"

"You read mine," she reminded me. "And I needed to know why you were in such a state, more than usual. I had every right. My family's health and safety are at risk here. I will do whatever a mother needs to do to keep my children safe. Now I'm taking the kiddies and we're going to Silly Bunnies because god knows we all need a bit of happiness. You'd better get it together if you're going to face Ava, I'll tell you that much for nothing. You look so much thinner, like you lost weight overnight. It's weird. You don't look good. Big shadows under your eyes, too. Maybe you should make a doctor's appointment and get yourself checked out. You're not in a good way, Sharps."

And with that she left, taking Sophie and Baxter, neither of whom even gave me a backward glance. I stayed on the floor until I heard the car start up.

"Shasta!" I squeaked. I had tried to yell but my voice squeaked out instead, and I cleared my throat.

"What the hell were you thinking?" My volume increased incrementally.

She crawled out from under the sofa, patches of dust stuck to her cheek and forehead. "I'm sorry. I wanted to time travel. I wasn't totally erased. I remembered the drive to St. Adrian's, the forest, the shower, the soup, everything. And then I saw you at the bar and you said you'd been hanging out at St. Drogo's station, and I knew that meant you had to travel from there. I've been camped out here for ten days. At least I think it's been ten days; it's very hard to keep track. I knew you wouldn't be able to access the front entrance so I took a gamble and stayed in the back at the closest gate. I nearly died in there. I was peeing in a can but then it overflowed, and everybody was just peeing and shitting and I didn't want to lose my spot and so I stayed, and I stole food and other people's water. Even from babies and old people. But I knew you would come and you did, and now we're here. But Sharps, here's the thing: I know your wife. I know her!"

I stared at her. I was worn out and trembling. My hands were fluttering like an old drunk's. "Shasta, can you see what you did? Do you know that you could have killed me? Both of us? My brain's already bleeding from coming over. My white blood cell count is off the radar. There's an artery roping around the growths in my head. And going back, the nausea was so bad, I nearly died. I'm not joking. And you just hitched a ride like Bob's your uncle without even asking me what the consequences might be."

"Because you would have said I couldn't come. And I needed to come, now more than ever."

I couldn't listen to her. I had to think. "Not now. Listen. You stink. You really stink. You heard Celeste. They'll be gone a while. Go and take a shower. Borrow some of Celeste's clothes."

"I wouldn't wear that bitch's clothes if hell froze over," she snarled. I was taken aback, but I couldn't get into it, whatever was bothering her. My head was going to explode, and my skin was burning and itching at the same time. I had to calm my body down.

"Then take mine, whatever. Or go down to the basement. I think Nanny Flo left a bunch of her stuff down there."

Shasta growled and clenched her fists. "No! Not hers either!"

"I don't care what you do or don't do," I shouted at her, and my voice was back, good and strong. "Go and get clean and give me some space, okay? I'm dying here, and I don't mean metaphorically. Physically. You nearly killed me. I have to get some protein and electrolytes into my body. And I guess I should call work and tell them I'm not coming in. But first, I'm going to caffeinate and rehydrate."

Shasta looked sulky, but she went upstairs and I heard the shower running.

I opened the fridge and cupboards and mixed myself a power protein smoothie. My hands were shaking so much that it was hard to get the powder into the blender. I wanted to grab some ibuprofen from the cabinet in the upstairs washroom, but I didn't want to weirdly walk in on Shasta. I rummaged around the kitchen and found a bottle of muscle relaxants behind a bottle of vodka, which made sense, and I swallowed four pills with my smoothie. *Come on, body, I need you to regroup. We have to finish this.* I found some extra-strength old-school aspirin, and I chewed a couple.

I flashed a message to Ava.

Am sick, will be in later if I can, sorry.

So fire my ass, if you like, bitch.

She fired back.

Sure you're sick. Delaying this won't change anything.

I didn't bother to reply. I heard the doorbell ring, and I turned to it. Celeste wouldn't ring the doorbell. I went over and pulled the door open.

It was Jazza. And he had no idea why, but I started laughing.

I laughed my ass off. "Hey buddy," I said, full of the joys of life and *bonhomie*. "Look who's here! Come on in! Do you want a smoothie? I make a mean protein bevvie, trust me."

Jazza looked completely nonplussed. "Uh, no," he said. "Why aren't you at work?"

"Sick, buddy, sick to my soul. I am the very darkness impersonated. Wait, is that the darkness incarcerated? Who the hell knows? Who the hell cares? Come on in. Let's have a party."

He was so startled he did what I told him and went over to the sofa. He sat down, his mouth hanging open.

And then Shasta walked down the stairs and I thought Jazza would come in his pants right there and then. She was wearing a pair of my boxers, with the waistband rolled down, and she'd tied the T-shirt to reveal her taut midriff. She looked sizzling hot.

"You see," I said and there was a note of hysteria in my voice, "we're all here! Party time! Jazza meet Shazza! And may your hearts entwine and may you live in health and prosperity forever, amen. Although, Jazza, last time I noticed, you were doing a bear dance with a rabid squirrel, *n'est pas?*"

"Sharps," Jazza commented evenly, "you've lost your mind."

This made me laugh even harder. I sank into the sofa and sobbed with laughter, and Shasta and Jazza exchanged a look.

"I'm Shasta. I know him from the bar," Shasta told Jazza, and he looked confused.

"What bar? And when did you get a tattoo?" He leaned forward. "What the fuck are you doing with Janaelle's name on your wrist?"

"You know Janaelle? How do you know Janaelle?" That cut off any hilarity. I sat up and glared at him. "How the fuck do you know Janaelle?"

"Buddy! Of course I don't *know* her. I know *of* her. The evil queen of doomsday. She's from the video game, *Alterna Inferma*. It's that mastermind life-is-chess war game, man—you loved it! And she's The General. If you kill her, you live forever! But you know that, Sharps. We used to play before you met

Celeste. You had this major crush on Janaelle! Everybody did. That was the point: get to the end and you had sex with the evil but stunning queen of doomsday!"

I threw up. Spewed projectile green smoothie vomit all over my carpet. So much for the dust bunnies being the most of my cleaning problems. And I guess I lost my super pills. Shasta and Jazza shot away from me.

I knelt next to my vomit, pounded my thighs with my fists, and howled. "I've lost my mind. I have. You're right Jazza, I've lost it. And we've only got twenty-four hours this time, and I don't know what's real any more. You came here to kill my family, didn't you? I was supposed to come and get you, but here you are."

Jazza looked stunned. "What do you mean?" he stammered. "I would never hurt anybody."

"Liar!" I rushed at him and wrestled him down, rolling him in my vomit. Frantically, I body searched him and found a gun in the waistband of his jeans. "You see!" I shrieked. "You were! You were! My babies! You killed them!" I sat back on my haunches, holding the gun, my chest heaving.

"I think we need to take a moment," Shasta said, and she ran upstairs and came down with a bottle of pills in her hand while I stayed where I was, gun shaking up and down with every breath, my eyes unblinking, staring at Jazza.

"What happened, man?" I asked him. "Seriously. What's up? Last time I saw you, you were in love with Ava and delighted to have her sit on your lap and encourage you to embezzle funds, pin the blame on me, and live happily ever. Then all of a sudden, you killed yourself. Then the next time you killed my family."

He looked baffled. "You are so fucked," he said. "But you aren't entirely wrong. I did think about killing myself. But then I thought I'd destroy your life well and truly first."

"Okay," I said slowly, "but why? Why not live with Ava forever and amen? Oops, awomen?"

"Because she wouldn't have me! She used me, Sharps! You were right. She said I had not proven myself worthy, all because of one mistake! One fucking mistake! That I told you about her and me! And she stopped giving me my post-scour meds the nanosecond after I pressed TRANSFER on the bank funds. She dumped me and cut off my meds."

"What meds did she give you?"

"I have no idea. But they balanced out my brain. Without them—argh, fuck it Sharps, I'm beyond repair. I have desires, Sharps, desires that sicken me! That's why I had to kill myself. But then I thought, no, YOU must suffer before I go because this is all your fault, your fault!" He growled and howled like an animal in pain, and Shasta held out the bottle of pills.

"Clonazepam," she said. "Because we need to take this down a level."

"Where'd you get them?" I knew the contents of our bathroom closet inside out because I needed to keep an eye on Celeste. "There are no drugs in this house. In Celeste's purse, yes, but not in this house. Well, some sleeping pills in her bedside table, but that's it."

"I knew where to look," Shasta said. "The CrystalMeBooty pink shoebox." She gave me a pill. I stared at it. I didn't want to take it. "The pink shoebox?" I sank back on my heels and then sat down cross-legged. "I feel like we're all so confused here. Like a bunch of *déjà vu* moments are cross-pollinating and making crazy patterns in my mind. I need a moment. Everybody shut the fuck up!"

38. IS IT ALL A GAME?

ITRIED TO GATHER MY THOUGHTS. "But wait!" I shouted. "I know! Jazza! *Alterna Inferma*. There were all these countries around the world, and you dropped through a black hole to access another city in another timeline. And you were given a task and you chose a crew and you had to go through a maze and cross borders and the crew was always the same but the places and tasks were different. I had Mr. Kung Fu, Mr. CleanMachine, and The Beauty Queen, and I was The Fixer. We went back in time, too, right back to the Victorian era when kids worked in sweathouses, and I freed them. And then I was in Africa. But there was always a clue that twisted the game. Like one time, I nearly got to the highest level—I was about to meet Janaelle and be knighted and have mind-blowing sex—and then I realized I wasn't The Fixer, I was just Mr. CleanMachine, and I knew because I found his inline skates in my suitcase and his bruise on my knee." I started crying. "That was the game, wasn't it? And we were chased by The Shadows, like stingrays in the sky, and we got trapped in abandoned buildings and had to find our way out. And there were nuns in long black habits with big white penguin cowls. The nuns were like big whiskered rats. And The Grackle was supposed to be my best friend, but he left me. And I had my arsenal, furniture polish, bleach, and silver polish, and I kept everything clean, even ironing the sheets that I had washed in extra hot water. I scored points that way."

"Sure, buddy," Jazza said, and I noticed he exchanged a glance with Shasta. I slammed my hand down on the coffee table.

I threw the gun and the pill onto the floor next to me and I rubbed my eyes hard. "Don't humour me. What was the game if not that?"

"It was about cheating death," Jazza said. "Coming back to life. We died and we lived again, but only if we died the right way. But you are right, we saved orphans. You liked to save orphans."

I hit myself on the forehead. "That's it! Because of Mother! She said it herself, she's not my mother. She chose me, she said. Or did she say my father chose me, and she thought he had made a mistake? I can't remember. Either way, I was a mistake. Maybe that's why I killed her. No! I killed her because she was going to turn me in. But did I turn her in for gardening? I did not. You see. I remember. I went back, and I remember why."

"Sharps, your mother is alive," Jazza said, and he sounded tired, like he was getting bored by this game, only it wasn't a game.

"She is now. I know that," I said. "I'm not stupid, Jazza! I know that! But she will be dead, and she'll deserve it too. But not my kids, not them."

I looked at my watch. "Where is Celeste? She should be back by now."

"They haven't even been gone an hour," Shasta said. "It's not even ten a.m."

I grabbed the portable comm. "She mustn't come home. We need to save the children."

Shasta laughed. "Yeah, like Celeste is the one to save the kids. She's sick, your wife."

I looked at her. I wasn't sure how much more I could take. I put my hands over my ears. "I don't care," I said. "I can't hear it."

"She made me watch porn with her!" Shasta shouted. "She paid me to watch porn with her—how sick is that? In Bax's room, when it was just him. Then up in Sophie's bedroom, full of FluffSqueaks and pink toys. She liked watching porn in the kid's rooms. She hated your bedroom, with that creepy painting of that ugly old guy, and she took the portable comm into Sophie or Bax's room and paid me to watch."

"I can't hear this!" I yelled. I looked over at Jazza, and he must have grabbed the gun when I wasn't looking because he had it in his lap. He was transfixed by Shasta.

"That's why I had to come back," Shasta said. "I recognized you the minute I saw you that night. And then you got talking about time travel, and I thought it would be a way for me to come back and get Celeste to own up to what she did. That's why I stalked you. Do you think I care about the science or you? I wanted to punish your wife. She ruined me. She drugged me. She gave me date rape drugs. Eugh. That voice. *Sweetie baby honey, schnookums. Let me lick your face, smell your fresh baby girl smell.* Eughh, yeah, it was her. I want to kill her myself."

I stared at Shasta. "I do know you," I said slowly. "From church. And yes, you used to babysit."

"The church was the connection," Shasta sneered. "There you were, singing your stupid ass off, and meanwhile it was where the parents abusing kids made their plans to meet and fuck—it was the base for their sick operations. Pretty much all the women were in on it. The men were so fucking stupid—none of you had a clue. But the rich women liked to pay the girls and the boys too."

"Why didn't you say anything? How were we supposed to know?"

"Who could we tell? Anyway, it wasn't bad at first. It was good money, and it even seemed like fun. Kinda like our own secret world. We could buy all the shit we wanted. But then it got gross. But who would believe us? My own mother had parties. I tried to talk to her, but she just said, 'Shasta, if you don't want to play the game, then don't. But don't you rain on my parade. And don't try telling your father because I'll have him send you to Dr. Oliver and Dr. Oliver has his own habits, which I know about. So if you try anything, honey, you'll end up worse off than before, in rehab for the emotionally disturbed.' My mother's parties were all boys. She said she loved the smell of teenage boys. And I guess your wife loved the smell of me. And now she'll pay."

I leaned down and picked up the pill I had dropped. "But she's not here. And I don't know what's real anymore. I don't know who to trust."

I turned to Jazza. "You stole the money and pinned it on me and if you don't kill my family and then yourself, it will be pinned on me, and then my kids will live but their mother is a pervert and I'll go away for rest of my life."

"Maybe I don't want to kill myself anymore," Jazza said and he looked a lot more cheerful than he did when he arrived. "This is so screwed up it's renewed my interest in life. And now Shaz is here, and that changes everything. I mean, look what just walked into my life, oh so pretty. Like I told you, Sharps, I have desires, and cheerleader girls are right up there." He held the gun more firmly, and as I watched, his expression changed, a bruised storm moving across a sky, a bully with a lethal weapon.

"And now it's time for some fun," he said and pointed the gun at Shasta. "We've all been so serious up to now. Shop talk all the way. Shazzie, how about you do a striptease for us, pretty please? Come on, nice and slow. Pretend you're listening to your favourite song."

"You're nothing but big talk and no action," Shasta said defiantly, and Jazza aimed the gun at me. "You think so? You want to try me? I owe him nothing. He didn't even make me his son's godfather. Do you know this is only the second time I've ever been here? The first time was to help unpack. Like I was a mover! I'd love you to give me a reason to shoot him and then you'll be stuck here with me and I will do whatever

THE RAGE ROOM   249

I want with you and then I might leave the kiddies to live with Celeste the Sicko."

Shasta peeled off her T-shirt. Her long, firm breasts were larger than I had thought they'd be, and her nipples were huge and dark brown, which surprised me.

"Good. Now the shorts."

Shasta started to pull them off and I looked away, but Jazza waved the gun at me. "We're in this together; watch the show. Don't want to hurt her feelings now, do you?"

I forced myself to look at Shasta. She was standing still, her hands hanging limply at her sides. "We need some music," Jazza said. "Only problem is that Sharps has terrible taste in music, don't you, buddy? But hey, maybe you can find one song that'll make the cut. Find us a song. And in the meantime, Shasta, move around, do something—you look stupid just standing there."

Shasta began to sway a bit, this way and that. Her eyes were glazed and she was covered in goosebumps and her nipples were hard, a detail I didn't want to notice but did.

"You know what," I shouted at him, "this is why I didn't make you godfather of my kids. You're sick, and I always knew it. Sure, you're clever—you're such a clever boy—but you're disgusting. It wasn't the scour that ruined you! You were born ruined! And you were stupid enough to think Ava could love you! Ha! I always knew you were a loser."

Jazza shrugged. "Whatever. I'm in control now. Find us a song."

I leaned towards the VinylMobile entertainment system, and as I did, the portable comm attached to it began to ring. The coincidental timing of my reaching for it and the ring tone caught us off guard, and we all stared at the comm.

"It's Celeste," I said, seeing her beauty badge flash across the screen. "I have to get this."

Jazza jumped up and held the gun at Shasta's temple. "Say a word about any of this and she's dead."

I grabbed the receiver and cupped it under my chin and into my ear. Celeste's face boomed onto the screen of the VinylMobile. I motioned the others to be quiet, and I said my wife's name as if it was a question. "Yes, Celeste?" I was so proud of myself for how calm I sounded.

39. THE BEGINNING OF THE REAL END

"SHARPS," CELESTE SAID, AND HER FACE had that weird up-the-nostril angle, "the kiddie winkles and me are going to Mummy and Daddy for the holidays. Honey, you've been behaving so strangely lately, you've been worrying me. And then you hit me. You hit me! I mean really, Sharps, Daddy wasn't happy to hear about that. He's flying us to Real Life Florida now. We're at the airport. I told the ticket seller it was a family emergency, and I was right. You're our emergency and we're leaving you."

"You're leaving me? You can't leave me! I know I shouldn't have hit you, but you forgave me."

"I never forgave you." Her face was pulled into an expression of disgust, and the comm was so close I could see the fine hairs on her upper lip. I would have thought she'd have those zapped long ago. I was distracted by that fluffy down—was she even a blonde? But she forced me back to the present crisis. "I wanted you to go to work thinking everything was fine. I was going to pack up properly, but then you wouldn't leave. I thought you had left, but then there you were, slumped on the floor. So I couldn't even pack properly! But Daddy said we'll buy new stuff. He said for me to tell you he's very disappointed in you, Sharps. And he knows about the money. He said he couldn't imagine you showing that kind of initiative, that you were the world's biggest procrastinator, and I agreed. I told him the only thing you were proactive about was cleaning the counter like a maniac before I even did anything on it!" Her voice sounded indignant. "But anyway, that's all by the by. We'll let you know what's going to happen. We may stay in Real Life Florida with Mummy and Daddy and never come back—we'll see."

"But they're my kids!" I yelled. "Not just yours. You can't take them from me!"

"You struck me, Sharps. I've taken pictures of the bruise. And there's the years of emotional abuse, which all my friends will testify to. Years of it! And do you have money for a lawyer? No, you don't! So if I were you, I'd let us go. Besides you've got other things to deal with, like Daddy said."

"Mrs. Barkley!" Shasta shouted but the screen went dead and Jazza and Shasta both stared at me.

"She left. With the kids." I threw myself on the sofa and buried my face in my hands. But I was just acting. I knew Jazza had lost concentration. I'd seen the gun dangling slightly from his hand. I let my body slump completely, as if I had given up on everything, and then I lunged up in a single movement and tackled him to the ground. I needed to get the gun away from him

Shasta jumped to one side and watched us, her hands up by her face.

Not only did Jazza have a weight advantage over me, but I was weakened by the jumps, and I was thinner than ever, frail. My head was throbbing with pain, and every heartbeat pushed a wall of jagged iron pieces into the soft flesh of my eyeballs. There was a black cloth shrouding my vision, and I saw fuzzy shapes more than anything.

Jazza gained on me, twisting me underneath him, and I heard him laughing. He dropped the gun and started strangling me, and I, crushed by his weight, felt the life being squeezed out of me. I couldn't breathe, and my eyes were going to pop right out of my head. The pressure in my head was unbearable, and then, *whack*, there was a loud thump, and Jazza fell off me.

Shasta had hit him with a statue of Jesus, aka the Chris Hemsworth avatar, who resided, ever present and beatific, in our living room. I looked at Jesus and his sad gaze, blood dripping down from his face onto his six-pack abs and his muscular, sculpted thighs. I took him from Shasta and set him gently in his right spot. I took the liberty of leaning on him for a moment to catch my breath, and my blood mixed with his. *Oh my head.* The unspeakable pain.

Shasta was scrambling back into her clothes. I let go of Jesus and looked over at Jazza. "Is he dead?" I asked, and Shasta shrugged. *What to do, oh what to do?* "He's so heavy," I said. "We can't get him out of here. He was going to kill us. I don't know what to do."

"Do you have any rope?"

"Why would I have rope?"

"Ties then? Come on, Sharps, whatever, think! We need to tie him up first, just in case. Otherwise it will be like those horror movies where they come back from the dead and kill you again."

I crawled upstairs and grabbed a fistful of ties. My heart fell like a lump of lead when I passed my boy's room and my girl's. My babies. I paused at the entrance of Bax's room, and I heard Shasta's voice.

"Hurry up, Sharps! Don't leave me down here. Come on! What are you doing?" She sounded increasingly frantic. "He's moving! Sharps! Where are you?"

And then I heard the shot. It was more like a weak firecracker than a bang, but I knew what it was.

I dropped the ties and ran down the stairs. Jazza was slumped on his side, blood pooling on the carpet. His right eye was a gaping black hole. Shasta had shot him at close range. I noticed that Jazza's gun had a silencer on it. He had indeed been ready to kill my family. But regardless, I had needed him alive.

I sat down. "Oh shit," I said. "I had a clear directive from OctoOne to NOT kill him! Shit, Shasta! WTF! How will I clear my name now? I can't prove he did it now! And I'm never going to get this carpet clean. What were you thinking, shooting him? I needed him! He had to tell them it wasn't me! Before, with the suicide notes, he told them what really happened. Now you've killed him and it all points to me. And you don't exist, so I killed him. Not only am I a thief, I'm a murderer. And a wife beater. And I've lost my children." I jumped up. "I have to find Norman. Oh god, my head is killing me."

"Our Norman? Where is he? How much time do we have left? Here, take these." She held out some tablets.

"Yes, our Norman. He's in a rage room. I don't know how long we have left and I don't care. Hours. Who knows? What are these? This is all so screwed. We are so fucking screwed."

"Take the pills, Sharps. It's codeine plus a bunch of other stuff. Chew them. Trust me."

I took the pills and chewed them. Chemical chalk dust filled my throat, and Shasta ran to get me a glass of water.

"Come on," I said, "let's get the fuck outta here."

I ran out to my car, and Shasta followed me. She was shivering. It was winter and she and I had both forgotten that. We'd travelled from the stifling, stinking, forty-degree heat and we were freezing.

I struggled to get the car started and I balked at having to touch the cold steering wheel. "We should go back and get some warm clothes," Shasta said, and her teeth were chattering. We both looked at the house. "I don't want to go back," I said. On a good note, the pills she had given me were helping. The pain was there but wrapped in cotton batting.

"I don't either. But I don't want to freeze to death. I need more than a T-shirt and your boxers."

We got out of the car reluctantly, and rushed back up the path and inside the house. I looked over at Jazza. He had died with a look of surprise on his face and his legs twisted under him in an awkward way. His sweatshirt was askew and his very lacy lavender bra strap showed. And then there was the gun.

I went over and grabbed it and I ran upstairs. I grabbed socks and sweaters and a pair of sweatpants. I yanked off my vomit-smeared clothes and got changed. I tucked the gun into the front of my trousers like I'd seen tough guys do in the movies. I just hoped to hell that tough guys didn't shoot their balls off.

Shasta gratefully pulled on one of my hoodies, pulling the drawstring tight. She tugged a thick scarf from the rack by the front door.

"Here." I threw a coat at Shasta and pulled on some boots. Then, just as we were about to leave, a figure appeared in the doorway. It was Strawberry Merv, my Christmas lights rival. He stood there, looking into the house, over at Jazza's body and the vast pool of blood around it. His gaze moved to Shasta. "Hey," he said, "you look familiar?"

Shasta shrugged like a sulky teenager called into the headmaster's office.

I was at a loss. This was so bad. Strawberry Merv had seen Jazza. "What's going on here?" He came into the house. I looked at Shasta. She shrugged.

"Who's this guy?" Strawberry Merv asked, pointing at Jazza.

"We had a home invasion," I said. "A drug addict from Dukes Road, I bet. He burst in with a gun, and he held me and my daughter hostage."

"Daughter? She's not your daughter. I know who she is. She used to live at the corner house, the one with the big gables. I remember now. She ran away years ago. And now," he said to Shasta, "you're back."

Oh shit. I'd screwed up big time. "You know what Merv, this is none of your business. Why don't you just leave?"

But Merv had taken out his portable comm. "I'm going to call the SSOs," he said, pursing his prune-ass little mouth.

I had to stop him. I reached for the gun and got tangled with my hoodie, fumbling underneath it, finally grabbing the gun from my waistband. *Oh shit*. How do you even shoot a gun? Right, get the safety off, yank things, just do whatever, keep trying. I finally got it right. I shot him and I heard myself panting like a dog that had run too fast and too hard.

I'd had no choice. The stupid man.

Strawberry Merv made a grunting noise as he fell to the floor, like the wind had got knocked out of him. *Oh shit.* Another body to deal with.

40. BACK TO THE RAGE ROOM

I LOOKED AT SHASTA. "YOU HAD NO CHOICE," she said. "Listen Sharps, don't worry about any of this. It isn't real, right? We go back, it resets to what it was."

"No, it doesn't." I was hysterical. "Not exactly. Every time I visit, things change in ways I can't control. Some uncontrollable variable sows the seed for future disaster. Or present disaster but in another present but not the same virgin one it once was. Every time I come back, it's different. What happened here moves forward, or some tiny random part of it does. That's the whole point—it's random. As of now, my kids are with my pervert wife, and I'm a thief and a murderer."

"And you killed Knox in the future we came from," Shasta said and I was startled.

"How do you know about that?"

"It was everywhere. He was a doofus, but I liked him. He was kind to me."

"Yeah. I'd forgotten about that. Well, sorry, what can I say? I thought he was an annoying prick, and he was trying to steal from me. There I was, buying him drugs out of the goodness of my heart and he tried to rob me! But yep, I killed him. And I killed my mother." I pulled on my jacket. "It seems I'm pretty darn useless at everything except killing. Who knew? C'mon, help me get this guy's legs out of the doorway."

We pulled Merv into the house and drove off, leaving the door unlocked.

"So we're going to find Norman?" Shasta was huddled into her seat, her coat zipped tight, the fluffy hood pulled close to her face. The car was still freezing. She was wearing Celeste's couture MountainFeathersFleece coat. I guess warmth and survival had triumphed over her hatred of the woman and anything associated with her.

I nodded curtly. She settled in and stared out the window, and I drove to the rage room only to find that Norman wasn't there. I was running out of time and I couldn't find a key player in the game.

To my credit, I stayed very calm. I didn't raise my voice when I told the attendant that I needed a room and I needed it now. He told me all the rooms were booked. I looked at him very calmly, showed him the gun, and told him to make a room available pronto.

Which he did. He asked me which soundtrack I wanted, and I said I wanted silence.

I refused the white suit, the gloves, and the goggles, and he didn't argue with me about that either.

I went into the rage room and pointed the gun at the ceiling. "Janaelle! Are you there? I know you're there! Tell me I'm not losing my mind! I know you're watching. If you're real, then you're watching! I'm on The Eye—I know I am! Talk to me!"

But nothing happened. I waited, and I shouted again and still, nothing happened.

"There are no cameras here, buddy, you know that." The attendant and Shasta hovered in the doorway.

"There are! They hacked in. They gather the data and they use it. The Eden Collective's going to destroy the world as we know it, and they use the data. I've seen the lab! I've seen The Eye! I know about the World Wide Warriors and what Head Office is going to do to the satellites!"

I realized how insane I sounded, and I slumped down. "I'm going to leave now," I said. "Are you guys going to let me go or have me arrested?"

"I'm happy to make like this never happened," the man said. He looked at Shasta. "What about you?" he asked.

"I'm going with him," she said. She must have found a pack of Celeste's gum in one of the pockets because she was snapping her jaws like a sea turtle, wafting grape scents as she spoke. "I want to."

"Whatever." He ushered us out.

"I'll drive," Shasta said, and I gave her the fob. I didn't care where we went.

"You got any cash on you?"

I dug out my wallet. "Can we stop at a Silly Bunnies?" she asked, and I laughed.

"No, Shasta, we cannot. By now they'll be looking for us. Strawberry Merv's wife is as nosy as he is. Dollars to doughnuts she was hot on his heels, found her dead hubby and dead Jazza, and rang every alarm bell she could. Fucking great. Now I'll be wanted on both sides of the time zone."

"So if you go back and then you come back here again, what will the situation be?" Shasta had momentarily forgotten her drive-thru idea, for which I was relieved.

"I don't know. It changes every time. The first time, in pure untouched real time, Jazza killed himself and I found him. Then I used his gun to kill my family and went on the run. Then when I jumped back, the first jump, I tried to change things at grassroots level and not kill anybody. I came back much earlier, thinking I could nip this thing in the bud, before Sophie was even born. But that failed. Then I came back and Jazza killed my family and he killed himself. This time, Celeste took the kids and you shot Jazza and I shot Strawberry Merv. And I'm guilty of stealing the money and everybody will think I killed Jazza. And I also learned that the love of my life is an avatar from a video game and none of this is real."

"I'm really hungry," Shasta said, hunching over the steering wheel, her hood still pulled high like a cowl.

I stared at her in disbelief. "I'm so glad you're tuning in to just how bad my life is. Thank you, Shasta, for being so fucking sensitive and AWARE."

I hit the fuzzy yellow dashboard, but Shasta didn't flinch. "What's wrong with you?" I asked. "You do realize there's a good chance we'll get stuck in displaced time when we jump back, thanks to you? You've added weight, and the program wasn't built for two bodies. When I started, I was here for a week, but my resilience is failing. This time I've only got a twenty-four-hour limit, and you screwed it up. Who knows, I might not even be able to come back for jump four, if we even make it out. Do you want to be stuck in displaced time? Apparently it's the spinning ball of hell and you're stuck in a fog where you can't see anything and you can't breathe. That's what Sting Ray Bob said anyway."

"Sting Ray Bob, Strawberry Merv. The names you guys come up with. Maybe we should drive down to Cherry Beach and kill ourselves."

"What? No! Why?"

"Because we are all so screwed anyway. Look at me. I ran away—that guy was right. I've been living on the streets since I was fifteen. And no, it wasn't just what your wife did to me, but she factored in. I'm only seventeen now. I look older; you would too, if you were me. Your wife had her lick-fest porn sessions when I was fourteen, and I tried to tell my dad after my mother told me to shut the fuck up, but he said rubbish, Mrs. Barkley is a bastion of Christian charity and didn't I know that her father, Mr. Williamson, was a head honcho at Integratron and he'd get my father fired if he said anything? So best I keep my mouth shut. And then my brother pimped me out to his friends to score money for drugs, and that's when I left."

"But you work in a bar! You must have papers, be legal."

"I screw the guy. He thinks I'm older. I got fake ID."

"How can you afford coke?" It was a stupid question, and I regretted it. "Oh. Sorry."

"I'm really hungry," she said again.

"I know!" I shouted. "But what are we supposed to do? I just don't think stopping for takeout is a solid idea."

"We need to be together when it's time to go," she changed the subject, gnawing on a thumbnail that could ill afford it. "You can't leave me. What will happen if you go without me? You've freaked me out about getting stuck in a beach ball fog for the rest of my life. What's the time? Why aren't you keeping better track of things?"

I checked. It was four in the afternoon, and it was getting dark. "I've got no idea how much time's left," I said honestly. "I wish I did. Oh God. My head's killing me again. My brain's probably dissolving inside my head. A puddle of mush is all I'll be left with. A puddle of mush that hurts like hell."

"I'm stopping at the next Silly Bunnies." Shasta's hunger trumped my intercranial bleeding. "They're the best bet. I have to eat. Look, there's one. I'm pulling over. Don't shout at me."

Defeated, I slumped down and pulled up the collar of my coat. As if that would help disguise me or fix the situation. Shasta looked over at me. "You're getting really grumpy. It's time to bring out the big guns."

She took two pills out of a large baggie, and I wondered when she had pocketed it. She was right. The pills I had taken were wearing off, and the pain was making me punchy. "What are these?" I asked, looking at the pills.

"It's old school fentanyl. I lied earlier when I told you I gave you codeine. That was fentanyl too. But by now you really need to eat or it'll hurt so bad you'll think you've got stomach cancer. Don't take them till I get back."

I watched Shasta go into the Silly Bunnies. I hated the place. All the servers wore rabbit suits. Rabbit suits in the fast-food joints, rabbit suits in the rage rooms. We were all just fucked up rabbits hopping around never-never land. Why did I even want to live? It was a good question. I had lost everything. It was so messed up. I studied the tattoo on my wrist. I dug at the skin, but the ink was real. The tattoo looked new and fresh. I had to have done that for a reason. But Janaelle didn't exist. Jazza had said so. Who was the woman I had met? And who were Jaxen and Sting Ray Bob? They weren't based on any video game. They were real too; I couldn't have just imagined them. And would we make it back through the jump okay? I wasn't lying when I told Shasta she had added weight to the load. And I hated to think of landing back in that station. And I'd need to jump back immediately because there was no way I was living in that shit-infested hole filled with the dregs of desperate humanity, waiting out two healing weeks before I could return. But what was my plan? I didn't have a plan.

My heart ached when I thought about Janaelle. She felt far away, like a movie that I'd watched a long time ago. Being happy and safe and clean and warm felt as alien to me as my former life. I wondered how Bax and Sophie were doing and if they even missed me.

Shasta arrived with lattes, wraps, doughnuts, jelly rolls, and cookies. I made her drive around to the back of the strip mall, and we fell on the food like starving piranhas.

"Good thinking," I said with my mouth full, but then I spotted an SSO car gliding around to the front of the mall. "They're most likely getting a coffee, but we should go somewhere else, just in case."

Shasta shot up, put the car into drive and pulled out smoothly, still chewing on her doughnut. I had to hand it to her, she was great under pressure. She drove to the outskirts of St. Polycarp and turned into another small strip mall.

"How many nail bars do you think there are in just this neighbourhood?" she asked, finishing her coffee.

"Not a clue. Maybe they're all money laundering schemes or something." I looked at the dashboard. "I'd say we've got about four hours to go," I said. "But really, I've got no idea."

"I'm so tired," she said. "Food coma. It's been a crazy day. I need to sleep, Sharps."

"Tell you what, let me put the seats down in the back and

we'll lie down and tie our feet together and one wrist. That way we'll be ready to go together. I'm exhausted too." The food and drugs made it hard for me to keep my eyes open.

"Can we keep the car running? It will get so cold."

"Then we both need to be in the front. I can't risk you being in the back and me being the front, in case it happens."

She tilted her seat back and we tied our wrists together, her right, my left. I wanted to stay awake, in case anyone rapped on the window and asked us why we were parked there for so long, but I fell asleep and when I woke it was with a jolt. My wrist was screaming and the ground was wet with recent rain and we were standing in the mud of an open field.

"WHAT HAPPENED?" SHASTA ASKED, and I looked around in panic. "We must be stuck in displaced time. Oh shit. Let's look for shelter or something."

"There!" Shasta pointed, and she pulled my wrist high with hers.

We ran toward an abandoned red brick fortress that cast a dark shadow, a shadow that ate up the earth and left a dark stain. The place was as inviting as a shark's mouth, with jagged broken glass windows. I didn't want to go in, but there was no other choice.

"Can we untie our wrists?" Shasta asked, and I tugged at the shoelace that bound us together, wishing I hadn't done such a firm job of securing it.

"No," I said, "I can't untie it and anyway we must stick together. We have to go inside," I said, but my feet were unwilling to move.

"It looks haunted," Shasta whispered. "I bet it was an insane asylum."

Neither of us moved for a while. The sky was the underbelly of a highway overpass, low-hanging and dark.

"It's going to rain," Shasta said in a small voice. "I don't want to get wet on top of everything else."

"We have to go inside," I said. "Come on. We'll get out of the rain and wait for Sting Ray Bob to rescue us."

I paused at the edge of the building's shadow, a shadow that fell like the delineation between good and evil. I took a step forward, half expecting my foot to fall into an empty hole in the darkness, but the ground was solid and firm and unremarkable. I turned to Shasta and tried to smile. "It's fine," I said, my voice betraying the lie . We walked across the black earth and up to the gothic front entrance that reminded me of my first school, the one where Mother had left me all alone.

We climbed the cracked concrete steps to the open mouth of the mausoleum, and as we did, the sun burst through the thick gloom and three golden rays flowed down from the sky, three pillars of radiant light. "Maybe it's a sign?" Shasta sounded hopeful.

"Of what? There's nothing here." I looked around.

The shark-tooth windows were set high up and tiny in the brick walls, and there was nothing inside the warehouse. No offices, rooms, partitions, or old machinery, just a layer of dust and grime.

Shasta stared beyond me and I turned, but there was just a steady cone of dust swirling in the golden sunlight. Momentarily distracted by the flow and dance of the light, I turned to Shasta, only to find that she had vanished. My arm was free.

"Shasta?" I was panic-stricken. "Where are you?" How had she got loose, and where could she have gone? There was nowhere for her to go. I shuddered. Being here alone was terrifying. "Shasta?" I swung around in a circle, and as I did, the sun died with a flick of a switch and I was left standing in the thick darkness.

I swung around to the entrance, to reassure myself that it was still there, and yes, it was. I could run outside any time I chose.

I was freezing and my skin was clammy. Goosebumps sandpapered my arms and my chest, and I shivered. My body was slick with greasy sweat, soaking my T-shirt. I hugged my arms around me trying to find some semblance of warmth.

I fell to my knees, crying. Hot tears that turned ice cold. I sobbed until I had nothing left. I had to stop feeling sorry for myself and find a way out of there. I stood up, and as I did, the three pillars of light snapped on and I spotted Shasta in the far corner, kneeling, holding something.

I ran to her. "Shasta! Where did you go? What are you doing? What's going on?"

I fired questions at her, but she didn't acknowledge me.

I knelt down and looked at her. "Shasta? Please, talk to me."

She was holding a child's shoe. It was Baxter's shoe, and I snatched it from her. "You loved him more than anything," Shasta said. "You loved him so much it hurt."

"I did," I said. "Where did you find it?" I asked.

"Here," she said vaguely.

"But there's nothing here." I looked around again, desperate to make sense of what was going on.

"I didn't want to leave home," she said. "I didn't want what happened to my life. I wanted to be somebody. I've figured out where we are. *Alterna Inferma.* My father used to play it all the time, too. He was also obsessed with the General, Janaelle. Sorry to tell you, Sharps, but you weren't alone in thinking she was hot shit."

She was right! Level 5, The Hidden Maze of the Mausoleum. My heart sank. It was one of the toughest levels.

A zeppelin shadow hovered above us. I sensed it before I saw it. I knew the play: the creature with a thousand flitting eyes would swoop down and suffocate us. I looked up to see it fanning its cape-like fins, preparing to drop and devour, but then it jerked away and dissolved into the high ceiling of the building. Why did it let us live? The zeppelins never let you live. I had wanted to point it out to Shasta, but it vanished too quickly and she was still staring at the shoe. I put my arm around Shasta and pulled her close.

My vision faded to soft around the edges, and renewed rivers of cold sweat ran down my scalp and my body. My heart was a panicked pulse in my eardrums, and my clothes were sodden. I didn't want Shasta to feel my weakness. I let go of her and leaned forward with my head on the ground and held my breath. It was as if spiders were crawling under my skin. How else to explain the bites erupting out of nowhere on my arms, legs, belly? Time travel was killing me, but I had to find a way back to save my boy and Sophie. I had to survive. I had to make it through this. The shoe was an omen, a message.

When I looked up, Shasta was gone and the only thing left was the shoe. What was happening? And why wasn't Sting Ray Bob saving us? *Oh shit.* I remembered what he'd told me way back when: "If the device fails, you have to dig it out of your wrist with a scalpel and rinse it off. You'll need to reset the software and stick it back in. It will hurt like hell."

Great. I didn't have a scalpel. I didn't have saline solution. All I had was the filth and the cold. I pulled up the sleeve of my coat, wondering if the device was still functional and thinking that getting a tattoo on top of it probably wasn't the most sensible of ideas. I rubbed my wrist in desperation, petrified that the implant might not be there, but to my relief, my thumb felt a small nub, an inch-long worm under my skin, buried deep. I rubbed at my wrist, hoping to reset the software by vigorous action, but nothing happened. My legs reminded me I was no spring chicken. I unlocked my joints and sat down cross-legged, which was marginally better, although I was shocked by how stiff my hips were. I reminded myself that stiffness and aging were the least of my worries at this point. I tapped the device, hard. Still nothing. Feeling like an idiot, I licked my skin, hoping the warmth of my tongue, such as it was in the ice-cold tomb, would help the device. But no. I sighed. I didn't have a scalpel. I had nothing. Except my nails. *Oh shit.* I looked at my fingernails. They were black and grimy. I tested my fingertips, but they were buffed and smooth which was no good. I needed something sharp. Sharps needed something sharp, *ha ha*, not funny. I laughed anyway, and my breath hung like a lacy curtain in front of my face. I realized that while I had been reflecting on my manicure, the temperature had plummeted. I'd better get a move on. And noticing my breath had done me no favours because it was as if my body suddenly realized how cold it was and I began to shiver like a poisoned dog.

I gnawed on the thumbnail of my right hand. It was the longest nail and the strongest. I bit off one side, creating a tiny triangle of a weapon, sharp enough, I hoped, to do the job.

I pushed the nail as hard as I could against my skin, but I only dented it. *Shit.* This was impossible. I leaned my head back and screamed. I didn't mean to make a noise and I startled myself, howling like a madman. I guided my thumbnail to the device and, still howling, I rolled onto my side and used the weight of my body to force the thumbnail into my left wrist.

I sawed the edge of the nail back and forth, and the blood flowed, hot and sticky. I'd done it! But where was the device? I brought my wrist close to my face. I could see it! A tiny glint of silver. I dug it out with my forefinger and my thumb, and I was shaking so hard, I nearly dropped it. I caught it under my fingernail and pressed it to the pad of my thumb. *Concentrate. Focus. Don't swallow it. Rinse it in your mouth. Find the reset button, and stick it back in.*

I hadn't counted on the blood tasting so vile. I nearly gagged and closed my throat just in time. My reflex was to spit the thing out but I rolled it around in my mouth and tried to rinse it, warm it up, do anything to make it work.

By now I was shaking so hard that I was convinced I wouldn't be able to get the device back in my wrist. I was curled up in the fetal position with my knees locked to my chest. I had to do it. I felt around in my mouth with my fingers and grabbed the device. I squinted closely and saw a tiny raised area like Sting Ray Bob had said. Could they possibly have made this any more difficult? I pressed my nail down hard, closed my eyes, and counted to ten. This had better work or it was all over for me. I didn't want to die or be stuck in this freezing hell. Trying not to think about what I had to do, I took the silver worm between my thumb and fingernail and pushed it deep back into the tiny wound. Then I passed out, with my thumb still pressed to my wrist.

42. FOURTH TIME LUCKY

WHEN I WOKE UP, SHASTA WAS LEANING over me. We were back at St. Drogo's. The mass of bodies was still the same only it smelled much worse than I remembered.

"Are you okay?" she asked, and I nodded.

"But I have to go back," I said. Instinct kept my thumb pressed to my wrist. "I have to go now. Don't come with me."

"God, no!" she said. "That was horrible. Getting stuck in the ArcadeCrystalChik Mall was a nightmare. I thought I loved the place, but I never want to see it again as long as I live."

The mall? Her displaced time, I guess. And mine was *Alterna Inferma,* Level 5, The Hidden Maze of the Mausoleum.

"Good luck," she said and kissed me. "You can do it, champ, I know you can."

I wished I had her faith in me. My body wanted to lie down and die; it was worn out, strung out, wrung out. But my mind was made up, and my desire fuelled me one last time. I had to jump now. I had to save the kids from Celeste, and I couldn't waste a single second. I had to jump before Sting Ray Bob or Jaxen showed up and hauled me away.

I knew this jump would be my last, even if there was still one left in my allotment. I couldn't manage any more after this.

I pointed my wrist at the gate, with my thumb firmly in place over the device. It worked! I landed back in my house. I took quick stock of the situation. I was upstairs in the bedroom. From the sounds of it, Celeste was making smoothies for everyone.

THE RAGE ROOM   271

I looked down at myself. I was covered in blood and dirt.

"Will you make me a blueberry faux-yoghurt with spinach?" I yelled down the stairs as if nothing had happened the night before, as if I hadn't hit her. "Please, CeeCee? I'll be down soon. I'm just going to take a shower."

I locked myself in the bathroom and took out the MediKit. I poured disinfectant into the gash in my wrist and winced at the pain, trying not to make a sound. I cleaned the wound thoroughly and rinsed it clean. I wrapped it in a bandage and tied it tightly. I didn't want the tiny silver grain to get lost when I was in the shower.

I scrubbed and washed every inch of my body, double soaping and loving the feel of the scalding water.

Once out the shower, I poked at the wound and recoiled in pain. A stupid move, but I needed to check the device was still there. It was. I bandaged it neatly and cleaned up, making sure all evidence of my first aid administrations were removed. The bathroom looked perfectly normal—a bit untidy for my liking but, nothing out of the ordinary.

I pulled on my suit and knotted my tie. I bundled my filthy clothes and shoved them to the bottom of the hamper. Time to get this show on the road. I felt surprisingly good; my head was clear and pain free, which was surprising, but I'd take it.

I flashed a message to Ava.

Am sick, will be in later if I can, sorry.

So fire my ass, if you like, bitch.

She shot back.

Sure you're sick. Delaying this won't change anything. I've got evidence that nails you and Williamson. I'm going to be promoted while your ass(es) will be fired! I don't need you to come in. The lawyers will be in touch. I'm going to rule the fucking world, Sharps.

I stared at the comm. This was a disconcerting and new development. Ava didn't need me to come in? That wasn't supposed to happen. But I didn't have time to think about it, and I didn't bother to reply. I rushed over to the pink Crys-talMeBooty shoe box. The box was full of drugs just like Shasta had said! Not only Clonazepam but a dozen others, and the names were all Diazepam this, or Sertraline that. I riffled through them quickly. Holy shit, which one to use? My plan was to crush the pills somehow and get them into Celeste's smoothie or her morning coffee.

But then, at the bottom of the box I scored a motherload. Nirvana! *WTF!* Nirvana was a designer drug, stronger than a mix of heroin, cocaine, and fentanyl. Six syringes, all loaded and ready to go. I grabbed two and closed the box.

"Cee," I called down, "can you come up? I need to tell you something."

She didn't reply, but I heard her coming up the stairs.

"What?" She wasn't happy with me and she stood in the doorway, hands on her hips.

"Cee," I said, "I lost it last night. What I did was unforgive-able. But Ava's accusing me of stealing from the company when it was Jazza, but I can't prove it yet. Please forgive me. I got the comm from Ava last night—she wants to see me today."

"What?" Her eyes widened and she walked towards me, her truculence replaced by clouded confusion. "Does Daddy know? Sharps, what's wrong with your eyes?"

I shook my head. "What do you mean?"

"They're all red. Have a look."

"I was just in the shower and everything was fine." I tried to brush her off, wondering what the hell she was talking about and thinking that whatever it was, I'd deal with it later. But she led me back into the still-steamy washroom and rubbed the mirror clean with a towel.

Oh shit. The whites of my eyeballs were a solid Halloween zombie red. It was off-putting to say the least. "Oh shit. I guess I blew a few blood vessels," I said lamely. "I'll get it checked out as soon as I've dealt with Ava. But listen, Cee, don't leave me. You and the kids mean everything to me." Good, so she hadn't heard about Ava's allegations and neither had Daddy. That was good, at least.

"Well," she said and moved slightly closer to me, "you have been behaving really weirdly lately. I was going to take the kids to Real Life Florida and give you some time to yourself, but your work situation explains a lot. Honey, you aren't really going to be fired, are you?"

"I've got it all under control." I sounded so convincing that I even believed myself. "Please, Cee, let me hold you. I know you've got no reason to be kind to me but it's been terrible."

She softened slightly but she was still resistant. I moved towards her and put my arms around her. "I'm sorry," I said. "Cee, haven't I always provided for you? Understood you like no one else? Loved you? I always have and I always will. Come on, baby, we're a team, you know that." She sank into my arms, and I caressed her and pulled her close and murmured in her ear. I brushed the hair away from her neck, as if I was going to kiss her neck, then I plunged the syringe in deep. I held her with all my might as she bucked and tried to get away. She only fought for a second or two, and then she sagged heavily, nearly pulling me down with her.

I managed to drag her to the bed and arrange her on her side, removing one of her slippers. I took the second syringe and shot it between her toes and replaced the slipper. She turned a weird shade of grey-green purple and started foaming at the mouth, her eyes wide and bulging. She took longer to die than I had expected. She thrashed around, and I hoped the kids couldn't hear anything.

She finally lay still. She was twisted and dishevelled, her mouth an open O.

I flashed a message to Jazza.

> Running late. Don't do anything stupid. As in, do NOT kill yourself or anyone else. Got it? Wait for me. I've got a plan.

Then I called #Emr. "My wife, I think she's taken drugs. I came upstairs and she was having a fit, and now she's not moving at all." I tried to sound hysterical and infuse my voice with emotion, but I sounded like an awkward kid at a recital, worried he'd forget his words. I knew the SSOs used voice stress analysis in homicide cases, and I hoped my inflections would be credible.

I went downstairs to wait. I did an unheard-of thing, I put on the ChirpyChippiesForWinkles channel, cartoons for the kiddies, something only used by me to entertain them when I was utterly desperate to quiet them or on very special occasions. I put Bax on the sofa with his very own box of Chompy Chocoroos and propped Sophie up in her high chair with a bottle. She was a little old for the bottle, but she still loved it and I needed to keep the peace.

The officers got there in no time at all.

"We were all here in the kitchen," I told one of the guys while the medics worked on Celeste upstairs. "Having breakfast, as you can see. Celeste said she needed to get something from our bedroom before I went to work and that I was to watch the kids for a few minutes. But then she didn't come down and I went up and found her."

I had cleaned the first syringe of my prints, pressed Celeste's fingers around it, and left it, fallen by the bedside. And I buried the second syringe in a bag of Sophie's used diapers that I thought was as safe a place as any. "No, I didn't know my wife was a drug user. It really scares me that I left her alone with the kids all this time."

I realized I needed to show more shock and devastation. "I don't even know what to say," I told the mullet-haired officer. "I'll be honest, none of this feels real. I feel absolutely numb." I ran my fingers through my hair, my eyes wide, unblinking. "To find her like that was such a terrible shock. I had no idea she did drugs. I'll never forget what she looked like. I feel like she'll come downstairs at any moment and carry on with breakfast. She loves Christmas—it's her favourite time of the year. Her parents are in Real Life Florida. Oh man, this will kill them. And the kiddies, look at them. So innocent." I knew I was babbling.

A woman officer was chatting to the kids, and they were both looking at her with delighted googly-eyed wonder.

"Do you have anybody who can help you with the children?" Mr. Mullet asked and I nodded. "My mother."

I called Mother. "Celeste is dead and I need you," I said without preamble. "Turns out she took drugs. Please come, Mother."

There was silence. "I'm on my way," she said, and we swiped our comms closed.

"She's not the warmest person in the world," I told Mr. Mullet, "but she'll step up in a crisis. I'm just trying to keep it together in front of the kids. I feel numb." I knew I'd said that before, but I had to try to explain my lack of emotion. "I can't lose it."

The man looked at me like he had seen and heard it all before, and maybe he had.

"It's a pandemic," he said. "Nirvana. Terrible stuff. Killing dozens every day. I'm sorry to say this, sir, but it's not unusual, even in suburbia, even for rich families."

"I knew my wife drank," I said. "I'm not being disloyal by telling you that—the evidence is there, she's been to rehab a few times. But I never knew she did drugs." Which was true. Until Shasta told me, I'd had no idea.

"You should check the house to see that there aren't any drugs or drug paraphernalia that the children could find," Mr. Mullet said. "You realize I have to ask you about your eyes," he added, and he motioned one of the medics over.

"I woke up like this," I explained as the man examined me. "I have been working long hours on a new campaign and work's been very stressful. Could it be that?"

The paramedic shook his head. "It's a subconjunctival hae-morrhage. The cause isn't always known, and I haven't seen it in both eyes like this. Tell me, sir, have you had any violent coughing fits, powerful sneezing, straining, vomiting? Have you rubbed your eyes or experienced any trauma to the eyes, such as the insertion of a foreign object into them?" The man sounded like a robot. I looked at him closely. Nope, he was real.

I shook my head. "No to all of them." I pulled my shirt sleeve down low. The last thing I needed was for anyone to see the bandage on my left wrist. They'd think I tried to kill myself and that'd be the end of all my plans. I could always tell them the tattoo got infected.

"And do you suffer from either of the following: diabetes or high blood pressure, also known as hypertension? Do you take any blood-thinning medications, such as Warfarin, Coumadin, Jantoven or aspirin? Do you have a blood-clotting disorder?"

"What? No, I don't. No to any of them. Look, I'm fine. I have to see if my kids are okay. I'll get this checked out later with my optometrist. Please, this doesn't matter now."

I went over to see Bax and Sophie. Bax looked at me warily while Sophie hugged me unreservedly. "I know my eyes are funny," I said to Bax, but I knew it wasn't that, it was that I'd hit Celeste. "Buddy, come here, Daddy loves you so much. Things have been a bit tough, Bax. Life's not easy, kiddo. Please, come give Daddy a hug, okay?" He did, wrapping his arms around me, and I buried my face in him, my other arm still clinging to Sophie. These little guys. I got all choked up and was about to start howling, which would have really scared them, but then Mother arrived.

I wiped my eyes gently, wishing the eyeball thing hadn't happened as it called unwanted attention to myself, but I'd have to live with it.

Mother took charge, and the SSOs removed Celeste's body and left. Mother had brought an overnight bag. "I'm here for you, Sharps," she said. "As long as you and the children need me."

"Thank you, Mother," I said. "And I know it's really bad timing, but I have to go into work."

"You go," she said, waving a hand around. "I'll clean up." She paused. "Sharps, I need to tell you something. Something I've been keeping from you for a long time." She took a deep breath. "Your father and I stole you. I wanted a baby so badly and I couldn't have one. So your father went and stole you. I don't really remember if it was him or me who chose you. There was a home for unwed mothers in a place called No Daddy Street. The locals called it that. We figured that we'd give a child a better home than a young, teenage mother, so I got a job in the kitchen there. The place was a revolving door, and hardly any fuss was raised when a baby went missing. There were dozens of babies like you. No one kept track of the girls—they came and went how they liked—so after you disappeared, they just figured they had miscounted or the girl and her baby had left."

"Didn't my real mother make a fuss? Surely she would have said something?"

Mother shook her head. "For some of those girls, their baby going missing would have been a relief. Most of them opted to have their babies adopted, and they got out of there as soon as they could. The place was a birthing stable, and like I said, it was hard to keep track. Some girls left as soon as their babies were born, so again, it wasn't that strange a thing to happen."

No Daddy Street. The origins of my illustrious beginnings, born to a teenage girl who didn't care about me. Stolen by a man who was damaging and cruel. But Mother had always loved me in her own inimitable way. I knew that was true. I'd hated her when she booted me out, but I knew she had done it for my own good. I hated her when she rejected Celeste, but she'd been right about that too. She had always cared while I'd only felt judged and lacking. Which wasn't on her. It was on me, I saw that now. I was the one filled with self-loathing, not Mother. And I'd felt vindicated when she had seemingly withdrawn from my life, but that was just good old angry me finding yet another thing to be angry about.

I went to her and hugged her, and she held me close. "Thank you, Mother."

I ran upstairs and emptied the contents of Celeste's pink shoe box into a gym bag, grabbed my keys, kissed the kids, and left. "I'll be back as soon as I can," I shouted.

43. AND TO JAZZA'S WE GO

I WAS TIRED AS FUCK. I SAT IN MY CAR. One down, one to go. I looked at my eyes in the rearview mirror. I looked like something out of a horror movie. And maybe it was the adrenaline wearing off, but my whole body was aching, like a giant-sized flu bug had jumped up and bitten me in the ass.

I got to Jazza's building and hauled myself to the elevator. My face was slick with oily stinging sweat. *Shit.* Come on, body, hold it together. I leaned on the wall as I made my way to Jazza's door.

He was waiting for me, his arms folded. "You look fucking terrible, man," he said. "And by the way, fyi, why would I kill myself or anybody else? Weird fucking message, man. I suppose you want to know why I did it? Why I set you up so damn bad?"

But I shook my head. "I don't care why. But you are going to fix this."

"Or what, big man? You're going to kill me? *Ha ha,* you couldn't kill a fruit fly."

"That's because I like fruit flies more than I like you," I said. "You are going to flash a breaking news alert to Integratron Universal and tell them you did it. Repeat the alert, with alarm bells code black." In other words, the loudest. We all had access to send breaking news to Integratron Universal, in case of emergency. We each had one code, one shot at saving the world. Or, in this case, saving my ass.

"Am not!"

"Are so!" I punched him hard in the gut with all my weakened feeble force, and he, taken by surprise, doubled over, wheezing. "And you know why you will, Jazza baby? Because there, on your portable comm, is the evidence I need. I know it's there. Bank transactions, you name it. And if I need to kill you to get it, I will. All your comm souvenirs are there. Sure, I signed off on the money, but I thought it was for a marketing campaign. You're the one who pressed the TRANSFER button for your bitch, Ava. Let's not forget that. That's why you're going to send the alert."

He stared at me. I could see the ones and zeros of his brain trying to flush out a solution, but he came up empty.

"I'm going to stand behind you," I said. "But first, you see this?" I showed him a syringe of Nirvana I had taken from Celeste's sho box. "I'm going to jab you with it if you make the slightest move. But before we even do that, tell me, don't show me, tell me where you keep your gun."

"Gun? *Ha ha,* you're nuts today, Sharps," he joked, but his eyes flashed over to a faux-Peruvian wooden box on the coffee table.

I reached over and I flipped it open. I grabbed the gun and the silencer that was inside, keeping an eye on him all the while. "I'm scoring everywhere today," I said. "Must be my lucky day. I should buy a FeathersFromHeaven lottery ticket, what with all this luck that I'm having, and go and live on a Real Life beach. So now I'm double armed—how cool is that? I tell you what, Jazza, let's send the world a bunch of proof, so get your shit together." I checked the time. It was nearly three thirty, and I had to hurry.

Because I had to go back to my future, I had no choice. Even if I wanted to, I wouldn't be able to just stay here. I had asked Sting Ray Bob if there was a way for me to stay in past present time when I went back, but he'd said no. He'd said I didn't have to jump but once I had, I had no choice but to come back. I'd thought about digging the gadget out, but I had the feeling that that wouldn't work. The gadget owned me, and Janaelle and the others were in control. This wasn't real time. I had to get back to real time and figure out how to join the two timelines. Sting Ray Bob had yet to explain how that would work.

"Pick up the pace buddy, okay? Capchas, transactions. Let's get moving."

By four thirty the comm had been sent and by that time, I could hardly move. I had to get out of there before Jazza attacked me. He probably didn't realize it, but he could have swatted me with a feather duster and I would have fallen over.

"I'm going to have to lock you in that closet," I said, motioning. "Come on, in you go. It won't take you long to break out. Go on, in you go."

He went in reluctantly, the gun at his back. I locked the door, picked up the portable comm, and fled. Well, fled is an exaggeration. I stumbled, hobbled, limped, and practically crawled to my car. Five p.m. I needed to hide until I went back.

But first I had to message Mother.

I can't explain this but I need a day to fix things. Please don't lose faith in me Mother. I need u to stand by me.

She got back to me right away.

Don't worry, Sharps. I'm always here for u. In all possible worlds.

It was one of the weirdest, most loving things she had ever said to me. I'd take it.

And then I waited, wondering how bad it would be this time.

44. JANAELLE HAS SOME 'SPLAINING TO DO

STING RAY BOB WAS READY FOR ME on the other side. He and Jaxen carried me out of the subway and into a waiting van. They hooked me up to IV bags and covered me with a weighted blanket, and I knew everything was going to be okay. My kids were safe with Mother. Celeste was dead. I had cleared my name. I could finally rest. Jazza was alive, which would hopefully score me points with OctoPuss.

When I came to, I was lying in a camp bed and the rain was pouring outside. I sat up, groggy. Jaxen and Sting Ray Bob were slouched in old-fashioned canvas camping chairs. I pushed myself up on one elbow. "How long was I out for this time?"

"Four days," Sting Ray Bob said. "You were depleted, one percent activity. We could hardly boot you up. You're lucky you're not dead."

I looked around. "Why are we in a tent and not in the fancy lab? I hadn't figured you guys for campers. I know I'm not. Not that I'm being ungrateful, but this isn't the five-star luxury I've come to know, love, and expect."

"Well, kiddo, this shit's about to get real!" Jaxen said, cheerfully. "Here's the thing, we've got a bit of 'splaining to do, as they say. Let's go back in time. Do you remember when you guys were on your way to St. Adrian's, the very first time?"

"Of course. It was Knox, Norman, me, and Shasta."

"Affirmative. And you stopped to get supplies—junk food

for Shasta mainly—and you pulled over in the parking lot for a quick forty winks?"

"I didn't remember, but now that you mention it, yes, I do, vaguely."

"When you woke up, it was actually two days later. You probably didn't notice a heavy-load transporter truck parked near you? Of course not; there were a bunch of them. One of them was ours. We kept you three inside, drugged and sedated. We implanted electro-magnetic optical, auditory, and sensory chip cards into your brains to reprogram what you saw. We did it to Shasta and Knox too and took them along for the ride right up till the sherry tomato soup had been shared and the grilled cheese bread broken, then we kicked them to the curb and sent them back to St. Polycarp. Following that, we inserted the electromagnetic semiconductor that you needed for time travel."

"That's impossible!"

"What, the chip cards or the electromagnetic semiconductor or the fact that we kept you drugged for three days?"

"All of them. But mainly the chip cards."

"It's much less complicated than you might think. OctoOne wrote the scripts for it, and we implanted them. How do they work? The cards, tinier than you can imagine, fire impulses in the brain that make you think what you see, hear, taste, and touch are all real."

"Impossible." And yet ... Daddy ... and Mummy ... and Celeste. They were holograms of their younger selves, or selves that they wanted the world to see. I'd realized that, so why was this so astounding? Because this was an entire world, not just a person. These were relationships. This was more than a bio-genetically enhanced body and facial suit that absorbed light rays and reflected a handpicked doll self, like an avatar come to life.

"It changed the visuals. For example, the lab. This," Sting Ray Bob gestured outside as he spoke, "this is the lab. What you saw—the high tech building, the lab with all the technicians in white—doesn't exist. This is the reality."

"No shit! I don't believe it!"

"I thought you might say that," Jaxen said, and he took out a micro-programmer. "Hold onto your panties, big boy, this is going to blow your mind."

He typed onto the screen and paused. "When I press enter, the world as you know it will change radically."

"Come on already," I said. He pressed enter and next thing, we were back in the lab. I was in my room, on my bed, in my white sweatpants that I most certainly had not being wearing seconds earlier. "But it's real," I said, grabbing the coverlet. "Feel it!"

I got up and felt the wall. It felt real. "But the space! This room is three times the size of the tent! And the light is different, and it even smells different!"

"All data that's being fed to your brain. An alternate reality created by planting new circuitry into your synapses."

"Turn it off," I said. "Please turn it off." He did, and we were back in the tent. "But how do I know this is real and you're not messing with me?"

Jaxen laughed. "Seriously, Sharps, do you think we'd choose to live in a leaking canvas tent when we could be residing in a state-of-the art palace designed by an architectural genius?"

"But you've got all the money that Jazza stole for Ava for you guys!"

"Yes, we do, and OctoOne's got plans to rebuild down the line, but first she wants the world to recalibrate. In the meantime, and that means for at least a decade, the money's going towards scientists monitoring the world, and creating data banks of information, as well as support for farming and fishing. Basically taking stock of where things are at. How many animals are left? We need to take inventory of the forests. Can the oceans be revived? Things like that. And what else is out there? Anything new? The world has to be mapped again just like it was centuries ago because we've destroyed so much. So the money, as large a sum as it was, is just a drop in the bucket of what's needed to get Mother Earth back on track. Thankfully, we've got soldiers in every cell of Integratron Global and our reserves are pretty big."

A thought occurred to me. "What else isn't real?"

"That, buddy, is the million-dollar question. All shall be revealed, and we apologize in advance for any inconvenience that this experiment has caused you."

"Experiment?"

"Yes. And you succeeded where many others have failed! You should be very proud of yourself! And before you ask, yes, your kids are alive, Celeste is dead, and Jazza is alive. Your mother is looking after the kids."

"Where does Mother think I am?"

"She thinks Jazza shot you. You're in the hospital in a coma."

"What? That's impossible. You can't implant optical transfers or whatever into anyone you feel like! How did you get her to believe that?"

Jaxen sighed. He was clearly getting tired of my stupidity. "Sharps. Come on. The SSOs told her not to go to the hospital because you were in a medically-induced coma, which she believed. So your absence is taken care of, and she is looking forward to your healthy return, which will be soon."

"And who are you guys, really?"

"We are The MosaliTitans. A world army made up of international chapters including the Eden Collective and the World Wide Warriors. Mosali means 'women' in Sesotho. We took our lead from the women in Real Life South Africa who wanted a party that really represented the people. That's our flag."

I looked up at a black flag with a large white acorn, crisscrossed by a sword and a rifle with a tiny crescent moon and a star to the right. It looked Islamic and yet African at the same time.

"And it all went according to plan," Sting Ray Bob added. "Although, we admit that the early timing of the Kickstart

Evolution was a surprise. It wasn't supposed to have happened for a while, but, *c'est la vie*. OctoOne said it was better anyway. She said she'd heard the rumours that Minnie was getting wind that the Evolution was coming and so better safe than sorry to get a jump on the reboot."

"Restoring the world to its natural state might not have been the best thing," I commented. "It's a muddy mess."

"You may jest, and things will be tough for a while, but they'll get better." Sting Ray Bob was confident.

"Where's Minnie?"

"In a padded cell. She lost her marbles when it all went down. And here's the thing, Mama's been dead for decades! It was all an illusion."

Something occurred to me. "What do you guys look like for real?" I asked, and there was silence.

"The thing is," Sting Ray Bob said, "we are geniuses, you realize that? Remember the old saying about not judging books by their covers, *etcetera etcetera*."

"Listen, you guys." I was struggling for words. "You, for some inexplicable reason, had faith in me. And you got me my kids back. And you taught me the meaning of life. I know we don't know each other in any kind of social sense, but I'd like to think that we're friends as well as business partners or guinea pigs or whatever. I don't care what you look like."

"You say that now," Jaxen said. "Fine, here we go."

45. JAXEN IS MOTHER!

JAXEN VANISHED BEFORE MY EYES. And in his place appeared Mother! Mother! Tall, hefty, somewhat mannish Mother with her long grey hair, prominent nose, and close-set dark eyes. Mother had always been proud of the fact that her older self resembled Patti Smith in her seventies. And here she was. Jaxen was Mother.

I sank down onto my cot and covered my face with my hands. Where to even start? "You know I killed you?" I muttered.

She sat down next to me and patted me on the shoulder. "Your actions have been very interesting, Sharps," she said, and her tone was gentle. "It was fascinating to watch your amorality unfold."

"Fascinating? I KILLED YOU!" I screamed, jumped up, and then rushed as far away from her as I could, which wasn't very far.

"If my life had been sacrificed for the cause, then I would have been okay with that." She was calm. "We all wanted to see what you would do. In fact, me most of all." She sighed. "Sharps, I told the Eden Collective about you. I told them you'd make the perfect subject for this project. I also truly thought this could help you."

"Help me? How?"

"Well, you did kill your children. We gave you the chance of redemption. I red-flagged you years ago, but when you killed your children, which by the way none of us had any inkling you'd do, we realized that not only could we use you, but that we had to."

Her eyes filled with tears. "Do you have any idea how I felt? I'd let them down. I felt like I'd killed them myself. I left you and that woman with them."

"Left them with us? We were their parents!"

I realized, as I said that, that my argument was sensationally flawed.

"But," she continued, "short of kidnapping them, what could I have done? It didn't exactly work out, me kidnapping you. It's not like I was a contender for the Best Mother Award, although I tried my best. Children are fresh slates, so I must have done something wrong."

I sat down next to her. "No, Mother, you didn't do anything wrong. I've never been right. You know it and I know it. But I tried so hard too. I tried harder than anyone I know to be the perfect dad and husband. It's all I wanted—don't you see? To be the perfect man."

"And," Mother said, "according to Ava, you are exactly that."

I stared at her. "What do you mean?"

"You are the embodiment of what man is. You and your actions are the embodiment of the quintessential, primal, patriarchal persona, from start to finish, top to bottom. It's as if you were distilled to have all the qualities of a man. But," she hastened to add, "this doesn't mean you are without good points. You did love your children; you did love Celeste—well, you tried. You did the tough work by going back and trying to save them, to make up for what you'd done. You repented, you chose alternative action, and you fought your baser nature, and that's what also makes you the perfect man. Don't you see, Sharps?"

I groaned and rubbed my eyes. Even here, even now, I couldn't ditch Ava. "What about Sting Ray Bob?" I asked. "And Janaelle?"

"I'm Sting Ray," came the reply and a willowy woman

appeared, with a broad smile. She had deep coffee-coloured skin, a long rustic mane of greying dreadlocks, a prominent nose and teeth that seemed unusually large, but perhaps I was just imagining it. "Sting Ray Barb, not Bob. Not sure I was too happy that you mixed me up with your Hockney man, but such is life. I designed a way more handsome avatar, but your cortex blocked my suggestions. All your visions were influenced by your own memories, hopes, and fears. They came as much from you as us. That's why you saw your mother as a big muscle man. That's what you wanted her to be."

I wondered if that had anything to do with my father, but I didn't have a single spare brain cell to think about that.

"And Janaelle?" It was the question I'd been dying to ask the most, and it was the question I was most afraid to ask.

"She's out there." Mother pointed to outside the tent. "Her name's Noelle. And be nice to her, Sharps, no matter what you think. She's really into you."

"Of course I'll be nice!" But I was petrified. Janaelle was gone. Who would be in her place? "Does she even have steel legs?"

"Of course she does," Sting Ray Barb said, and she sounded annoyed. "You can only take visual distortions so far."

"Where is she?" She pointed and I took a deep breath and looked.

The woman turned to me as if she sensed I was looking at her. She was short, the same height as Janaelle, but that's where the resemblance ended. This woman had spiky platinum hair, and her face was covered in piercings. And she was as broad as she as high. She could probably hoist me with one arm no problem, whereas I'd seen her as a delicate flower. She was dressed in camouflage, not a long-skirted dress. Her features were stronger, with broad cheekbones, sensual lips, and heavily-lidded eyes. She looked exotic, a warrior who could snap me in two like a toothpick, should the whim take her.

"You liked the dress idea," she said, coming up to me. "That came from you. Camo, that's more me!"

She grinned, flashing silver incisors. When she smiled, her face opened like a flower, dimples creased her cheeks, and she was transformed to stunning. Up close, her eyes were green with gold flecks, and she had the longest eyelashes I had ever seen. She was incredible, but she wasn't my Janaelle.

"What on earth were you doing with me?" I asked, and she laughed.

"Enjoying every minute," she said. "I got to date the prom king, the quarterback hero of my fantasies. Any regrets from your side?"

I hesitated and she saw, and her face slammed shut. I tried to find the love I'd felt for her, but it wasn't there. She wasn't Janaelle, and I couldn't help that.

"I thought you had faith?" I challenged her. "Would a person of faith be so duplicitous?"

"I am a woman of faith. There is only one Creator and Her Name is Truth and we shall set Her free. Namaste. That never changed. I abide by and respect the fundamental principles of human morality and a sense of order within the world that was created by a being more extraordinary than we can ever imagine."

"So what now?" I asked, not interested in her or her theology. "How do I get back to my kids? Do I just go over to the house and see them? Say, 'Hey Mother, I'm home. Isn't this weather crappy,' and pretend like I don't know about any of this shit?"

Sting Ray Barb nodded. "We can take you back to just as you were about to leave to go to Jazza's place. You'll feel a strong sense of *déjà vu* for the first few hours—you may even feel some dizziness and nausea—but it will pass and then your lives will be connected."

"Isn't there a way to avoid the jump? Why must I go back?" I sounded whiny and I knew it.

"The time circle has to close," Sting Ray Barb said, and I thought I saw Mother and Noelle exchange a glance. "It cannot remain stranded, unhinged like that." Was she lying to me? Yet again I was powerless to challenge their assertions.

I nodded and looked around the skanky campgrounds. The rain continued to pour, and I was damp to the bone. The aging canvas tent didn't offer much by way of shelter. I wondered where they'd got it. Probably from some war museum. All their equipment looked antique and quaint, like it came from the early twentieth century.

"This world's rough," I commented. "I preferred the luxurious model we had before."

"At least this is real," Mother said. "Nature's recalibrating; the Earth needs to heal. And we'll get used to this. It'll be interesting to have a real winter. All of life's going to be a Real Life adventure, Sharps, in a real life way!"

I suppose she was right, but being cold and damp for the rest of my life didn't thrill me.

Sting Ray Barb laughed and those unfortunate teeth laughed with her. Big horsey teeth. How come Sting Ray Barb didn't have the standard issue teeth? That was weird. We all had the same teeth. I was mesmerized for a moment, and all I could think was *all the better to eat you with*. I was losing it. I shook my attention away from her teeth. "I gotta say, this has been a lot to take in," I said. "And I have some questions, if that's okay."

"Sure, Sharps." I could hear that Noelle was trying to be patient, but there was an undercurrent to her tone as if I was yesterday's news slapping her in the face like a wet fish. "We've got all the time in the world to sit here chatting while the real world burns."

I ignored her sarcasm. Maybe she was upset that I wasn't attracted to her, but she'd lied to me about who she was and I had earned my right to know the truth. "How does it work, what you're doing? Why unplug the world? And why did you need me to time travel and succeed? Why did you access the data in the rage rooms? I still don't understand. You owe me that much at least."

46. WHY TIME TRAVEL?

"I'VE GOT THIS," STING RAY BARB SAID. "Going back in time, a decade or so after she'd been in power, Minnie and the Sacred Board realized that the sun was dying. Sayonara solar power and, therefore, goodbye to the only world we had left. The rest of nature was long gone, all we had left was the sun and, alas, our great solar star was quickly heading towards extinction too.

"The Sacred Board appointed an emergency commission to look into alternate ways of harnessing energy and—guess what? It turned out that we had to look no farther than our own noses. The winning idea was human. Electricity from humans was the way to go—body power. Think about it, Sharps! Our bodies are potential torches, brimming with energy, so much so that spontaneous human combustion is a real thing. And what creates more power and electricity than rage? Nothing. That was the real reason Minnie invented the rage rooms. She wanted to monitor her subjects—keep an eye on what was happening, how her subjects were feeling—and give them an outlet for anger, but more importantly, she believed there was a real possibility that gathering the electrical output could create a viable resource to fuel the world."

"And did it work?"

"Yes. Because by god, there's so much anger out there! You've got no idea. World energy problems solved! The sun was weakening, but it was still around, which meant that Minnie had time to stockpile a reservoir of energy that would be ready to rock when the great celestial light kicked the bucket. But you know what they say, Sharps, about the best laid plans of mice and men.... The sun rejuvenated! Scientists are still scratching their heads as to the hows and whys, but the sun rebounded with ten-fold its original energy. Minnie kept the rage rooms going because people needed them and also because, as she put it, the sun had proven a streaky player in the game. Who knew when it would snuff out and leave us in the dark? Hence the continuation of the rage rooms. Thank god she did, or we'd have lost access to our data and our subjects."

"Okay," I said. "But what did the rage rooms have to do time travel?"

"Nothing at first." Sting Ray Barb said. "The rage rooms were just the rage rooms. And time travel was just a hypothesis that Minnie quashed as soon as it raised its ugly scientific head. Too politically dangerous, she said. It made her vulnerable to attacks from timelines she couldn't control, and also, according to her ethos, time travel was interfering with God's Will and Mama would have none of that.

"Meanwhile, my mother and her professor friend, Doctor Horvarth, came across a largely redacted time travel hypothesis, and of course, to them time travel was irresistible. They had to test it out. The first attempt ended in catastrophe. The volunteer subject couldn't successfully reintegrate on return, and she died. But the collateral data showed a massive energy spike when the woman jumped. Huge! My mother and Dr. Horvarth realized they had discovered the pot of gold at the end of the rainbow. The guinea pig was Jazza's mother by the way, for which she received a posthumous medal from Head Office."

"And that's why Jazza had to be saved. He's the son of the big hero."

They all nodded. "His mother is one of our most revered heroines in this war," Sting Ray Barb said, "but the whole thing had to be kept a secret and not just because jumping killed people. Of course all the heads-of-state knew that the energy harnessed in the rage rooms was a great source of electrical power—and we were quietly skimming and collecting as much of the excess as we could—but they had no idea that the output, when combined with time travel, was excessive beyond all expectations. One jump produced enough energy to power a small city for a month.

"It had to be kept a secret because of the ethical issues. I mean, people would have to be sacrificed in order for the rest of the world to survive. It was like that old movie, *Soylent Green*. 'Green is people!' In that admittedly fictional instance, people were recycled into food. In reality, human sacrifice for the greater good isn't really anything new but it is morally questionable, no doubt."

"So your solution was to use 'expendable' humans like me?"

"Generally speaking, yes, but I knew you'd survive," Mother said. "All the data pointed to it. I hoped you'd use the opportunity to go back and make better choices, Sharps. I hoped it would help you. I'd never have put you through it had I believed it would kill you."

"Sure, Mother." I glared at her with hatred. "Exactly what data are you referring to?"

"You need to have a unique gene coupled with a compatible psychological, intellectual, and emotional profile. You've heard it said all humans are 99.9% identical? That was true at one point, but as soon as scientists were no longer limited by the amounts of sequenced DNA available for study, we were able to discover there's a gene for almost every trait, including time travel. We each carry three billion pairs of information inside us—isn't that beautiful?"

"Stunning. But seriously, there's a time travel gene?"

"Yes," Sting Ray Barb admitted, but her tone was reluctant and her gaze was vague. "It's got more to do with cell capacity for dis- and re-integration. It's hard to explain. Anyway, we identified a location with an intermittent magnetic field that generated plasma by way of a coronal discharge. That was one of the two thing Dr. Horvarth discovered we needed when Jazza's mother took her ill-fated ride. The perfect location turned out to be St. Drogo's train station because it has the weakest temporal structure in the city. It has the most effective geographical coordinates to bridge time. It's just a junction where the veil of time is most transparent, most fragile."

This was too much to take in, and my brain felt fuzzy, but Sting Ray Barb forged on and I tried to focus on what she was saying.

"Dr. Horvarth further calculated that we needed to create the same kind of environment found in the Integratron in California. It's a Multiple Wave Oscillator that was invented by Georges Lakhovsky, a scientist who believed that ultra radio frequencies were a cure for cancer." She noticed my blank look. "I find the history of all this fascinating, but I know we don't have the time—*ha ha,* bad joke! What you need to know is that we flooded St. Drogo's with the same radio frequencies as the Integratron because it was designed for time travel."

"But wait! What do you mean? Integratron is the corporation I work for." These guys were losing me more and more with every utterance.

Mother barked out a laugh echoed by Sting Ray Barb and Noelle. "Oh, Sharps! Ever naïve! There's no originality in today's world! They ripped off the name! And of course it's ironic that it's the glaring antithesis of the very thing from which it stole the name. Our world hides behind bloated catchphrases that espouse goodwill and spirituality while essentially selling useless junk to the masses with aching holes in their guts, wanting more, more, more. Of which, Sharps, need I remind you, you were a primary purveyor?"

"How about we get back to the discussion we were actually having." I glared at Mother. "Did anyone ever actually time travel from the original Integratron?" I was curious.

"No, but we believe the scientific theory was sound. The Multiple Wave Oscillator," she continued, "is a combination of a high-voltage Tesla coil and a Split-ring resonator that generates ultra wideband electromagnetic frequencies. Van Tassel, the guy who designed the Integratron, had a theory that electromagnetism affects biological cells, and he believed that every biological cell has a unique resonant electromagnetic frequency. According to Van Tassel, the generation of strong ultra wideband EMF by the Integratron resonates with the cell's frequency and recharges the cellular structure as if it were an electrical battery. Van Tassel claimed that human cells 'rejuvenated' while inside the structure, but we've taken it a couple of steps further. Well, my mother and Dr. Horvath did."

"But how was the rage room energy collected and stored?" I was trying to picture it in my mind.

"In electrochemical capacitors. They used to be called double-layer Supercapacitors but now they're called Iracapacitators, *ira* being Latin for rage. They store electrical charges at a surface-electrolyte interface of high-surface-area carbon electrodes. But Sharps, we're veering off topic here."

She was right. I had no idea what the heck she was talking about. I decided to stick with topics I had an actual grasp on.

"And no one noticed your mother and Dr. Horvarth and you guys doing all this stuff?" I asked.

"It was fairly easy to fly under the radar. However, my mother and Dr. Horvarth constantly lived in terror that they would be found out and killed for the intel. Money wasn't what motivated my mother or Dr. Horvarth, but you imagine the dollar bills this could have brought in. There are people out there on the black market, survivalists who'll do anything to stock up their underground larders. But Sharps, you haven't connected the dots yet, and I'm a little disappointed."

"What do you mean?"

"The teeth! It's all about the teeth!"

Now I really had no idea what was going on.

47. TEETH

"REMEMBER WHEN EVERYBODY'S TEETH fell out?" Sting Ray Barb asked, and I nodded. "That was no accident. Minnie's fav buddy on the Sacred Board was a crazy dictator from some 'stan' empire: Türkmenistan, Kazakhstan, Uzbekistan, Afghanistan—one of those eastern countries who refused to be sainted or dubbed Real Life this or that. God knows the guy's name; it's one of those unpronounceable three-sentence, a-hundred-syllable epics. He was a dentist before he was a dictator, and he came up with the idea for dental implant hard drives. Sure, we all had Crystal Path chips, but it took Minnie about three seconds to realize that she wanted more control than the Path's capacity could afford her. Besides, the chips had started to show their age and couldn't take any further upgrades, so *voilà*, in came the great water scandal. We all lost our teeth and were given new dentures jam-packed with a new super powerful hidden internal hard drive. They poisoned the water in order to fit us up with two petabytes of memory."

"A petabyte?"

"A million terabytes a person!"

"But why on earth would we need all that memory in our teeth?" None of it made any sense to me.

"We didn't, really," Mother said. "Even Minnie didn't need that much for her new software. She just figured it might come in handy down the line. And while she didn't end up utilizing it, we did. She did us a favour."

I must have looked as confused as I felt.

"Let's backtrack a bit," Mother said, and she sounded as if she was feeding mashed-up bananas to an infant. I was waiting for *here comes the airplane, open wide*—although come to think of it, she'd never been that gentle. "You're hooked up to the Crystal Path via the chip in your brain. You with me so far?"

"No need for sarcasm," I shot back, remembering in that moment why I killed her. We stared at one other.

"So you hacked the Crystal Lattice?" I asked. "And the Crystal Lattice is stored in our teeth?"

"No!" Mother said, looking exasperated. "The Crystal Lattice is just a highway of information; we didn't hack it. We needed access to the single repository, the location with everyone's info. In other words, Minnie's Vatican. Of course she'd dub her mainframe with a name like The Vatican. The woman was consistent to say the least. Miles and miles of hard drives—bigger, in total, than the size of St. Magnus, the great state formerly known as Texas—all hard at work recording every file sent, every image taken, and every message exchanged. First, we had to install software in your dental hard drive, which would allow us to process and store the data, then we hacked into The Vatican and downloaded the data into the time travel candidate's teeth."

"The time travel candidate," I echoed. "How warm and fuzzy of you, Mother."

She shrugged. "That's what Sting Ray Barb was doing when you thought your teeth were falling apart. She was installing software and downloading the data of your life. All of which hurts like the blazers. One candidate mentioned it was like having your nerve endings pulverized by dirty bombs."

My tongue moved around my teeth in a swift motion and I nodded emphatically.

"Who are you really?" I mumbled at Sting Ray Barb, keeping my mouth firmly closed.

"I'm on the military side," she replied vaguely. "In an unofficial capacity. I'm really an autodidact, and my mother helped me fill in the gaps."

"You've got a heavy hand with a scalpel, I'll tell you that much," I snapped at her. "I thought I was going to die of pain and go nuts from the hallucinations."

"Yep. Sorry about that. I had to reload the data a few times and reboot. You kept crashing on me. I even had to force quit a few times, and I was worried that the open files had corrupted. I had to delete them once you were up and running again, then gracefully shut down and try the install again."

"What do you mean, I crashed? I'm not a computer!"

"Sorry, the Easter Bunny crashed, not you. The Easter Bunny is the software program installed on the tooth. For some reason, I really struggled to manage the software install. It's a complex program and takes a lot of processing power from both the hard drive and the candidate. It wasn't as easy as it should have been, given that you were subject forty-nine. I thought perhaps I was encountering some kind of unconscious resistance, but that didn't make any sense. Then I realized I was struggling because the tooth's hard drive, while separate from the Crystal Path chip, is intrinsically and unavoidably piggybacked onto the chip's software. This is far from ideal, given the aging nature of that technology, in addition to which the chip reacts to brain activity in a way that the dental hard drives cannot. There's no way around it, not currently anyway. But I was correct, you were fighting me tooth and nail, *ha ha*, which is why you kept crashing."

She looked off into the distance as if she was trying to figure out a theorem, and I snapped my fingers at her.

"You were putting an Easter Bunny in my mouth," I reminded her. She glared at me and continued.

"Yes. Mom started out as a dentist in the Secret Service Army, but she was also a tech geek, and when she met up with Dr. Horvarth, they were unstoppable. The Easter Bunny, an advanced processing system, was their invention. Basically, if a person's life, and the lives of those they encountered, were downloaded into a single individual, then that person, contingent upon them fitting the other parameters, as outlined previously by your mother, opened the door, if you'll excuse the bad pun, to travel through time." She looked embarrassed. "I really need to work on the elevator pitch for that," she admitted. "But, in a long-winded nutshell, that's how it works. And, in this way, vast stores of energy were cached, ready for satellite shutdown. You guys created our backup generator."

"Fortunately for us," Noelle interjected, "the Sacred Dental Procedure became mandatory, even for those born after the water scandal, or if they had somehow escaped it. Everyone with the right genes was a potential candidate for time travel."

"Not everyone!" Sting Ray Barb chuckled. "My mother made sure I kept my original teeth just like good ole Minnie kept hers. My teeth are some of the only originals left. I'm a rare creature! And while not everyone was really a potential candidate for time travel, they all came with new teeth, like it or not. The software alone ate up more than a terabyte, and then you had to add the data of everyone's lives."

"Which meant only one person could jump at a time; the system couldn't cope otherwise. It was crazy how we, the underground warriors, ended up with the most powerful tool at our disposal and the big guns had no idea!" Mother laughed, a beautiful sound I hadn't heard in years.

"Back to recent events. Shasta nearly screwed things up by jumping with you," Noelle said. "But it turns out we learned a lot from her. Something in the equation changed, and her shotgun ride proved that more than one person can jump at a time."

Shasta. I hadn't even thought about her. "What happened to her?" I asked, and Sting Ray Barb waved towards the campgrounds. "We recruited her. She's as good as new. She loves it here. She's got a great future too, all the markings of a leader."

Shasta? Really? "One happy ending at least," I said, sarcastically, although I was glad to hear that Shasta was all right. "Meanwhile I'm just a hamster on a wheel, and every time I run, you get the energy and power you need. You guys are monsters!"

"No need to see it in such a negative light," Noelle said. "We had great sex, you learned you could get it up without a hole in the wall, and you saved your kids from being killed by their loving dad or warped by their pervert of a mother. Win-win, if you ask me."

"I don't want to jump back," I said. I was exhausted. "You say you've rejuvenated me but I feel shot to hell." On top of which, I had lost everything. My clean, tidy, sunny world. My friends. The woman I thought I had loved. Nothing was real. All I had left was the fact that I'd been used and hung out to dry. And I was soaking wet and freezing cold in a muddy field. No, I didn't see the results as a win, the only exception being my kids.

"Of course you're tired," Mother said, and she put her hand on my shoulder. There it was again, Jaxen's kindness. It was odd to feel that kind of warmth from Mother and I burst into tears. I sobbed, my face in my hands, and when I finally came up for air, Sting Ray Barb was holding out a large sheet of paper towel and Noelle was looking away, as if embarrassed and discomforted by what she'd seen.

"Sorry," I said, but Mother shook her head. "It's a lot to take in. You're doing very well, Sharps. You are." High praise that made me feel a bit better.

A thought occurred to me. "What happened to the Blowflies? With all this?" I waved my hand around, and you'd have thought I'd won an award for stand-up comedy, with the way Mother, Sting Ray Barb, and Noelle reacted.

"Oh, Sharps!" Sting Ray Barb finally said when she could talk again and I was getting annoyed. "We *are* Blowflies. All of us here. You don't think you guys started the revolution, do you? Why would you? Why would you destroy your comfortable, pretty, shiny lives? That's hilarious."

Noelle was still grinning, but there was malice in her smile as she moved closer to me. "You think we liked living in high-rise prisons? You think we liked the fact that you were quietly killing us? We stopped eating your food and grew our own, in places like this, off the grid, and no one noticed and no one cared. We stopped taking your drugs. We educated ourselves since we weren't welcome in your universities."

"And I defected," Mother said. "And the rest is history. Listen, great chatting, but come on. Sharps, let's get you back to St. Drogo's for one last jump. You may not feel like it, but you're physically sound and good to go."

I looked around. I had no friends here. There was nothing I could do but acquiesce. I rubbed my face hard, digging my fingers into my eye sockets and pushing the pressure points until I saw stars. I decided it was best to go along with whatever they said and then try to figure out a Plan B that saved my ass and got me away from these crazy psycho bitches. They were without mercy. And they thought I was the one with issues? I needed to get out of their clutches. "Okey dokey," I said meekly. "Let's do this thing then."

Noelle didn't come with us. Oh, how I mourned the loss of my Janaelle. My heart was broken, shattered. I truly wished I could love Noelle the way I'd loved Janaelle, but I wasn't to blame for that, was I? Noelle hadn't even really said good-bye; she gave a mock salute and a twisted smile and then disappeared into a canvas tent. And it wasn't because she looked different, although certainly that was disconcerting to say the least. Where had all her tenderness and love gone? But I knew the answer to that: he who hesitates is lost and I hesitated and lost. But she had lied to me on so many levels. Had she simply been role-playing? She'd been so convincing. I'd meant to ask her about her tattoo, but I didn't get the chance. For all I knew, she'd had something else done and

I'd seen what I wanted to. I guess I'd never know the truth when it came to her.

I wasn't impressed by the surroundings when they walked me to the car. The campgrounds were filthy, and the she-soldiers, as Mother told me they were called, all stank to high heaven. It was an army of women, not a man in sight.

"No men at all?" I asked.

"Not yet. They have to prove their worth. The women in Real Life South Africa made that decision. Men can join the resistance, but they're part of a lower-echelon and they do jobs more suited to them, heavy lifting, assembling weapons and equipment, and building housing. We're the thinkers, the planners."

I stopped to watch bio implants being administrated by a scary-looking nurse who moved with speedy precision.

"What are those for?" I asked Sting Ray Barb, watching the stern-faced woman prep a syringe with a small metal pellet and shoot it into a she-soldier's webbed flesh between her forefinger and thumb.

"Location microchipping along with identification and personal stats. We're going back in time as much as we can, but the reality is that we still need to be able to keep track. The day will come when the individual goes back to being purely organic, but it will take a while. We have to be vigilant because there will be a war, Sharps. World War III. A clash of the ages. We've been gearing up for it. Those microchips will tell us the locations and mental, emotional, and physical status of the she-soldiers."

"Where will this war be fought?"

"Here. In St. Polycarp, over in St. Isidore, all around the world. That's what a world war is, Sharps—everybody gets involved."

"But for what? It's not like we have countries worth saving anymore, we're one big united mess. What are we fighting for?"

"*Pro Patria*!" Sting Ray Barb shouted, and she'd lost her

smile. "What on earth do you think? Why did we even bother with you, Sharps?" She turned to Mother. "You said if this guy achieved it, it would prove that we'd be victorious. You said that."

What did she mean? "Victorious about what, Mother?" I asked, and my chest immediately filled with my old friend, anger. My lethargy and heartbreak circled back into my old familiar friend, blood red, scalp-prickling fury. I clenched my fists and stared at Mother, feeling betrayed all over again.

"You helped us prove a crucial theory about cause and effect," Mother said calmly. "Ground-breaking insights and data about the variables of consequence. You've helped us more than you can possibly imagine. In that way, you've done me proud. We learned so much more from you than genetics could reveal or psych evaluations could uncover. We've increased our insights into human frailty, expectations, vulnerability, and how all of those immeasurable and yet unavoidable elements can make or break the practical application of a hypothesis. We also learned how the memories and fears of one person will affect his perception of a given event and how that might differ from what actually happened. And we know why you succeeded where forty-eight others didn't. It wasn't genetics either."

"And what was it? Why did I succeed?"

Mother looked at me and shook her head. "Because you're the perfect anger machine. I don't know why, Sharps, but your fundamental, instinctive, feral rage is a rare thing. There are some things that even science can't explain."

The pinprick of her words deflated me. Yes. That was me: Mr. Angry. From the cradle to the grave.

I turned back to watch the nurse shoot another pellet into an outstretched hand then slap a bandage on the she-soldier's hand and wave her on.

I wondered why they weren't micro-chipping me, but then I realized they already had.

48. NO ESCAPE

I SAT IN THE BACK OF THE STATION BUBBLE as we drove from St. Adrian to the outskirts of St. Cornelius. The view along the way wasn't promising. The homeless and the hungry prowled the highways, wandering into the roads, and we had to weave around them as the rain continued to pour down, a relentless curtain of oily grey slush.

"Here's your bike," Sting Ray Barb thrust it at me as she lifted it down from the rack. "Good luck."

"See you later 'gator," I said to Mother, trying to inject a modicum of levity into our farewell and failing. She grabbed me and hugged me. "Don't forget, Sharps," she said, "that every moment of every day is a new chance to be the man you really want to be. Don't let your past overwhelm you."

Easy for you to say, I wanted to retort but I didn't say anything. I didn't even say goodbye. I looked at her for a moment, shouldered my backpack with supplies, and rode away as fast as I could. I didn't look back.

This trip was far worse than the first one I made after the Evolution had hit hard. Rats, squirrels, and feral dogs had somehow repopulated, and they roamed the streets, but the worst were the cats. They chased me, ravenous, with hungry looks in their eyes, and their long curved teeth bared. They looked more like cheetahs or panthers, roaming for kill. I had to kick them away as I cycled. Half-covered pits held random fires that added to the heat, and the smoky stench of smouldering tires, wood, and gasoline mingled with the rain which fell in a thick syrupy glop, like alien saliva in a B-grade sci-fi movie. The world was a stew of sweat, smoke, and mucus, and I fought my way through it, hardly able to breathe.

I passed the Sky The Tower and I saw a giant MosaliTitans flag proclaiming victory. The wind rippled through it and it fluttered with proud defiance. Yeah, you won, I thought. But at what cost?

I finally made it to the station. The place was full of people, but they were all dead. The realization struck me as soon as I hit the entrance. I had no idea how to survive the stench long enough to reach the gate. The bodies were rotting and maggot-infested and so foul that even the rats let them be. I peeled off my T-shirt and wrapped it around my face. And then I ran. I ran over those bodies, their mushy mouldy pulp exploding under me. I slipped and fell, and my hands pushed against slimy intestines, exposing terrible bone. I gagged and cried as I slid, pulling myself forward through the gory slush.

When I reached the gate, I shut my eyes for that brief moment. Stinging tears, brought on by the stench, burned down my cheeks.

Sting Ray Barb had told me I'd land back with Mother and my children and that we'd all live happily ever after. That my lives would be united and that the circle of time would close.

But that meant one thing. That this post-sanitized world, this disgusting, unhygienic, filthy, disgusting mess was my future and the future world of my hapless children. Three and a half months from now, this would be all of our worlds.

No. I couldn't live like this. And I couldn't let my children live like this either. There was only one solution. I had to go back and kill them. Kill Mother and Bax and Sophie and then kill myself. Because nothing was worse than this revolting world. Nothing. I had never been so certain of anything in my life.

I held my wrist out. The gates opened, and through I went. But when I opened my eyes, I wasn't in my house. I was in the rage room. "O Fortuna" was pounding, and sweat was dripping into my eyes. I smelled oil, plastic, and diesel. I held a hammer, and I was poised, mid-swing.

This was all wrong. I was supposed to be back in my house, back in the clean world where I'd be in control. What was going on?

I stood still, cold, oily sweat running down my body, which was odd since I didn't remember even hitting anything or working up a sweat. I was filled with panic and claustrophobia. This was all wrong.

The music shut off abruptly, and I shrank against a wall, just to feel the reassuring solid support behind my back. My heart pounded in my ears and my breathing was shallow. Why was I here? I dropped the hammer, jumping at the sound as it hit the floor.

Hissing static and broken bits of audio stuttered into the room, and pixels flashed, forming a shimmering wall of light like a dying video card. Then, *wham*, a screen popped up in front of my face. But the technology wasn't supposed to be working anymore. I reached out to touch the screen, and my hand shot through it as if I'd stuck my hand through a light projection. I pulled back, and Janaelle's face appeared, widescreen. My Janaelle! My heart leapt. She was back! But wait, she wasn't real and besides, she'd fucked me over just like everyone else. I glared at her.

"Ah, Sharps," she said, and she sounded sad. "The others didn't think you deserved to know why you're in this room, but I did. They thought you should be left here alone with the torment of confusion as your friend."

"Yeah, I can hear Mother saying that," I said, leaning in, just glad to see my Janaelle.

"But I just wanted to see you, so they let me have this time."

"You aren't real," I said weakly.

"I'm as real as anything in your life, Sharps. Whatever we believe constitutes our reality. And our avatar selves, our online personas, they're real, right? You were SmashingSablink007, and you really experienced all those things, didn't you?"

It was true. I had real memories and emotions of those digital adventures. "But you were my invention," I said. "You never chose Janaelle. You got that from me."

"I did, yes. But I've been forty-eight other avatars with forty-eight other subjects and I never felt like any of them fit, or that I wanted to be with the subject. And I did fit with you. But you couldn't love me as Noelle. And yet, of course, I still loved you. I fell in love with you the minute I saw you."

My whole body was aching to hold the woman on the screen, avatar or not.

"I did love you," she said. "I still love you. The others weren't happy when I fell for you, but they said as long as it didn't interfere with our bigger plans, that I could screw you until the cows came home. Look," she said, and held up her wrist. "Your name tattooed onto me. I saw the man you could have been, should have been, maybe like that woman who married Ted Bundy or all those women who marry men on death row. Maybe I, like them, can't handle anything except those kinds of relationships. And, if you need me to be Janaelle when I'm with you, then I'm okay with that. I mean, what's really real anyway?"

But I wasn't interested in her sob stories or pontifications. She was safe and sound while I was stuck in a box in outer space.

"Why am I here?" I asked. "Is this like *Alterna Inferma*? Do I need to reset the gadget?"

I looked at my wrist, at the visible rice-grain-sized lump and Janaelle laughed. "No, Sharps. The gadget was nothing more than a placebo to help you understand, or think you understand, how time travel worked."

I sat down on the floor. "Then explain it to me," I said. "C'mon, spill the rest of the beans. I don't even think you can shock me anymore."

She bit her lip. "I've thought about this so many times,

how to tell you the truth. It's all got to do with the deconstruction and reconstruction of atoms. You, me, everybody,
everything, we're all just atoms. So time travel is basically
deconstruction at one point and reconstruction at another
point, all determined by data."

"I literally disintegrated. Oh my god." Of course. It made
perfect sense. "The pain, the nausea, the disorientation. The
reconstruction. Oh my god! That's why I saw my foot dissolving that time! Sting Ray Barb told me my head always had to
go first, that I had to lean forward slightly, but I forgot and
I stuck my foot out in front of me and I saw it pixelate and
dissolve! I totally forgot about it until now."

"You didn't forget; we wiped you clean. But I felt you should
know the truth so I reloaded that memory into your data."

I jumped to my feet and punched her. At least, I tried to
punch her. I swung at the air and knocked myself off balance.

"You bitch!" I yelled. "Who the fuck do you think you are,
taking memories away or putting them back? How do I even
know this conversation is real? Or anything? Maybe none of
this happened. Maybe my whole fucking life never happened."

"I'd be angry too," she said, and she sounded like a Comfort
Centre EmoBot, reciting scripted dialogue.

"Oh don't insult me with your fake empathy," I yelled. "You
ripped me apart. You disintegrated me! You didn't send me
back the way I thought you were." I took a deep breath. "I
thought I was just going back in a straight line meanwhile you
created a parallel universe with a different timeline."

"Wrong. It's all the same timeline, just different iterations.
When you were sent back, a new timeline was created and
when you returned, the timelines converged. Changes in the
past reflect onto your present reality. So actually, the loop
doesn't need to be closed; it's a closed loop to begin with. We
just told you that to get you to this place, to make you do a
final jump. There really is only ever one timeline.

"We're all just information, Sharps. Atoms that make up

information that make up our worlds. Our entire existence comes down to three things: data transfer, data storage, and data retrieval. Well, that's in Queen Minnie's world anyway. Talk about complete control. We were just her pawns. But, no more, we're taking it all back, going back to the land and reclaiming our individuality. No more interconnectivity or shit like that. We went too far, Sharps. We were morphing into a single AI creature, just like The Vatican. You know it was starting to turn on Minnie? Her own creation started plotting her demise. We could see it 'thinking' of ways to knock her off her throne, and she couldn't shut it down. It was only a matter of time before The Vatican ruled the world. Minnie had lost control, although she'd never admit that. Which is also why we needed to shut it down and thanks to all our years of planning, we could succeed where she couldn't. We had to shut down all the AIs, Sharps. They let us think we controlled them, but we didn't!"

Her voice had a slightly hysterical edge to it and I needed her to focus.

"Yeah, great. So you get world peace, love, and the integrity of every individual fellow man—sorry, fellow woman—and all good things. Sayonara AI, we're kicking your asses, it's time to get organic. I get it. So you go back to the land, but what's the plan for me?"

She looked down as if studying something fascinating on her fingers. "You're where you need to be," she said, which was what I had expected her to say, although I had been hoping for charity.

Something occurred to me. "Subjects one to forty-nine. Something I meant to clarify. All men, huh? We're nothing more to you than disposable fuel and data, right?"

"We've lived with the consequences of your patriarchal bullshit all our lives, Sharps. Now it's our time, and if there are a few male casualties along the way, well, *c'est la vie*—you earned it."

"Janaelle," I asked urgently, and I moved closer to the screen and looked as genuinely earnest as I felt, "you have to get me out of here. I know you can. You've got access to the data. You just told me you did." And she'd told me she loved me. She had to set me free. After all, she was weak. What kind of woman would be willing to live as an avatar for a man she loved? The kind who'd help me escape, that's who.

"Maybe. But it's not up to me." She looked away. "Have you ever had a boss who scared the shit out of you, Sharps?"

"Yeah. Ava, remember?"

"Imagine someone a thousand times more scary than Ava. More vicious. Ruthless. That's what we report to. We're just a Level Two Quad-Tentacle Team—me, Jaxen, Sting Ray Barb, and Mother. One tiny quad-tentacle among millions of others worldwide. OctoOne knows everything we do. They said I could have half an hour with you." She looked at her watch. "And we're nearly out of time. It's all so much bigger than you think. We're just pawns. Goodbye, Sharps, and know this, I will always love you."

"Wait! Will you come back? Are you going to leave me here? Janaelle? Noelle? Don't leave me here. I loved you too. You know I did. I would have given up everything for you. Don't leave me here!"

I tried to read her expression, but she wasn't giving me anything.

Her face flickered, and the hiss of static returned. I could see Janaelle talking and I thought she said something about checking in on me as soon as she could, but I couldn't hear her clearly, and then her image exploded into a thousand tiny pixel pieces and flew away like the confetti moth shards of my teeth.

Subject Forty Nine. I looked over at the mirrored glass. *So what now?*

But I knew the answer to that question. I sank to my haunches. "So here you are, buddy," I said out loud in one of the many one-to-one conversations I knew I'd be having all by my lonesome in the future. "You really managed this well, didn't you?"

I looked around. A thought occurred to me, and I jumped to my feet and grabbed a hammer. I swung at an old TV and froze, hammer aloft. A TV? They weren't allowed. *Screen-based materials are forbidden in the rage room. Glass cannot be utilized or destroyed in the rage room. We always consider your safety first! Because we care about you! All in accordance with Docket102.V, Health and Safety Code 0009: By Order of the Sacred Board, Gloria in Excelsis Deo.*

Where was the robo-voice now, and why wasn't it sounding all kinds of alarms? The sick feeling in my gut radiated outwards, and once again sweat, my closet friend, *ha ha*, drenched my clothes. "Dollars to doughnuts," I said out loud, "if I smash the TV, it won't stay broken. And even if glass flies, I will be fine—uncut, unscathed, and unscarred. I'm invincible. I'm the superhero of my own worst nightmares!" I yelled the last and swung at the TV with all my might, hoping I was wrong.

Glass shattered. Blood flew as puzzle pieces lacerated my face and my skin, and it hurt like hell. "Mother of god!" I shrieked, and I dropped like a stone. But the pain receded and just as I had suspected, pieces of glass flew from my body and went back to form a beautiful, unsullied screen, and my wounds healed as if by magic.

I was stuck in lost time in a rage room. "Living the dream," I whispered weakly. "Got what you love the most, time in a rage room. Well done, buddy, well fucking done."

ACKNOWLEDGEMENTS

Such grateful thanks to Inanna Publications for always making my most important dreams come true and this year, even more than ever. What conditions.... All I can say is thank you for this book in a time of Covid-19. Thank you, dear Luciana Ricciutelli for your wonderful editing and your constant faith in me. Endless thanks to Renée Knapp, Inanna's tireless and talented publicist.

Thanks to my lovely Bradford Dunlop for your eternal patience and support, and much love to my family, always.

Immeasurable thanks to Colin Frings for helping me map out the technology and the time travel.

Thanks to Lora Grady for introducing me to rage rooms, to Jason Abrams for a pivotal discussion about teeth, and to Joanna Wood for reading the early manuscripts and giving me invaluable advice.

Huge thanks to the early readers for supporting this book: David Albertyn, Melodie Campbell, Catherine Dunphy, Terry Fallis, Amy Jones, Shirley McDaniel, Evan Munday, Lorna Poplak, Kelly S. Thompson, and Suzana Tratnik.

Much love to my comrades in arms, the Mesdames of Mayhem.

And, to you Dear Reader, I hope you enjoyed this adventure as much as I loved writing it.

Photo: Bradford Dunlop

Lisa de Nikolits is the internationally acclaimed, award-winning author of nine novels: *The Hungry Mirror; West of Wawa; A Glittering Chaos; The Witchdoctor's Bones; Between The Cracks She Fell; The Nearly Girl; No Fury Like That; Rotten Peaches;* and *The Occult Persuasion and the Anarchist's Solution. No Fury Like That* was also published in Italian in 2019 by Edizione le Assassine, under the title *Una furia dell'altro mondo.* Her short fiction and poetry have also been published in various anthologies and journals. She is a member of the Mesdames of Mayhem, Sisters in Crime, and the International Thriller Writers. Originally from South Africa, Lisa de Nikolits came to Canada in 2000. She lives and writes in Toronto.